The Trinity
of Fundamentals

Wisam Rafeedie

Published in January 2024 by
1804 Books, New York, NY

1804Books.com

By Wisam Rafeedie
Translated from the Arabic-language original, الأقانيم الثلاثة
Translated by Dr. Muhammad Tutunji
Project of the Palestinian Youth Movement

© Palestinian Youth Movement. All rights reserved.
ISBN: 979-8-9882602-1-9
Library of Congress Control Number: 2023949984

Cover by Hannah Priscilla Craig and Vivek Venkatraman

Table of Contents

Foreword	v
Preface	vii
Introduction to the Novel	xix
A Note from Comrades	xxiii
Publisher's Note	xxvii
Dedication	xxix
Cast of Characters	xxxi
Chapter 1	1
Chapter 2	39
Chapter 3	65
Chapter 4	89
Chapter 5	117
Chapter 6	137
Chapter 7	183
Chapter 8	203
Chapter 9	241
Chapter 10	271
Chapter 11	307
Glossary	319
Endnotes	325

Foreword
George Habash

The Trinity of Fundamentals: an exhilarating experience. It is a unique novel that recounts a Palestinian revolutionary experience. I write this not to praise or engage in literary criticism. Rather, I feel compelled to record my impressions and my emotional reactions to what I read: the feelings ingrained in my memory of joy and sorrow at certain times, and pain or hope at other times. On other occasions, I shed tears, and I would not be exaggerating if I were to say that it awoke dormant memories and catalyzed feelings and reactions which had almost been filed away...

From my perspective, this novel belongs generally to the genre of thriller and suspense. In the novel, Kan'an is the optimistic Palestinian who overcomes his difficult circumstances, subduing his inner self and his individual concerns for the sake of the nation, the cause, the party to which he belongs, and the objectives and values to which he adheres. All of which gives rise to conflicting emotions, and intense and extraordinary feelings within him as a revolutionary and human being.

The novel is an autobiography by the optimistic protagonist who storms the abyss of the unknown and accepts the challenge. He is not intimidated or spiritually defeated by the events or looming dangers because he is a revolutionary and a human being who, in the revolution as in life, is a bundle of sentiments, emotions, demands, and needs, starting with a loaf of bread, going on to women and love, ending with freedom and everything in between.

It is no wonder that we should say that the stages of our national struggle and its complexities have sometimes demanded a choice hero, a dazzling hero, which is what Wadie[*] was and what Kan'an approximates to an extent.

In all living revolutions, certain stages of the struggle have required a model hero, one who rises out of specific personal and material circumstances for the sake of the continuation and triumph of the revolutionary cause and the supreme objectives of the nation.

The novel is mixed with the fabric of revolutionary realism, and is packed with the spirit of resistance and confronting the enemy in search of national liberation and independence. Consequently, it deserves to be read as the gospel of Kan'an the man, Kan'an the revolutionary who is, first and foremost, a Palestinian living in the time of fierce confrontation in the era of struggle.

The battle for the liberation of our people has begun, but it is not over . . . It was and still is in need of the likes of Kan'an, the revolutionary and the human being.

In dedication:
To the truly uplifting comrades, in the times of hardship and challenge, I conclude my remarks.

—Written in 2000

---

[*] Wadie Haddad was one of the founders of the Popular Front for the Liberation of Palestine (PFLP) and the leader of the PFLP's armed wing.

Preface
Ahmad Qatamesh

Reviewing the draft and final version of the novel by comrade Wisam Rafeedie was a truly invigorating experience. I fell under the story's spell. It stirred emotions in me and awakened what was asleep in my memory. Certain parts even made tears well up in my eyes. It is a novel of a special kind, bringing together various aspects of the clandestine existence through which the author lived for years.

The novel depicts the flames of his burning rage and the furnace in which he slept. It contains, in its essence, an exploration of the general standards for leading a clandestine life under the prevailing circumstances in our country. It also has unique attributes that help the reader grasp how certain elements of life expand in scope, others shrink, and others are absent still. It portrays the epic experience itself, from the perspective of the fugitive, as it relates to his characteristics: his age, experience, attributes, and personal maturity.

In the final analysis, comrade Rafeedie explores the personal dimension of his experience working under the constraints of general laws. Under no circumstances, regardless of the creative efforts, should anyone form the impression that what the author has penned here is a photographic image of his experiences, for the novel is an abstraction of an experience of rich dimensions, great endurance, and immeasurable sacrifices. While the art of the novel possesses great horizons and far-reaching possibilities, it stands in humility, like a guilty child, when confronted with extraordinary concepts like going into hiding or war or love or motherhood. Thus, even as one must acknowledge the superior qualities of the novel compared to other art forms, there are defining moments in life that are even more superior in their drama and makeup to any dramatic constructs or art.

The message in the novel is clear. It revolves around a prominent axis, and its structure is manifest and well knit together. In sum, it transcends a documentary and rises to the status of a literary work with a special flavor, the contents of which were not difficult to shape aside from linguistic forms, its internal cohesion, and the beautiful, well-chosen, often poetic terms. It contains events that occurred in Kan'an's life which dictated the uniqueness of its course as he sailed through the gulfs of the self and navigated his isolation, both of which are reflected in the novel's architecture. The author was able to overcome the paucity of social relationships and interactions by providing a cascade of internal monologues. The interest of the reader is maintained throughout by the protagonist's development and constant suspense as the narrative weaves back and forth to particular dramatic scenes from his life.

In following the life of Kan'an, the character pursued by the occupation forces, the author turns the novel's spotlight on one of its central pillars, namely the struggle, which manifests itself primarily through the antagonistic relationship between Kan'an and the tyrannical occupier, as well as the sharp contradiction between Kan'an's natural, human needs and the conditions in which he slips into oblivion. All this is conveyed in a chronological order, beginning with the raid on Kan'an's family's house by the occupation forces and stretching to the raid on his hideout and his arrest.

The novel relies on profound psychological depth that goes beyond mere storytelling to serve its aesthetics and message. Simply put, the novel is neither a mathematical formula nor a historical document. It is a mixture of imagination with reality, the logical with the illogical, advancing and retreating, stopping at the surface and exploring the depths, all of which are natural in literature. Making the moment of the raid a key point of the novel is no doubt a factor which captivates the reader from the moment they read the first paragraph. This captivation is renewed every time the reader's enthusiasm flags or they attempt to catch their breath to drink a cup of tea or sip a cup of coffee. The success of this literary device, an excellent choice, is no coincidence, given that the moment under analysis contains extremely fast-flowing and contradictory emotions as one course of events ends and another begins. The moment of Kan'an's capture is a rich hub of innumerable sentiments and ideas, both familiar and unfamiliar, ordinary and exceptional, protected by a determination that has been forged into steel over years of glory and solitude, of productivity and challenge. The author does not dwell on regret or spiritual defeat nor laments the loss incurred. Even an inquiry into the factors that led to Kan'an's arrest are downplayed, quickly replaced by the requirements of Kan'an's new predicament when he becomes a captive.

The backdrop of the novel is connected to the reality in Palestine and the events our people experience in the occupied homeland. Namely, this includes the spirit of resistance, a progressive trend that seeks to replace the existing tyrannical reality with one that will lead to the emancipation, freedom, and independence of our people. This novel belongs to the revolutionary realist school which does not stop at diagnosis, but seeks to agitate and bring about change. Revolutionaries in politically repressive countries have resorted to the tactic of living in hiding in cities, particularly in small countries where it is difficult to launch a resistance from the countryside. The Tupamaros movement in Paraguay and the Cindero Luminoso movement in Peru are the most famous examples of this. The Palestinian experience, however, is unique, and this tactic has had a less positive effect given the limited geography and demography of the territories occupied in 1967, not to mention the absence of a suitable topography—a given and objective factor that cannot be ignored no matter the brilliance and intelligence of the actors who have adopted or may adopt this option. During the upheaval of the Intifada, individual refusals to comply with arrest warrants took the shape of a collective phenomenon; consequently, every city and village and camp was swarming with fugitives, an experience which is a simplified and short-lasting version of what Kan'an represented and endured.

The leftist position does not usually limit itself to revolutionary premises only; rather, it aims to be at the forefront of knowledge too. Consequently, it is pointless to minimize the personality of the individual and, subsequently, the revolutionary personality, and turn it upside-down as though it were simply a flesh of politics and struggle alone. This pointless representation appears as a *fait accompli* and is ineffectual with respect to the novel. In life, as in the novel, the revolutionary is a human being first and foremost—a human being with a body, mind, and soul, with needs that include a loaf of bread, as well as freedom and love. Without the loaf of bread, he will die, and without love, humankind would cease to reproduce and exist, and it would lose its most important source of pleasure. Even though freedom is a civilizational request, its genes are also planted in the elementary forms of life as well.

The two basic instincts that humanity has are self-defense and the instinct for survival, which implies procreation. Any other instincts are branches of these two huge stems. Consequently, a woman's need for a man and a man's need for a woman are original instincts without which the human species would become extinct. Going back to the ancient Babylonians, about four thousand years ago, according to the epic of Gilgamesh, Gilgamesh's friend Enkidu was human in shape but lived like a beast in his conduct and associations. He did not become fully human until he enjoyed the pleasure of a sexual relationship with a woman. Contemporary philosophers go so far as to say that a thing does not attain self-consciousness until it discovers its opposite: good and evil, socialism and capitalism, liberation and colonialism, knowledge and ignorance ... Consequently, a man discovers the extent of his humanity and a woman discovers her humanity through their relationship with each other, not to mention what a woman may represent to a revolutionary man and a man to a revolutionary woman, in terms of mutual help, shared dreams, psychological comfort, and solidarity at times of retreat and difficulty—when one supports the other and they fight with the strength of two instead of one. So, love is a progressive value, particularly if it is mutual and deep. Separation is a major calamity for both, far above any considerations of finances or prestige. Love, in other words, is a free choice in the turmoil of intimacy and cooperation.

A woman to a revolutionary man is more than just a source of beauty and delicacy and tenderness; she is the very root and branch of beauty and delicacy and tenderness. Everything else is connected to her and branches off from her. This goes beyond being a warm embrace and a wellspring of feelings of love, yearning, fascination, desire, and lust; beyond being the cleanser of the soul from the impurities of time and the dregs of life. She is all of that and more, rising to the level of a total equal in the course of his life, so that it is difficult to see him succeeding or any revolutionary act succeeding without her.

It is clear that the third fundamental element, as Kan'an calls it, namely women, was always the present absentee throughout the nine years. As long as Kan'an was in limbo, yearning for the third element, it was natural that it should figure prominently in his concerns and attention span. But that is intuitive and totally unconnected to the Freudian interpretation which considers the libido, meaning the innate sexual energy in a human being, to be the mover of his behavior. Man is first and foremost the product of his environment and his age. Kan'an himself is the product of specific circumstances that sought to mold his path, circumstances which he defied. That is what drove Kan'an to rebel against the occupation. As the saying goes, "if the circumstances are what make a human, we shall make humane circumstances." This entails, among other things, a recognition of the principle that man is an object and a subject at the same time.

Just as all humanity seeks to harness the raw resources of nature to satisfy its needs, it also seeks to defeat tyranny, injustice, repression, and exile which take man's humanity hostage, exploiting and degrading him. It seeks to remove the obstacles which hinder the innate attraction between a man and a woman.

Kan'an was searching for his third element, prodding himself on as is his natural right. As the chapters of the novel make clear, his incentive was genuine, in keeping with his statement "without mad love there can be no escape from constant anxiety."[*] However, he was compelled out of necessity to subdue that desire like a long-term prisoner or a monk or a spinster in a conservative society. The self can be domesticated in this fashion, so the desire can be subdued but not extinguished, as if one is adapting to unfair circumstances. It helps to subjugate the mind so that it agrees to surrender to the reality of deprivation and to keep busy for longer hours each day. Work is the cure of the soul, which paves the way to reigning in natural needs and inventing new responses befitting the conditions of being a fugitive, prisoner, etc. This then leads to a reconciliation with the self and the postponement of its innate tendencies.

However, suppose that Kan'an's character had pacified his demand for the third fundamental element. If that is permissible, one could then imagine a different character for Kan'an, narrating what it used to be, what it has become, and what it has sought to modify. Such circumstances would probably lead to a more bearable situation involving less anxiety and would be better grounded for leading a secret life. He would have had a distinctive journey with himself which would inevitably be included in the events of the novel, making it more aesthetic, polished, and humanly austere, as in the case of a Buddhist monk. Suppose as well that Kan'an had encountered his third fundamental element and emerged from his loneliness, sharpened his character, reached self-fulfillment, and completed the clandestine experience as a couple. That would change the context and enrich the literary text. In fact, the archetype of a woman would become more positive and concrete, and the bitterness which one can taste in Kan'an's expressions about the

---

[*] These sentences are paraphrased from the novel.

duplicity of the feminine sex, which are sprinkled in the text, along with the multitude of negative examples he encounters (his former fiancée Muna, Umm 'Isa, Sakinah, Hind who appeared and disappeared in the blink of an eye), would be dissipated and one could feel that the negative memories were the exception rather than the rule. The rule, however, is the facts and the reality that women are the fertile affirmation of life, in fact there is no more positive fertility in life than the fecundity of women.

It is simplistic to think that Muna was just a woman who broke off her engagement; she transcends that in the sense that she is a loved one and a collection of memories. Beyond that, she represents all women, and in keeping her distance and given Kan'an's special circumstances of isolation, she took all women with her. To be fair, she most likely did not turn away from Kan'an the human. In fact, she was, and still is, charmed by him. However, she spared Kan'an the difficult decision because she could not rise to the challenge given her ordinary qualifications. Hind, on the other hand, is the hope that was realized after nine years of patience and endurance, yet no sooner had she tasted the flame than she ran away, never to return—who endures in the flame of the fire?

Even though the novel presents Kan'an as a revolutionary who bears the cross of the nation and the people on his back in the glare of day and loneliness of night, it is difficult to pin down the connotations of the term "madness" in connection with hiding and being professional. Kan'an describes going into hiding and being a professional revolutionary as madness, whereas one could rank it as one of the highest levels of revolutionary action, which grants happiness like no other. It grants a productive, effective, and unique happiness, yet it is combined with the pain of hardship, like a mother in childbirth, or a mother who stays up long nights to care for her sickly child, or toils for consecutive years and sacrifices the ripeness of youth for a dozen or so sons and daughters. She is happy and exuberant under all circumstances—at least happiness and exuberance are the principal image in her spiritual structure, whereas fatigue and exertion and torment take second, or even tenth, place in her priorities, or they are transformed into happiness in the cistern of her soul. It is the paradoxical dialectical unity.

A serious choice, a very serious one, gives you as much as you give it. It cleanses the soul and rejects its distortions. It strengthens its internal structure and turns it into tempered steel. It remolds its owner in a better and more refined way and opens doors wide for him to take on a role that is twice, even multiple times better. It is as if it removes all the empty spaces in the atoms of the revolutionary, keeping only the stable nuclei. This is what we see in the novel as Kan'an's anxious, hesitant, and downtrodden personality matures under the pressure of the inevitable requirements he faces, from the beginning of going into hiding up to the decisive moment in which he had to take a position. Then came the raid campaign of 1985 which was another jumping off point for serious transformation.

Kan'an could not have done otherwise, seeing as he had just left his studies at the university, an experience associated with vitality, relationships, activities, and the joy of youth; he left his sweet fiancée to become the unknown soldier, undergoing a complete transformation and immersion from head-to-toe, in a milieu at odds with all of the above and man as a social being. We must not rebuke Kan'an when he presents himself in 1986 as contrary to what he had been in 1982—he desperately needed four years to make the inevitable leap in the course of his development.

The characteristics of a revolutionary are like a living being that grows. At the beginning it is stumbling, faltering, and restless, dominated by the "I," hesitant, disputatious, and complaining. However, the fire of practice, the experience gained with time, the effect of revolutionary thought, and the collective spirit, given what it encompasses in terms of the recurring power of example, uplifts the "I" to heightened levels of awareness, determination, and firmness in principle. It is absorbed into the "we" and acquires the work skills, solid character, and all the provisions needed for the revolutionary enterprise. This is the general essence that is achieved by the pure revolutionary, each in his own way.

Revolutionary professionalism takes place when one dedicates themselves, with all their personality and all their might, to their convictions and principles. When they take a lofty position and become passionate about acquiring real skills and gifts, they are elevated to the category of vanguardism, where they surpass others in competence and become worthy of being labeled trusted guardians.

However, professionalism in the Palestinian arena is often falsified and emptied of content to the extent that any full-time worker and employee is called a professional! The contemporary revolution has suffered from the conceit and ruckus of the army of full-timers, creating a heavy burden on the people and their objectives, and giving rise to endless criticisms, not least of which is that, in their midst, there has grown a stratum of bureaucrats that has spread corruption and ultimately aborted political decision-making and the spirit of resistance of the struggling masses. Kan'an is an alternate type that is valiant, brilliant, and free of the dust and corruption of self-interest and parochialism.

Kan'an's experience, which lasted almost a decade, was not only an olive tree bearing the fruit of struggle and achievement, not only flour kneaded with the yeast of pure suffering. It was also distinguished by the intelligence, insight, preparedness, and original thought which allowed him to avoid the traps laid by the intelligence services and to foil their feverish quest to arrest him for over nine years.

It has to be admitted, however, that the political transformations and the post-Madrid settlement* have unsheathed their sword and slain this model of clandestine existence, which has been mercilessly bled. Is it true that this model is no longer desired? This model was, at an earlier stage of history, the highest form of response to the relentless contradictions and a challenge to the tyrannical law. However, in light of the settlement, there has arisen a negotiating authority and a political movement calling for democracy and civil

---

* This is in reference to the 1991 Madrid Conference. See Chapter 11, Footnote 56 for more.

society. All these commitments are pushing to guarantee the calm and gradual development of society in the direction of dependency and tutelage. Consequently, this model is no longer dazzling or an objective demand. However, should economic, political, and cultural globalization fail to freeze the struggle, even if only in the mid and long term, then one could speculate that the national contradiction and the social contradiction will come to a head and that developments at the regional level could make this model worthy of study, inspiration, and emulation. Generally speaking, this model of resistance was born in the womb of fixed objective circumstances and was the most noble of the noble.

As reading the novel and in between the lines informs us, it was difficult for this model to be born without bringing the party into play. The party: the collective mind, collective guide, collective educator, collective ideology, and the conscience of the people, which appears in the novel as a helping hand whenever Kan'an calls on it. It controls his reactions, eliminates his confusion, and supports him whenever he is debilitated by illness. It secures the necessities of life for him and supplies whatever he needs, whether in the form of a letter, a circular, directives, a visit, or companionship. It is evident that such a party cannot serve such a role unless it possesses a high degree of power to inspire and the ability to convince and resurrect hopes.

Kan'an does not suffer from hubris. He acknowledges the contributions of his colleagues and carries out the instructions of the party and arms himself with them: "wash your inner self with soap and water and be patient" and "it is difficult to forge a secret life without the help of the party."* This is totally warranted, considering that belonging to the group and its values, dreams, objectives, and regulations is the foundation of the resistance fighter's vigor. If the party shakes, everything shakes, and if it is confused, the resistance fighter is confused, and his priorities, standards, and point of view on things change too.

---

* These sentences are paraphrased from the novel.

One can feel how cruel and mean the years in hiding were for Kan'an with regards to his constant relocations, for he never settled in one place, and we should remember the small size of the city in which he was hiding, which forced him to be constantly watchful and to utilize his security intuition so as not to run across anyone who could compromise his secrecy. There are other vivid examples, such as the house in which he spent three months without being able to turn on the lights at night, the mattress that was stuffed with stones, and the wall with which he grew accustomed to speaking, like the poet [Nizar] Qabbani once said, "I escape from wall to wall." Although this was not merely metaphorical, it was Kan'an's reality, as for years he addressed a deaf and mute wall. He overflowed with thirst and hunger for people. Such a deformed conversation is in fact necessary and a defense mechanism to alleviate the dynamics of misty memories which arise in the womb of loneliness and isolation. In addition, Kan'an concluded his "mad" journey by swallowing papers which had been drenched with kerosene and facing the assault by the soldiers prior to his arrest and investigation.

When I met Kan'an-Wisam in prison a year and a half later, I noticed how emaciated his body and face looked, how sunken his cheeks and how dull his eyes were, except for a daring gleam which glowed under the force of his willpower and the purity of his revolutionary spirit. When I embraced him, my fingers could feel his ribs, one by one. I was dumbfounded for a moment once the impact of that meeting after twenty years of separation had pervaded my heart. The effect of that happy and tragic meeting remained with me, made me realize the extent of the burdens and suffering made distant by the years. What gave me comfort was his conviction in the validity of his choices and his reverberating laugh, as though there was nothing disturbing his mood.

I must note that during his journey of "madness," the face and prayers of his mother appeared daily. Kan'an's spirit was splintered by yearning for his mother and would only find satisfaction or heal once they could hug each other. His good, devoted, and patient mother did not falter in igniting determination and energy in her son. She was worried about him wherever she went and he worried about her, like spiritual twins. He purified his wounds in her pure and resplendent waters and found shelter in her shade from the flames of his revolutionary dreams which burnt his skin and lit an inextinguishable flame in his chest.

—Al-Naqab-Ansar 3 Detention Center
February 1995

Introduction to the Novel
Wisam Rafeedie

In *Return to Haifa*, Ghassan Kanafani wrote, "After all, in the final analysis, man is a cause." Kanafani did not intend his categorical assertion to be confined to Palestinians, despite the fact that his novella poses the question of identity from a Palestinian perspective. He was positing the situation of man as a human being in a world bursting with conflicts of all sorts. On which side of a conflict does a man stand? At the ramparts of the oppressors or the ramparts of the oppressed? That is the main issue—a person is ultimately defined by the choice of their cause: those who struggle against imperialism, Zionism, capitalism, and the forces of reaction have chosen their ramparts and are united in the struggle against this criminal camp. That is what we Marxists call "international solidarity," a solidarity that unites all the strugglers for the sake of a world where national, class, social, and sexual exploitation are banished: a communist world, heaven on earth for human beings. A beatific dream? Very well, so be it! It suffices that not only does that constitute an incentive for struggle, but also for steadfastness of principles, guided by what Marx wrote in his instructions to the militants of the First (Communist) International Workingmen's Association: "Beware of compromising your principles; beware of theoretical concessions."

In that Marxist, class-oriented school of thought, my consciousness began to take shape at the age of sixteen, when I became a member of the Palestine Communist Party, and subsequently of the Popular Front for the Liberation of Palestine. From that day, up to this very moment, I feel within me all of the injustices that befall each persecuted person in the world. I consider everyone who struggles against that injustice to be my comrade, and my legitimate resentment of imperialists and capitalists in all of their varieties continues to build.

It is within this context of international solidarity that I situate the efforts of my comrades to translate my novel *The Trinity of Fundamentals* into English. And it is within the same context that I felt a great sense of enthusiasm for the project and offered them all that I could to ensure its success. I wish to express my appreciation to them at the opening of this introduction.

It is true that all experience is personal, but—in an embodiment of the Hegelian saying about the general and the specific—everything personal contains what is general. Living in hiding during that historical period (meaning the Palestinian circumstances of the 1980s) makes that experience specific; however, living in hiding as a form of clandestine action (which is revolutionary professionalism in the Leninist sense) is a general phenomenon among peoples in many revolutionary situations. Lenin went into hiding for months, Tito did so for years, as did Ibrahim Nuqud in Sudan. Similarly Palestinian communists during the period of Jordanian rule and under Zionist occupation also went into hiding.

It is granted that each individual experience has its specific characteristics with regards to the structure of the party, the forms of struggle, the geographic and demographic nature of the situation, as well as the extent of development of the technological capabilities available to the intelligence agencies. Yet, it is also true that there are general characteristics which surely unite all of these experiences, for they are experiences of struggle against capitalists and imperialists. The Zionist movement (which is the offspring of white European imperialism) gave birth to the Zionist project in Palestine, which took the form of a state and of settler-colonial occupation. It was described by our departed comrade Dr. George

Habash as "little imperialism"; its aggression touched all peoples of the entire region. Its purpose as the regional arm of world imperialism renders that description a logical reality. Zionism, although it colonized Palestine, also occupied territories belonging to three states. Its blatant military aggression reached three other states while its unannounced aggression, through its destructive intelligence agencies, has reached all of the Arab states, in cooperation with the intelligence agencies of the reactionary states.

Because living in hiding is a special kind of experience within clandestine action, it has become yet another "meal" on the table of revolutionary skills for revolutionaries throughout the world, including those splendid militant comrades, of various nationalities, who serve as the real embodiment of international solidarity and the diversity of revolutionaries within the very domain of American imperialism. Imperialism and capitalism serve to unite us revolutionaries, and the least we can do is exchange experiences and expertise.

At the personal level, as one who lived in hiding for nine years, I have become familiar with the skills of living clandestinely, firstly with the help of the party and secondly through self-education based on the partial availability of details of other experiences: Lenin disguised himself as a laborer for a few months; Tito lived in the mountains with the fighters against the Nazis; Julius Fucik in Prague; Nuqud in Sudan, moved between its north and south; Fu'ad Qissis, the Palestinian communist who experienced life with the Bedouins while seeking to escape Jordanian intelligence; and the Palestinian communist 'Arabi 'Awwad who stayed on the move between rural areas . . . All of those experiences were like extra "helpings" that allowed me to master the skills and techniques of clandestine action. I would like to emphasize that I acquired the most important of those skills and techniques through my party experience and through my relations with the party, which allowed me to arrive eventually at what I regard as the first law of clandestine action: neutralize coincidences as much as possible.

It is in this context that I see the importance of the translation of this "fictionalized-narrative-of-life-in-hiding novel," as I like to call it. To elaborate, under current circumstances the translation serves as a link between two generations, not in the sense of lifespans, to which I attach no importance, and which is used for neoliberal propaganda, but in the sense of historical periods. The period of the 1970s and 1980s, during which my convictions and achievements took shape and I lived a clandestine life, was radically different from the current period. The liberal quest to bury revolutionary concepts and points of departure, and to sow doubts about them has reached unprecedented lengths today. The alternative: individualism, consumerism, and the values of the market as opposed to the concepts of revolution and class and sacrifice and collectivity and justice and struggle. That is not even to mention colonialism. Unfortunately, many revolutionaries changed their convictions with the speed in which they take off their pants, to use Fidel Castro's apt expression. They went from one extreme to the other, and they should be ashamed of themselves.

On the other side, those who hold on to the choice of revolution and revolutionary struggle are like one holding embers in their hands. Despite their small numbers today, they are the hope of the future, the future of revolutionary struggle against imperialism, capitalism, and Zionism and the struggle for socialism and communism. That is why passing on the skills of my generation to youthful generations today has extraordinary significance. I rightly look with awe and appreciation at what these young people are doing in the stronghold of American imperialism, those who are imbued with revolutionary fervor and brilliant intelligence and energy and vigor in the service of our people's cause and the causes of oppressed peoples and classes. What joy I feel when I see people in the full bloom of youth siding with the struggle against imperialism, capitalism, and Zionism, not just because I am glad to see the base of revolutionaries widen, but also because I am happy to see that there are those today who are raising the flag for which we fought.

Thank you, comrades, for your efforts. You have made my heart overcome with joy.

A Note from Comrades
Palestinian Youth Movement

> "We reject what is, and strive to construct an alternative; we give shape to the historical alternative."
> —Wisam Rafeedie

During the summer of 2022, the Palestinian Youth Movement (PYM) decided to take up the task of translating Wisam Rafeedie's historical novel *The Trinity of Fundamentals* into the English language. This decision marked an important moment for the Popular University—the PYM's popular education committee—and the organization as a whole. It allowed us, as the PYM, to advance the goal of overcoming an important aspect of Palestinian fragmentation produced through Zionist colonialization of our land, namely the political, sociocultural, and linguistic barriers that exist between us as Palestinians across the diaspora.

The project of translating and publishing *The Trinity of Fundamentals* involved a unique process and approach. With the support of a professional translator, PYM members spent more than a year developing the translation of *The Trinity of Fundamentals* through serious and lengthy engagement with the historical, political, and linguistic context of the novel. For the first time in known history, a group of Palestinian youth active in their liberation struggle took it upon themselves to build a bridge between Palestinian history and present reality, between the English and Arabic languages, and between the homeland and the far diaspora.

Through this process, we came to understand the significance of *The Trinity of Fundamentals* for our own understanding of our history, our cause, and our commitments and struggles. We learned that the novel—written within the confines of Zionist prisons—was a fictionalized account of a real historical experience of a Palestinian revolutionary during the First Intifada who went into hiding for nine long years. We found that *The Trinity of Fundamentals* not only narrates Wisam's experience but comprises a revolutionary manifesto—one whose pages overflow with political lessons, personal reflections, theory, cultural references, and history.

Through the fictionalized character of Kan'an, Wisam exposes us to his experience of commitment and sacrifice, dissolving any idealistic romanticism we may attach to revolutionary struggle, while hardening our revolutionary optimism and resolve. It provides an opportunity to appraise the inevitable contradictions that arise in a life of committed struggle, as Wisam (Kan'an) narrates the contradictions between his "trinity of fundamentals"—the three pillars that define his life in hiding—life, revolution, and love. Most importantly, *The Trinity of Fundamentals* illuminates the essence of our struggle: that the revolutionary drive for victory and liberation will never be shattered.

As strugglers for liberation, we understand that we pick up this novel within the currents of history. We recognize we are a product of a shared history; that is, decades of struggle—including those undertaken by Wisam—that leads our people to the present moment as historical actors. Our people have experienced catastrophes (an-Nakba) and setbacks (an-Naksa); peace-processes (Oslo Accords) and uprisings (intifadas); and moments that have completely altered our peoples' vision for what is possible, from the 1936 revolt to the birth of the Palestinian revolution to Unity Intifada and Al-Aqsa Flood. It is upon this legacy and in this moment, our generation intervenes.

We find ourselves in a difficult stage in the Palestinian cause for liberation. For that reason, we must arm ourselves with a high level of consciousness and revolutionary relentlessness that will allow us to confront this stage in our struggle. We affirm, to draw from Wisam, that we have immense potential, one only "expanded by ideological conviction" for the liberation of Palestine. It is our hope that *The Trinity of Fundamentals* can serve as a weapon of knowledge and inspiration for all those who share in the belief that our victory rests upon our ability to be organized, to be committed to a revolutionary path with determination and conviction, and to be transformed through struggle from passive objects of history into active subjects in service of national liberation. For all who share in these convictions, you will find an eternal home in *The Trinity of Fundamentals*.

Publisher's Note

The Trinity of Fundamentals is a story of revolution, and to be entrusted with this story is a gift. Kan'an's secret life unfolds before us: from learning to cook and living in silence, to treating aching and festering wounds, to breathless whispers murmured between comrades from hidden corners. As we sink deeper into Kan'an's story, we realize we are being gifted with the opportunity to understand what it truly means to become a revolutionary, a fighter, a comrade.

Kan'an often refers to his experience as "unique" and "distinct," and when faced with the difficulties before him, it becomes clear that the task of living a clandestine life is one that does not come to all and certainly does not come easily. To live completely separated from everyday society, especially a society in struggle, is a restriction on the very human urge to be with others, and we watch Kan'an battle with and against his impulses to give in to that urge. Ultimately, in his clandestinity he is alone in many ways, but despite the hardships that come with isolation in the midst of an ongoing uprising, he makes the difficult and necessary choice to be together with his comrades, to follow the strategy of his party, and to become a part of revolutionary history.

With each challenge Kan'an faces, both the dramatic and the banal, we bear witness to the inner debates of a revolutionary in formation. As the political landscape changes, we watch a revolutionary organization and movement adapt and transform to meet the people's needs. The contradictions and struggles are ever-present, rushing at Kan'an and his party from all sides, but each time Kan'an chooses his secret life and his commitment to humanity, and each time his choice only reaffirms his commitment to liberation.

Kan'an's story is a gift, but it is also a charge: knowing what it means to be a revolutionary, will you be able to do the same? While we as readers face different conditions than the ones Kan'an lives through, the book still calls us to action, challenging us to understand the stakes of our tasks as revolutionaries wherever we may be. It is an invitation to get to know Kan'an, to know the intifada, to know the dignity of the struggle for Palestine. To know and understand what the fight for liberation requires of us is to embrace the humanity of the struggle for liberation across the world.

Dedication

To my mother, the friend dearest to my heart...
In the time of hardship and challenge,
And to my comrades, the true pillars of support...
In the time of hardship and challenge

Acknowledgements

I wish to thank my friend, the author Hassan Abdullah, for his attention which went beyond encouragement, and my comrade and friend Ahmad Qatamesh, not only for his support but also for his close attention to even the smallest of details that had to be dealt with.

Last but not least, I owe thanks to my three splendid comrades, 'Omar Tayeh, Yousef al-'Ati, and Yousef 'Abdul-'Al at Al-Nafha Prison, who took upon themselves the laborious tedious task of copying this novel on fifty-four capsules* and arranging to smuggle them through six prisons and delivering them safely into my hands.

—Wisam al-Rafeedie

---

* A method used by the Palestinian prisoners' movement to fold and wrap paper into the size of medicine capsules in order to transfer information within and outside of Zionist prisons.

Cast of Characters

KAN'AN SUBHI
The story's protagonist and member of the Popular Front for the Liberation of Palestine (often referred to as simply "the party" in the novel). He receives a letter from the party with orders to undergo a clandestine experience, or "secret life," in support of the Palestinian liberation struggle.

UMM KAN'AN
Kan'an's mother and resilient supporter.

MUNA
Kan'an's first love and fiancée.

HISHAM
Kan'an's close and dependable comrade who was assigned by the party and chosen by Kan'an to assist him with political duties during his clandestine experience.

UMM 'ISA
The nosy and intrusive owner of Kan'an's first secret house.

UMM MAHMUD
A neighbor who seemed to recognize Kan'an as he stayed in a safe house in Al-Bireh and thus taught him to never open the peephole of the door to an old woman from Al-Bireh.

FAYAD
The protagonist of Hanna Mina's novel *The Snow Comes through the Window*. Kan'an read the novel multiple times in hiding and found resonance between his and Fayad's clandestine stories.

BIGFOOT
A party member whom Kan'an refers to as the "comrade with the giant foot." He assisted Kan'an with emergent relocations.

SAKINAH
The prying owner of one of the apartments in Al-Bireh the party used as a safe house.

'ABIR
A beautiful neighbor Kan'an nicknames the "sun-maiden."

HIND
Kan'an's love interest for six weeks in his final year of hiding.

Chapter 1

Relentless blows on the door to the safe house. Thunderous banging that shatters a beautiful and serene summer night. The harbingers of what could be a drastic transformation of his life. Is this how his latest birthday was to be celebrated, with smashing steel-toe military boots and rifle butts? What sort of life do these vigorous announcements foretell? One born only to be extinguished.

Will the anniversary of his birth, that celebration of beginnings, spell his life's end as well?

They were pounding on the door like celebrants of some primitive, pagan ritual, like members of a cannibalistic tribe engaged in a debauched, mad dance to the accompaniment of mindless screams and shrieks that tear apart the stillness of the jungle. Amidst the beating of drums, they announced a thirst and hunger to tear apart flesh and devour their prey. That was how Kan'an imagined them on that August night as he crouched motionless in his secret den next to Hisham. It was half past midnight when the soldiers began their attempt to break in.

The quick succession of fierce blows disturbed the hush of the large, sparse house and the surrounding industrial neighborhood. Silence had prevailed there, save for the barking of dogs at the nearby barley mill. The dogs fell mute when the ritual began, petrified by those evening poltergeists who had drowned out the yelps with their clamor. As the pounding intruded, the monotonies of his secret life faded away.

In their desire to breach his den which had eluded their intelligence services for years, the intruders were akin to lecherous men assaulting a virgin, seeking to violate her horrifically. The soldiers' blows would derail the life he had become accustomed to. What was to come? What would forge the course of the strange and exceptional life ahead? Would it be the habits of his old life, accumulated from the hours, the days, the years he had spent evading the soldiers' grip? They had their customs and he had his own. He had spent year after year living just beyond their clutches. Throughout that time, he had built the schedule of his days; he owned those days, he pressed their hours into the service of a revolutionary enterprise. That secret life became his profession, until eventually it was the womb which birthed all of his experiences, an amniotic of searing hardships and revolutionary action.

The blows had grown very loud. Their echoes bounced off the walls, the doors of his house, his chairs and books, his papers and pens, his loaf of bread and glass of water, his red prayer beads and his cigarettes. They reverberated through the past nine years of his life. The sounds flitted down the streets and neighborhoods of Ramallah, the houses and alleys of the city which had embraced him and held him close to its chest. Ramallah, where he had sought refuge and disappeared from the gaze of its occupiers. The echoes fell on his head like the blows of a hammer, shaking every one of his brain cells, calling for mobilization and action, as though yelling to say:

> *Act quickly, Kan'an, the unthinkable has happened! The blows this time are different than two years ago when the soldiers grew tired of knocking and left. This is the dawn of a new era, Kan'an, a confrontation which represents a different sort of challenge from what*

you have grown accustomed to for many years now. This is a battle you must win. Nothing but victory will do, nothing short of victory!

A new era and a new confrontation, a juncture which turned the last page on the past. Nevertheless, each line on each page of his diary was emblazoned onto his memory, recorded as if on a cinematic reel of film.

The turning points in a man's life cannot obliterate the past, no matter how long ago it all began. The past is deeply etched in memory; it refuses to leave, and the mind recalls its events whenever it wishes.

A first love is a turning point. Does a lover forget how it began? Does he forget his first stammering words, the trembling of his hand when it touched hers, his confusion as to where to put his nose when he kissed her for the first time?

Enlisting in a clandestine party is another turning point. Does one forget the first words of the man who introduced him to the life of struggle and the path of secrecy, where they were walking, or where they were sitting when the conversation began? Does one forget the first secret meeting, the first communiqué he distributed like a fugitive, or the first operation he was assigned to carry out?

The birth of a first child is a turning point for the mother. Does she forget the pangs of labor and the pain of childbirth? Does she forget the moment she first saw the tearful eyes of her baby, the small, cherubic mouth suckling on her breast which she offered to him for his first feeding?

December 1982 marked one such great transformation in Kan'an's life. On a cold and lonely dark night at eight o'clock in the evening, he received a warning: "Your man has been arrested and may confess. Do not spend the night in your house. Fend for yourself until we can make out where things are headed."

The cloak of mourning hung over the house. Death had visited the family a week earlier, snatching away his father and leaving in its wake not only sorrow, but also new family obligations dropped on Kan'an's shoulders by fate, and a hope kindled in his mother's heart that he would step into the shoes of his departed father.

"It seems as though calamities come in multitudes. What a coincidence," Kan'an said upon receiving the news. He sensed dark days lay ahead.

Dark days? No, more like dark years. After that cold, lonely December night, your family home will no longer be open to you, you may no longer step across its threshold. You will leave and never return. Things have taken a turn for the worst. Your name had not been known to them, but now it has been revealed—not just your name, but your party position, the missions you carried out, the identities of those you contacted. You could not have divined what lay beyond the horizon no matter how gifted you were at discerning the future.

As soon as he received the warning, he left the house, determined not to frequent it at all for fear that he may fall into their hands. He knew many students with houses around the university and in the two cities. He used to spend one night with one student acquaintance and the next night with another, constantly on the move. Slinging his leather satchel on his shoulder, he carried around his books as well as his nightwear and extra packets of cigarettes. They were a precaution against the unforeseen in the event that he could not get around the checkpoints set up by the soldiers or make detours to avoid the Occupation's army patrols. He continued to go to the university in spite of it all.

In December of each year, the university would turn into a beehive of activity. Tensions ran high as the annual elections were held for the student union. They coincided with the anniversary of the founding of the Popular Front for the Liberation of Palestine (PFLP) as well as preparations for the commemoration of the revolution and the launching of the Fatah movement. Consequently, classrooms appeared almost empty. Everyone was busy either participating in union or syndicate politics or engaging in endless debates (which grew louder day by day), or listening to and observing what was going on around them.

Kan'an did not openly participate in the preparations for the December activities. Instructions from the party were to keep a low profile, and his party affiliation remained unknown to many. The reality was that Kan'an and his comrades were deeply involved in the decision-making and implementation of various activities, whether in regard to preparing for the anniversary celebrations of the party's founding or commemorating the launching of the revolution and the Fatah movement.

This was why he was rarely able to meet up with Muna on campus those days. But they would find a few minutes here and there to spend together over lunch or a quick cup of tea at the university canteen which, at times, buzzed with large numbers of students far exceeding its capacity. The students argued and clamored as though the scene was a vegetable market or a hornets' nest. The circles of debaters were transformed into something resembling pyramids: the circle would start with two students, and then a few more would join in, and then they would begin climbing on tables and chairs and one head would tower over all of the other heads and so on. At this stage of the squabble, it was difficult to see the debaters or make out who was speaking or what they were even saying.

Muna would get annoyed whenever she saw Kan'an weighed down with the concerns and worries of the season, his clothes rumpled, his eyes red from the lack of sleep, fuzz covering his unshaven cheeks and his stumbling gait revealing his fatigue.

"What a sight you are. If only you could see yourself in a mirror. Your clothes, the stubble on your cheeks, the bags under your eyes—it's like you've climbed out of a grave. Go get some sleep, change your clothes, shave."

"As you know, we're in the middle of the elections, the anniversary commemorations, and on top of everything, an attack on the party and a comrade under interrogation. Who knows if he'll crack?"

"I don't think he will break down and implicate you in his confession," she said firmly without any basis.

That was wishful thinking. He looked at her tenderly, his lips forming a tired, satirical smile. His beloved was expressing her hopes and wishes.

※※※※※

A week after Kan'an left his family's home, the occupiers mounted a surprise attack on a house adjacent to the one he was staying at with some students. The minute he heard the commotion across the street, he thought he was under surveillance, that they knew his location and were searching the houses in the area looking for him. Without hesitating, he quickly opened the door and scaled the wall around the house. He jumped and took off running between the houses near the edge of Qaddura camp,[1] heading for his family's home—he wanted to know if they had raided it. Hiding at a safe distance, he watched the house from under the cover of some trees. At midnight he knocked at his mother's bedroom window.

"It's Kan'an. Has anything happened?"

His mother rose from her bed, disturbed and breathing hard, not having fallen asleep yet. How was she to sleep having learned from Kan'an that the house could be raided by those looking for him? Ever since Kan'an embarked upon the political path and the Occupation's boots trod the floor of their home, her ears had become attuned to military trucks driving by, and she told him so many times. The sounds made her uneasy and, since the family house lay on the route regularly taken by the Occupation, there was no end to her disquiet.

"No, they did not come. Come in, come in, it's cold outside. I will put the teapot on the fire. Where are you roaming to at this time of the night? They did not come. Come in!" She too was engaging in wishful thinking.

At any rate, if they were to come they would have already come before midnight. I should go in! He thought to himself. He made up his mind and shuffled in through the kitchen door. He was led by his nostalgia for sleep and a cup of tea. The self savors peace and quiet, but "the revolutionary" who allows himself to be led by its wishes is sometimes led to his death.

Half past midnight, as he sat drinking tea with his mother and brother, his eyes kept drifting towards the street nervously. Suddenly, he caught sight of soldiers headed towards the house. He quickly recognized an intelligence officer leading the group of soldiers. Vaulting towards the kitchen door as though stung, Kan'an whispered an order to his mother: "Don't leave the third cup on the windowsill."

Sneaking out the door, he ran towards the wall surrounding the house. As he climbed over, he looked back to see the soldiers surrounding his home before forcing their way in. He ran across the neighbor's vegetable garden and up the frosted hill overlooking his house, then climbed a tree and crouched down, watching the house. After two hours of sitting like a monkey in the tree, he was sure that they had left. He climbed down and walked towards his home, then tapped on the windowpane again.

"Open, open!"

The only reason he had returned to the house was to say goodbye to his mother and to find out what the soldiers had done. Did they mistreat his mother, brother, and family? Did they search the house? What had they said? All of these details could prove useful. Kan'an started questioning his mother as soon as he entered the darkened house.

"So, what did they say? What did they do?"

His mother was agitated, though she had not been moved by their deceptive assurances.

"They did not stay long, and they did not search. They asked about you and said they wanted you for five minutes, no more, 'just to ask him a few questions and he can go back home.'"

Kan'an smiled, communicating his understanding, and his mother nodded as though to say she too understood.

"What will you do now? I told you time and time again, Kan'an, the political path is difficult, but you did not listen. Go ahead, tell me what you are going to do now."

"I won't turn myself in. I have to go now." He tossed this grenade of a sentence in his mother's face with no warning or time for explanation.

"Don't be stupid! I told them that you were studying late in the library and would probably spend the night there. Tomorrow morning, go turn yourself in and may God protect you." She said this as though she had not heard and did not wish to hear what he had said.

"There is no time for explanations. Later, when things quiet down, I'll send for you. For now, I'm not turning myself in."

There was no convincing her. She argued in a troubled voice, shifting between scolding and pleading. He was pained by her state and his own at the same time. The tension grew, though neither was successful in convincing the other. They ignored each other's words as though they were addressed to someone else.

"Let me leave with my mind at ease. Don't be mad, it will be a hard burden to bear if I were to leave while you're angry. I must go!" He settled the matter by embracing and kissing her, struggling to fight back the tears welling up in his eyes. She kissed him, trembling from a mixture of fear and tenderness. She insisted on giving him money but he refused. She settled the matter in her usual way by shoving the money into the pocket of his winter overcoat. He turned and walked towards the back door. As he opened it, Kan'an suddenly heard her voice behind him:

"Go, my son! May God be pleased with you."

He left to face his new life, bearing with him his mother's prayer.

A week later Kan'an received a letter from the party which he read with extreme care, line by line, word by word. It was not an ordinary letter by any standard. The party organization in the region was in the midst of a struggle with the occupiers. The letter smelled of clashes and conflict. It contained an assessment of the intelligence services' aggressive campaign on the organization, with references concerning "the importance of each and every comrade" staying on top of their responsibilities and not allowing the Occupation authorities to stymie their efforts. It stressed the dire need for professionals who will grant the party not just the hours in their days, but perhaps their very lives. The letter concluded with the following official message:

> **It has been decided that you will not turn yourself in. Rather, you shall go into hiding and lead a secret existence, adopting the measures, precautions, requirements, and rules of conduct which must be followed to the letter. To begin with, do not receive any visitors and do not visit anyone.**

"**The importance of a comrade, every comrade, being on top of their responsibilities!**" Kan'an knew the party's experiences in the homeland were informing this important security decision. The occupier's attacks on party organizations and the imprisonment of its leaders prevented party members from amassing experience, as the letter also said "**Protecting the accumulation of experience through the preservation of cadres and foundational pillars is now the first line of defense for an increasingly effective and more stable party structure.**"

During 1980-81, the party justifiably adopted the slogan of "solving the institutional problem" as a pragmatic decision. It alerted its members to the necessity of building party organizations which, after they became firmly established, could serve as a basis on which all branches of party activity, especially the popular, political, informational, and combative branches, could be centralized.

What was achieved at the beginning of the 1980s was meager but nevertheless promising. The activities of the dispersed nuclei of the party, consisting of university students, intellectuals, and some workers, began to be organized under a somewhat unified resolution, even if they were not yet within an integrated party network. In this way, the party in the homeland was like a toddler on all fours learning to walk upright. The party paper was being published, albeit haphazardly, and focused on directing and discussing organizational policy. One could see the buds of the student and women's unions sprouting in the universities, institutions, and cities, while party activities among the large arena of rural workers were still in their infancy. These union organizations had begun to replace committees of volunteers which, since the mid-1970s, had been one of the only channels for recruiting, politicizing, and mobilizing activists towards party activities. The party worked with these union organizations, seeing them as instruments for expanding among the masses without any serious focus on their syndical programs and tasks.

The pursuit of that goal—a unified party organization in the homeland with a constructive outlook and with popular, political, and media branches engaged in resistance activities—was a multipronged effort. It required the party to prevent the disruption of the accumulation of institutionalized knowledge, which would occur as a result of the arrest of party members. It also imposed upon the party the need to grow the professional cadres and leaders who would be dedicated exclusively to dealing with the party's problems and the struggle. Indeed, there can be no revolutionary party without a professional team. There was a firm conviction that the party would be built, not by amateurs, but by professionals who would collectively shoulder the responsibility of coping with the problems facing the revolution from beginning to end.

In 1982, developments in the struggle against the Occupation trended in that same direction. That year, the Occupation dealt a strong military blow against the revolution, which had demonstrated a heroic resistance by any standard. As a result, the revolution was forced to halt its military activities in Lebanon, which had served as its most important base, and to evacuate thousands of its fighters to the outer regions of the Arab world. This brought the significance of the Occupied Territories to the forefront, a notion that gained widespread popularity overnight due to the realization that poor political decisions had, thus far, neglected the homeland as a viable base from which to build a resistance front.

Up until that point, the party had been resigned to treat the Occupied Territories as no more than an important site, rather than as the principal arena for resistance. The party's policy had emphasized setting up small groups of *fedayeen** who were quickly liquidated either before they became active or shortly thereafter. This strategy was not aimed at building a popular organizational and political structure as a bulwark of the national resistance's military action. It initially originated due to the fact that the revolution had erupted outside the country and was compelled to fight constant battles to protect its sheer existence. This eventually meant that efforts in the homeland itself fell short, part of which was also the result of the underdevelopment of Palestinian political thought and its immaturity in organizational matters and in creating modes of resistance. The resistance had to wait until the 1980s for the political organizations to begin competing against one another to mold that organizational structure. The military defeat in 1982 should have set off proverbial alarm bells: signaling the importance of the Occupied Territories for building the structure of resistance and the need to consider the homeland as the primary arena of struggle.

In 1975, Kan'an's party had attempted to build such a developed structure, but using an approach that lacked an administrative scientific party methodology. This led to the enemy's intel-

---

* Resistance fighters.

ligence wiping out that weak, new experiment in 1976 through a comprehensive campaign of repression. Dozens were arrested and the weak and deficient organizations, unable to defend themselves, were broken up. On June 1, 1976, Muhammad Yousef Al-Khawaja[2] was martyred at the hands of Israeli intelligence operatives, while defending his organization in the interrogation cells of Ramallah prison.

By the end of the 1970s, a new attempt at party restructuring was made, but this time using a different methodology, one which viewed the building of the party as a political-organizational program, rather than an administrative one. In that context, the methodology focused on two needs: the need for a professional team, and the need for self-preservation through protecting essential connections outside of prison and consolidating party traditions as an educational environment for the formation of a coordinated character of the party.

Kan'an received his letter from the party containing its decision while he was staying in a house near the university waiting for Muna's class to end. He had hid himself between the narrow walls, leaving behind him all of those noisy debates of student life, on topics ranging from the Israeli invasion of Lebanon to the commemorations of December.

Since the fourth of June, the university was no longer what it had once been. Its walls were covered with all sorts of posters, provocative slogans, communiqués about the results of battles, and notices about activities in solidarity with the prisoners. The Israeli slogan, "Saboteurs, stop and think!" had no effect whatsoever on the political and moral disposition of students. Neither did the empty bravado of Menachem Begin, Ariel Sharon, and the enemy's military leaders, who threatened the liquidation of the saboteurs in forty-eight hours!

Each organization on campus took to commenting and acting as it saw fit, but the propaganda and solidarity efforts of the organizations were soon unified under the supervision of the student union. As for the students—that body of humanity dizzied by tireless and endless discussions—they were transformed overnight into experts on military affairs: one person would issue an assessment on Israel's military capabilities and its combat formations, and another would explain the use of guerrilla warfare tactics by the resistance. And a third even had the audacity to give his two cents concerning the distribution of combat units across fronts due to his "extensive" knowledge about the geography of Beirut and its suburbs! In war, all the spectators turn into military analysts, just as all patients in a hospital become doctors and all assistant attorneys become lawyers and all detainees become court experts and crime scene investigators.

Students were caught between the intentionally demoralizing Israeli military propaganda and the overly optimistic propaganda of the Palestinian factions. Student opinion coalesced around the latter, building new aspirations on top of the old, turning the Palestinian resistance into an invincible force and the Israeli military machine into a paper tiger. But after three months, the brave fighters, defending the honor of the Arab nation, were forced to exit Beirut with their small arms and light weapons while Yasser Arafat and the Palestinian leadership placed their confidence in the promises of the American envoy, Philip Habib, who negotiated the withdrawal! The result was twofold: on the one hand, the spirit of the revolution and the bulk of its fighters were saved, and on the other, an Israeli-Phalangist massacre of Palestinian refugees in Sabra and Shatila[3] occurred, in which the heads and limbs of women, old men and children were hacked off and cast into the mud in the alleys of the two camps!

The students and the people at large were not shaken by the military defeat and the withdrawal. Wherever one went, whomever one asked, the opinion of the masses, students, and the public alike confirmed this.

"May God give them health and strength. They did what was expected of them and more. They were under siege for eighty-four days and possibly more, fighting the sixth largest military power in the world while the Arabs watched idly. Who else fought like they did?"

"Our regimes claim to be nationalist and amass weapons, yet when the hour of battle is at hand they say, 'We will choose the time and place of the battle and will not allow the Israelis to choose for us.' They forget that a soldier does not always have a choice as to when and where to fight, otherwise there would never have been wars in the first place."

"The Israelis are liars. They surely lost thousands of troops!"

"The withdrawal of eleven thousand combatants is not such a big deal! In Lebanon, even children carry RPGs. The revolution is still alive there."

"Now the secret armed resistance will begin. The Popular Front for the Liberation of Palestine, the Democratic Front for the Liberation of Palestine, the Lebanese Communist Party, and the Communist Action Organization have announced the formation of 'The National Lebanese Resistance Front,'[4] and have begun to fight. They will transform Lebanon into a new Vietnam!"

The people and the students did not understand the dangerous political consequences of the blow to the Palestine Liberation Organization's (PLO) military infrastructure. These consequences soon found expression in the Reagan Plan, which was announced directly following the Palestinian withdrawal. The popular forces turned away from the plan as they rightly saw it as the political aftermath of the military outcome, while the official leadership of the PLO declared its flirtatious middle-of-the-road position within the logic of "yes-and-no."

About five months after the withdrawal, the party issued a circular emanating from its Central Committee meeting, which took up, among other things, the issue of the Occupied Territories. It made quick references to the future role entrusted to the Occupied Territories after the destruction of the PLO's infrastructure[5] in a way that kept with the trends of building a united and solid organizational infrastructure in the homeland.

❆❆❆❆❆

(1)

Kan'an was on pins and needles as he waited for Muna. He felt as though her class lecture had taken an entire decade. What would she do? Ever since he received instructions from the party to take precautions, the insistent question badgered him: How would she react? Thinking about her evoked memories of the three years they spent together.

They met for the first time in 1979. He first laid eyes on her while he was giving a talk on Jimmy Carter's visit to the region. He could not stop looking at her. His words gushed out of his mouth in stutters and stammers, flustering him more than he already was. She looked at him from among the rows of listeners. Her gaze pierced into him, but her mind was not focused on what he was saying.

"What's her name?"

"Muna," his friend replied.

"Does she have a phone number?"

"I don't know. I'll check the lists of club members."

That same day Kan'an called and asked her to meet him.

"How did it occur to you to invent the ploys you used in order to talk to me? Didn't you consider that I might say no?" she asked him, shyness and hesitation gripping her from her head to the tips of her toes. He was in no better shape than she was; nevertheless, nature's logic and magnetic pull pushed all obstacles aside. They were sitting on the edge of a water fountain in the garden of the club. Her blue jeans and white shirt showed off her captivating, svelte form.

"I wanted to see you and talk to you. I have been thinking about you ever since I first saw you. But your eyes were also calling out to me, weren't they?"

She was too shy to reply. They changed the subject of their conversation to something innocuous, a topic here, a reference there. He uttered whatever words spilled out of his mouth, trying to banish the shy silence which had descended upon them. They approached each other like toddlers, not yet having learned how to advance upright, knowing only how to crawl.

(2)

On Tuesdays, Kan'an would finish the last class at the secondary school and hurry home. Then he would bathe, shave, dress quickly, and set off for the university to meet her at two o'clock. For a whole year, every Tuesday was their day. He would usually find her sitting with other students next to the door of the snack bar, waiting for him but not showing it. She would join in the conversation with those around her from time to time while looking at the passageway where he would appear. He would arrive and sit down, and she would continue to act as if no one had just entered. Her shyness about her emotions and a thrilling fear of these new feelings took root inside of her.

"We've been meeting for months. Tuesday is our sacred day. But you? Where are you?"

"What do you mean? You come and you find me here," she said, embarrassed.

"Is that so?"

(3)

The more he continued to meet her, the more attached he grew. He found her shyness to be a captivating grace. Her fear resulted from her isolation and her life experiences, and his role was to challenge that. Her yearning for him would shatter the bottleneck. Desire could not be suppressed forever.

"I brought you a book. I can explain anything you may find confusing."

"The guys here explain a lot of things to me. I read and pay attention to what is going on for your sake."

At that time the university served as a hub for nationalist actions in the Occupied Territories. Everything was politicized—union activity, social relations, even the gathering of a few students to study together! The students clustered around organizations that were engaged in a heated struggle for the hearts and minds of the youth in an atmosphere of democratic and intellectual competition among varying agendas and opinions. The university's policy of wide support for the students proved transformative, shifting the entire setting from that of an educational establishment for the children of the bourgeoisie to a learning institution that attracted hundreds of residents of refugee camps and the rural areas each year—the children of the popular classes. This shift sped up the process of politicization even more.

The political organizations belonging to the resistance movement quickly capitalized on this trend, sending tens of freed political prisoners to form secret organizational cells which then spread like wildfire among the students. Clusters of unions began to appear, fronts for the political organizations that later changed into democratic student organizations. Birzeit University was not only a hotbed of resistance and political organization, it was also an example of a modern and enlightened society that was not closed in on itself. The university was open to new ideas and the free exchange of opinions, a society in which the full spectrum of ideologies—the nationalist-bourgeoisie, the leftists, the religious, the communists, even the Trotskyites—had someone to carry their banner, even if the ideology itself had no followers. And the anarchists, who were enamored with life along chaotic European lines of thought, flocked together like a clique which elicited nothing other than annoyance.

The annual election season on campus brewed an environment of stormy political developments, and arguments and disputes would break out when, for example, a banned book was distributed or a communiqué from a leader was read aloud. Although the practices of the university's student movement were impetuous, this did not nullify the dominant characteristic of the learning establishment as a sanctuary for nationalist struggle and a democratic arena for intellectual dispute. The university provided fertile soil for the formation of a stratum of politicized and militant students who could be relied upon to play a future role in the makeup of the party and the politics of the people.

Those who lived in and devoted themselves to this atmosphere at the university during the early 1980s were fortunate. The rebels lived within its walls, battling against the Occupation and against convention, such that that their lives were a medley filled with secret organizational affiliations, love, the songs of Sheikh Imam and Marcel Khalife, the books of Lenin, Nawal el-Saadawi, Hisham Sharabi, and Che Guevara, and a student lifestyle that contradicted all traditions even if it was just for the sake of being contradictory.

Little by little, Kan'an tried to attract Muna to this environment as an alternative to her schooling and rearing by nuns, women who dedicated themselves solely to the hereafter and not to this world. It was also an alternative to her family which, like most Palestinian families, provided circumstances propitious for nothing other than the crushing and marginalizing of personalities. But Muna was moving in his direction, albeit very slowly and held back by an immense fear.

(4)

They sat on one of the stone benches under an evergreen cypress tree in the courtyard of the classroom building. It was as though the bench was reserved for lovers. In fact, it was widely accepted as such—seldom did anyone have the cheek to question this and transgress the established ownership of those seats! He used to call them "the seats of rebellion against convention."

"You are not your usual self," he said while gazing into her sleepy eyes.

"What do you mean?" she asked with a dazzling smile.

"You are radiant and smiling all over."

"I'm happy. I missed you. I've been waiting for Tuesday."

"I would come every day, if I could. You know I have school until noon, and afterwards I'm busy with my affairs."

"You are a party member, aren't you?" She said it quickly with no preliminaries as though she was talking about something routine and simple, not something whose discovery could lead to years in prison.

"How did you know? I never shared any of my affiliations with you. You only know my convictions."

"I understand what's going on around me. I don't need you to reveal things to me!"

He had spoken to her about the party often without acknowledging that he was a member. She supported the party and its activities and positions. Women in the party paid attention to her. They sat and discussed things with her as Kan'an had asked them to do.

"When I think of you, I fear for the future. My family will not approve of my relationship with someone like you. You are known to them. Ever since you visited my brother he changed. He began to listen to Sheikh Imam and to buy books. My father says, 'Kan'an is like a germ. He brought Lenin into my house.'" She imitated her father's voice as she said this, then she laughed and followed it up with a question: "Since when have you been listening to Sheikh Imam anyway?"

"Ever since I became one of those 'workers of the world, unite!' people in 1975. Anyway, it is too early for you to think about how your family feels. We have years of studying before us and then we'll see. Don't anticipate calamities before they occur. I'm with you. Do not be afraid of anything."

She looked at him with concern and changed the subject. "Many of the new students support you. I try to sway some of them too."

"Support '*you*'? I thought you were one of us? Why do you try to sway them if you are not one of us?" he teased her disapprovingly. She fell silent, embarrassed.

(5)

"You know I love you. I've said it more than once. We've been spending time together for a year now and I find that there is a lot between us, yet you haven't spoken openly about your feelings even once."

"I'm scared. Don't be annoyed with me. Don't get agitated. Please, we are together here in the university, we're always together. What more do you want?"

"What more?" Kan'an could not control his emotions. "I have the right to know how you feel, where you stand. Are we joined together by something special or not?"

"Joined together." She said it, finally.

"On what basis?" It was as though he was pleading with her, trying to extract a confession of her love for him.

"On whatever basis you want." She said it in a low stammer, she had admitted it finally, maybe not with her words but with her actions. He smiled and touched her hand under the table in the restaurant. A shudder of buried desire ran through their bones.

(6)

"Here's the underground newspaper. Burn it as soon as you are done reading it. Don't let anyone see it."

Muna stuck it in her bookbag and they walked towards their seat under the cypress tree. "Do you think you will succeed in the negotiations to form a united national front?"

He gave her an angry look, which she did not understand.

"I will overlook the fact that you said '*you* will succeed' instead of '*we*' as though you belong to a world different from ours. '*We*' will succeed in the end. There is no other option. It would be a disgrace if the PLO did not control the student union. A victory for the Islamic bloc would mean the paralysis of the student union and would prevent it from clashing with the Occupation authorities, seeing as the Islamic political trend has yet to engage in the struggle so far. As usual, the real fight is between us and Fatah. The influence of the communists has waned, and the Democratic Front is too small. Even if the decision has to be delegated to George Habash and Yasser Arafat, we can't allow any organization other than the PLO to gain control of the council."

"Where did the Islamic bloc come from?" she asked derisively.

"They have popular support as one of the already established movements, but the bloc relies too heavily on money from Saudi Arabia and the Muslim World League.[6] The money comes to them through Jordan with the knowledge of the Jordanian government. From there, it reaches the Islamic collective in Gaza with the knowledge of the Israelis, who turn a blind eye. That is the Islamic bloc's payoff for opposing the resistance and the PLO and the left. Have you read the book they distributed recently, *Nationalism and How it is Understood*?"

"No. The students burned the copies they sent us in the courtyard. They haven't redistributed it since."

"Naturally they will not redistribute it. It's causing a scandal for them. It was stupid to distribute it in the first place. They consider nationalism to be an 'animal instinct' that we adapted from the Western Crusaders. As for Palestine, the book says it is a dot on the map, barely visible, and God grants it to whomever He chooses! Of course, there is the influence of Iran's revolution, our shortcomings, and the policies of Abu 'Ammar.* These factors created fertile soil in which the Islamic bloc can exist. As long as they do not fight against the Occupation, they will remain isolated and suspect. They become dangerous when they threaten Palestinian unity. We have to take that into consideration. The university is a lofty educational, democratic, and modern edifice. We cannot afford to forfeit the student union to those who adopt ideas such as 'the Crusader administration,' the separation of male from female students in the cafeteria and lecture halls and laboratories, elimination of the cultural studies program and the rest of that nonsense that does not belong in this day and age."

(7)

"We will find a way! We will examine the university statutes, registration, and find a way!"

---

* Yasser Arafat. This is an example of the *kunya*, or an honorific Arabic name, referring usually to a person's first-born son.

Muna had been horrified to receive a warning that she may be expelled from the university, and Kan'an was trying to comfort her. She cried with her head on his shoulder as they sat in his house. Her political interests and union activity, which were limited anyway, were catching up to her and hurting her grades. Like many others, she could not balance her political activities with her studies. She had changed her major, and now, threatened with expulsion, was at risk of drifting to a third major. She couldn't handle that, especially considering she had earned an 86 in the high school diploma exam.*

"My political activities at the university have hurt my academic record."

"Many others are more politically active than you and have taken on many responsibilities, yet they still made the honors list."

"My affairs are all upside down," she said, lamenting her bad luck.

"We will find a way, don't worry. Tomorrow you should go ask for a copy of the university's bylaws and study them carefully. The important thing is that you should put your affairs in order so that we can go celebrate Labor Day at the Umariya School in Jerusalem."

"I'm worried we won't get back till late."

"Find a way to convince your parents to stay out late. Tell them you will be studying at the library."

Muna went to the celebration and came home late. A week later, she chose a third major and managed to salvage her academic career.

(8)

Politics could not find a way to preoccupy Muna's thoughts, where resistance activity only had a superficial influence, like lipstick. She remained connected to politics and resistance because of her relationship with Kan'an and in keeping with the dominant

---

* Tawjihi is the General Secondary Education Certification Examination, and the grade earned dictates which majors you are able to enroll in at university. Muna's need to change majors meant that she was enrolling in majors requiring higher Tawjihi grades than the one she earned.

fashion at the time. One had to be categorized, in some way or the other, as belonging to this group or that group—there was no floating middle ground. She was Kan'an's girlfriend and he was known to her and her acquaintances, so of course, she was part of his group. As a matter of principle, she subscribed to the dominant social norm that women were subordinate to men. Women adopted the way of life of their men, regardless of the ways of life that existed around them. A woman who broke with this norm was an exception, nothing more. Muna could not be an exception considering the amount of defiance, strength, independence, and individualism it took to do so.

Three types of political commitment characterize the behavior of students. The first type of commitment is deeply rooted in ideological conviction; such commitment survives in its owner beyond university life as they join broader society. The second type of commitment is dependent on the current fashion, which emerges from tumultuous university life and the clamor for novelty. This terrain created ripe conditions for the emergence of this second type, branded by the ideologically-committed students of the first type as "revolution until graduation." The third type of commitment results from dependence on a loved one, friend, or relative, and therefore takes a variety of possible trajectories: their commitment persists after graduation because their relationship of dependence persists, their commitment is transformed by experience into an ideological commitment, or they end up subject to the second type: "revolution until graduation."

(9)

"How did I lose my mind and fall in love with you? What possessed me to attend your talk three years ago today?"

Muna was already asking herself these questions, but actually said the words out loud as she resignedly laid her head on his shoulder. He had one hand on her neck while the languid fingers of the other traced the features of her face with delight, like they were discovering them for the first time. He would sink into languor like a pianist gently playing a delicate tune while he imagined himself soaring in infinite space.

That day they acted as though there was no one else in the world. They were joined by love and laughter and kisses and wine, like children resuming their harmonious play after a quarrel. In her, Kan'an found refuge from politics and the party and hideouts and newspaper clippings and arguments—she was a haven from studies and books and endless exams. In him, Muna found refuge from crushing authoritarian supervision and from the words of the nuns, her teachers, which were etched into her memory, words that rang the rusty alarm bell to beware of sin whenever her desire welled up inside her. They both found escape in the warmth of a feverish embrace, a secret delight in the hours they managed to snatch each week. He would turn his back on his world full of tiring daily details while she would smash the alarm bell in her mind that warns against sin. They lived for a few hours each week as though there was no one else in the world. Each would bring out the inner child in the other so that only nature remained. Everything comes from nature and everything returns to her, even if only for a few despairing hours.

"Love entering our lives is madness. We have been stricken by it. In our life, resistance is madness, and to be alive as human beings means to be mad. And there is nothing more perfect than insane resistance!"

He kissed her passionately.

❖❖❖❖❖

Kan'an waited for her by the window of his house until her lectures ended and she came to him. It had been a week since he last saw her, on the day they raided his house. For a week, he bounced from house to house to escape their eyes and their raids as he waited for the party to make arrangements for his shelter. For a week, he missed her incessantly every second. For a week, he yearned for her daily, desiring her with his mind, his whole being, and all his senses. He would ask about her just to set his mind at ease. She had been officially involved with him for months now, something which the whole city and her acquaintances in the student body knew.

Muna came to him breathing hard, her face ripe with longing. She was in a hurry as though she feared losing him and missing her date with him forever. They embraced for a long time, and he squeezed her slim waist forcefully between his hands. He kissed her earnestly and she too yearned for him.

"I missed you terribly, you rascal," she reprimanded him gently. "Why do you do that to me? As usual, you don't care about your beloved."

Kan'an sat her down next to him, stroking her hair and embracing her. She laid her head on his shoulder contentedly.

"I couldn't see you for your sake and mine. Don't forget that I'm a wanted man. Every step I take has to be calculated."

"How did you spend the last week?" she asked gently, revealing her sympathy, her hand on his chest.

"Moving here and there, from one house to the other, avoiding surveillance and raids."

"How long will this last?" she asked seriously.

"Until certain arrangements are finalized."

"What do you mean: 'certain arrangements?' When will I see you again?" She fired her questions at him, beset by confusion.

"I mean a fixed and secret safe house, known only to a few and difficult to reach. As for our next meeting, it depends on what your position is with regards to my new status."

She raised her head from his shoulder and sat up straight.

"I don't understand anything. A fixed safe house they cannot reach? My position? Your new status? What are all these riddles?"

Kan'an knew that it would not be easy to explain these things to her—she would not be able to digest what he had to tell her in any case. He anticipated the end of the conversation would mark the end of his love and their relationship. He tried to make her understand gently, without shocking her. He tried to explain to her that she had to accept a one-eighty-degree change in the course of her relationship with him, because his life had turned one-eighty-degrees! But how could he do it? He tried to say what had to be said. He leaned towards her and gently kissed her forehead.

"Muna, please understand me well. There will be a fundamental change in my life and our lives together as a consequence. I will not turn myself in. I will be living a secret life. I don't want the enemy to neutralize my potential. There is no point in my going to prison. My role has been decided. In my new life, I see you as more than a friend and more than a lover. I see you as everything. I see you as a support for me, like I am a support for you."

She was stunned, her mouth wide open, listening to his words, not believing what she had just heard. It pained him to see her beautiful face contorted like this. He was being torn apart, but he knew that he was doing the right thing. His rational mind said "one could only do what is right," regardless of the catastrophic consequences.

"I don't understand. Why you in particular? Everyone turns themselves in. Is the confession made against you such a big deal? I don't understand. Where am I in your plans? Why are you neglecting me?"

> *You are not the only one who will not understand what is going on,* he thought. *No one who knows me will understand. None of my friends will understand. I do not blame you, my love. What I am about to undergo will be a new experience. I myself do not understand what the details will be. I excuse you because what I am about to undergo is incomprehensible, mad even.*

"The issue is not the magnitude of the confession made against me, big or small. It is a matter of choosing a life dedicated to resistance, a life out of their sight and their prisons, a new path and experience.

As to why me in particular: that is the result of the progression of their campaign of attack. It reached me in a way I didn't expect. I do not decide how their arrests and confessions should go. There is a first time for everything. Consider me the first."

"What about me?" Muna yelled bitterly as her tears began to flow. "What about our plans? Completing my education, marriage, the children you want to play with? Did you forget all that? Did you forget we are engaged? Am I to tie my fate to the unknown?"

He wiped her tears with his thumb. He held her face between his palms and drew her face to him.

"You are in my heart and my mind. You are Muna who made me stammer when I first saw you. I latched onto you the minute I laid eyes on you. We shall remain together. You are mine and I am yours. I shall be an unknown for the occupiers and for the world, but I shall be present for you. We shall meet and love and live. Our plans will be put on hold. We are not the first couple to encounter the stubbornness of fate. But our love will be unconventional—there won't be anything like it. Didn't you always want a unique love and an extraordinary relationship, an experience unlike any other?"

"I can't. What about my family and society?" she continued through her tears.

"Please don't cry!" he went on joking with her. "As usual you try to influence my stance with your tears. You know I can't stand to see you cry." He tried to stop her from choking up and to lighten the atmosphere created by their discussion.

"I can't. What shall I tell my family? Even without this, they hate you. You are a political radical, but they had finally accepted that. However, if you go into hiding, what could I tell them? Their pressures will consume me."

"Put your family aside for once. Make a decision without the sword of your family dangling over your head. I am here, so is the party and so are the comrades. We will support you against the pressures of your family. What more do you want? Tell them one thing: 'he is my fiancée. When he comes out into the open, we will get married.'"

"You oversimplify things. You have grown accustomed to doing that with me. You make light of problems more than you should. You habitually simplify what is complicated."

"Well, to be consistent with my habitual self, I say: Things are simple, but that depends on your willpower and decision. Arm yourself with determination and that will make the impossible possible."

"I can't. I can't."

"Yes, you can," he said feverishly as he kissed her forehead and wiped away the tears.

"How long are you going to be leading this secret life, to be missing? Until Palestine is liberated?"

"I don't know. At any rate, it is far too soon to ask that question."

"Say one year, two years, a hundred, even! But don't say you don't know. Am I to go on living like this, knowing nothing about my future with you? Lighten my burden a little, at least talk about how long it might take."

"It is not in my power to decide how long. Believe me, if I could I would, I just can't. I won't deceive you by saying one or two years and then ignoring that number. The party's needs, my abilities, the resources of the party, our situation in general—these are what will decide the outcome. I don't control the variables and the unknowns."

"What about me and my future?"

"Your future is with me. We are tied together. That is our future. Whether we get married in one or two or ten years is secondary. The important thing is that we have a binding relationship. Isn't that our future?"

"This is not what we agreed! We were going to get married in two years. You have abandoned me!"

"Let's stop talking because this conversation will never end. The one who gives up on the other in their hour of need is the one who abandons the other. Love is meaningless if one doesn't support one's lover in the time of his or her difficulties. You love in the time of peace and run away in the time of conflict. Don't talk to me about abandonment. You knew very well what the resistance means to me. I am not some amateur."

"I never knew things would go this far. You're crazy! And my misfortune is that I fell in love with you."

"Is it my fault that you have set a ceiling for my resistance activities? Personally, if I felt that a ceiling was being built above me, I would tear it down immediately. I refuse any limits to my partisanship. There should be no upper limit to my struggle."

"I can't . . . I can't. I love you but I can't. You have to decide: me or the party."

He restrained himself so that he would not yell in her face. It took an effort for him to speak quietly.

"Be a little more humble. Don't be stupid. Who are you, in the final analysis, to place yourself on one side of the scales and the party on the other? The party consists of thousands of resistance fighters, thousands of detainees, thousands of martyrs. The party has a historic mission. Much blood has been shed. Would you put yourself on the same level of sacrifice as that? If our relationship has to end, let's do it calmly and not abuse each other. You have a choice. I understand the reasons for it and, at the same time, I don't. I have made a choice. I hope you will understand it, and that you will really let the understanding sink in."

"I am not the girl for you. Let the party marry you off to a resistance fighter, she would be able to withstand your life and your choices." She finished in a sarcastic tone, hiding her resentment over his choice. He hugged her at the door, kissing her quickly before parting.

"I'm not saying goodbye. Let us say: Till we meet again." She nodded her head in agreement. "Keep this engagement ring for the sake of remembrance." He tore it off his finger and gave it to her. "Contemplate your choices in life. I fear you may pay a high price for decisions that are not well calculated."

He said those final words sensing that she would wrap herself in a cocoon, a traditional lifestyle which would not be suitable for her as an educated woman, pitying her for her depressing decision, for choosing marital stability and respectability at the expense of her love and her lover. Her eyes teared up again when they reached the door, and he had to fight to keep from shedding a tear. He quickly opened the door, and she went through it and out of his life.

❋ ❋ ❋ ❋ ❋

He sat on the couch not knowing what to do. Tonight he would go to the safe house. He pulled out the letter from the party once again: "**measures, precautions, requirements, and rules.**" He had heard about them. The party had spoken to him repeatedly about them. The letter contained condensed words, abstract, deaf words, dry words fitting for a report. At the time Kan'an did not understand their real meaning, how they would become concrete in his daily life and seared into his skin. That would be months later. He would suffer for months before those words revealed their full meaning, until they would be fleshed out, the tangible reality of his days and hours. Then and only then would he comment, "Talking about it is one thing, living it is another."

When he read that clear and harsh order in the letter "**do not receive any guests, do not visit anyone,**" he was overcome by the sweet taste of adventure, its uniqueness, its distinctiveness. He saw himself as strong, wily, and capable, challenging an entire system. They will search and search and they will not find him. His secret measures would be masterful, no one will know anything about him except a few trusted people, which will make the Occupation dizzy. Finally, they will stop, they will surrender. What could be more delightful than the defeat of the organization that always boasted its successes in breaking up secret cells in the homeland?

He received the keys to the safe house and set out on his journey. In the evening, in an isolated street far from the noise, a secret meeting took place with a comrade who introduced himself using the code word previously agreed upon in the last letter. The meeting did not last long. As is customary in such meetings, brevity was the order of the day—a word and a response sufficed.

"Here's the address. Everything is ready in the house, clothing, food, and a small radio. The owner of the house, Umm 'Isa, likes to stick her nose in everything, she personifies the gray-haired old lady. She must not see you. Do not open the door if she knocks. Ignore her. If she asks questions, we will take care of it. We will bring you a TV set in a few days. It will be useful to you. Read and write, do nothing except read and write. Take care of your health and remain well-nourished. We will go into your mission and your duties later. The important thing now is that your name should be forgotten."

His name would not be easily forgotten. They had been looking for him for a week. They had been carrying out daily raids on his family home, they had threatened them, warning, "If he does not turn himself in tomorrow, we will find him and kill him. If he tries to cross the border, we will arrest him or kill him and take him off your hands. We have his picture, and no one sneaks across our borders. Convince him to turn himself in so that you do not lose him."

Their raids were adding to the anxiety his mother was already feeling. She did not reply, save for the sentences she repeated on the occasion of every raid: "I don't know where to reach him to convince him of anything. Only he knows what he is doing. When you find him, let me know." As usual, she was composed and brave. They put checkpoints at the entrances to the university and closely checked students' ID cards and raided their houses, hoping to catch him. But he was smarter than they were. He knew they were looking for him so he avoided the places they were raiding or that they may be watching.

They resorted to tricks to learn where he was and to arrest him. One evening, following daily raids on his home, his poor widowed mother, who had to suffer because of his mission, heard a knock on the door. She opened the door and found a woman who looked over fifty, bent over and clad in a traditional black *thobe*.* The woman

---

* A *thobe* is a traditional Palestinian dress, often decorated with embroidery.

asked without raising her head or looking at her, "Is this the house of Umm Kan'an?"*

"It is. Who are you and what do you want?" his worried mother asked.

"Hurry to him, my sister. He is bleeding in the stomach. God knows if you will reach him in time to see him or if he will die before you reach him. Hurry to him!"

Tense and affected, she spat out these words in rapid fire in Kan'an's mother's face, quickly turning her back and descending down the stairs in front of the house. The horror story hit his mother like a bolt of lightning, and her limbs began to quake. Not knowing what to do, she quickly walked out of the house, not headed in any particular direction. They were following her with their eyes and in their cars: a military patrol and a car carrying an intelligence officer. They assumed she would go to check on her son, based on yet another assumption: that she knew where he was hiding. His mother was in fact walking aimlessly while they were tailing her. She decided to go to the house of a family friend to tell them her worries. After hearing her story and knowing her pain, one of the family members sympathetically and decisively reassured her.

"I don't know how his people go about their business, but I am confident of one thing: they would not hesitate to inform you should something bad happen to him, God forbid. Most likely that woman's story was concocted by their intelligence services to put you on edge as a family. Rest assured. Personally, that woman's story doesn't sit well with me anyway."

Perhaps his mother only needed a few quiet, encouraging words in a moment free of tension to regain control over her thoughts. Her memory began to stir and from its recesses, a picture began to form of the intelligence officer who had come to arrest Kan'an a few days earlier.

---

* Kan'an's mother. In Arabic, "umm" when placed in front of a name means "the mother of."

"It's him! It's him!" she shouted as she discovered the connection. "He was the woman who came today. The intelligence officer who came earlier. He kept his head down so that I could not see his face, but I caught a glimpse of his eyes for a moment. They were his eyes, it was his body frame. It was him! May God punish them! I was about to collapse out of fear for Kan'an. It was Ronny, that intelligence officer, disguised as a woman."

❖ ❖ ❖ ❖ ❖

Following his quick meeting with his friend, Kan'an moved rapidly down a long street lined with trees, cloaked by the darkness of night, and headed to the safe house. He looked closely at the few passersby, imagining they were all assigned to chase after him and follow his trail. They were wrapped in heavy winter clothing for protection from the December cold and rain. Their clothes covered their heads, and in some cases their faces, which increased his suspicions that they were following him. He did not go directly to the house, deliberately taking detours to make sure he did not have a tail, going from one empty alley to the other, keeping his head covered with his spotted red *kufiyyeh*** which he had grown accustomed to wearing for protection from the cold and from prying eyes. He kept a lit cigarette in his mouth which kept the fingers of his right hand and his throat warm.

He was still taken by the delight of this adventure—its uniqueness and distinctiveness. This was the era of those of who thought nothing of turning themselves in to the occupier, to them it was quite ordinary. No one criticized this act or thought it brought shame to those who did it. Those who did not turn themselves in sought to flee across the border, either to escape a confrontation or to change the arena of resistance. Those who chose to remain

---

** The Palestinian *kuffiyeh* is a black-and-white checkered simple square-meter fabric, typically folded diagonally into a triangle. Traditionally it was worn draped over the head of rural Palestinian men. It now acts as a symbol of the Palestinian cause and nationhood and is worn across the world.

embedded among the people were very few indeed, yet the people knew nothing about them. They were the unknown soldiers in advanced positions, about whom the Occupation knew nothing. He was devoted to the third option, to be implanted here among his people.

When Kan'an received the party's invitation to lead a secret life, it wasn't only the thirst for adventure that convinced him to accept. He was also motivated by a deep conviction that in the final analysis there was only one true course of action: the party needed resistance fighters, so the right thing to do was not to turn oneself in. He did not over-rationalize the decision, he did not turn it over in his mind constantly. Excessive calculation tended to sap determination and tie down initiative. Activism is an alternative to dormancy, apathy, and compromise. A revolutionary never fits in or surrenders—he rebels. What kind of revolutionary fears adventure? Since when was revolutionary action truly revolutionary if it was completely sane and devoid of adventure? In moments that called for decisiveness his mind cried out: "There is only one true course of action." This cry trumped all calculations.

There was no way he could have imagined, as he hurtled towards his safe house, what sort of life he would be transitioning to. We come to know bridges well after we cross them, not before. We own an experience when we live it, just as one comes to know a woman when he is intoxicated by her and with her. He had no idea what the details of his life would look like. Whether out of ignorance or lack of experience, it is all the same; after all, ignorance, in the final analysis, is lack of experience.

"Know where you are stepping before you put your foot down." It was a bit of valuable advice that he admired from the prince of Arab storytellers, Naguib Mahfouz.[7] But he now understood that you only know where you are stepping once you set your foot down, not before.

He reached the address he had been given, the ground floor of an old two-story house. The top floor was inhabited by the owner of the house, Umm 'Isa. The house was nestled in the middle of an orchard, amid the type of fruit trees most-often grown by houses far from the town center, and its remoteness gave it just the right touch for a safe house, like a bird's nest. The December rain was still coming down strongly upon his arrival that moonless night, giving the house a desolate and awe-inspiring look. A pitch-black night, torrential rain, a house surrounded by trees in a remote area far from all of the noise and lights—all of this made Kan'an feel like he was approaching a house of myths and legends full of djinn, ghosts, and wizards. That is how he imagined the house as he walked down the tiled passageway leading to the door. A sense of loneliness had begun to envelop him. He turned the key in the lock, entered, and shut the door behind him.

> *Kan'an, do you know what awaits you behind this door that you just closed? Chronicle this rainy December night, for your history begins as of now. On December 21, 1982, a door opened and closed again. When it reopens, a most critical development will have occurred in your life. An opening and a closing of a life that is not a life, a world that is not a world. Make a record of what came before December 21 and what came after December 21. This date will be for you what the birth of Christ was for humanity, a turning point from which people date events. Humanity has its calendar, you have yours.*

Kan'an turned on the light. There were two small bedrooms and a kitchen and bathroom. One of the two rooms contained a table and a worn-down couch that must have been sold for a cheap price after its owner grew tired of it. The other room contained two old beds with wooden frames. The beds were large and could accommodate a married couple comfortably without one complaining to the other for more space. There was an old rickety piece of furniture that had difficulty remaining upright on its four legs, which he decided was intended to be a wardrobe. There were also a number of chairs and small tables. The kitchen was small, with hardly enough room for two people to cook or wash dishes, and a small refrigerator which was sufficient for his needs at any rate. There was an oven and kitchen utensils and copper and zinc plates and other necessities. On top of the fridge were two bottles of wine of a popular variety produced by monks from the Latroun Monastery. Kan'an smiled.

"The comrades did not forget the approaching Christian new year and its customary celebrations. Without wine, New Year's Eve loses its meaning."

He opened one bottle and knocked back a cup of wine in one go, feeling the warmth in his belly. His intellectual nourishment had not been neglected either: there were a handful of novels and theoretical works, newspapers, magazines, notebooks, and pens. The most prominent nourishment was the fictionalized autobiography of Nikolai Ostrovsky, *How the Steel Was Tempered (Kayfa saqaina al-foulath)*, which the party had printed and distributed in the homeland. He smiled again when he saw the book, remembering what he playfully nicknamed it out of admiration the first time he read it: *How We Irrigated the Fava Beans (Kaifa saqaina al-foulat)*.[8]

The windows on both sides of the house looked out on the orchard, predominantly consisting of fig trees and white mulberry trees, and on the third side they overlooked an arbor of jasmine vines covering the passageway leading to the door of the house. The thick trees and the low-lying house made it difficult for sunlight to penetrate through the windows. Kan'an completed his preliminary introduction to his safe house, and he stretched out on the bed after he had taken off his clothes and his wet shoes.

> *Kan'an, have you acquainted yourself fully with the contents of your house,*

its features and details? You will live in it for the years to come, you will memorize every nook and cranny; they will become the companions of your resistance and your life. Get well acquainted, Kan'an, for now your journey has begun, a journey that you never suspected could last so long, until you come to love it like you would a woman. You will live through it withstanding all of your wounds, you will become intoxicated by the idea of possessing it. Just now you have closed the door to your house, and you do not know if it will ever open again. You closed it and turned your back on the life you had been living ever since the old French midwife pulled you out of your mother's womb. Now, your party and comrades are the midwife, and you are opening up a new life with the closing of a door and a willpower that you will build brick by brick. Get well acquainted, Kan'an. Your future life will not be all adventure. Do you realize that Umm 'Isa will monitor the sound of your urine as it flows from your bladder into the toilet bowl and will rush to knock on the door and subject you to interrogation? Get well acquainted so that with your comrades and your party you will become a hoe with which to dig the path of a novel revolutionary experience, not a destructive tool that tears down the walls of your reserve

> *strength and makes you a burden on the organization on top of all its self-regenerating burdens.*

Yet he was still taken by the sweetness of adventure, its uniqueness and distinctiveness. He did not know what lay behind the door. What meaning would his life acquire? When will the door open again.

Chapter 2

A furtive glance from his bedroom window revealed the shadowy figures of soldiers at the main door to the house, retreating only to surge forward again, kicking the door with their boots in an effort to dislocate it. The pagan ritual was beginning. Military vehicles took up positions at the three openings to the house, which were clearly visible from Kan'an's window. He looked at Hisham who was standing next to him, also looking out the window.

"I think we have fallen, comrade." Thinking out loud, Kan'an spoke quickly. "The number of soldiers and the trucks don't give the impression that they are just looking to arrest stone-throwers. We won't open the door. Let them open it themselves if they want to come in. I will hurry to the hiding place with my papers, and we'll do what we had agreed earlier. I hope they did not see the two of us when we went out on the balcony for reconnaissance."

Panting and agitated, his words spilled out rapidly, but they were not confused or hesitant, rather they were confident and determined. It seemed like he had long practiced speaking these words, as though he had memorized them. He did not feel any confusion—the natural and human response to an impending danger, a result of human weakness. Instead, he felt bitter and crushed as he addressed Hisham, aware of the ritual the soldiers were conducting at the door. It would cause him great pain to see that door breached, to know that they had defeated him after nine years. He looked at Hisham as he spoke and saw no sign of confusion—what he saw were the features of a face that was alert, watchful, and waiting. Both of them displayed the composure and self-control of those who had fought many trials, who had not only tested themselves and their strength, but tested others while exploring their potential and limits.

> **The fearlessness of the party, the composure of its organizations and its comrades, is what is needed now to repel the attack on the party. The loss of courage means the loss of balance which leads to a fall; it means confusion and flailing about. What is destroyed now can be rebuilt even stronger. There is no need to panic. Let us defend the party and ourselves now, and later we will rebuild several times over what was destroyed. Confusion amounts to collapse in the dens of interrogation. Your mission now is to protect yourself. Again, it is to protect yourself.**

That was what they wrote him in 1985, the year the intelligence services tore apart the party's organizations from Rafah to Qalqilya. The party kept reiterating those words until they were etched into the recesses of his brain, reinforced by the recurring confrontations of the enemy.

Kan'an quickly picked up his stack of secret papers and a pack of cigarettes from the workbench near his bed. He turned to a familiar location: the large wardrobe against the wall, opposite from the bathroom. His training kicked in and he went to work with organized, automatic motions. He opened the door of the wardrobe and removed one of the shelves where the bath towels and cleaning equipment were stacked, placing it on the floor. He picked up a small nail which he had put there specifically for this moment and inserted it into a barely visible hole in a movable panel of wood at the back of the wardrobe. He pushed the panel upwards revealing a cranny in the wall just wide enough for him to pass through. He squeezed through the opening into a small, dark enclosure and quickly replaced the shelf. Extending his arm, he grabbed the wardrobe's door and closed it. He lowered the panel into place and the enclosure was enveloped in such a thick darkness that he could not even see his hand in front of his face.

Kan'an crouched motionless at the edge of the crevice, waiting. Hoping for their primitive ritual to end, he listened for what was happening outside and sank into thought. The shadowy figures were still trying to open the door, trying to tear apart his secret life. He hoped that he could escape their grip like he had once done years ago. Anything would be tolerable except if his secret papers fell into their hands. *Let them take my life but not my papers!* He clenched them even tighter, as though he were clutching his life in his hands to prevent the enemy from snatching it away, like a mother embracing her sick newborn for fear that death may steal him from her.

In the darkness, he fumbled with his fingers to reassure himself that the cigarette lighter and the kerosene tin were there. He had prepared everything according to the ground rules of secrecy that he had grown accustomed to, rules for taking precautions against the unexpected. One of the elementary principles was secret activities and secure communications: he always made arrangements for agreed-upon signals with those coming to the safe house, and he would instruct them on how to knock on the door. His comrades' furtive knocks meant that life was about to enter the house. Everyone coming from the outside carried this pulse of life with them: news of comrades, friends, family, and other people; their lives, local developments, events, even jokes; what people were talking about, discussions, rumors; whatever struck their fancy and occupied their thoughts.

He felt that he had a "right" to this information, insisting on it if a visitor tried to cut the conversation short, as though sharing the information was akin to tearing off a bit of their flesh. Curiosity was his incentive; he did not want to be mentally severed from the events and worries of life even while he was physically estranged from them. He sought to reassure his inner self that he was living with and among people. This was his motivation! He denied many of his self's demands, but he was careful to satisfy this one. Unfortunately, what he was hearing now was not the beloved, planned knocking of his comrades. This time, the knocks were hostile, perhaps a warning of death, evoking a savagery that could tear into his body, torturing him. These knocks were determined, decisive, foreboding—something that could turn his life upside down.

It was akin to the daring and decisive decision in the December letter nine years earlier, a decision that had uprooted him from one life and thrust him into another. The party decided and he agreed enthusiastically with that decision. This time it was the enemy who would decide the future course of his life. That they, and not he, should make the decision created a lump in his throat and made him feel sick in his heart. A person who has had the power to make their own life-altering decisions for years and years will not accept that others control them without paying the price. That price is their defeat—that he will not allow them to benefit from his arrest.

The pounding—growing louder in its force and violence—affirmed their insistence. It signaled their provocation caused by the door's refusal to bend to their will, to be unhinged and opened. He could now also hear familiar noises: the ugly sound of wireless equipment.

He wondered anxiously, out of a sense of solidarity with his comrade and friend: *What is Hisham doing now? No doubt he is monitoring their movements from the windows, having made sure that no papers had been left uncollected.*

It never crossed Kan'an's mind that one day the knocks on the door would bear the foreboding significance that they did now. He had thought about being arrested earlier, and on the instructions of the party, had taken a series of precautionary measures. Arrest is almost a forgone conclusion for a resistance fighter. The long years of his life, his strict adherence to the rules of secrecy, his trust in the party, the sternness of those working with him who knew his secret, and the inextricable revolutionary essence of his life . . . all of these things meant that he felt reassured that nothing could put a limit on his political life! His missions, struggles, experiences, and productivity made him unable to imagine himself living outside the ranks of the party and the struggle. He had experienced a sensory state that imposes a certain type of life on a person, his being, feelings, senses, and the hours of his day. It had molded him. He had experienced it to the extent that he could no longer imagine that his life of resistance could come to an end. He felt its distinctiveness and solitude with the fullness of his being—a truly unique and revolutionary experience.

No doubt the idea of arrest had intruded on his daydreams. How rich are the daydreams of he who lives behind the walls? They became the artery that nourished his spirit, allowing it to resist the petrification of the encircling walls. They were the secret link that connected him to life outside his house. It was a freedom from the mental constraints of a secret life, while remaining steadfast in adherence to it. He "experienced" the victory of the workers of the world against the false idols of capitalism. He "rejoiced" when his country was liberated and he "began" to build socialism under the leadership of his party. He "delighted" in the companionship of the woman of his dreams; they walked side by side, he joked with her, stole a kiss in a fleeting moment! His life was buoyed by all these optimistic, joyful visions that allowed him to embrace a bright future.

In his daydreams, arrest signified resistance and steadfastness. He imagined himself a martyr in the clutches of interrogators. In his mind's eye, he witnessed his funeral procession that transformed into a demonstration while the party praised his resolve and mourned him. These were the internal, personal mobilizations he engaged in while pacing between one wall and the other, or while he sat on the balcony during a summer's night, or while he lay his head on his pillow before he fell asleep. In his daydreams, he was arrested when he walked down a street in disguise, heading to a secret house to meet someone. He imagined himself captured, just as he received a letter from an agreed-upon secret source.

Despite the richness of his dreams—fertile, like the famous red soil of the Bin 'Amer meadow—none of them included a premonition of the incessant knocking of the past half hour. Just as his secret life had led him to places he could not have fathomed, he felt the beginning of another life approaching; it appeared to him now, as if a question mark.

For weeks now he had been sounding the depths of his secret life, a life that he could not see for all that was visible to him was a locked door and deaf walls. He was well aware of the basic value of his life: rebelling against the arrest warrant, continuing the struggle, and not allowing his potential to be locked between prison walls. But wherever he went there were doors, and when he turned away and averted his gaze there were walls—it was as though the entire world had been abbreviated into doors and walls, nothing more. This world recurred day after day, yesterday was like today and tomorrow. This was the situation he had put himself in!

What kind of a world was this in which a man wakes up in the morning and does not go out of the house, instead sitting at a table or pacing from wall to wall, afraid to open the door? People woke up in the morning and opened their doors: some went to school, others to their place of work, another to shop, and yet another to gossip with their neighbor. Kan'an was unable to even wish his neighbors good morning. What sort of world was this in which a man lives with no friends, cannot play with a child or sit down with a woman? Oh, to just sit down with a woman! A world where he could not see his family or his relatives, could not converse with someone, anyone! Even a prisoner could do all those things from behind barbed wire, when it was time for his periodic visit with his relatives and friends.

Who could appreciate the monumental significance of life's ordinariness? Only a person denied the routines of a social existence could assess their cascading significance, feel a pressing need for them in his being. This floors him, knocks him down daily, hour after hour, minute after minute. Because it was so, he only now began to sense, through his skin, with his nerves, the full meaning of that coarse order, blunt and hard as concrete: "**Do not receive anyone, do not visit anyone.**"

The result was a sprawling monotony: he paced in the house between the wall and the door, or he lay on the bed or opened a book or watched the street and the neighbors from his window. He cooked his food or listened to the radio or the tape recorder or chewed a piece of bread or darted from one room to the other, or concealed himself behind the walls to escape the eyes of the gray-haired hag Umm 'Isa, or ... or ... or ... His new life antagonized every cell in his body; he was tense, his nerves high strung and stretched to the limit.

> *What sort of a sentence is that? How could someone write that? Do they understand what it means in real life when its letters and words are translated into actual reality? Do they know how that order can be implemented in lived hours and minutes? That is not an ordinary sentence, it is a slow death sentence. Man is a social being. How can he retain his humanity if he isolates himself from society and social life? What sort of madman were you to be enthusiastic about that damned order:* "**Do not turn yourself in to the Occupation authorities?**" *What party does that to its members?*

He paced back and forth, posing these questions to himself, and then he sat and he smoked. He did this only to take up pacing once again and throw himself onto the bed while questions tortured the cells of his brain and gushed out of his mouth; tense and emotional questions, which turned into swear words spat out at whatever crossed his mind or meets his eyes. He went on like this—like a corn kernel on a hot roof—all day long. His tired nerves spoke and his body sighed from exhaustion. He went on like this, debilitated by his tongue, its rapid words, its cuss words, until he fell asleep, exhausted. Sleep would prove fitful: he twisted and turned, tossed from side to side, until he was so tired that he fell asleep once more, only to wake up a few hours later. His nerves would go through the routine once again, repeating their sharp-tongued sermons... While his tired nerves narrated, his inner self would barricade itself behind its requirements, firing back at him:

> *Overnight everything was all over. One sentence determined my life, nullified it:* **"It has been decided that you should not turn yourself in."** *Concentrated, abstract, deaf, judgmental, and dry words. A coarse, commanding sentence that wasted an entire life. Everything is behind me. I do not belong to what is around me and it does not belong to me. Did I engage in resistance out of a sense of belonging to doors and walls and utensils and plates? Did I resist only to end up calculating the sound that my urine makes so as not to be detected by Umm 'Isa? Lonesomeness is killing me; no mother, no brother, no sister, no lover, no friends or acquaintances. How did I leave all that behind? What sort of madman was I? Nothing except these walls and a handful of damned doors. One of them closes, not to open again except for bread deliveries, and then closes again. Prison would be a*

thousand times better. I expected to spend one, maybe two years in prison and then come out to engage in resistance once again. That is what everyone does. So what happened to me in this instance? My needs grow and grow until they collide with the walls and bounce back on my chest. My desires grow and grow and are transformed into sharp fangs that tear into my flesh, brain, and blood, transforming into a savage Dracula. If my desires try to sneak out, they encounter a bolted door and a coarse, commanding sentence and dry, concentrated, deaf, judgmental, abstract words which kick my desires in the rear. It is this secret life which transforms my needs and desires into impossibilities, but in a normal life they would be quite ordinary and possible, in fact they would be achieved!

Between the anxiety attack and the shriek of his inner self in his throat, his mind would intervene with a wise and balanced opinion:

Bear up, Kan'an. Endure. If it is your duty to become acquainted with this house and life, then do it and endure. Your party and your experience make you a revolutionary. Can that be done without sacrifice? Bear up, then. Being revolutionary requires certain things, so do them. Show tolerance. Have you not read about the lives of great rev-

> olutionaries? What have you offered so far compared to them? What have you contributed compared to those who fought for the revolution in Lebanon, who include warriors from your own party? Are you not convinced that the hardened revolutionary will lay down his life for the sake of the revolution, he will contribute something much more valuable than the hours you spend prattling? Tolerate it and then let experience mold you into a hardened revolutionary. You are committed to the revolution, so be a man and pay the price without being frivolous. The revolution changes you, so help it do so by accommodating yourself to its logic. Don't allow your nerves to turn you into a counter-revolutionary, a knife that stabs you in the back.

There was a struggle between reason and taut nerves. Each side stood behind its fortified position and aimed its rifle at the other. Each fought desperately but could not kill the other. Even at this level of the conflict, his nerves had the upper hand and his inner self was dominant, yet the mind was not defeated. The mind had its moments, but the tiring and vacillating inner self had its hours and days and weeks, for its needs were dictated by human nature, and those needs are satisfied for everyone who can walk upright and is able to use speech and abstraction; the mind, on the other hand, relied on conviction, which is shaken on many occasions as a result of the lack of experience and the cruelty of variables. He could hear the nerves of his inner self yelling at him, so he took tired steps from wall to wall, swaying like a drunkard, with a lit cigarette forever dangling between his lips. He used to smoke three packs a day so that he was like the smokestack of a train, which stopped emitting smoke only when its wheels came to a standstill, and he fell asleep.

The struggle is between the demands of the "I" which has its needs and desires, and the "we" which presents its own demands. The cursed "I" is incapable of anything! The secret existence dwarfs its needs to the lowest level possible: food and drink. The "we" had a long list of demands, which were even greater than those of the "I" and quite numerous; they were endless and required his endless giving. The weeks marched on and on and turned into months, and the occupiers never give up the pursuit.

❖❖❖❖❖

During the fifth month of his secret life, intelligence officers visited his family home for the last time. His mother was suffering from exhaustion and was unable to get out of bed. His comrades kept reassuring him whenever he asked about her: "She is fine, rest assured there is nothing new with her!" When he asked them to relay a message to her, they had a ready response: "Be patient until things quiet down a bit more. The moment is not suitable now!"

A little before midnight, two officers knocked on the door to his family's house.

"Good evening! May we come in for a bit?" They entered without waiting for an answer to their question, which was merely a pretense for politeness—a unique form of insolence and a technique mastered only by intelligence officers. "Sorry to disturb you. Where is Umm Kan'an? Can we see her?"

"She is sick and cannot get out of bed," answered his brother, who was not accustomed to seeing or talking to them.

"May she get well soon! Can we see her?"

Without waiting for permission, the officer started moving towards her bedroom, and with an artificial and affected gentleness they both went on to ask his mother about her health and her ailment, wishing her a speedy recovery. After these preambles they moved on to the reason for their visit.

"How is Kan'an doing?"

"How should we know? Since he left five months ago he has not been back. Don't you know something about him? Swear to God that you have not arrested him?"

His mother answered and asked questions with steady nerves. She was putting on an act to hide the inescapable anxiety she felt from the presence of strangers in her house and next to her bed.

"Are you making fun of us? Would we come asking about him if we had him in custody?" one of them replied irritably, revealing his lack of experience. The other one, realizing this, tried to cover for the irritability of the first.

"It strains credulity that you should be so sick that you're unable to get out of bed, and he doesn't come to visit you?"

"It is credible. That is, you assume he knows I am sick. May God ease his path wherever he is. I want nothing from him. I have people to help me, he has many brothers."

"No, no, that is not credible! You are his mother. Doesn't he come to check on you just for a moment? What sort of son is that? Does he not come, even for five minutes, to wish you a happy holiday? Wasn't it Easter just a few days ago? What sort of son does not visit his mother for the holiday when she is sick?"

"I told you I know nothing about his whereabouts, and no, he did not come. Why do you go on for so long with this pointless conversation?"

The two officers struggled in vain to control their reactions so as to avoid provocation, but they failed.

"We have his pictures; the Popular Front cannot help him," one of them bellowed, revealing his true nature and showing the fangs of the occupier. "We will bring him to you on a stretcher with ten bullets in his head!" He released all the bile inside him before the sick mother, then left.

A week later, the party sent him a message that buoyed his spirit and gave him some stability:

"Write to your mother and let her know that she can write back to you. We will arrange some way for you to exchange letters with her without risk."

He started walking, talking to himself:

What will you write about, Kan'an? About why you left her a week after your father's death and why you were no longer to be seen? How will you tell her that the phrase "for now" would be deleted from the sentence "I will not turn myself in for now"? Do you suppose that she will understand your party's need for professional revolutionaries, or its need for a revolutionary organizational structure in the homeland, or your infatuation with adventure and distinction? What will you tell her about Muna, whom she loved like her own daughter? The Muna to whom you got engaged to envelop her in your arms as your bride, only to exile yourself between four walls? Will you describe your life to her for the last months, and the struggle between the "I" and the "we" in the recesses of your brain? What will you write, Kan'an?

Kan'an was pacing, pen in hand, clicking it with his middle finger. A blank page of paper on the table was waiting for the distillation of his thoughts and anxieties, waiting for letters, words and sentences he would pen for his father's widow to read, the one suffering because of him, the one afflicted by her chronic disease. What sort of position was he in now? When he was permitted to write to her, he was happier than he had been for months, but he now found this task to be a burden. He had previously written to her from prison about missing her and about life in captivity. He usually told her: "It's all right, endure my dearest mother; soon I will be with you." If his pen could not come to his rescue back then, his tongue was up to the task when he saw her during the monthly prison visits. But now, there was so much before him to explain that was unfathomable, like swimming in a sea with no shore or traveling as an astronaut in the infinity of space, not knowing when he would arrive! If the pen could not come to his rescue, when would he see her in person, considering the eyes that were keeping watch over the house and monitoring his mother's movements? He sat down again but jumped right back up. He looked out of the window at the trees in the garden, clicking his pen. He finally sat down at the table and wrote:

> **My dearest mother, I send you many, many kisses. Before I go on, do not forget to burn this letter after you are through reading it. Do not mention it to anyone, neither in detail nor in passing conversations. This concerns my secret life, and any mistake could put me in danger.**

He put the pen down on the table, his tongue coagulating from the tension he felt and his resentment for his current situation.

> *Even the simplest manifestations of my relationship with my mother acquires a party dimension, due to the fact that the letter I write requires a decision by the party and the agreement of the party. My first sentence to her is a command, giving instructions, as though I were addressing a cell or a comrade. My*

letter will get to her through security arrangements and her reply will reach me through a similar arrangement. What is left? Should I have begun my letter in the following fashion?

> "Dear comrade mother,
> A warm comradely salute to you ... "
> And should I conclude it like this:
> "Onwards!
> Your comrade son,
> —K!"

He smiled bitterly at his sarcasm.

Kan'an started to realize, some months back, ever since he began his secret life, that all relations in his secret environment would be under the patronage of the party, that his secret life would reformulate those relationships. However, realizing this is one thing and living it is quite another. From the first line he wrote, his mother was instructed to appreciate the seriousness of his position, so that she could learn the rules of the game! He was aware of the significance of his imperative introduction. One word out of place here or there would begin the logical unraveling, a word would work itself into the prattle of old folks and busybodies. The ears of the intelligence services would pick up the gossip in the street and their eyes would set about for more surveillance operations. Surveillance is the death of secret political organizing; surveillance tears it apart and attacks its communications, activities, and hideouts. The eyes of the enemy infiltrate into the fortress of the party, and soon the party and its internal world would be laid out on their table. What sort of clandestine work would that be? The coarseness of the preamble, its imperative nature, and its arrangements constitute a strategic guarantee, for, in the final analysis, if an experience is not transformed into history it is not worth a red cent. He went back to writing once his consternation and the congestion of his thoughts passed.

> Take care of your health and do not worry; the party and the comrades are looking after me very well. I am eating well. I can cook *mulukhiyah** and *kousa mahshi*.** Did you ever imagine your son would become so creative? I am sleeping well, my time is fully occupied and I do not suffer from boredom.

He was lying in order to make it a bit easier for her to bear. In fact, he could not cook anything at that stage of his secret life. Sleep was elusive, flirting with him, yet averting his advances. Boredom was killing him and his nerves were incapacitating him!

> ... I hope that you will understand my position, even if it entails difficulties for you. I have chosen my path in life, the path of resistance in the name of our people and the freedom of our homeland. Your little son has grown up and has the right to choose his path in life, and you are fully entitled to be proud of my path. You have made a man out of me. What sort of a man would I be if I remained an idle spectator while our homeland was occupied and our people enslaved and I did nothing... All I want from you is to take care of your health. You can best support me by repeating that dear expression which I have been carrying with me since I left the house five months ago: "Go, my son. May God be pleased with you." Repeat it constantly to yourself, and be confident that I can hear you.

---

* *Mulukhiyah* is a dish widely eaten across Palestine, Egypt, Syria, and Lebanon. It is made from a spinach-like plant (called "jute mallow" in English) that is dried and cooked into a stew-like dish. There is slight variation in terms of preparation of the dish in terms of sides and seasonings across the region.
** Stuffed zucchini with rice and meat.

He wrote and he wrote. He tried to convince her that his choice was right, but he knew that all the reasons concocted by the philosophers of the world could not convince a mother to push her son far from her embrace, whether he be a crawling toddler or a man of mature age whose hair was turning gray!

He concluded the letter with instructions, as at the beginning, adding:

> **Please stick strictly to the arrangements my comrades make to pick up your letter, for your sake and mine. I send you my warmest kisses.**
> **Your faithful son, K.**

A week after she received his letter, she sent a reply. The waiting killed him. He waited to see what she would say; he was eager to see the words she penned as they climbed and descended above and below the line, her words in the vernacular mixed with classical Arabic.

> **My dear son, my heart is satisfied with you and I pray God is satisfied too. How are you? How are you living? May God curse this world for separating us. Don't worry about me. What's important is you. Cook and nourish yourself. Tell the comrades to buy you everything you need. Ask them to do so. Keep yourself warm; it gets cold at night. May God be pleased with you wherever you may be. You are a man, and you know what is good for you . . .**

He teared up as he read her words, confronted with her motherly tenderness. He lost himself imagining her: in the kitchen, scolding him when he stole a bit of what she was cooking; dozing off in front of the television; sitting with him on the balcony, peeling oranges and handing him some to try. She always gave him the sweet bits while she ate the sour ones. He recalled when she would try to wake him up in the early hours of dawn so he could study. He remembered her respecting his privacy when he was with Muna.

"She is going to be traveling for rest and to treat her illness, which is a good thing. She asked about the possibility of future correspondence." He informed his comrades of her request.

"You know that correspondence after she leaves is going to be difficult. A letter can go astray if not delivered by hand. You know this better than anyone."

"I know, I know," he said, defeated, and continued, "I cannot write that to her. You must tell her yourselves."

"Alright."

❖❖❖❖❖

Contradictions still challenged him. The party had taught him about the law of the unity and struggle of opposites, the theory of dialectical materialism. He had learned all of this at a young age, hovering with a group of teenagers around a former prisoner who answered all of their questions while they smoked unfiltered "Omar" cigarettes. But Kan'an could not understand the current situation, the opposites struggling in his brain. Mind against tense nerves, "I" against "we," human needs and political obligations. The conflict between these terms raged on in his life for the first few months. The party was part of the conflict, the party was the embodiment of the "we," the mind and the requirements of the job. From time to time, he too aimed his rifle and fired a word at the tense nerves, a message for calm, for reconciliation, for silence. He called those messages "morphine injections." He accepted the word of the party with an eagerness that rarely left him. However, when the tense nerves were particularly well entrenched and his needs and desires bit into his flesh, he merely shrugged his shoulders and paid no heed to what the party was saying.

"Read and write, for the magazine is in need of writers. Write letters to the base, compose studies."

"I can't. My nerves are tired and exhausted. I have writer's block."

"Read. Read the novels."

"There isn't one that I haven't read."

"Exercise. That will activate the body and the mind. Weren't you an athlete once?"

"Where should I swim, in the bathtub? Or should I play soccer in the kitchen?"

"Physical fitness training does not require a playing field. Exercise nourishes the soul as well as the body."

"The issue is more complicated than that. Sitting still like this drives me crazy."

"You will get used to it."

"How?! You people don't know what you are talking about. How do I get used to having no life? Am I not a human being?"

"Yes, we do know. The experience of the group is more significant than the experience of the individual. You will get used to it."

"I am the one buried in here, not you. I'm the one who is imprisoned behind locked doors, not you."

"We understand and appreciate that. We are in solidarity with you but you need to calm down, you need to think calmly. You will get used to it."

"I am calm, but I want tasks."

"Tasks will come later. You must allow things to settle down now after the assault. You must allow your case to turn cold. Wait until your name is forgotten."

"I did not enter the house to sit down. I want to act!"

"You have years of action ahead of you. Don't be hasty. Think of the long run, not the moment."

"But the current situation is killing me. It is unbearable. Did I revolt in order to turn into a housewife? To sweep, cook, and clean?"

"That will end. You will remember what you are saying now and laugh. Be a man and endure it."

"My needs and desires are consuming me, like wolves tearing into my flesh."

"This is understood and quite natural. You must beat them. Don't let them get the best of you, otherwise they will overwhelm you. Deprivation is blowing them out of proportion."

"This talk does not concern me! I am a human being, I am not made of stone."

"That is why you are fit to be a revolutionary. It is because you are a human being that you are capable of freezing your needs and desires for a greater cause."

"Can human instincts and needs be frozen?"

"Yes, they can. That is what experience has shown us. Through patience and endurance one can cleanse the self. Endure and cleanse your inner self well. Being revolutionary requires this, it will increase your enthusiasm for a secret life. Your agreement to the December decision is like carrying soap and a brush. Now scrub. Scrub well and cleanse the inner self, the ego. Clean it of the dirt of the 'I'."

He knew the party was right. But how could his tired nerves and riled-up ego accept that? The experience had not delivered its final judgment yet. It had not molded him in its own special way and hadn't leavened him with its own yeast. He had yet to become an example of the party's vision. For that, he understood that he would need to be calm, he would need to reawaken his gentle nature and carry out the struggle with a revolutionary self that is not aggressive and inflamed.

The party was planning for the long term, not for the present moment. It was trying to make a revolutionary out of him, tempering him on a low fire, like a piece of iron which had yet to be heated. Kan'an was thinking about his present—his nerves were raw, his excited inner self was speaking, his ego, not his mind, was governing his tongue. Experience has its foundations and laws, its requirements and rules, and its horizons. All these terms must be satisfied. The experience has to be lived from beginning to end, like a novel which one enjoys reading. Years of experience cannot be skipped over; one cannot tear through its stages. Can one ask a child to grow a mustache?

What do you say now Kan'an? Are you savoring the sweetness of the adventure, its uniqueness and distinctiveness? Face it head on and don't be merciful. Face your needs and desires and don't be compromising. Be on the side of the mind, the party, "we," and what the job requires. Get used to waking up not to open the door and leave the house but to wash, eat breakfast, and sit or walk or watch the passersby in the street! It is no longer the case, ever since your arrest warrant was issued, that there is a beautiful love with a breathtaking figure waiting for you at the bus stop to accompany you to the university. Your morning meeting with her was your incentive to wake up and hurry, happy and energized. Will you wake up like that today, happy and energized?

He used to enjoy seeing those sleepy eyes each morning. Her hair was a mixture of wine red and light brown. They would board the bus, and he intentionally used to squeeze her between himself and the window, beginning the playful morning game of which he had become addicted: he would get closer to her, brush against her more, his elbow secretly toying with her tender and compact waist, his lingering foot touching hers delicately and provocatively. They used to have excitement for breakfast, she being shy as usual, twisting and feigning annoyance while wanting him to go on. She looked forward to this delightful breakfast of playful banter even more than he did.

"Shame on you. This is embarrassing." However, her eyes would laugh, betraying that her warning was not serious.

"I am merely practicing my natural and legitimate right," he would answer disdainfully. "Love has rights for which I am ready to fight the whole world."

She answered with a look that aroused him more than it scared him—her eyes always had that effect on him.

> *All these are memories now, Kan'an. For months now all that has been in the past. No breakfast bantering, no elbow toying, no thigh touching, no arousing eyes. Tomorrow that will still be just a memory. It is a beautiful memory, but it is just so. Understand that and stop torturing yourself. Do not bring up memories and arouse your instincts; that is a torment which brings pain to your nervous system, and your body. Talk, Kan'an, about how you enjoyed the sweet taste of adventure, its uniqueness and distinctiveness. There is no room anymore for it; for family and friends, for people, the bus, the university, your breakfasts. Your mind tells you to get used to paying the bill for your adventure. Did you think it would be without a cost? Can't you feel it on your skin, throughout your days and hours? Pay it without hesitation and go forward. Did you not sacrifice your love for the choice you made? Pay it, everything will be easy now that you have paid the price of losing Muna. Was there anything in your life more precious than she was? You loved her madly, as you told her. There is a different kind of madness ahead of you now. Pay and proceed.*

He paid for the loss of Muna after much suffering, though still he ruminated on what it cost him. He opened the door for her and she walked out of his life. She left and he entered.

> *She still occupies a place in your heart and your mind. Months after she walked out the door, you used to fall asleep at the break of dawn overcome by fatigue, thinking about her, insomnia wreaking havoc on your nerves as you turned over each moment you had spent with her: the breakfast banter, sitting in close contact with each other at the university cafeteria, the daily lunch of falafel sandwiches with tea; walking together on your way back from the university, the moments of discussion, joking, singing, dispute; the moments of pleasure and elation; the days of university strikes which you two made use of; the days alone together, in love.*
>
> *You did not harbor a grudge against her, or hate her, rather you retained a beautiful memory and image of her. Having loved someone, can one hate one's former lover? A single critical remark once from a friend instigated a sharp response from you.*

All that was still engraved in his mind after months and months. When he remembered her, he remembered something beautiful. It was as though she had not left him alone to struggle with the walls and the doors at the moment that he needed her. He did not find her next to him at the moment he wanted to destroy the walls with his bare hands. Had she been there, she could have drawn his head to her bosom and told him: "Calm down and endure!" He did not find her in the moments when he desired her.

Kan'an had forgiven her, perhaps because he understood why she had done what she did; he understood, and he forgave! Perhaps he forgave because he loved her. To love is to forgive those we love. He told her: "I understand without trying to understand." In fact, he did understand and did not give way to resentment or hatred. Often, he felt pity for her. Whoever hangs on to trivial choices arouses pity. Now she sits at home and waits for her future husband! What sort of choice is that? What sort of misery did she bring down on herself as a woman? He used to conjure her up before him; he often talked to her and discussed things with her. What he found most suffocating was that she had put herself at the mercy of fate. She was waiting for the future husband that her father would bring home, as though they were buying a watermelon. Either it would be ripe and red or it would be bad and gritty—the luck of the draw. Either her father's purchase would be successful or not. It was a matter of luck, no more.

"What miserable position have you found yourself in? Testing your luck with a man as you would with a watermelon?"

He used to pity her and to curse in his imagination. The weak deserve to be pitied. One of his comrades once gave an assessment of Muna in front of him:

"She is weak to the point of extinction as a being."

Kan'an could not accept that and got angry, although he knew it was an accurate assessment. He would often be frank with her: weakness is the loss of the ability to rebel, it is taking orders and being led around, it is the obliteration of the personality; all these are synonyms for a person who accepts not to have a place under the sun. She was that person.

> *Now you are on the threshold of ending your years of secrecy, holed up in your*

stone den while they attempt to break down your door. Have you wondered why you have kept tabs on her for nine years? Is your love for her still alive in your heart? Certainly not. Do you see it as your yearning for the woman she was, leading to nothingness and a moment of pain? Perhaps. Was your interest in her the result of beautiful memories? Perhaps, perhaps.

You kept up with her life as one would open the file on a prime suspect, thoroughly following her news every chance you got. She finished her studies and got a job, and you were happy for her. She was waiting at home for the man on a "white horse," so you pitied her for her miserable choice. Her mother wanted her daughter's watermelon to be a man in a "high position." You recalled her dependency and the obliteration of her personality. You read in a newspaper that she had gotten engaged to a man in a "high position" and you tore up the paper. You lit a cigarette—your faithful friend—and you started pacing from wall to wall in a burning rage. Then she got married, and her choice of a life fit for triviality and misery was complete. All you could do was smoke and curse! She moved to another city, and you followed her with your inquiries and monitoring agents. She gave birth to a girl and to conceal your bitterness you joked: "We had agreed on having a boy." You also opened a file for the man in a "high position" and investigated his history and relationships and his world and their life together. You did not lose your interest in her. You had formed a picture of her as the only woman in your life, and you lived with that picture year after year. Such is the secret life: pictures in your memory of the girlfriend, the mother, the comrade ...

Chapter 3

His mind would not stop racing. Neither would their boots and fists, whose ceaseless beating on the safe house door bore down on him. His dark hiding place was no more than eighty centimeters in width, about two-and-a-half meters long, and two meters and eighty centimeters high. The floor was littered with chunks of hardened concrete left over from the wall he built there, and the crevice was full of the odor of cement.

Kan'an waited in his den, his ears cocked for sounds from the outside. Time began to weigh on him as he lit a cigarette and waited for the unknown. That unknown could be death, maybe from torture at the hands of his interrogators or being murdered in his cell. He often thought of death in his waking dreams as he paced around the safe house, comparing his life to those of great revolutionaries.

A pleasure must follow death, and though probably unfelt by the deceased, it must be a relief to not wear oneself out thinking about what has happened, why it happened, how it happened. The past is nullified, and that is good. Kan'an philosophized his position on death in this peculiar way and put a halt to any further thoughts about death. He concluded that some people die for a reason, others for none at all—it is best, then, to look for a good reason to die.

Kan'an was engrossed in contemplation, then he burst out laughing to himself as he recalled reading the tragic news item in *Al-Quds* newspaper about the inhabitants of a remote village in Bangladesh who fell victim to an epidemic of dysentery—yes, dysentery! The village lost 260 people in a single day. He imagined the tragedy of the scene and laughed at how horrible a calamity it must have been: people twisting from the pain in their intestines while excrement poured out of their rear ends, and they collapsed. Perhaps they passed away as they defecated, or maybe afterwards. Imagine the spectacle of those unfortunates with liquid feces collecting under their bodies strewn between the mud huts. What sort of a death is that? Is this "death" comparable to that of a poor man who confronts his class enemy and becomes a martyr? Could the life of the great being of humanity, who aspires to invade Mars and settle on the moon, who has begun to run societies with computers and remote controls, be ended by diarrhea?

A person, by prior conviction, should choose to die in an honorable way that is fitting for them as a human being. A humane death is one that is remembered and lives on after the deceased. It garners the respect and awe of the people. It is a death that is not remembered in jest as people recount the story as they might joke recounting the death of someone who drowned in a septic tank, or a man who died from a heart attack on his wedding night, overcome with excitement upon seeing his naked bride for the first time! That person has lost his worldly life as a man and half of his faith as a believer! He has neither truly lived on this earth, nor will he experience the sweetness of the afterlife.

These thoughts came to him throughout his life just as they came to his mind now as the savage knocking continued. His reconciliation with death made him look on the prospect of his demise indifferently to a certain extent. He wondered: What brought them? Had they noticed a certain activity? Did the house arouse suspicion, or did they hear noises that led them to monitor the house? Did a collaborator* catch a glimpse of him and write a report about it?

---

* A spy or someone who works in collaboration with the Occupation forces to gather intelligence and leak information to them.

These sudden questions took him by surprise. Up until that moment, he hadn't wondered for an instant why they came to the house. It was as though the matter was of no concern to him, as though those incessant blows were not raining down on his house, his hiding place, but on someone else's, someone else whose life would change completely if they were to be found. He quickly refocused and addressed himself:

"Now is not the time for these questions. Now, only one thing should be dominating my thoughts, my determination and all my senses: remaining steadfast in the battle being waged between me and them. I must transform a victory they would gain in arresting me into a loss for them as a result of my endurance. Think about how to protect the party, the comrades, and the secrets."

He clutched the papers in his hands even harder.

Kan'an, prepare yourself for a new stage requiring a new response to the challenge. The important thing now is for them to know what it means to tangle with our party and its revolutionaries in the halls of inquisition—as they have discovered time and again in the past.

The intense pounding continued as Kan'an crouched in the dark, clutching the wad of papers in his hands, listening carefully and thinking. He lit another cigarette. They were trying to destroy the door. He heard heavy metal cudgels beating it, producing a furor whose echo resounded ever more strongly. The door was resisting them. Once they break past this one, they would still have to get through the inner door also made of iron. Getting inside was the first obstacle and their arduous effort heartened him: since they'd come to arrest him, it was only right they pay the price of entry. He had always questioned the national custom of opening doors for the occupiers. Let them blow up the door and pull it off its hinges, but we should never open it for them ourselves. Should we open the door for those who come to steal our freedom and lead us to the dungeons of torture? Should we open it for those who have come to tear the son away from the embrace of his mother, the father from his children, and the woman from her newborn? He always thought of that as a form of "Arab generosity," reflecting the awe and fear that ought to be rooted out to plant the values of resistance and rebellion in their place.

That was his first step on the long path to challenging the occupiers. He had already decided on the second and third steps, each in their own good time. Their sources of strength are their soldiers, their arms, all their prisons, their cudgels and crowbars, their specialized intelligence and investigation techniques ... all the things that they have brought to the threshold of his house, all the things they would use to incite and interrogate him should they get hold of him. Their state has modern and scientific technology that makes use of all these things in hunting down and liquidating revolutionary actors and interrogating prisoners. They are constantly reviewing their methods and techniques, developing them to be more effective. All of these are undoubtedly sources of strength for them.

Kan'an knew these things from the experiences of many resistance fighters and factions, and from his own life. But above all, he knew that the resistance fighter is strong in and of himself: in his conviction, his determination, his trust in his struggle, his faith in the justice of his people's cause, and in his confidence that his people, his party, and his comrades are in solidarity with him in his forward trench. All of these are the prerequisites for his steadfastness and acceptance of the challenge. But what is most important in the final analysis: to be strong through the support of others or to draw strength from oneself? He was certain that his party would be behind him if he were arrested, if he were in *sahat al-shabeh*,* in the interrogation room, in the filthy prison cell—in the moments when he needs it most. He real-

---

* This is a term used by Palestinians, especially prisoners, to refer to a form of positional torture used in the Occupation's prisons. Prisoners are placed in stress positions for prolonged periods of time during interrogation, often with their hands bound behind their backs and their feet shackled.

ized its decisive importance in reinforcing his strength and resolve, but he also knew he would have to fight alone on behalf of the collective—his comrades, his party, and his people. He would be alone except in his will and the solidarity of his comrades, like that soldier who is asked to defend his forward trench alone.

"Challenge and determination are the keywords. Nothing else."

He arrived at that conclusion years ago, and repeated it to himself now, clutching his papers, listening hard, thinking and smoking. He had made that decision while pacing from wall to wall, from window to wall, from door to wall, while sitting at his table in front of his papers, while smoking and contemplating, while sitting on his bed in the darkness of night.

Kan'an flicked his cigarette lighter so he could read the time on his watch, which he wore every day for fifteen years. It was night, 1:20 a.m. It had been thirty minutes since they began their wrestling match with the door using cudgels and crowbars. Just as he looked at his watch, he heard pounding of a different kind, less loud and further away. He held his breath, keeping his mouth wide open, to hear better. Then he let out a vilifying curse as a wave of sorrow swept over him and his agitation. He tried to speculate about the location of the new pounding and felt his heart jump. His ears were not mistaken. They had become like radar over years of training during his secret life and now they heard true—he resorted to his inexhaustible supply of curses once again.

"Two blows on the head would have hurt more." He thought this out loud and let out a long and regretful sigh without thinking.

"Comrade! Comrade Kan'an!" Hisham said in an audible whisper, and the anxiety was evident in his tone. Hisham had cracked open the wardrobe door, his voice coming from outside the den.

"Yes. What is it?"

"I think they are surrounding the other house and trying to break down its door. Things are not looking good!"

Kan'an felt certain of that. His ears were not deceiving him. Hisham understood the significance of them storming the other house and that was why he hurried to inform Kan'an.

"Hisham, what do you think? How long will it take them to break down both doors?"

"An hour at least. I will go monitor what they are doing. How's it going in your cave? By the way, there is an entire military barrack surrounding the house, it's like they've declared war or something."

That's Hisham for you; he could make light of things even at the darkest hour, Kan'an thought silently.

"We merit a declaration of war, my comrade. We are not to be trifled with. My cave will probably pass the test, my efforts in building it will not be wasted. Make sure the shelf is in place and be sure to close the wardrobe door well before you leave."

A military barrack around the house! He found this highly significant. It said a lot about the reason for their presence. Certainly, they wouldn't employ these tactics in pursuit of a stone-thrower or someone who set car tires on fire, not even someone who threw Molotov cocktails. Those activities were common in the neighborhood, but based on the way the soldiers were moving now and the positioning of their vehicles—he had enough experience to know that this pursuit was different.

❖❖❖❖❖

As 1983 drew to a close, the outcome of the conflict between opposites was becoming more decisive: with the passing months, the outcome favored the "we", the mind, and the requirements of action and resistance. He had grown much thinner during the first year in hiding. He had lost his appetite because his brain was exhausted, he was tense for months on end, he suffered from chronic insomnia, and his mouth smelled like a chimney because he smoked three packs a day. Besides, it was strange, even non-human, to eat alone! He could not remember doing that except for a few times in his normal life. Now month after month, he found himself in that unusual situation. The combination of a lethal loneliness, nervousness, and exhaustion had turned the act of eating into no more than a mere daily biological necessity, just to preserve life, with no desire and no enjoyment to be found in the act. He asked his comrades to bring him sleeping pills because of his insomnia, but they refused.

"Forget about that; it is bad for your health. Calm down and you will sleep. Read so your eyes will get tired, and you will sleep."

When he tried to sleep, sleep became like a woman trying to seduce him. His attempts at slumber turned into rounds of struggle between him and the thoughts that crippled his mind: his impulsive inner self, the "I" and its needs and desires. When he would turn on his right side, he recalled his mother and her loneliness after he left her. He was, at the very least, comforted by his correspondence with her before she traveled. His reproaching conscience kept him awake at night, which exhausted him, but when that happened, it was his emotions that denied him sleep. When his mother needed him most, the demands of resistance had forced him to abandon her. When he would turn on his left side, he remembered Muna and their memories together. He saw her in his imagination, he desired her, and he reached out for her, but he grasped at nothing except recollections and images, which had started to fade and lose their glow with the passing months. He tried to conjure up an adequate picture of her in his imagination—her face, her eyes, her hair, mouth, lips, her figure, the way she spoke, her smile, the way she walked . . . and he found that some elements of the picture were beginning to be erased.

He spent his days anxious, his mood in upheaval, and his nights were sleepless until dawn. He would sit on the bed and smoke. He would walk from wall to wall, but the wall snubbed him with its silence. He would take advantage of Umm 'Isa's absence and stand at the window watching passersby. He would observe the trees in the garden and allow his thoughts to wander to the world outside the house, the world from which he had turned his back.

Through all of that, new facts began to dawn on him. Behold how time works. It is capable of erasing all ailments and fractures of the soul that spread like weeds! Time is the most skilled surgeon in history and is capable of patching up any wound no matter how deep.

The party absorbed the results of the attack it endured, and life began to course anew through the synapses of its neurons. The party stabilized—communications were reestablished and blood flowed through the arteries of party activities once more. Kan'an began to buckle down gradually to the task at hand. He participated in decision-making, received directions, engaged in dialogue, argued, wrote, and made proposals. He moved from point to point, keeping with what the secrecy and security required of the job. Work began to consume part of the hours of his day, and he came to sense the importance of remaining between the walls, far away from their eyes and out of their reach. His productivity increased, and his political positions and visions acquired a different meaning and new vigor arising from the revolutionary nature of his reality. With each new day, he became more aware of his importance to the party and his revolutionary significance. His lived experience found the significance it had lacked for many months. But, on the other hand, this showed him that daily stability in this kind of life is not guaranteed, and that non-stability is the law governing a secret life.

One day at the beginning of 1984, his comrade arrived in a hurry, looking dead serious.

"I must get you out of here. I think someone is following me. I tried to make sure that I wasn't being followed when I came here, but it is necessary to take precautions."

He described in detail what had made him suspicious. There was this stranger in the city who wandered through the streets by Al-Mughtarabin Square, constantly watching and on the lookout. He had followed Kan'an's comrade tonight, but the comrade intentionally led him away from the route he normally took to the safe house, then slipped away from him and escaped.

Kan'an picked up his belongings and left with his comrade and they walked uphill towards the boundaries of Qaddura Camp. Some students who were friends of the party lived in a small apartment there. The party had asked them to vacate the apartment for two days and they agreed. At the time, the party did not have a lot of secret houses. Kan'an's comrade walked in front of him so that he could warn him just in case.

At 9 p.m. they arrived at the small flat on the second floor of a three-story building. His comrade led him there and left. Kan'an entered the apartment. Everything in it indicated that the residents were students. There was little by way of furniture and what was there was in a sorry state. The apartment was a chaotic mess, and the dirt seemed to be an inextricable part of it!

The building was wedged between the makeshift houses belonging to the camp. If you went to a window, you would find yourself in the middle of an active and boisterous crowd: here a woman hanging her laundry and gossiping with her neighbors, there a bunch of people hovering over cups of tea, shouting and discussing private matters, children hopping about between the houses and on the roofs all day long, and the alleys crowded with pedestrians. The house in which Kan'an found himself was one of these houses, one incapable of guarding the privacy of its residents, like all houses in the camp.

"How long will I be here? This house is the perfect example of a house unfit for hiding. I will be discovered within a week here, unless I lie still all day and do not move about."

These thoughts worried Kan'an as he woke up on the first day and looked out the windows of his new hideout, trying to familiarize himself with where he was, but his stay there was not to last long.

At 7 p.m. in the evening he was sitting with the lights on in the room, listening to Umm Kulthum singing on the radio, leafing through some of the many books in the house. His engrossment in the books made him unaware how loud the radio was. Then the doorbell rang. He turned off the radio and sat still.

"Open up! It's Umm Mahmud! Open the door, Ayman!"

It was clearly the voice of the owner of the house. He did not open the door, and she yelled again, her shrill voice a warning of her tactless nature.

"Why don't you open up? I am Umm Mahmud!"

It became clear to Kan'an that she was not going to go away. She had heard the sound of the radio, and if he did not answer she would become suspicious.

"God only knows what she will do. She will summon all the residents of the camp with her screeching." He decided to respond.

"Yes, yes! I'm coming!" He opened the peep window in the main door.

"Good evening! Why don't you open the door?" She was a quarrelsome old woman.

"Good evening. If you could just be patient. I was in the bathroom."

He tried to intimidate her with his decisive tone. She was looking at him closely. Seconds passed while she studied his face. Then she dropped a bomb.

"Aren't you the son of Umm . . . You look like her. Are you the one they are looking for?"

She was demonstrating her observance and caught him off guard for a moment. But he recovered quickly.

"Who is this Umm . . . ? What are you saying, Umm Mahmud? There's a lot of people who look alike. I am from Jerusalem. I came to study with Ayman."

"From Jerusalem?!" She asked with a disapproving tone, reflecting her skepticism. She continued, "Your face is . . . Anyway! Here is the water bill. Give it to Ayman."

She left and he closed the peep window.

Kan'an started pacing nervously. She had recognized his resemblance to his mother, so he had to leave quickly. He knew the nature of old women from Al-Bireh. They pursue what they want to know with the insistence of a fly you can't shoo away. Within days, even mere hours, tongues would be wagging delightedly with "he said" and "she said." This experience suggested a needed revision of his instructions, which should be "Don't visit anyone, do not receive anyone, and do not open the peep window of the door to an old woman from Al-Bireh."

In two hours' time he was walking behind his friend heading towards one of the quarters north of Al-Bireh on the way to a safe house used by the party and owned by a woman called Sakinah. As they drew near their destination, he entered a side street leading to the house and found himself face-to-face with family friends—a man and woman with their daughter who was also a student at Birzeit University! They were only a few meters away. Kan'an decided to communicate his message to them through the method he had devised in cases of emergency such as this one. When they drew closer, he turned his face away from them and towards a house along the street. The message was clear: I cannot speak with you, so don't call out my name. He passed them, in awe of his comrade who was supposed to be scouting out the path to warn Kan'an of such situations. His comrade continued down the street while Kan'an turned onto another, so he fell behind and Kan'an found himself acting as the scout for his comrade! When they reached Sakinah's house, Kan'an bid his comrade farewell.

"Tell our comrades to warn the family I ran into to keep silent, especially the woman. She is intelligent and understands the peril of the situation, but she may let a word slip here or there."

Two days later he heard from the party that there were no suspicions concerning "the strange face in the city." He could return to the house of Umm 'Isa. He went back, this time telling his guide which route to take, step by step.

❋❋❋❋❋

At the beginning of 1984, as he buckled down to work, Kan'an's life began to flow according to a new pattern which led increasingly to personal stability. He moved to a new, sunny safe house owned by a man who did not stick his nose in his tenants' affairs. This gradually made it easier to spend twenty-four hours a day between walls.

Kan'an would wake up at nine, eat breakfast, and work till noon. Work for the party had begun to diversify and required more energy.

Its organizations were taking ever deeper roots and its popular base was expanding. Meanwhile, the features of democratic organizations were becoming clearer with each passing day and there was a need for writers. The party published the monthly student newspaper, *Al-Taqaddum*.[9] At lunchtime, Kan'an would hastily put together a meal, which actually took some time, involving a mixture of merriment and frustration as he attempted to master the art of cooking. Pounds of rice were wasted until he was able to produce well-cooked rice, not mounds of clumpy, sticky, shapeless stuff. Large quantities of *mulukhiyah* were lost as his pots overflowed like volcanoes until he discovered that he should not cover the pot while cooking it! He would take a nap after lunch and wake up and resume reading and writing. In between work and cooking, when he was bored, he would listen to the radio and sing along with Sheikh Imam:

> *"If we are hungry, we will eventually be full*
> *Everything will sort itself out.*
> *We don't sell our word for a hundred pieces of silver.*
> *This is how we are, and how we shall remain.*
> *Conscious and clear-eyed!*
> *We know whom to support and of whom to beware!*
> *Always aware!*
> *Not a bit of this and a bit of that.*
> *This is how we are and how we shall remain!"**

Other times he would stand by the window, observing and thinking about the passersby. It is impossible for those leading a secret life not to spy on the people going by their house! It is a cherished activity, even if frowned upon by those leading normal lives. It made him feel like he was part of people's lives—and it also had immense security benefits: one could learn a lot by observing a neighbor or listening to women's idle chatter or the scolding or questioning of a child.

---

* The lyrics are from Sheikh Imam's song *"Hanghanny wa dayman hanghanny,"* translated to "We will sing and we will always sing."

At night, the television was invaluable. It amused him and kept him up-to-date with events and developments. Following a show or watching a film relaxes tired nerves, not to mention cultivates artistic and aesthetic taste.

His duties and responsibilities to the resistance continued to increase as the scope of his party work expanded. His personal daily affairs developed with the solidarity of his comrades and their support. In the course of carrying out these responsibilities, his life began to flow in accordance with these newly established traditions that left their mark on his existence.

Who said that nature dominates nurture? Experience taught Kan'an that this popular saying was ridiculous. Through endurance and forbearance, a human being can adapt contrary to his nature. He can rise to the challenge of new variables in his life and arm himself with determination, and this nurture can lead to a new nature making it difficult to return to one's old way of being. This logic of perpetual change is constant and absolute. A human being cannot detach himself from this logic.

He lived month after month according to the logic of his new life. The inner self, however, had not been fully silenced! Is that to be expected? he wondered. His inner self was his humanity, and how could he detach himself from his humanity? What was new, however, was that when the inner self pressured him, demanding that its needs be met, it could no longer fortify itself behind a barricade, arm itself with a rifle, and open fire on the mind. The self would now whine and complain, and he used to listen and reason calmly with it, but now if it did not obey, he would resort to harshly shutting it up. When he remembered Muna he would feel bitter, enduring the loss, but his mind would intervene.

Yes, she is good and loving and devoted, yes you loved her madly, but she is weak, very weak. Her school and her home life impaired her ability to rebel, to develop an independent personal-

> ity. Her personality is submissive, she cannot endure shocks and difficulties and rebellion and madness. How can a resistance fighter going through a rebellion like yourself be attached to someone who is afraid and incapable of it? Your struggle will not permit an attachment to someone who will turn into a burden. It would also be exhausting for her, it will crush her and subject her to a trial she cannot endure. What happened was natural . . . someone whose life has no room for rebellion will find it difficult to attach herself to the experience of a secret life.

Having always thirsted for knowledge, he felt sorry because he had been unable to complete his education.

> Often the hands of a fighter cannot carry two watermelons at the same time. The circumstances of resistance required putting the "watermelon" of his studies aside. You are part of a revolutionary movement, your value in life is how much you can contribute to that movement and that experience. You can quench your thirst for knowledge in any field you choose, right here between the walls. You do not need a university.

❖ ❖ ❖ ❖ ❖

Early one morning in the summer of 1984, Kan'an was scurrying about his house, like an ant looking for its hill. He tidied up his room, dusted the chairs and the TV set, the bed frame, headboard, and the table. He polished the kitchen sink as well as the cooking range. He opened the fridge and examined its contents. It was replenished with more than he could eat, seeing as he was living alone: various assortments of meat, vegetables and fruit, cheeses, milk products, and goods he would never have thought to buy. He could live for a whole month on these provisions. He was not used to buying supplies for more than a week, nor was he used to this cleaning fever. That day was unlike any other since he had taken up the path of secrecy a year and a half earlier. He was preparing to welcome a guest in a way he never had before nor would again in the future.

So, he woke up early from a restless sleep, eager for the much-awaited daybreak. The previous day was busy—he had mopped the floor of the whole house with soap and water until he was exhausted. He even mopped the unused rooms empty of furniture and the glassed-in balcony. Nor did he forget to clean the glass of the windows. He finished what he had to do by 8:30 in the morning. He looked at his watch: there was half an hour left before his guest would arrive. He shaved, showered, put on his best clothes, and stood by the window looking at the street leading up the hill to his safe house while he quickly thumbed his prayer beads.

"How will the meeting go? Oh! How I've missed you!" he thought, feeling a mixture of yearning, pity, shame for his shortcomings, joy at the thought of embracing his guest.

He was waiting for his mother who had returned from her journey. The party informed him of her return two weeks after she got back and followed up with a decision to allow them to meet. Kan'an almost jumped for joy—in the moment he needed her most, he would finally get to see her. His inner self had been repeatedly asking for her . . . now that wish was about to be realized and he could find peace in her company.

The party had left it up to him and his comrades to make the arrangements, meticulously formulated in secrecy. He sent her a letter delivered by a comrade she did not know. She would be able to tell that the letter was not one of the machinations of the

Occupation's intelligence services and the carrier not an intelligence agent: she could recognize Kan'an's handwriting and the inside references he made to incidents only they knew about. He asked her to take a side street that ran between the Friends School building and playground. His comrade would monitor the street and pick her up in a car between 8:45 and 9:00 a.m., taking a long and circuitous route to the safe house.

He felt bad for involving her in secret arrangements governed by exact timing and descriptions and measures. It was the same way he had felt a year earlier when he wrote her that first letter. She was on the threshold of her sixtieth year and about to enter a world that was entirely strange to her. However, he trusted her intelligence and knew she would follow his directions out of concern that he might be in danger. She was not like the women who knew nothing of the world except their husbands and children and the chatter of old women. She had some education, she could read and write well, she had traveled abroad more than once, and gained a bit of life experience.

His mother had known for years, due to her family background, what it meant for her son to be "embroiled in secret activities," as she angrily put it. She knew enough to calculate the steps she took so as not to affect the life of her son. He therefore trusted that she would not only adhere precisely to his instructions on how to contact and meet him, but she would also understand the way their relationship would be from now on. She knew how to visit prisons and had encounters with intelligence officials more than once. She saw him hide contraband inside and outside the house and in his clothes when he went out. For years now, she had been in contact with his secret world, complaining, yelling, and getting angry about it, but at the same time relenting and showing compassion and sympathy. Whenever a real or imagined danger loomed, she did what would thwart the danger. She never accepted that her youngest child would follow a political path, but, in view of his insistence, she placed her trust in God and prayed that he would be pleased with her son.

At 9:04 a.m., the car he was waiting for began to climb the hill towards his safe house. Kan'an's heart began to beat faster and a shiver ran through him as he waited for his comrade to open the door. He heard the key turn in the lock. The door opened and his mother clutched him in her arms with the emotion of one who had found her lost child. She rained kisses on his cheeks, he cradled her head in his arms and brought it to his chest. He could feel the trembling of her lips as she kissed him and held back her tears with difficulty. She had always withheld her tears in front of him in order to make him stronger. She never cried in difficult circumstances: not when she visited him in captivity, nor when he came home and she kissed him to console him as his father lay wrapped in a shroud in his coffin, nor when he said goodbye to her a year and a half earlier and left. On this occasion too, she did not break her promise to be brave. She cried when she was alone, when her head was on the pillow as she went to sleep. She did not cry in front of him.

They were standing before the door which was still wide open.

"Go in quickly so the landlord doesn't see you. I'll leave now and come back at four," his comrade warned them before he left.

"Get me a seat—my legs are shaky, damn you! How are you?" his mother said in a voice tinged with sorrow and pain as a tremble ran down her spine and gave away her nervousness. Cursing him was an expression of her sweeping love, enveloped in mock anger.

"Okay, calm down first. I'll bring you some orange juice to calm your nerves."

"Never mind the juice. Tell me how you are. What's your life like? What are you eating? What do you drink? How long will this life go on?"

She bombarded him with a barrage of questions which would have taken him an hour to answer. She kept turning her head, seeking to inspect her surroundings, agitated. He could not help smiling in view of his happiness with her and amusement at the insistent "interrogation" technique she had perfected. She was his mother, whose interrogations, insistence, and reprimands he had missed.

"If I were to answer all your questions in one go, there would be nothing left to talk about," he said, trying to relax her.

Kan'an joked with her as was his custom, enjoying it especially when she brought up the most serious issues in his life to make her feel that there were no answers to her questions. Instead of a reprimand in reply to her questions, he was indirectly saying "don't ask!" That was what he used to do when she asked him where he was going as he left the house at night to attend one of his secret meetings. Playing down the gravity of her questions and reassuring her, he would only reply, "I am going to walk in the direction of Haifa and come back." That silenced her.

He did this with her ever since he first trod the political path and became embroiled (as she put it). But then she caught onto his games and never stopped asking questions.

"The talking never ends. Speak, speak quickly," she interrupted him as he talked.

No sooner would he begin a sentence than she would interject a question or change the subject. He was sitting near her on the bed, and she covered the whole spectrum of topics, even the washing of his underwear, giving him her best practices. He enjoyed the distinctive smell of his mother. How he had longed to smell her and kiss the wrinkles of her cheeks and to place his tired head on her chest while she ran her fingers through his coarse hair, repeating one of her favorite phrases: "your hair is like a horse's hair."

Now that his wishes had been granted upon seeing his mother, he temporarily forgot that he had gone into hiding; forgot the requirements, the rules, the precautionary measures . . . She had transported him to her world outside the realm of secrecy and safe houses, her world which is full of insistent questioning and free-flowing tenderness and small details with which a mother deals to perfection.

"Now, let's get serious." She became alert, and he continued. "If I were to tell you my life was great, I would be lying. However, I am happy to live according to my convictions and my principles. I want only one thing from you: that you should support me and repeat what you said the day they raided the house: 'Go, my son. May God be pleased with you!' That is worth the whole world to me. Don't you want me to be a man that you can be proud of having given birth to? Be proud now. Don't you want me to be happy? I am happy. As for how long I will be here, I do not know nor do I even think about it."

"Happy while you are confined between four walls?" she asked disapprovingly.

"Happiness is satisfaction with oneself, and I am satisfied with myself. I am happy when I am engaged in resistance activities. That is enough for me."

She listened to him, shaking her head with a look of resignation in her eyes.

"What about Muna? You lost that fine girl. She broke off her engagement to you. Did you know?" Her question picked at a fresh scab, conjuring up an image, the details of which had not yet been fully erased from his mind.

"I didn't lose anything, she is the one that lost." But he had already admitted to himself the enormous size of his loss. He was aware of it each and every day for a year and a half, and he knew it today.

"A fine girl. What a loss." She repeated this as though she was talking to herself in a tone indicating regret.

"I know she is a fine girl but I also know that she is weak. She loves at times of peace and runs away at times of war. We are at war. Our homeland is occupied, would you have me acting as if it was of no consequence to me?"

She went around the house, entering each room, familiarizing herself with it.

"So you have a house! And I am visiting you in it." She understood the change in his life and in the relationship between them. Her youngest child had grown up. She entered the kitchen and was pleased to see a gas range and an electric oven. She opened the fridge and its secrets were revealed. She raised her eyebrows in surprise. "Really! Your fridge is full? Can you cook well? Come see what I brought you! Where is the sack? Did we forget it in the car?" She slapped her cheeks in dismay as she asked the last question.

"It's by the door. I left it there. What did you bring? I told you in my letter not to bring anything. I don't need anything."

She did not stop to hear the rest of his infuriating words. It did not matter to her. She had gone to fetch the sack. She opened it and began to take out its contents, small parcels like the ones the village elders carried under the belts of their *thobes* to hold coins. One parcel contained fresh white cheese from the local farms, another contained anise seed cookies, a third contained pickled eggplant, a fourth and a fifth and a tenth . . . He was secretly happy with these small gifts. They were things that either he could not make well or that he had simply forgotten about. However, when she produced her last bundle, the largest one, he lost his temper.

"A chicken? A chicken?" he yelled at her. "The city is full of chickens. Do you think that I have not eaten chicken for a year and a half?" He was pained that she had gone to the trouble.

"My son, may God be pleased with you. This is a country hen from our stock. It will make a delicious soup. It is great for stuffing too. I cleaned it so that it is ready for the pot." She was dejected and hurt, her tone full of apprehension from his yelling.

He wished he had cut off his tongue before yelling at her like that, and at their first meeting no less. *I should let her express her motherly instincts in these small ways*, he thought. *So long as it makes her happy, I should let it go. What spirit of stupidity possessed me?*

"You're right, I'm sorry," he apologized. "Don't be upset. A country hen from our village deserves a parade. A country hen that can be stuffed with delicious ingredients, now this is a real present." He kissed her and she brightened up and smiled. "Stuff it and sew it up well so that the rice does not spill out, and bake it in the oven."

They had lunch together. He got up to collect the dishes, but she took charge.

"Sit down!" she said. He obeyed and sat down while she washed the pots and dishes and cleaned the sink and the kitchen.

"What would you like me to make you? We have three hours until the comrade comes back. What shall I cook for you?"

"I know how to cook. Sit down so that we can talk." He convinced her with difficulty.

"Alright, when will I come back to you?"

"Whenever you want. Just make arrangements with the comrade who brought you so that I can be prepared and make sure no one comes while you are here."

"Don't burden yourself. Find a time suitable for you," she said in a resigned tone, putting things in his hands.

"I have time to see you every day, but I don't want your movements, I mean your trips outside the house, to be an object of suspicion by the family. What's important is that certain things are followed carefully."

"Whatever you want," she said and waited for him to continue.

"Under no circumstances should anyone know anything about our meetings. 'How's Kan'an doing?' 'We don't know!' It is best to keep quiet. That way they will forget my name." She began nodding her head in agreement. "Never come on your own without prior arrangement. Whatever you may hear from here and there, don't come. Remember what they did to you months ago: they expected you to know where I was. You would have been the trap into which I fell. You fix the day with the one who brought you, then I will send you my response and you can come. Find a reason to leave the house when you come to me: one time make it a visit to an acquaintance, another time a trip to the hospital, or a visit to the doctor . . . Vary the reasons for your trips and be careful that they do not notice what you are carrying, otherwise don't bring anything except your handbag. And as a precaution, wear your prescription glasses when you come."

As he was dictating his conditions to her a feeling of sympathy came over him. He felt at several points that his revolutionary experience had added a new dimension to her personality. His relationship with her became more than that of a son to his mother; rather, she became a friend close to his heart who provided the warmth and tenderness of motherhood and the gift of her sensitive humanity. Still, he resented the circumstances that made meeting his own mother so complicated due to the need for secrecy.

At four in the afternoon, she left his safe house.

❖❖❖❖❖

The party was doing everything in its power to secure internal peace and stability for Kan'an. The party was ready to provide whatever Kan'an needed so long as it did not have a negative bearing on his secret life and personal safety. Kan'an and the party were in constant communication and letters flowed freely between them. Solidarity and support were daily and definite. It would be difficult to imagine a successful life in hiding if the party did not do everything that it could to demonstrate and reinforce concern for the owner of that life. He who leaves one life and transitions to another life, one that is difficult and cursed yet necessary, must be cared for. In this regard, the party and Kan'an's comrades were truly uplifting his spirit.

He was reading a lot, and his conviction concerning his decision and his life grew stronger every day. He read literature in particular, authors such as Jorge Amado, Hanna Mina, Ghassan Kanafani, Mahmoud Darwish . . . and Soviet writers. He would spend hours and hours reading, and he would read the novels that he liked twice, even three times on occasion. That was what he did with Mikhail Sholokhov's *And Quiet Flows the Don*, and *How the Steel Was Tempered* by Nikolai Ostrovsky, as well as *The Snow Comes through the Window* by Hanna Mina.

The last novel played an important part in his secret life. When he read the book, he said with every page, "Hanna Mina wrote this about me . . . he is talking about me." Every page, every line, every word in that book was a brilliant depiction of the warrior's secret life, of the struggle between strength and frailty, the difficulty of constantly moving from place to place, instability, women, the struggle, the mission ... but up to that time he did not have a "young woman of the window" as Fayad, the hero of the novel, did. The party was to Kan'an what Khalil was to Fayad. Khalil toned down Fayad's reactions, directed him, controlled his impetuousness, reshaped him. Fayad's Khalil was a laborer, Kan'an's Khalil was a revolutionary policy. When he finished reading the novel in the summer of 1984, still under its spell, he asked himself: Fayad's beginning is not like my beginning, I did not flee the homeland in order to return to it in the end. Will the end of my experience be like the end of his: arrest, caught red-handed in possession of the party's printing press? What a coincidence that would be.

Literature nourished him, gave him pleasure, strengthened his moral fiber, cultivated his taste for art and beauty, fanned the flames of enmity within him towards the tyrants, boosted his opposition to all manifestations of oppression. It nurtured a sense of compassion and empathy with the toiling masses, and there is nothing better than this for a man in hiding. The development of a refined sensitivity for justice and the adherence to sublime human values will lighten the weight of daily existence's hardships. The party appreciated the importance of comprehensive and varied education and gave him a blank check to buy books.

"Do not hesitate. Buy what books you want and read them. Don't worry about budgetary considerations." When his comrades came across a significant book, such as a good novel, they did not hesitate to recommend it to him: "Drop whatever you are doing and read about the life of the great Dzerzhinsky. Have you read *The Sun on a Cloudy Day* by Hanna Mina? You will really enjoy it. We discovered some books by Jorge Amado—buy *Gabriela, Clove and Cinnamon*, and *The Land of Golden Fruits*. Did you receive *Cities of Salt* and *A Zoroastrian Love Story* by Abdul Rahman Munif?"

Kan'an used to read and read whenever his work allowed for it. Occasionally he would drop whatever he was doing to immerse himself in some novel. He read while cooking, before going to sleep, or even in front of the television when what was on didn't interest him. He felt a special pleasure when he picked up an enjoyable novel at the end of a tiring day of party work or for the sake of relief from the pressures of daily tasks.

"**Measures, precautions, requirements, and rules.**" He had not forgotten the words that informed him of the decision to transition to a secret life. After a year and a half, they no longer stirred up resentment within him. He no longer reacted with a shrug of the shoulders and biting sarcasm as he had done in the early days, weeks, and months. They had become the law of his secret existence which he guarded as he guarded his own life—in fact it had become his life. He observed that law now with conviction of its vital importance. He understood its necessity in his life and for his struggle, even though he did not like it or enjoy life according to its rules. At any rate, he was beginning to discover that there is a difference between enjoyment and necessity.

"**Do not receive any visitors and do not visit anyone**," along with the amendment he added seven months prior: "Do not open the peep window of the door to an old woman from Al-Bireh." He got used to that commanding order, which was as hard as concrete, that encapsulated his relationship with those outside his house, his big den. He repeated it not because he liked it, but because it had become a daily routine, and time guarantees that any difficulty can become habit. With the passing of the days, he had gradually begun to be convinced of its importance. He was starting to understand the difference between time and necessity.

Chapter 4

Military barracks were now surrounding the house, as Hisham had said. Their vehicles were like a necklace around the entire quarter. There would be time later to analyze the reason for the raid. What was important now was whether the soldiers saw one person or two on the balcony when Kan'an and Hisham had heard footsteps and stuck out their heads to see what was happening. Kan'an cursed himself for the amateurism of looking out without taking sufficient precautions.

Kan'an felt the papers he had placed in front of himself again, alongside the bottle of kerosene and the lighter. He made sure he knew where everything was so that his sense of touch would not betray him at the last moment and prevent him from acting quickly. He had prepared everything for an emergency. Half the party's security depended on not betraying secrets during the confrontations in the interrogation room; the other half depended on rules and measures taken prior to the confrontation in the interrogation room. These rules and measures were designed to prevent chance occurrences, which can sometimes be more catastrophic than party members falling apart during interrogation.

Clandestine activities in their entirety depend on preventing these chance events as much as possible. A chance event like forgetting the lighter, in this case, would have severe consequences, as would losing a piece of paper and not destroying it. Kan'an owed his success in maintaining a secret life for many years to this golden rule, among others. What a crime it would be for his documents to fall into the hands of the occupiers! He would not want that crime to be recorded on his file. What significance does this stack of papers sitting in front of him now, next to the kerosene can, have in his life? His daily thoughts, his work, sustenance, tasks, comrades, party, struggle, his secrets—all recorded on those pages. He clutched them in his hands when he moved. They rested on a small stool next to his bed as he slept. They were with him when he worked, and he either read them or wrote on them. They were often the third presence in the room when he had a visitor. Years and days of his life were spent with them. His papers were what his eyes saw the most, what his hands carried the most, what he committed to memory the most, what he feared for the most. Through them Kan'an ventured into his experience and with them he connected with his people's struggle. His pen was his tongue. With it he conducted a dialogue: incentivized, educated, objected, argued, proposed, discussed, decided . . . It was a substitute for his chained hand and his real tongue, which was otherwise imprisoned in his throat and used only for chewing food.

Were they just like any other papers? They were teeming with life, archives of struggle, and tasks. They intensified his political life, laying it out in those smooth, soft, line-filled pages. Kan'an would not surrender them even if the enemy pointed a gun at his head. How can one surrender part of his body to anyone? His head, heart, lungs, feet, hands . . . ? He could not be too quick to destroy them. Destroying them would be a coup de grâce, like shooting a sick and aged horse in the head to preserve its dignity. He was determined to protect the dignity of his papers, so he decided he would not allow their fingers to touch them or their eyes to see them at all costs.

His nine-year clandestine existence could be summed up in a few concentrated words: doors, papers, walls, pen, chair, table . . . He spent hours working at his table. No wonder then that he was always especially careful in choosing it. He would peck and peck on its surface as he thought, or lean his elbow against it as he smoked, or eat on it while he worked so that olive oil and cigarette butts and ashes would be mixed in with the papers. His chair did not tire his buttocks which were as lean as a beanpole. His table and chair did not give him pain in his back, shoulders, or hands. As the years went by, the significance of the material things surrounding him in his life became greater until they practically became life itself. His secret life could be crammed past the opening of a door, one which he entered and locked years ago, one which could open within hours and through which he would leave—the ending of one life and the beginning of another, the essence of which was unfathomable.

Between one wall and the other were his footsteps, no more. One step, two, ten, and Kan'an would be up against another wall and turn around. His needs were crammed for years between a ceiling and a wall and could not pierce the barrier. If his needs resisted, they would stretch and stretch—only to encounter four walls lying in wait for them. They would collide with the walls, rebound off them, but the walls stood in the way of their realization.

Kan'an had his letter to Hind in his hand. He picked it up while he was feeling for his papers, as the clamor and attempts to force the door continued. He remembered her as he groped for the letter. He could still imagine feeling her short, rather coarse hair, or running his fingers over her forever-sunny face as though to capture her smile between his fingers, or touching her eyes, radiating intelligence and transfixing him whenever she was at his place. He sighed and squeezed the letter with a sense of pain and bitterness. He had been very careful to retrieve his letter to her when he heard the Occupation's pounding. He would not permit anyone to infiltrate the synapses of his brain or the membrane guarding his heart this way. It contained his joy and his sadness, his elation and his anger, his tenderness and his callousness. It contained all the contradictions that swayed his memories of their short time together. It contained things he had said only to her, for she was a good listener and expert conversationalist, so he wanted to talk to her, not to anyone else. He would not allow them to put his love life on the interrogation table and in the torture room. Even with his comrades, he was reserved on the subject, so how could he expose these things to his enemies? His comrades knocked on the door to his self but did not try to force it open; if he did not open up to them, they stopped.

A sensitive letter in delicate circumstances, it had shaped his thoughts and his mood and conduct for weeks. The letter felt as if she was sitting in front of him, always smiling. He did not know if her smile was for the sake of decorum, or if it was natural to her. She paid attention to what he had to say more out of an almost morbid curiosity than out of consideration for the friendship that he thought had sprung up between them. The letter was a final attempt, and the first in his secret life, to transform the image of the woman in his imagination into reality, an image based on features he had glimpsed in Hind. But she tore up the picture and strolled out the door. He shut it behind her and went back to living with the picture in his head that had entertained him for years!

What does Hind dream about these days when she sleeps after a tiring day of working and commuting while he remains in stasis, waiting for the approaching unknown in his dark, stony den? Did she listen to some gentle classical music before she went to sleep to relax her exhausted nerves? Or did she prefer the songs by Marcel Khalife that intoxicated her, or the latest reel by Fairuz, "*Kifak Inta*," a fever she had spread to his house? Did she keep the promise she made him to not eat dinner too late at night to preserve her figure—a fact he had once pointed out to her? That was the last promise she had made to herself!

❖❖❖❖❖

Suddenly the pounding drew closer and closer. He could now clearly hear their voices—they had finally succeeded in forcing the outer door open and now it was the inner door's turn.

It was now 1:40 a.m. It took them almost an hour to unhinge the first door and the second would not last an hour: it was smaller and thinner, made of weaker iron. The moment separating two worlds was drawing closer: the first, a secret world he dwelt in for many years, and a different world, the true nature of which he did not know, and in which he would live for an unknown time. The unknown was torturing him, killing him. He wanted it to reveal itself. Will they discover his den or not? Did they see one or two people on the balcony? He could escape and preserve his presence among his comrades and his party and in the hearts of his people and continue to carry out his mission. He held onto that hope. He could not do otherwise. He sensed it to be a flimsy hope, not knowing why.

Hisham was acting in accordance with their approach. He would not open the door. The pounding was close by and violent and strong. Their shrieks to open the door were loud.

What is Hisham thinking now? Is he thinking of the arrival of the unknown and the prospects for the future? Is he thinking of his beautiful boy—just one-year-and-five-months old—like a child's toy, with a head too big for his age? Is he thinking of his comrades or his sick parents . . . what is he thinking? Everything dear to one's heart force its way into these moments when one is surrounded by danger. The party, the family, the mother, the comrades, the woman . . . they all invaded the brain. Hisham will be the Hisham that I know—a man when men stand up to be counted. When you first met and you asked him if you should flee the safe house if he was ever arrested, did he not say "Don't leave it"? He was the sort of man for whom you would reserve a special place in your heart because of his kindness, his sentiments, his unwavering commitment, his courage and temerity, his comradely qualities, his innate sense of humor and constant jokes which animated whoever heard them, through which he reaffirms his belonging to and upbringing in Jenin.

It was precisely in these moments, as the occupiers approached, that Kan'an was confident that he and Hisham would rise to the challenge and be true to the expectations of their comrades.

Along with the pounding he could hear voices in a feeble Arabic accent that Kan'an always hated hearing from Israelis out of pity for his language. "Open, by order of the military governor! This is the army, open the door!" The door resisted. It seemed to him that even the door began to protect him with its body, its iron frame enduring their frenzied blows in his defense. It had grown accustomed to his company for years and years, day by day, hour by hour. It was as if everything in his house was indebted to protecting him from the eyes of the enemy and the curious: the doors, the windows from which he watched the streets and people, the walls to which he poured out his worries as he paced between them. There were his books which had not grown tired of moving from house to house over the years, of having their pages bent and turned, which had kept him company even when he was in the bathroom! Even the colored decorations on the tiles of the floor were his friends. He imagined drawings and figures in them, as a child might see a house or an orange or flowers or small letters in a cloud. There was a beautiful duck on the tiles of the bathroom which he contemplated as he sat on the toilet. Had he not asked the walls: My needs and desires increase and grow, won't you help bring them about? Had he not yelled at the door at moments of frustration, when he felt the pressures and cruelty of life: Won't you open some day? Will I not exit through you to live in nature like the first man did, to be without you, without the walls, the table, the chairs?

But his friend, the door, would collapse sooner or later. It would succumb to their blows. After all, what willpower did the door have to remain steadfast? For years, Kan'an had sown in his mind the values of confrontation and steadfastness, and it seemed to him that the time for their harvest was near. The second door was about to collapse. Kan'an would not collapse from their blows. His trust in his party and in the struggle would not be wrenched from his heart!

❄❄❄❄❄

The flow of his secret life was not free of disruptions, in fact they were part and parcel of it. A life in hiding knows nothing of stability.

Just before sunset after a blistering August afternoon, Kan'an was standing at his window contemplating whatever his eyes chanced upon. The window overlooked the industrial zone in the eastern part of Al-Bireh, but it was only an industrial zone in name. In reality it hardly belonged to the world of industry in the modern sense of the term. Carpentry and ironsmith workshops were spread throughout, as well as one or two factories producing cinder blocks and tiles, and a couple more producing processed food. Apart from these light industries and workshops, the area was dominated by car and auto shops. As far as the eye could see, there were frames of cars and trucks, their parts strewn throughout the side streets and in the garage and workshop yards. Because Al-Bireh had barely emerged from the womb of a rural environment into the world of the city, it was not bereft of the most prominent manifestation of the village: fields of fruit trees on both sides of the street running up the hill to his house—fig, almond, and plum trees in particular. The figs of Al-Bireh are as sweet as honey. These orchards bestowed the entire vista of the region with a beauty that penetrated even the world of garages and cars and noisy workshops. This beauty was a reminder that once, not too many years earlier, nature had full reign before it was deformed by haphazard construction and scattered workshops.

His window, his portal to the real world, was like any other window in any other safe house he had stayed in. Pondering the fig orchards took him back to the days of his childhood when all the orchards of Al-Bireh were public property for him and the other children, where they could not only savor the taste of the figs but also take up chasing after the Palestinian goldfinch, his hobby until adolescence. His memories and current state of mind were tangling together, the two intertwining like a spider's web, so that he imagined organizing a raid on the fig orchards of the house—escaping his pressures, responsibilities, and hardships into the happiness of his mischievous childhood.

The owner of the house was a good and friendly man, an exception among the landlords he had met so far, and he generously did not deny his tenants the benefit of his figs. Kan'an did not ask him for figs, perhaps because he was too shy to ask, or for the love of carrying out raids. Instead, he coordinated with a comrade with a giant foot to sneak into the orchard before daybreak, not because he wished to take advantage of the darkness, but because figs can only be eaten while covered with dew, when they still hold the night's invigorating cold. After Kan'an had carried out several raids, the landlord came to visit, carrying a basket of figs.

"The orchard below belongs to me, and you and your friends may treat it as your own," he told him out of goodwill (which made Kan'an feel a wave of shame from head to toe). "This house is your house and the orchard is your orchard." But this made Kan'an's raids "legitimate" and they therefore lost their appeal.

The owner of the house was unlike others Kan'an had met. It was difficult to classify him, based on his conduct, as a landlord. He was the sort who, finding himself in a new social class because he was a landlord, had not yet grown accustomed to behaving in the manner of his new class, like so many former working-class farmers, who were now members of the bourgeoisie. They had neither put on the social characteristics of the bourgeoisie nor had they gotten rid of their nature as farmers completely—they were like a woman dancing on the middle rung of a ladder! He did not love the arrival of the first day of the month, as landlords usually did, nor did he stick his nose in the affairs of his tenants, as owners of small tenements did. The most important thing, as far as Kan'an was concerned, was that he did not track his movements or the movements of his visitors. If you stretched out your hand to pay him the rent he would be embarrassed and insist, with no fakery, that he would not take it. When the money from the party was delayed for one reason or the other, Kan'an only had to go to him and say: My family was late in sending money and we have to pay tuition at the university—can we pay you the money in two weeks? The man never hesitated. Nor did his kindness turn into stupidity, as the case of one whose kindness exceeds its reasonable limits. However, he had reasonable suspicions that his tenants were activists, regardless if their cover of being students was not the most convincing.

"I have been called in for an interview by the intelligence services. What shall I say if I'm asked who my tenants are? Give me any name you like that is not suspicious."

Kan'an thanked him and gave him a fictitious name, and stayed away from his safe house for two weeks as a precaution against any senseless coincidences.

That scorching day, just after sunset, Kan'an stood looking out the window and suddenly he saw a column of troop carriers approaching from the army camp in the city, which crossed the main road linking Ramallah and Nablus and descended towards the industrial zone.

"What's all this? Daily arrests? Unlikely. There are no demonstrations here. Something may have happened!"

Standing by the window, Kan'an tried to work out an answer as he watched. The column was made up of military vehicles carrying officers and small trucks on tank treads. The formation continued moving in the direction of the crossroads, and when it got there, it stopped along the road that climbs the hill to the safe house. Different units began to disperse, and Kan'an noticed that the combat formation had taken the shape of a pincer with a spear in the middle: an officer's car and a soldier carrier went to the right and a similar combination took shape on the left. The vehicles stopped a hundred meters away.

Meanwhile, an army truck stayed at the crossroads while another, preceded by an officer's car, started up the street to the safe house. Soldiers got off at the crossroads and took up positions, resting their machine guns on the paved road. Those climbing the road leading to the hill kept going until they reached the end of the paved street and continued onto the dirt road. They stopped after a few meters directly behind the safe house, no more than thirty meters away!

"It is the encirclement which precedes the raid," Kan'an said out loud as his hands immediately began collecting his secret papers.

He felt as though there was a noose around his neck. His mind was preoccupied with one question: what's to be done? After ten minutes of agitated thinking with no resolution, pacing from window to window to monitor the movements of the troops, he heard the sound of the key turning in the lock of the door and his comrade with the giant foot entered, visibly tense and agitated. He was panting and barely able to catch his breath, his clothes soiled with dirt and dried grass. He put a sack of bread on the table and asked a stupid question.

"Have you seen what is going on outside?"

"Do you think my ears would not pick up the sound of tank treads screeching thirty meters away? I cannot see exactly what is happening." Kan'an tried to reassure his comrade, although he himself needed it too. It suddenly occurred to him. "But how did you get in? Quickly, tell me what you saw."

But his comrade had nothing to add to what Kan'an had seen, except for how he got there.

"When I approached the crossroads, I saw them. I left the road and entered the fields. I crawled between the trees and the houses to get here. Some people are moving about freely and no one is intercepting them."

His comrade never let him down in situations requiring courage and boldness. He was the sort who did not know fear, which neither entered his heart nor impeded his movements... Perhaps this was due in some part to his courageous nature or because his brain had not been flooded by calculations which inhibit courage, or because he could not do the calculations to begin with, or his tranquil soul did not experience doubt which could cause his determination to waver. He was the sort who possessed the ability to do what was asked of him without letting his mind meddle in the execution. He was the same sort of base of which the Marxist thinker Antonio Gramsci spoke, a base that is ready to carry out orders but does not possess sufficient political maturity to take initiative or to make decisions. His rural life and very limited background had shrunk the horizons of his thinking within the narrowest boundaries. On the one hand, he was weak in initiative, shrewdness, sagacity, education, and experience... On the other hand, those weaknesses were offset by his endurance, courage, and boldness. Therefore, as Kan'an had once estimated, while no torturer could extract a single word out of him, he could fall easy prey to ruses and tricks.

"What is this all about then? They surround but don't raid, they don't even stop passersby. They haven't imposed a curfew? What sort of raid is this really? Is there a critical issue requiring a daylight raid? They have been here for twenty minutes, what next?"

Kan'an did not wait for answers, he was thinking out loud. Finally he decided.

"At any rate, we should leave immediately. We can't remain surrounded by an army barracks ready to carry out some sort of raid. Let's hurry, seeing as nightfall is here. Let us sneak out the same way you came. Which safe house shall we go to?"

"To Umm 'Isa's. It is empty as far as I know. Isn't that right?"

"Empty. Fine, let's go to Umm 'Isa's house." Kan'an let out a knowing sigh. He remembered that he had to be careful there such that even the sound of his urine flowing from his bladder should not be heard!

Umm 'Isa's house was at the far end of Ramallah. That meant they had to walk more than four kilometers without even forged identification or the means to disguise his features. He had a light beard, which was not up to the task of disguise. As a precaution against emergencies, he had to take side streets not crowded with pedestrians and empty of army patrols. The streets also had to be such that one could enter any house or garden along the way, which is a feature the main streets lacked. This meant that the total distance could extend as far as six kilometers.

Kan'an's name was still on the lips of many people; he had not yet been forgotten. After a year and a half, his experience was still in its infancy and had not yet had a chance to deeply sink in its roots and its rules were not set yet. What made the situation more dangerous was that it was logical to conclude that his name might be in the pockets of army patrols in the streets of both cities.

Staying in place was a danger lying in wait in the form of soldiers bristling with arms only thirty meters away. Leaving the house was also a risk. However, its dangerous consequences could be avoided if one has a sharpened focus and exercises great alertness. A clandestine existence in its entirety is a constant risk—a chain of risks which the clever clandestine revolutionary must negotiate or leap over through means that may or may not be available. The landmarks of the experience were becoming ever clearer, day by day and month by month.

The two men sneaked out of the house under the shadows of the trees and in the darkness of night, crossing orchards and circling behind houses near the street, crawling on the ground like soldiers engaged in battle. They quickly broke out of the encirclement and marched through the streets of the industrial zone. Bigfoot scouted the way and Kan'an followed him, trying not to lose him. They circled around the collection of cafes in Al-Bireh, arriving at the cemetery. From there they descended to the municipal slaughterhouse, reaching Shurfa Street and then the edges of Al-Am'ari Camp. From there they ascended across the small forest leading to Ramallah Hospital, then the UNRWA Teachers

Training Roundabout, and then descended to the outskirts of the industrial zone in Ramallah where Umm 'Isa's house was situated.

A year earlier he had left this safe house for no reason! Nothing had changed, there were the same steps leading to the garden trellis.

"It was my mother's prayers that saved us tonight! Open the door comrade."

His comrade searched for the key. He did not find it in his first pocket; he tried the second, and signs of tension began to appear on his face; he looked in his shirt pocket and did not find it. Confusion showed on his face.

"Search carefully." Kan'an said, sighing as he sensed the inevitable approach of a predicament.

"I don't have it on me. I must have left it in town."

He was speaking out of embarrassment, confused like a child caught by his mother and implicated in a misdemeanor which he could not deny, weighing what his punishment would be.

Kan'an unloaded a profuse stream of harsh words on his comrade's head, shivering from the anger that got hold of him, and as he tried hard to keep his voice low out of fear that Umm 'Isa might catch him—she who could hear the sound of urination hitting the bottom of the toilet bowl!

"It is 10:30 at night. We walked from the outskirts of Al-Bireh to the outskirts of Ramallah just so you could tell me that you forgot the key? Where shall we go now? Where shall I spend the night?"

Their only choice was to head to the large field adjoining the safe house. They spent the night there in silence, each one communing with himself. The insects feasted on their blood. All that could be heard was the slapping of hands swatting insects followed by abject curses. In the early morning Kan'an was able to communicate to his comrades what had happened. They arrived before nine and transported him back to his safe house in Al-Bireh.

"There is no danger threatening the house. We discovered last night that the army had done the same thing on the outskirts of other cities. They seem to have been conducting exercises, no more." His comrades set his mind at ease. They told him things he did not know: the night before one of his comrades accidentally noticed an intensification of troop presence near Kan'an's house. He hurried to inform the party, which in turn hurried to mobilize a handful of his comrades. One of them snuck through the encirclement up to the safe house and peered into the windows but did not notice any signs of raids being conducted inside. What is more important is that he could not find Kan'an. His comrades started roaming the streets in their cars looking for him, anticipating that he would encounter risks by moving about at night in view of the intensive troop movements on the outskirts of cities.

❖❖❖❖❖

The door finally gave way. They broke it wide open by force, using their crowbars and heavy military boots. As soon as they entered, enraged, eager to sink their fangs in human flesh, they fell to beating Hisham. Their yells grew louder.
"Why didn't you open the door? Speak, you fucker, speak!"
"Strike, you fascist, strike! Go ahead and please your sadistic inclinations that they trained you in." Hisham shouted defiantly, accompanied by a string of vilifying invectives.
Curses are a linguistic treasure for the revolutionary which he draws on at moments when there is a clash, an overflow of anger and frustration which interact in his revolutionary chest. A revolutionary who does not curse in the dungeons of interrogation is as rare as an old currency. Kan'an felt his blood boiling with anger but he could do nothing for his comrade who was defending him, accepting their blows for both of them. He was overcome with sympathy for Hisham. The set arrangements for what to do in case of confrontation had put Hisham at the front lines.
The good comrade becomes apparent at the time of the most arduous mission. The party had reiterated that many times. Hisham, the good comrade at this time, put himself on the frontlines—he was defending his comrade who was ensconced in the stone den. Kan'an's papers were in front of him, he could hear the voices

speaking Hebrew and tried to make sense of it using his meager store of vocabulary. Above all, he prepared for battle should the time come and his den be discovered.

"What's your name? Speak! Where is the second guy? Where is the second guy? Speak!" yelled the voice in Hebrew.

Kan'an understood the question. *"Ivo Hashani?" Then they must have seen two people on the balcony, and they are looking for me. I shall not forgive myself for that amateur stupidity unbefitting to a professional. The hour of battle is therefore drawing near, it is inevitably coming.*

They saw two, but they only had one in hand: where did the other one go? They will pull up the floor of the house, tile by tile, until he shows up. They will tear down the walls until they find him, they will rip up the mattresses, everything. He must appear—it was all over for Kan'an. They will continue searching, they will uproot the closets and they will find him. Now it is just a matter of time. How soon until they reach him? When will he be in their hands?

It is really over, Kan'an. Your long years are about to end. All possibilities are now open: killing, mutilation, banishment, arrest. Now dawn is about to break. We shall see if the party's training proves useful, whether your self-mobilization and what you stored up while pacing between the walls or as you lay your head on your pillow is fruitful or not. It is time for the test, the test of your resistance, your experience, your position, your role. With tests a person is either honored or dishonored—honored for his steadfastness or demeaned for collapsing.

As he had planned earlier, he had not burned his papers yet. He was waiting until the last moment: when they begin prying open the closet that concealed his den, only then would he burn them. He corrected himself quickly—*if* they find the den!

Kan'an, holed up like a wolf that fears the huntsman's bullet, still had hopes of escape! He still hoped they would not find him, a man about whom no one knew anything, who had slipped through their fingers for years. He hoped with his whole being, not because his hope was supported by a real possibility, but because he was attached to his choice, his life, his experience, his struggle, and mission. He was attached to all of these things, like a monk's attachment to his hermitage, like a drowning man hangs on to a plank of wood, invisible amidst the crashing of endless waves. He felt like a mother hoping for a "divine gift" that would suddenly lift her only son from his grave, a whisper to her son, just like Christ said, "rise," and the person rose!

Clutching onto this fading hope, he decided not to destroy his papers until the last moment, papers which were his life. He could hear their iron cudgels pounding the walls of the house. They were looking for him, edging the wardrobe in his bedroom directly behind his den out of the way. The small drawers of the kitchen's cupboards were being opened and slammed shut, producing noise that reverberated throughout the house. They even looked for him inside the kitchen cupboards. Did they think he was inside a can of sardines? Or in a sack of salt hiding behind the grain? Or was he perhaps hidden behind a wall of sugar that he built before they began tearing down the walls of his house? They were confident there was a second man, and they would continue looking until they found him.

"Where is the second man? Speak quickly! Where is he?"

Their shouts were accompanied by the blows they were dealing out to Hisham, mixed with the angry curses he was hurling back at them. Hisham was crouched on the floor of the first room near the front door. They were searching Kan'an's house as he grew more and more resigned; they would certainly find him! He could only wait, wait for his pre-determined fate, wait for an official announcement that it was over. A mixture of feelings of tension, incitement, resentment, pain, sorrow, and determination were welling up inside of him as he waited for the soldiers to reach him physically. How difficult is waiting in such moments?

He had experienced a similar experience of "waiting" years earlier. Everyone has such "waiting periods" in their life, but Kan'an's had a special flavor, a distinct reality. His waiting periods arose out of the inability to do anything except wait. If Kan'an wanted something, he could do no more than wait for it to materialize because he was prevented from satisfying the need himself. If he asked for something that would help him do his job, he had to wait for someone to arrive with the specifics; if he ran out of cigarettes due to some silly quirk or stupid arrangements on his part, he had to wait for someone to bring them to him.

No sooner had he remembered the experience of waiting for cigarettes than he lit one and hungrily took a deep drag, evading the painful ramifications of "waiting." If he heard a rumor that aroused his curiosity and sometimes caused stress, he had to wait to verify it. His waiting confirmed his powerlessness! How the feeling of powerlessness drained him at moments like this. When he was waiting, he was like the hunter who held his breath while the bird hopped and sang merrily in the vicinity of the net, but not where he could reach it. He would quicken his pace as he walked from wall to wall, and he would smoke and smoke (if he was not waiting for a cigarette). He would strike the wall with his fist sometimes out of rage due to his powerlessness, or he would go to the kitchen and eat something, an example of unconscious behavior as though his inner mind wanted to escape the frustrating situation by keeping his hands occupied. At other times he would take the bed frames apart and move them somewhere other than their original place and rearrange them; he would change the place of the wardrobe for no reason other than to create work for himself. By the time his "waiting" ended he would be on the verge of exploding in the face of whomever drew him out of the state of feeling powerless!

However, as the years went by and the succession of his "waits" continued, he found that he had begun to get used to the tension.

In the end, as he learned from experience, the waits do end! Gradually he got used to controlling his reactions at moments when he felt powerless, and he eventually got to the stage of what is known in the vernacular as *Al-Marara Al-Matfyieh*,* meaning the state of steadfastness, patience, and forbearance. However, waiting to be arrested was not a situation that could be handled by the prescription implied in *Al-Marara Al-Matfyieh*. This was not the first time he had experienced such waiting. Years before his current predicament, he had discovered that waiting to be arrested was the most difficult kind of wait, but that time he did not fall into the hunter's net. This time, however, the net was tightening around his neck—between him and it: a meter, maybe less. Remembering his earlier wait, he took a deep pull from his cigarette, enjoying the smoke.

❖❖❖❖❖

Since April 1985, the intelligence services had launched their assault on national organizations in Gaza following the daring military operation by Fathi Al-Ghirbawi,[10] in which Al-Ghirbawi sacrificed his life. The attack on the party in Gaza began then and extended throughout 1985–86 and came to involve all nationalist organizations. The year 1985 was a turning point for the party in the homeland because the party's organizations faced the task of protecting what they had achieved over five years of struggle, persevering daily in their confrontation in the face of a focused attack against most of those organizations.

Between 1980 and 1984 the party's organizations and its extensions were engrossed in organizational activities under the banner of "solving the organizational question." The focus was on two main spheres: one, expanding the integration of new members and building a circle of friends and supporters of the party; and

---

* A vernacular expression that translates to "deactivated gallbladder." It is traditionally known that when someone gets very stressed and angry, their gallbladder stops working. After the gallbladder's deactivation, the person no longer feels anger or irritation.

two, building up the party cadres and developing their potential in accordance with their talents and skills, consistent with the situation of the party and its activities.

By the time 1985 rolled around, this mission had been successfully accomplished. Those organizations that, having given priority to the local over the general in their activities, had immersed and isolated themselves in their local circles and experiences, began between 1980 and 1984 to acquire a party character in their structure and activities in place of their narrow provincialism. By 1985, party organizations increasingly affirmed their Leninist character which came to serve as the guiding theoretical foundation for the task of party building. Their structures of leadership and cadres crystallized into various fields of specialization, specifically the organizational, grassroots, and feminist areas, and to a lesser extent, in the fields of politics, media, and even resistance activities. The structure of the cadres became stronger, whether in their ideological and political orientation, or in their security strength and experience in secret activities at various levels. At the same time, the party had surrounded itself with a broad fortification, one level of which was the cells of candidate members, so that the party increasingly implemented the two decision-slogans: "every member leads a circle of friends" and "the periphery is twice as big as the number of party members."

The connection with party supporters was organized in multiple ways: either through the educational circles led by party members, through political ties with individuals and groups, or through the most common and widespread form—organizing friends of the party in professional democratic organizations and unions, led by party members who were also interspersed at various levels. It is now uncommon to find a local party organization that is not paired with a branch of a democratic organization. If one does not exist, the decision is clear: the members must establish a branch of the democratic organization. This has been a major influence on the establishment of democratic workers, students, and women organizations, as instruments of national and syndical resistance, as a form of establishing a connection with those popular sectors, and as a way of scooping up those who are qualified to be candidates for membership in the party. The major category that was missing was that of the educated and professional groups, such as engineers, doctors, teachers, and lawyers.

As for education within the party, the unified educational program runs through the veins of party organizations and their extensions, whatever their level and reach, beginning on the outskirts with the circle of friends, then the cells of candidates, then the members, and finally the cadre. Emphasis was placed on the resolutions of the party's Fourth National Congress and the security education handbooks, Leninist literature, local memoranda and pamphlets, and the history of the national cause. The program included directions for self-teaching such as a clear emphasis on directives to read novels by a list of authors: Ghassan Kanafani, Hanna Mina, Al-Taher Wattar, Maxim Gorky, Gabriel Garcia Marques, Jorge Amado, Nicolai Ostrovsky, Mikhail Sholokhov....

The party magazine, *Al-Rifaq,* played an important role in this phase. Through its consistent publication, resistance know-how and experiences were disseminated, contributing to the unification of mechanisms and tasks, the creation of a common party mindset, and the formation of a unified self-party orientation. Its essential focus was on organizational articles and security education. The magazine was comparable to a maestro conducting and unifying an orchestra, playing a symphony called *Encouraging All Leaders and Cadres to Build Party Organization with Unified Structure, Decision-Making Abilities, and Activities.* By contrast, the lack of consistency of the secret mass newspaper, *Al-Thawra Mustamera,** was its main shortcoming in the field of political agitation. At the end of 1984, the party made the decision to design the central structure of the organization at the level of the nation, and the general development of party work over the previous five years allowed that to happen.

---

* *Al-Thawra Mustamera* which translates to *The Revolution is Ongoing* was a clandestine newspaper for the Popular Front for the Liberation of Palestine.

In the beginning of 1985, as soon as the new organizational structure was implemented, the organization found itself in a real war launched by the Occupation's apparatuses. The Occupation launched an attack on organizations in Jerusalem, Ramallah, Gaza, Beit Lahm, Beit Sahur, Nablus, Qalqilia, and Tulkarm, under a brazen slogan announced by the Israeli intelligence services: "The government has issued a decision: you must be liquidated!"

The attack came while the party was fighting its biggest political battle in defense of the phased nationalist goal of establishing an "independent state," and for independent Palestinian decision-making and representation (that is, that the PLO should be the sole legitimate representative of the Palestinian people).[11] According to the party, there was a violation of this goal in the agreement signed on February 11, 1985 between the leadership of the PLO and the Jordanian government.[12]

At the time, the party provided a detailed analysis of the agreement during the full session of the Central Committee in April of that year. The Central Committee attributed the causes for signing the agreement and the conditions that led up to it to the structural class and institutional changes within the PLO over the previous years. These changes were a result of the inflow of petrodollars and the consequential growth of a corrupt bureaucratic bourgeoisie within and at the top of inflated institutional agencies. This corrupt class came to see alignment and a common cause with the ruling Arab bourgeoisie as the course that would lead to the consolidation of their interests and privileges, amounting to a merger with the American master and placing themselves under his *'abaya*,** as they say!

The more that stratum within the PLO thirsted for new privileges and more money, the greater the number of new institutions it gave rise to and the more it inflated that roster. In turn, they demanded their own bureaucracy as they grew, giving rise to an increase in institutions on the one hand, and a swelling of the bureaucracy on the other. And in an effort to increase their

---

** A loose, full-length outer garment.

influence nationally, that stratum not only built its organizational resistance instruments, it also sought to reassert itself domestically via institutions that were being built on a daily basis in a confidential and rapid operation that began at the dawn of the 1980s. Due to their proliferation and the amount of capital plundered by that stratum, these institutions became an object of derision by the people and energized Palestinian political factions.

The bureaucratic contagion was like a virus that had begun to infect from the outside. The same funds from the Gulf were used to buy muscle and symbolic figures. Once a division appeared between the bureaucratic leadership, the PLO, and its larger organizational base—the Fatah movement on the one hand, and the collective forces on the other—concerning their position on the Amman agreement, the bureaucracy and its institutions took steps to line up the nation behind the agreement.

The instructions of the party were frank in the form of a letter Kan'an received: "**Abu 'Ammar must come to realize that the occupied land is not in his pocket, and that he was squandering the Arab recognition of the PLO as the sole legitimate representative of the Palestinian people and the goal of independence.**" Consequently, popular and political activities demonstrating the nation's rejection of the agreement became the pivot of the work of the democratic party organizations, so as to prove its dangerous consequences. These consequences were most significantly the call to convene the PLO's 17th National Council, which was restricted to the delegates of Fatah and independent elements of the leadership of the PLO in Amman, so as to endow the agreement with legitimacy after it had been signed.

The party, sometimes acting alone and other times in cooperation with others, activated its resources and organized marches and rallies in order to mobilize the people against convening the 17th National Council session and to protest the February 11 Amman Agreement so as to allow the voice of the nation to be heard. In many institutions, as usual, the political aspect dominated the alliances, and leftist democratic blocs were formed to contest the internal elections within those institutions on a platform rejecting the agreement. It became abundantly clear that the nation and the people were not united in support of the Amman Agreement or the policy of the leadership of the PLO despite the information blackout and the laughable, pitiful distortions by the national press. This was demonstrated when the Jerusalemite newspaper *Al-Fajr* published a picture of a women's protest in Ramallah organized by members and friends of the party against the February 11 agreement and the convening of the 17th Council with a caption that read: "March in Ramallah in support of convening the 17th Council session."

That year Kan'an moved to another small safe house with a low ceiling which obliged him to bow his head every time he rose to his feet. He bid farewell to his comrade Bigfoot and "convinced" him that he would leave the homeland if he grew tired of hiding! Meanwhile, his comrade traveled outside the country to study at the expense of the party!

On a winter's night at ten in the evening, Kan'an ended a quick meeting, tense given what they were discussing. The room they had been in emitted light from its windows and could be seen by the street. His visitor left and Kan'an turned off the light, moving to another room that was not visible to passersby.

Kan'an walked down the corridor leading to the door of the house, secluded from the street. The time was five past ten, and he paced with quick steps, smoking as was his custom when his mind was going full throttle. Suddenly, when he reached the end of the corridor, he saw a soldier standing next to the fence adjacent to the house, his back to the corridor and Kan'an. The soldier was urinating! It had been just under five minutes since his visitor left, and he had turned off the light in the room visible from the street. Kan'an's breath caught, his pulse quickened, and he was confused for a few seconds. Less than two meters separated him from the soldier—just two meters! His head and gaze swiftly swung right, towards the street and the house's main entrance, and he saw two military vehicles and soldiers dismounting and heading towards the house and descending the front steps. His nervous system leapt into action, pulling him out of his momentary confusion, and issued its orders: draw back without making any noise and revealing yourself. The distance between him and the soldier answering the call of nature was short enough for the soldier to hear his breathing. He could hear the stream of urine that was hitting the bottom of the fence. Kan'an moved quickly and noiselessly to his room. He locked the door using the key and the bolt; he picked up his secret papers, entered the bathroom, and closed the bathroom door.

> *If they unhinge the door to the house, they will still have to deal with the bathroom door. During the two attempts, I can burn the papers I have.*

There was nowhere in the house where he could hide during a raid. The house wasn't a safe house in the full sense—it was meant to be a temporary arrangement, to be used just for a few days, weeks at most. Seconds after he entered the bathroom, the soldiers began knocking on the door forcefully.

"Open! Open! It's the Military Governor. Open! Army!"

They continued to pound for a few minutes. Their pounding was the alternative to yelling. Then they began to force the door open in the traditional way, a characteristic of soldiers of the Occupation and American policemen: two or three soldiers step back and then charge the door together, kicking it with their heavy boots. He was crouching in the bathroom, waiting. The waiting and the inability to do anything were killing him.

> *Will my experience end after only three years? What sort of experience begins only to end? It is an "experience" that barely constitutes a legacy. What will the party say? Why did I come to this damned house?! What brought them here?*

For over ten minutes, they practiced their ritual, attacking the door with their heels in an attempt to break it down. Kan'an was waiting and preparing himself for the confrontation, which he anticipated would be very soon. Suddenly the attacks on the door stopped. His "wait" ended but another started in its place:

Did I escape their clutches? Did they leave or are they lying in wait outside the house in the hope that my calming down will induce me to move or make a sound so that they will become aware of my presence? Isn't it likely that some of them went to get some instrument for breaking the door down or blowing it up?

In the new "wait," his suspicion of their behavior became a source of confusion. What short endurance must they have if their attempt to break the door down lasts only a few minutes? He decided to take the initiative. He snuck out, walking on the tips of his toes from the bathroom, with his papers and cigarette lighter in hand, alert and listening for any faint sound from outside the house. He looked out the window but saw no sign of them. Suddenly he heard the sound of their military vehicles moving away.

It seems they have left. Shall I risk coming out? I fear they may be back! Is a trap likely? Or shall I stay where I am and risk being arrested if they come back?

Staying is a risk and leaving is a risk. A clandestine life in its entirety is a question of exiting one risky situation and entering another. Given the choice between the two, he quickly decided to take the second risk. He opened the door, trying not to make a sound. He headed towards the fence, walking slowly, his ears monitoring any sound that may be significant. He quickly climbed the fence and ran with long strides across the wide plain behind the house. He headed towards another house for shelter. The house he chose was that of Sakinah.

What happy coincidence caused his guest to leave at five past ten so that he turned off the light in the first room? What coincidence caused him to walk along the corridor so that he noticed the "vanguard" of the soldiers taking a piss? What happy coincidence caused that soldier's bladder to fill so that he stopped for a few seconds and Kan'an saw him? He remembered his mother's prayer in 1982: "Go, my son. May God be pleased with you!" Fate had arranged a series of happy coincidences all at one go, a wonderful arrangement that saved him from their claws. There are many happy coincidences like this in the life of a revolutionary, but it takes only one bad coincidence after which what one prays that God may forbid will come about. Then he could pay with his life for the turn that fate chose. Clandestine activities and the intelligence of the veteran resistance fighter prevent many bad coincidences, but life has too many of those coincidences in store. The possibilities of changes in the course of events are boundless, so that arrest and martyrdom are possibilities that are almost inevitable.

He reached Sakinah's house exhausted, out of breath, panting from agitation and the thousands of packs of cigarettes he smoked and the nicotine that had lined his arteries over the years. He made himself a cup of tea and stretched out on the bed, thinking about that night and its events. It seemed to him that it had been years, not minutes, between the time they began their ritual and the time he slipped away.

❋❋❋❋❋

His waiting now was different from that of 1985. Then his secret-life experience was only a few years old and had not changed him much. It was different now. Now he had lived through long cruel years, full of challenges and productivity which had shaped him, kneaded him, and given shape to his features. Between these two waits, that of 1985 and 1991, he had lived a three-dimensional life! He had carried his cross, the weight of his resistance, his responsibility to his people, standing upright, not bent over. He never said, and will not say, as Christ did before he gave up his spirit, "My God, my God, why hast Thou forsaken me?" And should he fall, he will not deny his teacher—the party—as St. Peter denied his teacher Christ three times.

His waiting now was more serious, more difficult and cruel. This time they were insistent. They tore down the second door, drawing closer to his crouched body in the dark stone den as he had visions of his secret life creeping away, slowly like a snake retreating from a stick brandished in its face. Half an hour after they started looking for him, he heard their footsteps near the wardrobe concealing his small stone den. Their footsteps were loud, the sound of heavy military boots. There were many soldiers and officers searching the house. Along with their footsteps he could hear their conversations which he did not understand. The only thing separating them from him was a wall containing an opening through which one could jump from the wardrobe to the den. Only a handful of centimeters separated two opposites, centimeters separating one life from another. A short distance in which nine long years are abbreviated, the time between opening and closing a door, which will most likely be reopened soon. Can such a short distance bear all that heavy significance? The end of one life and the beginning of another? How can those few centimeters carry such a heavy weight? He had carried the weight with great difficulty. Does the distance feel the burden it is carrying?

Chapter 5

The wardrobe door was opening. Their fingers were tapping on the sheet of wood, examining it, feeling it, smelling it, like dogs and their prey. Kan'an held his breath. His heart was racing.

Oh! How cruel waiting can be! It's all over! Now is the moment. They are feeling the back panel of the wardrobe. There are only millimeters between you and them, just the thickness of the sheet of wood. Not even a few lousy centimeters, just an even more hopeless couple of millimeters. Burn your papers lest you desecrate your secret life. Burn your secret life which has been reduced to letters and words on paper. Deliver the coup de grâce to your old horse and don't let them make a mockery of it. Don't allow them to lay the party out on the table.

They spoke in Hebrew as they tapped and examined the sheet of wood. Their ringing voices indicated their questioning, their surprise and suspicions. He flicked the lighter, igniting the flame.

They started attacking the wardrobe with their crowbars, prying it off its strong screws deeply rooted into the wall. They did not realize that the wooden panel slid up and down, so they decided to tear down the entire wardrobe to examine what lies behind it.

> *Hurry up. Beware that their crowbars aren't faster than you. Set fire to your "life-experience" laid out on the smooth paper.*

He brought the flame of the lighter in contact with the kerosene and the fire started. He quickly began to feed the pages into the flames. At the same time, he stuffed his letter to Hind in his mouth and began to shred it with his teeth, though not without difficulty. It had been folded repeatedly and wrapped in plastic-like paper such that the letter had taken the shape of a plum, making it difficult to burn. The flames hissed and singed his face and fingers, and the smoke, suffused with the smell of kerosene, invaded his nostrils and lungs. With the haste of a madman, he continued to feed the flames with papers while their crowbars continued to attack the wardrobe. Thick smoke arose. He started gasping. His breathing, heavy and labored, came in successive, tense gasps as the anxiety of battle took control of him. He had too many papers, his den was too small and narrow, and no air was entering it. Sweat was pouring down his face as he continued to throw papers into the burning box. The heat of the blaze seared him, the rising smoke stinging his eyes and hurting his lungs. He felt like he was on the verge of suffocating.

Their crowbars were still tackling the problem of the screws and wrenching the wardrobe away from the wall. Their voices and the movements of their hands were frantic. Suddenly, the unexpected happened. Fate presented its unhappy, vexing, stubborn, hostile, filthy, son-of-a-bitch coincidence: the thick, rising smoke created a layer of carbon dioxide that did not allow oxygen to reach the flames, so they went out. He felt as though his soul had left his body. What a cruel and filthy coincidence! What naïve security arrangements! He quickly tried to ignite the flames again but the lighter rebelled against his wishes and the papers did not reignite. He cursed, using the foulest profanity in the vernacular dictionary, a rich and copious dictionary. Such an outrageous coincidence at such a fateful moment suggested that all the bad luck in the world had conspired against him, as though it could find no one else to amuse itself with!

Hurry Kan'an! Hurry! You are in a race with their crowbars which are advancing more and more. Their crowbars will pry your soul loose if they reach you while your papers are alive and well. Quickly, find a solution.

He could only find one solution. He started picking up the remaining papers and stuffing them into his mouth, chewing them quickly and swallowing what he could—his stomach would just have to manage. His teeth worked like those of a gnawing rodent. He chomped and chewed and swallowed in record time, like a man denied food for days who had suddenly found cuts of meat. Some paper had been drenched with kerosene but had not burnt fully. He did not hesitate. He picked them up, shoved them in his mouth, bit off pieces, chewed them, and swallowed. He too had a ritual of his own which he was practicing now, a savage, primitive ritual suitable for a man-beast, a forest dweller. The pain of the heat and the thickness of the smoke were taking a toll on his lungs and he couldn't open his eyes. He closed them tightly and continued his savage ritual. He brought his nose close to the paper-thin crack between the wood of the wardrobe and the entrance to his den, trying with difficulty to suck in air to help him breathe. He caught a very thin wisp of air. Breathing with difficulty, his burning eyes shut tight, he stuffed his mouth with the papers he held in his hands. The battle he was fighting was at its height. Who would win? He who has nothing except canines and molars to grind and a stomach to digest, or those with iron crowbars?

His stomach began to hurt. The smoke and the disgusting taste of kerosene burnt his throat and esophagus. But he did not stop. He felt his surroundings like a blind man discovering where he was stepping, checking to ensure there was vacant space around him. He was hardly breathing. His stomach was digesting what it received in the form of paper and ink with difficulty. His eyes were on fire and he could not muster up the strength to open them. But he had won. He had won the race, the invisible confrontation. He finished the feast of chomping and chewing, swallowing and digesting before they had finished displacing the wardrobe.

Kan'an now sat at the edge of the entrance to his den which was elevated a few centimeters off the ground, resting his back on the side of the entrance. He was trying to inhale as much of the air that barely managed to seep through the paper-thin crack. He tried to breathe regularly so as to relieve his aching chest. His eyes were in immense pain, and he still could not open them.

Their attempts to wrench the wardrobe free were intense. He had gone to a lot of trouble to make, assemble, and fasten the wardrobe during what had been a bitterly cold winter. The four screws were sunk deep into the wood, making the wardrobe and the wall one body. The wardrobe had been faithful to him and intrepid in its resistance against the soldiers by clinging to the wall, allowing Kan'an enough time to defeat them. She too proved to be his friend, like the door and the walls and the table and chairs and pens ... everything in his large den. He won the race in the end. The only thing that had been on his mind was to get rid of his papers and he had succeeded. It did not occur to him that he could die of suffocation. He did not care if he died, he had never come as close to death in his life as he had in this moment. He fought like a sailor confronting a turbulent sea, and he managed to save both himself from drowning and his ship from sinking. He had won.

Despite the pain in his chest and stomach and his burning eyes, he was happy. Nothing was more wonderful than victory. Winning makes one forget the price paid for its honor. He was happy to have kept his secrets safe and for his victory in what he considered to be the first round. Everyone has their "traditions" for expressing their feelings. Smoking was his for all the emotions that swept through him: discomfort, tension, planning, contemplation, and inspiration. There was nothing better than a cigarette inhaled with enjoyment. As he sat at the edge of his den, he experienced the euphoria of winning the race.

"Let me smoke a cigarette. God knows when there will be time for another. I may never smoke another."

It was clear that prying the wardrobe loose was taking them some time. He probed with his hand for the pack of cigarettes that he had grabbed along with the papers as he thrust himself into his dark den. He thought he might stay there for some time and perhaps they would not find him, they could search for hours and not find him. In that case, the cigarettes would be his only friend to keep him company during his solitude in the den. The desire for a cigarette was overwhelming and could not be mollified. He picked one up and placed it between his lips with the lighter nearby. Would it fail him as it had done a short while ago? He tried to produce a spark without making noise. It failed him and frustrated his desire. He cursed it silently. He tried a second time and it let him down again. He appealed to it emotionally and brought it near the paper-thin crack between the wardrobe, which had widened slightly, to take advantage of the air that leaked through.

"Come on, you son of a bitch. Don't fail me. I beg you!" He struck a spark and it obeyed, producing a flame. He took a deep breath sensing the smoke invade all the air sacs and pulmonary arteries in his lungs. "A man has three personal pleasures: cigarettes, women, and a glass of *'arak*.'"* He had tried all three and became convinced that Hanna Mina, his favorite writer, was a brilliant novelist and a wise man as well. What pleasure could a person who spent years imprisoned within walls and subject to

---

* A distilled anise-flavored liquor.

an endless sequence of measures, precautions, requirements, and rules demand? The party had told him many times: "Your desires are simple. Do not hesitate to ask. They are easy to satisfy." A tape of new songs by Sheikh Imam. A plate of *baqdunesieh** with garlic and a glass of *'arak*. A ten-minute drive during which he could explore the landmarks of his city and sort out what was new. Five shawarma sandwiches and three bottles of beer, or "5x3," as he and Hisham called their favorite meal. A baby he could play with for a few hours. These were some of his pleasures and desires. The secret life cuts down the demands for pleasure and desires to a minimum, rendering simple things a delight despite their simplicity.

At that moment, as he sat waiting for them to reach his body, the cigarette was his source of enjoyment. It had always been the fuel that supplied the machine sitting above his shoulders. His pleasure at inhaling deeply from the cigarette and the awakening of his sensibilities mixed with the noise of their conversation as they gathered around the wardrobe and the sound of their crowbars splintering the wood, rubbing against the wall in the attempt to complete their mission. The unknown that was keeping him awake, as it does to anyone who is acutely aware of it, was swept aside. The unknown withered away—they would reach him within minutes. That was what calmed him down and diminished his reaction. He forgot about his eyes which were still burning from the heat, and he could no longer taste the disgusting kerosene in his throat. His chest, which was already filled with the foul smoke of the fire, nevertheless accepted the smoke of the cigarette as usual—that had not changed. He was smoking quietly and courageously, seemingly emotionally unaffected, only feeling severe fatigue as a result of his exertions in his first battle.

It took them a quarter of an hour to pry the wardrobe from the wall. As it gave way, they let it fall flat on the floor. It made an extremely loud crashing noise and some of its doors broke. The smoke that had been contained in the den billowed out rapidly

---

* Parsley in sesame seed oil.

and with force. He opened his eyes with difficulty, and he could barely make them out. He saw ghosts, mostly green, carrying their weapons and flashlights and wearing their headgear. He was unable to count those gathered around the wardrobe that now lay on the floor. For a moment the soldiers looked like they had been struck dumb by the scene before them: the wardrobe served as the stage curtain which had been lifted to reveal a scene which froze them for a few seconds. Their positions and their flashlights allowed them to see onstage a pale and tired person sitting on the edge of a door leading to a dark enclave, an exhausted person, whose eyes opened into slits in which one could clearly see red. Thick smoke streamed from the door of the den, and the cigarette, not finished, dangled from the lips of the pale, fatigued face. Black soot could be seen covering the wall opposite the entrance to the den. Directing their flashlights at Kan'an, they spent a few seconds taken aback by what they saw and lunged at him. They extended their arms as they rushed at him like competing beasts of prey pouncing to make a kill.

They tore him away from his seat. They felt that his conduct provoked aggression when they saw him with a cigarette dangling from his lips, staying seated when they reached him. They expected him to conduct himself with the fear and submission that they were used to seeing in some of the people they arrested. They grabbed him by his clothes and dragged him by his armpits and threw him on the ground with the savagery that sets apart every Occupation soldier. They landed blows all over his body with their boots and their rifle butts and their fists, concentrating on his back and his waist. He gathered all his strength and shook his body and got up quickly and hit one of them in the chest with his right elbow. The latter staggered and fell back trying to brace himself against the sink attached to the wall. One of them quickly hit him with the muzzle of his gun, the blow landed on his left eyebrow and caused serious injury fracturing his skull. Infuriated by his self-defense, they threw him on the ground again and beat him with greater savagery. One of them grabbed his head from the back and pounded it into the floor, others kicked him with their boots in his back, waist and legs. They continued to do their job for about five minutes during which time he heaped curses on them, both political and crude. With each curse they grew more savage, and he in turn increased his curses.

He heard a voice which he guessed was asking them to stop. They forced him on his feet. He could not move from the pain all over his body. Blood was streaming down his face from the wound on his left eyebrow. Surrounding him, they bound his hands behind his back with a zip tie which constricted the blood in his arms. They made him stand in the bathroom with his back to the wall while two of them aimed their M16 automatic rifles at his chest as though they were about to carry out an execution. One of them drew closer to him, and he guessed from his civilian clothes that this man was an intelligence officer. Kan'an addressed him.

"Listen, I am a revolutionary and Marxist fighter who is confident that one day we will win and gain our rights. This gives me strength and makes me refuse to submit to terrorism and the conduct of you and your soldiers. Do not think that this will be of any use to you, for you do not scare me."

He was speaking emotionally and with a loud voice. Yet he spoke clearly and insistently. He wanted them to know from the beginning what he was really like, unfiltered and without hesitation. He wanted them to know that he was strong. It was his first direct confrontation with them and he wanted to decide the outcome in his favor because a lot depends on that first confrontation. The intelligence officer responded in broken Arabic while he shook his finger threateningly in Kan'an's face.

"Be careful what you say. We are not terrorists or scoundrels. We are men of the law. A terrorist is one who hides like this," he gestured towards the opening to the den with his hand. "You are the one who was hostile and troublesome from the start. I didn't want things to turn out like this. Why didn't you open the doors to the house? Why were you here?"

"They are the doors to my house. I open them to whoever I choose and whenever I wish to do so. This is my house. This is my business and not yours, so don't ask me about it."

"What's your name? Who are you?"

"I won't tell you!"

The intelligence officer's eyes bulged out and he shook his head like something had just dawned on him.

"What did you burn here? Why all this smoke?" He said this pointing for the third time towards the den and the remaining smoke that was seeping out in small quantities. Despite his deep fatigue and the effect of the blows and the tension of the confrontation and the situation altogether, Kan'an could not help but smile at this stupid question. He answered as a small smile crept over his exhausted and bloodied face.

"You ask a strange question, amusing even. If I wanted you to know what I burned, then why would I have burned it in the first place?"

The officer did not say anything in reply but he scrutinized Kan'an closely and shook his head again. He turned towards his soldiers and said something to them in Hebrew which Kan'an did not understand. They laid him face down on the ground after blindfolding him and tying his feet together with a zip tie similar to the one they had used to bind his hands.

> *The last periods of waiting in your secret life are over. The door at which you once screamed, "Will you not open one day?!" has opened. You asked, "Will I not exit through you to live in nature?" Well behold, it has opened. What lies before you is not a transition to nature, but a transition to putrid prison cells. What comes after that— you do not know. The last night you spent in your safe house now bids you*

farewell with no possibility of return. Your dissipating hope that they would not find you has evaporated and here you are spread out on the bathroom floor while they search the house. The curtain has lifted on the unknown. They have dragged you out of your den. Before you lies one unknown after the other. Go back to playing the unknown "waiting" game. Sort your affairs now as you have over the years: through confrontation and challenge. Rain begins with a drizzle. The signs of their boots and their fists and their guns can be seen on your bleeding brow, on your back, your head, your waist. You predicted that your battle with them would be bloody, like the blood that is flowing and covering your face and the adjacent floor tiles. You expected a long and bloody battle. For rain begins with a drizzle. Rain begins with a drizzle ...

He heard their many footsteps moving about the house. Their voices filled the house which, less than two hours earlier, had been completely silent. Some of the voices were issuing orders, a couple of them were engaged in discussion, a third was asking questions and a fourth was calling after someone ... They were in constant, animated motion. Someone they had not expected had fallen into their hands tonight. The circumstances of his arrest in the den, the fire, the smoke, and the room with typewriters made them act quickly, energetically, happily. The ropes binding his hands restricted the flow of blood, hurting him. The soldier who had tied him up could not find a way of securing revenge other than to tighten the zip ties so much that they were painful—a silly little soldier seeking revenge in a silly way.

Kan'an tried to move his hands in order to ease the restraints a little. He was contemplating an image of himself lying flat on the bathroom floor. He had an unshakable conviction that it was the duty of his party to hold him accountable and to question his behavior. If one of his comrades was arrested he would always ask: Did he compromise on precautionary measures and cause his own arrest? Or did he do all that he could to escape and resist arrest? It was essential that he should hold himself accountable to his party. His party always said: "**The security of your house is your own responsibility. Check once, twice, even ten times. Institute rules for how you are going to live so as to take care of yourself.**" He did not hesitate in this regard.

I used to check once, twice, ten times. So what happened? How did they find me? How did I end up in this situation? Some of his questions took him by surprise; they demanded to be answered but he insisted that it was not yet time. *Let me take responsibility for being arrested first, responsibility for breaking rank, only then can one discuss the causes leading to my arrest.*

Their voices continued violating the yearslong peace and quiet that characterized his house. The mere comparison of the state of his house now as opposed to two hours earlier filled him with indescribable anger. Instead of barbecuing the meat that Hisham had brought with him, they had stayed up in the room where Hisham was now thrown on the floor. Kan'an had suggested postponing the barbecue to another day when it was light out. They had substituted the meat for a salad with oil, white cheese, and pickles. The large platter with the remains of their dinner was still in the same place, on the small table in front of the TV. They talked about everything, watched a British film, had dinner, and then moved to the bedroom at midnight. As was Kan'an's habit, he moved the TV with him to his bedroom and flipped through the channels looking for something to watch before falling asleep. He did not find anything tempting, so Hisham picked up a book to read while Kan'an slipped between the sheets to sleep. Only minutes later the raid happened. Kan'an remembered this all and felt bitter.

They wreaked havoc on his house-den, destroying everything in it. They had to pay the price. His first step, burning the papers, was just the start to them paying the price. His refusal to give his name was the second step, and more were to come. Still, whatever they paid, it would fall short of the full price. He could still recall the details of that first battle: the papers, the kerosene, the lighter, the chewing, the swallowing, his chest, his stomach, his eyes . . . an insane battle between him and their crowbars. How strange is man: at moments of peace all he can remember is his weakness, his hesitancy, his impotence. During the battle, however, he discovers that he has heroic—even indescribable—strength. When a human being is fighting for his life, as he sees it, with a deeply rooted determination and conviction in the justice and legitimacy of the cause for which he is fighting, he is transformed into a strange being in his strength and conduct. Under normal circumstances, Kan'an would not have done what he did in his den even if he had been promised all the treasures of the world. The smoke that choked him, the sudden flare of flames and kerosene that nearly burned his face—none of that dissuaded him. Inside a human being is a huge capacity to bear suffering. He had come to understand this on several occasions throughout the course of his secret life.

After half an hour of Kan'an being thrown on the floor, at about 2:30 in the morning, the intelligence officer returned. He picked Kan'an up off the floor, cut the zip ties binding his feet, and led him to the bedroom, accompanied by a soldier. When the soldier removed the blindfold covering his eyes, Kan'an was able to catch a glimpse of his bedroom: the wardrobe had been wrenched free, bits and pieces of it were strewn about, the mattresses had been torn open by a sharp object and the sponge interior strewn around the room. His clothes were on the floor, some of them torn. This reflected the stress they were under and their desire for revenge, for what could they find between the threads of his clothes to justify tearing them?

Only the TV and his table remained intact—confiscating them was more important than breaking them. His room was no longer his room. The soldier picked up a knife, went behind him and grabbed Kan'an's hands so as to cut his bonds. The intelligence officer was examining some of the books strewn on the floor of the room. Among them was Lenin's *Philosophical Notebooks* which Kan'an had read a few days earlier. The intelligence officer was closely examining the book, its pages and the notes along the margins.

While the soldier was cutting the ties binding Kan'an's hands, the knife cut deep into his flesh. He felt the blood flow from his hand and yelled at the soldier.

"Be careful with my hand, you son of a bitch!"

The intelligence officer noticed. "What happened? Why are you insulting him?" he asked.

Kan'an did not reply. He was looking at his hand which was bleeding profusely. The intelligence officer noticed the blood and drew closer, taking hold of his hand to examine it, then examining Kan'an's bloodied eyebrow and speaking to the soldier.

"I am sorry for what the soldier did," addressing Kan'an. "He did not mean to wound you. Once we get to the prison, I promise you will receive treatment for your eye and hand. The prison doctor will examine you, as per the law. Everything that has happened since we found you in your hideout are developments that we did not want."

"Your apology does not conceal what you really are, nor does it replenish the blood that is flowing. You raised your soldier to be a fascist and he is being true to your training." It did not seem as though the officer had heard what Kan'an said, either that or he was determined not to hear what was said.

"What's your name? Why don't you want to tell me?"

Kan'an was irritated by this naïve approach: an introduction full of promises and apologies followed by a question about what the officer wanted to know: his name. At the same time, Kan'an was upset that the intelligence officer thought that the deception would work on him. (*He doesn't know me well yet*, he thought to himself). During this time, the intelligence officer was carrying in his hands two personal ID cards: the real one bearing his name, Kan'an Subhi, the other one a fake under the name of 'Adel Amin. Kan'an knew that it would not be difficult for them to find out his real name—one call on the wireless would be sufficient to reveal the truth. Their intelligence services are adept in the use of computers and scientific methods. But he decided not to give them his name as a challenge to them.

"Once more: I will not tell you my name."

"Why?" asked the officer, trying to appear calm.

"First, because my house is not an interrogation room, and second because I do not want to."

The officer swallowed the insult of hubris that lay behind Kan'an's answer. "We can easily find out your identity by contacting headquarters," he said. "We can resolve the issue in seconds, but the matter does not warrant that. I have arrested you and I would like to record the name of the person I arrested. I am talking about an arrest warrant, do you understand? I mean you are either Kan'an Subhi as it says on this"—he waved the ID issued fifteen years earlier which he was holding in one hand—"or you are 'Adel Amin as it says on this"—he waved the counterfeit ID dated this year in his other hand. "All I want is your name . . . It is a simple matter."

But Kan'an decided not to make it a simple matter.

"I will not give it to you. When you begin your investigation I may tell you, or I may leave it up to you to solve this puzzle."

"Now, we are the ones who decide, not you. You need to understand that fully, otherwise you will have needless trouble. You are under arrest now. Understand that well."

"We shall see who makes the decisions."

"You will see that for yourself. Now, change your clothes, they're soaked in blood."

Kan'an's undershirt was stained with blood, and more spots appeared on his pajama bottoms. The intelligence officer exited, leaving a guard with a weapon trained on Kan'an's face. Kan'an moved about the room, looking for a shirt and trousers to wear.

It was necessary for him to search for these items as nothing in the room was left in its original state. Signs of their primitive rites were clearly imprinted on the contents of the room. He finished changing his clothes and wrapped a piece of cloth around his hand to stem the bleeding. He contemplated his room once again, taking advantage of the absence of a blindfold.

Here was the window, his window to the world. How much time had he spent here, standing or pacing between the window and the wall of his dark stone den? He used to observe the workers in the chocolate factory opposite the house as they strolled about during their lunch hour. He had heard that their average salary was not enough to pay for a worker's cigarettes and transportation costs if he was a rural resident, this at the time that the factory was famous for the excellence of its products and its penetration of the Israeli market. During the Intifada, the owner of the factory had scored two wins: his sales increased due to the halt of imports of the rival Israeli product, and he also lowered the salaries of his workers, taking advantage of widespread unemployment. In spite of this, he would later announce in a loud voice, like other capitalists: "We were hurt by the Intifada, we need support."

From this window, Kan'an came to resent the employees of the cinder block factory and their noisy machines that occasionally woke him at four in the morning after only two or three hours of sleep. From this window, he looked at the young women who walked along the streets leading to his house, at the people who frequented the nearby workshops, the rapid motion during the day in front of the neighboring restaurant, at a car that came by frequently, or another that parked some distance away and aroused questions in his mind. From this window, he cursed the day dogs first appeared on earth whenever they began their evening serenade for no reason, at times going on for hours.

From this window, during the Intifada's general strike, he saw a young man and woman enter the passageway leading to his door. They neither rang the electric doorbell or knocked on the door, nor did they retrace their steps. He was surprised by their conduct.

The streets were empty of passersby and trucks. He moved to the balcony from which one could see the door directly underneath. Looking surreptitiously and careful not to make any noise, he found that they were exchanging kisses, hiding behind the wall leading to the door. He withdrew silently, giving them a chance to seize a few moments of happiness which they were forced to steal in this repellent situation. They were just two unfortunates who thought the house was empty—because that is how it seemed. *Never you mind*, he thought then, *let them think it's vacant, even if this assumption could jeopardize the secrecy of the house.* The important thing was that they had won a moment of happiness. From this window, he used to watch Hind on her way to come visit him. He would see her turn right going from the main street to the side-street leading to his house and he would jump up out of joy, knowing it was only a matter of seconds before he would open the door for her and await her embrace.

From this window, just a few hours ago, he and Hisham had stood looking covertly at the street leading to the entrance of the house, when they heard the sounds of a frightening activity and discovered ghosts that they could not identify clearly.

After Kan'an had finished changing his clothes, the soldier tied his hands and feet once again, blindfolded him, and sat him down on the floor. As he looked for clothes to wear, Kan'an had observed the facial expressions and features of the soldier. He was a young soldier, barely eighteen years old, inexperienced in the full sense of the term, with a weak build and small stature. He had boyish facial features, a small nose that was barely noticeable on his face and a mouth that could pass for a small forgotten scar. In short, everything about him reminded one of small things. The expressions on his face suggested a person who had no idea what was going on around him. What's more, his facial features indicated he was terrified for some reason. Perhaps what had happened had struck fear in his heart: doors being unhinged, blood flowing, fire, smoke, fists swinging, and a hiding place behind a wardrobe.

In Kan'an's estimation, it was hard to believe such a soldier could have ever taken part in battle. It appeared that the raid on the house was the first battle in his military life. "What kind of soldier is this, he's just a child!" Kan'an thought to himself as he was getting dressed and directing harsh, deprecating, and threatening glances at the soldier. He was overcome by a sweeping desire to humiliate him. This soldier embodied a contradiction between the role assigned to him as a minion of the repressive Occupation and the childish features of his face which radiated fear and ignorance of what was happening. (*Is this the same soldier who just over two hours ago was practicing a collective, primitive, pagan ritual and performing a cannibalistic dance at the door of my house? Is this the person who put an end to my secret life on this night, who defiled my house?*) He felt frustrated and resentful as he sat bound and blindfolded, these questions welling up in his mind.

This soldier began to fool around. He wanted to convince himself that he possessed a power that he did not actually have in the face of the "terrorist vandal" that sat before him. He had noticed the power of the "terrorist vandal" from the time he began to practice his ritual up until their hand-to-hand clash. Everything that happened during the raid and the short confrontation with the intelligence officer demonstrated the power of the man sitting before him to the soldier. His inferiority complex was activated, and he began to give expression to it in a juvenile attempt to show off, to prove to himself that he had power. The soldier picked up a fifteen-kilogram iron disc used for weightlifting and put it on Kan'an's head. Kan'an sighed, grumbling audibly and moved his head so that the disc fell on the floor. The soldier repeated his action (*he wants to amuse himself, the son of a bitch*, thought Kan'an) and dropped the disc on the floor again. At that point the soldier removed the blindfold over Kan'an's eyes and aimed his rifle at him, bringing its muzzle close to his chest until it almost touched Kan'an. He said something in Hebrew which Kan'an did not understand except for the word *khablan* which means vandal and followed this up by yelling "Boom!" and imitating a shooting action with a theatrical gesture.

"Shut up and shove your rifle up your ass!" Kan'an said in a loud voice.

The soldier did not understand what was said to him. At that point the intelligence officer entered, seeming to have heard the commotion.

"What happened? Why are you yelling?"

"That childish fucker"—gesturing towards the soldier with his head—"wants to play. He put the weight on my head and pointed the rifle at my chest and threatened to shoot. I can't stand his child's play. Tell him to leave me alone and that his actions do not scare me."

"Don't be rude when you speak with the soldier. You appear to be educated and your house is full of books, but your tongue is filthy," he said, wagging his finger. "My patience is about to run out. Be careful. I will ask the soldier to stay away from you."

"You deserve insults because your actions are bloody and fascistic. Do you want me to thank him for his maliciousness?"

"I will ask him to keep away from you. We are done here."

He rebuked the soldier in a commanding tone and the latter shrank into himself like a child who had been punished. The officer left after he blindfolded Kan'an again. It was clear that the intelligence officer had put in play a strategy for the investigation, and he wanted to calm things down as much as possible. He had made a point of chastising the soldier in front of Kan'an in order to allow him to vent the frustration and resentment built up within him, and to lay the ground for building bridges for civil dialogue for his investigation. The difference between the intelligence officer and the soldier was stark: the former was thinking of the task ahead of him and had begun discharging his responsibilities from the first moment of the arrest, whereas the soldier's task had ended when the arrest had been made.

Kan'an remained sitting in the bedroom, bound and blindfolded, for another quarter of an hour and the soldier did not come near him during that time. Afterward, one of them pulled him up and dragged him to the larger room so forcefully that his bound hands trailed behind, and then they pushed him to the ground. As he lay on his stomach against the floor of his room in his desecrated den, the more important stage of waiting had now begun.

Chapter 6

Kan'an rubbed the blindfold against the floor, lowering it a bit. The floor tiles adjacent to his bloody forehead became stained from the copious bleeding. With a small movement of his head and right eye, he could see the soldiers' legs from behind the already slightly displaced blindfold. The eye of a detainee cannot stop trying to perform its function whether he is in the hands of soldiers in *sahat al-shabeh* or in the chambers of interrogation. It does not need training to do that; once the eye is covered by a blindfold or a bag, it will always struggle to break through any restraints and see.

They were wreaking havoc on his home-world. That which had eluded them for years and years had become fair game for their ugly, heavy combat boots. His life, which had been a secret even to those closest to him, was now revealed, and here they were desecrating it. Wherever they stepped, he could feel them stomping over years of his past, years in which he lived outside their grip and in the service of the party and the struggle. But now their restraints were wrapped around his wrists and feet, confining his movement and freedom. His wrists had once served as his tongue, allowing him to articulate his actions and efforts, and his feet had enabled his pacing from wall to wall as he pondered and lived the struggle. The blindfold prevented him from seeing his friends: his books and pens, the doors, the walls . . . His home had been a liberated territory in the midst of an occupied land. He had exercised authority over this territory, and it intoxicated him day by day until the sense of confrontation engulfed him.

In their trashing of his couches and mattresses, they desecrated his body and spirit. By ransacking the contents of his library, they were defiling his daily sustenance, denying him his nourishment. In this moment, his eyes had come to simplify the Occupation down to its footwear: an unsightly collection of sneakers, leather shoes, and combat boots. Wherever his eye traveled, it saw military footwear, combat boots in two colors, reddish brown and deep black. These were the ugliest, made of coarse leather, dusty and dirty in appearance. Its wearers were armed to the teeth from helmet to heavy heels, and their favorite weapon was American, specifically the M16 rifle. They would move left, then right, march away, pause, only to return and move again. The Occupation itself is merely a combat boot that decides and enacts laws, represses, arrests, displaces, kills, and governs. Just as one could encounter the dove and find a symbol of peace, where one encountered the combat boot they would find savagery.

His eyes could only see these boots, with a few leather shoes worn by policemen and sneakers worn by intelligence officers interspersed throughout. The authority belonged to the sneakers. They were the thinkers, planners, decision-makers, the issuers of orders, and the leaders of nocturnal campaigns. Meanwhile, the combat boots heeded, obeyed, and executed their orders. The leather shoes were there merely to give a superficial hue of legality for the conduct of the repressive military Occupation. This was the military's ranking system, with the sneakers at the top and the combat boots at the bottom and, in between, within the steps of the hierarchy, there were all sorts of shoes and soles, each corresponding to a rank and type and color.

Kan'an's eyes saw the Occupation in its entirety: a regime, a state, an authority, and laws, all of which could be condensed into a forest of shoes. Let those who do not know the Occupation look at that forest. This would serve as an introduction to its nature. As Kan'an lay bound on his stomach secretly stealing glances, he contemplated the scene like a director closely examining his actors through the camera lens. But he was a director that could issue no orders, instructions or directions—he could only observe. So, while in reality he was a viewer, not a director, he had decided that the scene before him was suited to a film about repression and resistance. The movie tumbled before him: the forest of combat boots and his body in a coffin—as it had appeared to him once in his contemplations—wrapped in flags, carried on the shoulders of members of the party and the masses.

But Kan'an understood that what his eyes saw was not a movie scene. What his eyes saw was a factual truth which lay heavily on his life and future.

> *Hey director, or rather, hey viewer, the combat boots in this scene have turned your life upside down, snatching you from your party, comrades, and duties at a critical and sensitive moment in your party's history. The combat boots will now decide your future far from the sun. They will take you to your putrid prison cell or your dark grave or your fatal exile,[13] they will carry you from the bosom of your house's walls and doors and lead you into the heart of darkness.*
>
> *They have put an end to your secret life, and with it, to what you thought was the third and final element of the trinity of fundamentals. A few days ago, it slipped through your fingers like water you tried to carry in your palms and hold to your chest. Only the depth of the future holds the answer to your third fundamental*

element, just as it holds the answer to your life as a resistance fighter. Observe, examine closely, and contemplate with the director or viewer's eye—it makes no difference! Continue to practice the contemplation that you had grown so accustomed to, deep contemplation only possible for one who leads a life like yours. Contemplate the forest of combat boots now as you have previously contemplated all things when you paced between wall and door, when you sat on the balcony with a glass of 'arak keeping you company and a cigarette dangling from your lips, when you lay on the bed, smoking in the darkness of night. Your thoughts carried you away while you were cooking, distracting you until you added sugar instead of salt to the rice, leaving you to throw it away, while cursing both your contemplations and your life.

Your imagination had gone as far as the graveyard: you saw yourself as a corpse mutilated by torture or torn by bullets, wrapped in the national flag and the workers' flag, carried on a bier while your comrades eulogized you and chanted your name. Your imagination had gone as far as the victory of socialism. Did your imaginations, your daydreams lead you to where you are now, stretched out on your stomach, hands and feet bound, eyes blindfolded, with a bloody forehead

> *amidst a forest of combat boots? Had the camera lens of your daydreams for the last nine years succeeded in capturing the current cinematic scene? Your daydreams fell short of real life. They failed you. They did not save you with their treasures of visualizations, dreams and imaginations ... Do not condemn them too quickly; they were full of imagination and limited by endless variables. Life is much fuller than the limits of the imagination and daydreams.*

I admit, I admit it! But my dreams are not to blame. They fell short but they were optimistic and beautiful.

> *What optimism are you referring to? You saw your body on a bier as you observed the combat boots.*

How can my dreams be optimistic when the combat boot is above my head? The combat boot and the forest of combat boots are a long way from optimism.

> *Then your dreams were not always optimistic. To imagine your body on a bier is neither optimism nor optimistic thinking.*

Martyrdom is a fitting end for the resistance fighter. He who dies at the right place and time is a hero. My bier was smiling, making fun of the killers.

> *Forget the philosopher in you. He drowned in a septic tank.*

But I strive for an honorable death. That is an optimistic dream, an optimistic endeavor.

> *Optimism is about striving for victory, not seeking death, even if it is martyrdom. Attachment to life wins in its struggle, didn't Mehdi Amel tell you that?*

Kan'an heard some activity in the room adjoining the iron door and he remembered Hisham.

What is Hisham doing now? Is he contemplating combat boots like I am? O Hisham, comrade in the era of strength and defiance, weren't we just enjoying a film last night that truly uplifted us? Comrade, enter the battle comrade while holding onto life, championing it so that life may be victorious in its struggle. I do not know when we will meet again, but we shall certainly meet victorious.

Like him, Hisham was lying on his stomach, bound hand and foot, and blindfolded. He too engaged in contemplation. One pair of combat boots kept going and coming back, stopped at Kan'an's head, cursed him and left. The size of the combat boots confirmed that it was worn by none other than a large pig. As they came and went, the pair of combat boots decided to introduce themselves clearly. They stopped at Kan'an's head and one combat boot lifted and came down on Kan'an's head, pressing it to the ground. The intention was not merely to hurt him but to enjoy rubbing his face in the blood from his eyebrow that had pooled into a large spot under his head. His heart was ignited with spite. He strained to lift his head while the combat boot pressed down with its full weight. A head struggling to lift itself and a combat boot pressing down on it. This went on for minutes until the combat boot worn by the pig finally retreated and went on to other tasks it had to carry out.

Spite is not inborn in human beings nor is it absorbed through a mother's milk. There are no hereditary genes for spite. A mother's milk is mixed with her tenderness and warmth and kisses, not with her rancor. Spite is created by aggressiveness and savagery, as a natural human reaction. Consequently, if one does not respond to aggression and savagery with spite, that person's humanity is deficient or nearly nonexistent. Spite rises with the increase of aggression and savagery. This ratio is a mathematical formula governing revolutionary action. The large combat boot had taught Kan'an a new lesson in spite and added an extra dose to his reservoir.

Whichever way they moved in his house, they wreaked havoc on his world and his memories. He recalled details of his past as though there were on a movie reel, screening events shaped by cruelty, deprivation, and resistance. His memory insisted on keeping the odds and ends of past events fresh, quenching the thirst of his present self, strengthening him, motivating him for the coming battle. In his hampered present, he drew strength against his bonds through the inspiration of his history of resistance and contestation, drawing on it like the Bedouin "intent on migration" (who fortifies himself by sipping a single drop of water before crossing the immense desert of Al-Rub' al Khali).* Ever since they tore down the wardrobe in front of his stone den, they initiated his journey towards Al-Rub' al Khali—the desert of the unknown, the desert of the new experience, the new challenge and the new confrontation. His past would serve as droplets of water.

---

* This is a reference to "*Al-Wataryiat al-Lailyiah*" (String Music of the Night) by the Iraqi poet Muzaffar Al-Nawwab.

❖ ❖ ❖ ❖ ❖

The confrontations between the occupiers and the party's organizations had expanded in 1985, and by December included most organizations of the homeland. The news of the arrests created an atmosphere that dominated the party and its organizations' outcomes. Decisions, directives, and measures affected everyone from Rafah to Naqura. For Kan'an, he was moved to a new safe house after spending only two nights in Sakinah's house. He froze his activities temporarily as a precaution.

One December morning, there was a knock on the door using the agreed-upon code. He had finished his breakfast and was sitting on the western balcony, catching some December sunlight which he deemed too shy to appear, for as soon as it did, it was quickly shrouded behind the accumulating clouds.

"I come bearing bad news!"

"I have been in a good mood for a week, despite what we face as a party. The house is wonderful—it has high ceilings, I can move around without having to bow my head, I can experience life outside. It has made me forget the misfortune of so-called 'Sakinah's house.' Are you conspiring against my mood to bring me bad news?"

"You'll have to vacate the house quickly." Kan'an held his breath in anticipation, waiting for his comrade to continue. "This house is not secure, as of now it is no longer safe as a result of the attack campaign. The danger has drawn much closer."

"Explain! Explain!" he pressed his comrade to speak. The latter explained in detail, but rapidly. Kan'an understood the danger of the situation. "Tonight, then?"

"It would be better now. The situation is unbearable. Prepare yourself to leave in fifteen minutes!"

He began packing his bags, collecting his papers and his necessities. The most important things he reached for in such moments—which were frequent—were the three items that stayed in his pockets wherever he went: his secret papers, cigarettes, and the red prayer beads, "the communist beads," as he used to call them jokingly. He packed those three things before doing anything else.

The house he had moved to a week earlier was a wonderful house with two balconies. From its windows he could see and hear everything he had missed for the past three years: the sounds of peddlers who chanted their calls advertising their products, streets crowded with passersby, peasant women carrying their baskets of vegetables balanced on their heads after they had finished their shopping, the roar of trucks and the yells of pushcart vendors, students who filled the streets in the mornings and the afternoons with their boisterous laughs and tumultuous discussions as they went to and came from their schools, classes of girls in their green school uniforms. He and his cohort in high school used to call those students "the green battalion" in jest and to flirt with them. He had not seen that battalion spreading beauty in the streets of the city for years.

This house allowed him the opportunity to experience life outside. On the western side, it overlooked crowded and noisy streets. On the east, the backyard overlooked rows of adjoining houses where there were children playing and women hanging newly washed laundry on clotheslines, or sweeping the rear courtyards with water, or yelling and chattering for some reason or no reason at all. He absorbed all that life that surrounded his safe house, alleviating the impact of the occupiers' assault on him, which had left him in great distress since the beginning of the summer months.

"The bad news is not over yet!" His comrade said this to prepare him for something worse. As he spoke, embarrassment and hesitation clearly marked his features as though he was personally responsible for the frustrations of secret life. "The order by the party is to suspend you from your duties and freeze your status for three months . . . Meaning that you will be isolated from your role, its communications and tasks, with the aim of protecting you from the thrust of this attack, seeing as developments may lead to the authorities tracing your scent!"

Things had come to a head. Kan'an was about to explode in his comrade's face, but he contained his reactions within himself.

"A raid, arrests, danger surrounds the party on all sides—and I'm frozen? Am I to spend my time during this period of confrontation cooking and watching television? Shouldn't I have been consulted before such a decision was taken?"

"It was a quick decision. There was no time for negotiations and consultations. It is a matter of party security. Do I need to explain that to you?"

He spoke the last sentence in a dismissive tone. Kan'an did not need things explained to him. When the matter concerned the safety of the party and his experience, there was no room for back and forth, for extensive consideration and discussion, particularly if the threat of arrest hangs over people's heads. Under circumstances of confrontation, the desire for discussion becomes a mere luxury for which there is no room. He knew that very well. Recent developments in the raid, which his comrade had explained to him, hit him like a thunderbolt. The house had lifted some of the depression stemming from last months' experiences; now he was forced to leave. The latest decision to suspend him was the greatest calamity. He lit a cigarette and paced back and forth, thumbing his prayer beads so that they clicked together, until he regained his composure.

"Where to this time?" he calmly asked.

"To the house of 'damned Sakinah,'" his comrade mumbled. "It is the most suitable at this time."

Kan'an sat down in the closest chair. He put out his cigarette before it had burnt down to the butt, contrary to his custom, and sighed. He picked up another cigarette and lit it. He did not know what to do, things were going from bad to worse. He dropped his head so that his face rested in his palms, propped up by his elbows resting on his thighs, like a despondent widow who had just lost her husband. The cigarette dangled from his lips and he closed his eyes to its stinging smoke.

"That is cruelty. How could one live next to that catastrophic woman for three months?" he said to himself in an audible voice while his comrade looked on in silence. He felt all the frustration in the world bundled up inside him. All the pressure and tension from which he had suffered in his earlier months had returned to grind his head down. "The grave is better than being near that so-called woman."

His comrade laughed and smiled ear to ear.

"Go ahead, laugh! Laugh! You are not the one who will be her tenant. I wish you were in my place so that I could see what you would do." His joking was an indication of his bitterness.

"I know exactly what you will be facing. But you must put up with it, comrade. You have to hurry up, we should leave."

So, Kan'an left quickly, heading to the house of that damned Sakinah, to live next to that odd species of a human being. He had met the landlady twice and his comrades had spoken to him about her often. He only went to her house for a few days under emergency circumstances or for a few short hours to conduct business and leave. But to live for three months in her house would get under his skin each and every day.

Everything now reminded Kan'an of his early days as though three years had not gone by and he was just embarking on his secret life. It was December again with its rain, its cold, and the sense of gloom it inspired. The atmosphere of the move to the house was the same: an intensified raid and arrests not of tens as in 1982, but of hundreds of members, supporters, and organizations eager for confrontation. Some members desecrated the flag, others honored it with their blood. Some experienced exile this time. The atmosphere of confrontation surrounded everyone, members and friends of the party and their families from the tip of the north of the country to the tip of the south.

He thought of the road he took that rainy December night in 1982. It was lined with trees, with the passersby wrapped up in their heavy winter overcoats, and with him, wearing his spotted *kuffiyeh* that covered his whole face except for his eyes. While he walked down the road he paid close attention to the passersby, to whoever was walking behind him, and whoever passed him. It was the same street, the same trees, the same watchful eyes. He asked himself, "Were they the same passersby? And the woman?" She was that damned Sakinah, instead of Umm 'Isa. There was some resemblance between them in essence. One could not really classify them as women! It was as though he was fated to deal with graying old women who added a touch of dreariness to his life every now and then.

Once he entered the dirt alley that led to the house, the similarity between the two Decembers, the two phases, became apparent. At the end was the one-story house, surrounded by trees dripping in the rain and cold, the wind swaying the branches in the dark, moonless night. The house appeared to be far from the noises of the city, enveloped in some kind of loneliness and surrounded by an aura of dread. It seemed to be more like a house in a legendary tale full of djinn, ghosts, and sorcerers.

What is it that history wants to say when it repeats itself? Did it seek to remind him of the troubled, tiresome, and exhausting days and months when the rebellious and out-of-control self managed to constrain the mind with sound and balanced calculations? Did history mean to send this message?

> *Your life will continue to be governed by instability and successive raids while you try to flee being caught in their trap. The cruelty of your daily life and your deprivations will not come to an end. The battle with the occupier escalates day by day and you are at the heart of it, an unknown soldier!*

Or could it be that the party was taking advantage of the rainy December—its winds, the dripping trees, the secret house, the savagery of the night and the cruelty of circumstances—to mold him further, to temper him with life's difficulties as if to take him back to the beginning of his secret life, to deny him any momentary bit of stability?

He arrived at the damned Sakinah's house at seven in the evening. He opened the huge iron door, once fashionable centuries ago. He entered and locked the door behind him. He felt he was sliding back in time to the moment he entered his first secret house, Umm 'Isa's house.

"Is it my fate to live in houses owned by old hags who by some accident belong to the gender that is supposed to be delicate? Is this a factor in the experiment of vanishing?" he muttered as he found himself in darkness inside the house. It was absolutely quiet while the sound of the rain and the rustling of tree leaves carried him far away towards a world of fairy tales.

Kan'an flicked open his lighter and began examining the rooms in the house. Now he had to live with the companionship of its walls, its furniture, its two iron doors, its tiles . . . everything in it for months.

The house originally consisted of three rooms along with a kitchen and a bathroom. Two of the rooms were not included in the rental and the damned Sakinah had sealed them off with two small padlocks. The good furniture, sofas, mattresses stuffed with cotton, light and heavy woolen blankets, cushions, all lay in the locked rooms . . . in other words, whatever the damned Sakinah carefully arranged to keep out of use in a room that would have been a much better bedroom for him! Instead, he had two worn-out bed frames on which lay two moldy mattresses. He tested the mattress with his hand and he encountered strange, large protrusions within it, solid and uneven and of various sizes. He decided to postpone his examination until morning and went to the kitchen, which turned out to be a misnomer. It contained some old utensils unsuitable for human use, consisting of cups, plates and pots and pans, a small refrigerator (barely functioning after a long life that had worn it out), a cooking stove with four burners (two of which were nonfunctional), and a clay oven . . . this is what the damned Sakinah offered her tenants in the guise of a furnished house.

He had heard a lot about her, about her greed and interference in all details of her tenant's lives, about her daily inspections of her furnished house that, in her eyes, was no less than a villa on the French Riviera. He had heard a lot: that she was the topic of conversation of entire quarters, and that whoever got into trouble with her on any issue, no matter how insignificant, could hardly get out of that predicament without gaining notoriety throughout the city from her sharp defamatory tongue. Such individuals emerge from their ordeal wishing that they could kill her!

He roamed the house using the faint light from his lighter. As part of his camouflage measures, not only did he have to avoid being seen from the window, but he also had to avoid turning on the lights in the house or going out to throw garbage in the neighborhood's dumpster. From the flames' glow he found a bag of provisions that his comrades had left him containing over thirty cans of tuna, over five kilograms each of apples and lemons, and dozens of bread loaves. The bag also contained a number of newspapers and magazines and forty packs of his preferred cigarette brand. In addition, the kitchen contained substantial quantities of olive oil and za'atar, dry onions, and pickled olives. *This is good*, he thought, *they know that the likelihood of me actually cooking is almost nil. As long as there is olive oil and za'atar and olives, all is well*. He tried jesting throughout his inspection of the house to regain some of the peace of mind he had lost with all the bad news.

Kan'an returned to the bedroom, or what was supposed to be his bedroom, and used his lighter again to examine the items on the table there. The table could hardly support itself. Its legs were dislocated and barely able to carry anything. It swayed if touched by a finger. A handful of books and articles were on the table: a book on the rebellion in Oman by the British scholar Fred Halliday, another a critique of bourgeois sociology, a third on the positions of Marx, Engels, Lenin, Mao, and others on women's liberation, among other books. Most of the articles were on the Muslim Brotherhood in Jordan in the 1950s and 1960s. *This is good*, he thought, *there is reading material available.*

He headed for the room with a window that overlooked the balcony and examined his surroundings as he was accustomed to. The building next door was a two-story house containing four residential units, and one of them on the northern side of the ground floor had no kitchen. While standing by the window, he noticed an old woman wearing a worn-out *thobe* going in and out of a side room, carrying a plate of food and a pot of tea. This annex served as a kitchen. *It appears that my neighbors are poor and their kitchen, and probably their bathroom as well, are outside the house. That much movement will not bode well for me.*

Kan'an had the opportunity to explore details that had not seemed noteworthy to him on his previous brief visits. He stood at the window observing the old woman who came out once every so often, heading for the kitchen and then returning to her house in a hurry to avoid the cold and the rain that was coming down in a light drizzle. He took his small radio out of his bag. It had been his constant companion since the beginning of his secret life. He switched it on and the voice of 'Abdel Halim Hafez blared out, singing Nizar Qabbani's poem: *"Your sweetheart, my son, has no land or homeland or address."* This brought on a sigh ending with a knowing smile, as he said to himself, "Take it easy, 'Abdel Halim!"

He turned the knob, searching for another station. Suddenly he heard the angelic voice of Fairuz singing: *"I have a yearning I do not know for whom. Night picks me out from among the sleepless ones."* He turned off the radio with a nervous gesture, cursing the singers. "Is this a conspiracy to unnerve me?" he wondered out loud. He fell asleep haphazardly, without changing his clothes, surrendering to oblivion under the cover of two woolen blankets.

Because he fell asleep early his first night, he woke up at 6 a.m. Every muscle in his body ached as though he had slept on a pile of stones and pebbles! Upon opening his eyes and feeling the pain his first thought had him asking himself where he slept. Shy rays of sunlight had entered the room. He sat up and felt the lumps in the mattress. They were sharp protuberances which stabbed him in his back, thighs, and waist ... He got off the bed and decided to investigate the matter. He pressed his hand on the bed once again, examining it. There were lumps wherever he pressed, like the ends of stakes. "I will open up this cursed thing to see what sort of catastrophe it is," he thought to himself. He quickly made up his mind, went to the kitchen, and came back with a knife. He tore open one end of the mattress and stuck his hand in. He was astonished. His hand encountered stones of various sizes. He widened the opening and started pulling out all the contents: stones and pieces of wood, interspersed with pieces of sponge. "O God! The games of the elderly have started. How can I sleep on this mattress for months?" he complained to himself.

He decided on revenge. He went to work on the lock to one of the closed-off rooms with a small knife. He broke it off, feeling triumphant and reveling in this act of revenge. "I shall nationalize her private property and place its contents at the disposal of the workers' party and in the service of its struggle," he declared to himself. He began to transfer whatever pleased him from that room to his bedroom. He furnished his room with a splendid Persian carpet, placing two thick and newly upholstered cotton mattresses on top of it. He also took several pillows and cushions to further satisfy his vengeful desire, despite knowing that he only used one pillow himself. He brought out several covers and linens of all sorts, two armchairs, one for him to sit on and the other on which to stretch his legs! Afterwards, he enjoyed his breakfast, consisting of za'atar, olive oil, olives, and four cups of tea. He started reading a book with the radio beside him broadcasting news to which he paid scarce attention.

Most days—from five in the morning, when he woke up, to nine in the evening, when he wrapped himself for warmth in the cold winter nights—he spent his time reading and listening to the radio or standing at the window or pacing between the wall and the door or between the wall and the window, thumbing his prayer beads, producing a clicking sound. Food preparation did not take up much of his time because they were simple dishes. His dinner was the same as his breakfast, except for this meal he opened a can of tuna on which he squeezed some lemon and sprinkled a few drops of olive oil. Once he finished a pot of tea, he made himself another. He had no television because it produced light that could be seen from outside. He spent his evenings in the dark, from almost four in the afternoon, around the time the sun went down, until he fell asleep. He lived without the benefit of light, so he memorized the routes he took and the location of everything in the house, like a blind man who knew his home intimately.

No one came to see him, except for a visit once every ten days when someone would bring a bag of food along with newspapers and some books and stay for a few minutes. They would talk briefly about the news of the party and the resistance, express their solidarity, and then they would leave. Kan'an could not even step outdoors to throw out the garbage because opening and closing the door created a noise that could be heard by the tenants of the house opposite them, which was only a few meters away with a fence between them. The bags of garbage accumulated in his kitchen would stink up the whole house. He would pace for hours between the wall and the door or between the eastern window and the wall facing it in his bedroom. He would pause by the window and watch the residents of the opposite house for a few minutes, then walk back to the wall. He listened to the radio, including songs, newscasts, and radio dramas, until he eventually came to memorize the programs of all the broadcast stations. He started his day with opinion pieces in the Arabic press on Sawt Al-'Arab at 5:10 a.m., and concluded his day with the Panorama news program on Monte Carlo radio. In between, he listened to Umm Kulthum at noon, the Occupation radio in the evening, and to Fairuz whenever he could pick up broadcasts of her songs.

He was devastated by loneliness and under constant tension, but the tensions now were not like before. During the first few months of his secret life, his inner self had to cope with the **"measures, precautions, requirements, and rules."** The tension this time was of a different sort because his inner self had changed and had different concerns: How far had the raid campaign progressed? What news was there about our comrades in the interrogation dungeons? Which ones have held out and which ones have betrayed their party and their comrades? How have the ones who remained free conducted themselves? Were they getting rattled, fostering doubts, weakness, and a breakdown of morale? Or were they keeping it together, enduring courageously, and defending their party and protecting what is left of it? How did the cells and organizations protect themselves and continue their activities so as to compensate for the losses? What communiqués have the party issued? What was their content? How have they been received by the members? These and many other questions consumed him.

Kan'an waited and waited but never received an answer. Waiting was the order of the day. He understood that the situation was difficult and that receiving decisive answers was impossible at this point. But at the same time, he did not understand. He wanted to satiate a thirst to feel that he was a part of the battle—at the heart of the battle—even if only by thinking and being concerned, but that required answers and information that he didn't have. He waited and waited but his burning thirst was not quenched. He waited for a comrade, a news item, anything, but nothing came . . . wait till tomorrow . . . Tomorrow, like the case of the colonel in the book by Gabriel García Marquez, waiting for a damned letter which would never come.[14]

He had been agitated since the beginning of the raids against his party, the same as any other member who felt that what was dear to him, and what he helped build, was being destroyed. He felt as though his father or his mother or his child were being slaughtered and that he was unable to seize the knife from the killer, as though he was just watching the battle from afar.

> **Stay where you are and read! The confrontation continues and we are hanging our hopes on endurance. More specifically, the cadres must endure and the precautionary measures will provide the safety valve.**

> The most important thing now is that you keep yourself safe. Your picture with the soldiers at the checkpoint on the Ramallah–Jerusalem road has been seen. Endurance now means saving yourself from falling into their hands during the raid campaign. You must not confine your potential within sacks of stone. Just one thing is demanded of you now, nothing more: to remain quiet until the next outbreak; quiet down and do not move.

This was what the party told him. Finally, a letter had arrived which partly explained things and offered some answers. It relayed what Shabak* interrogators had said in the interrogation dungeons: "This is your year. We are going to liquidate you and none of you will be left. There is a government order. We must put an end to you." The letter made clear the dimensions of the battle, the confrontation, and the defeat. Hundreds of members and supporters were in interrogation dungeons and in *sahat al-shabeh*, their heads covered with stinking sacks and their wrists bloodied by lead handcuffs as cold water lashed their naked bodies in the icy wind of winter.

It is a confrontation that knows no middle ground: shivering, weak, naked bodies cloaked in willpower and trust in their party and the justice of their national cause against a strong, capable intelligence body in possession of the most modern and scientific means to destroy whoever falls into their hands. The letter contained many details about those who mounted a confrontation and others who had collapsed. But there were no conclusions drawn. The battle was still at its height, and one had to be optimistic that the seed that was planted, after years of education, hardening, and nurturing, would bear ripe fruits, of course with an understanding of that elementary truth: that each tree produces some rotten fruits.

---

*   Otherwise known as Shin Bet, Shabak is the Zionist entity's internal intelligence agency.

Then the letter arrived that struck Kan'an like a thunderbolt: **"Our greatest loss has been that they managed to find part of our gold treasure, the undercover agents, and to arrest the heroes, comrades Fanoun and Al-Nahhas."**[15] He could not go on reading. He sat down on the chair unable to control the feeling that his bones had been torn from his body. He had not met them, nor did the party release their names to those engaged in the clandestine experience, and he was not the sort to ask, as the rules of the game were clear to him: it was not permissible to ask about those who left their homes and disappeared. Despite this, he felt deep inside that these were his "colleagues" in a shared profession, people who lived as he had lived, who fought from their positions as he fought from his, living lives of hardship and challenge, pacing within their safe houses, rejoicing, getting angry, and suppressing their inner selves on a daily basis. He therefore felt the need to support them. No matter what experience or life one may be living, to feel that one has companions in that experience creates a bond and feeling of mutual support.

Everyone is in the heat of battle except
for me. I . . . I . . . shall remain still until
the time for action comes.

He was unable to shake a sense of inadequacy. It was as though he wished he would be arrested so that he could be at the center of the confrontation. The desire to defend the party in the moment of battle is to forget, in that moment of emotional reaction, that *sumud*[*] also means to be still and await the coming advancement.

He received a letter a month after he started living in Sakinah's house, which put his mind at ease and lit within him the fire of desire for years and years of struggle. The letter encapsulated the voice of the party, its pulse and perseverance. Its wording made clear to him how difficult the situation was: **"The member who**

---
* Steadfastness in Arabic. The meaning of *sumud*, in the Palestinian context, carries with it the meaning of enduring like the olive tree. Sumud as a national liberation concept focuses on the development of self-sufficiency.

persists with us after this assault campaign will continue with us for a long time." That sentence reflected the intensity of the raid campaign and its repercussions. Consequently, the confrontation of 1985 had had the same impact on him as it did on others in the cadres; it hardened them, further intensified their allegiance, while it drove others to collapse. He could feel the daily effects of the confrontation in fostering and consolidating his inner strength.

He no longer entertained the same beautiful and romantic images of revolutionary work as he had in the prime of his youth, in the school days of clandestine leftist cells and the printing of communiqués and secret newspapers, using a homemade press in the dirty houses of rural students . . . Romantic imaginings of revolutionary action are good as the setting for a fiery song or beautiful poem. However, they are not adequate for educating a person who is going to take up revolution as his profession because he will find out sooner than later that a revolution is one thing and romanticism is quite another. Those imaginings do not arise in the mind of someone who immerses themself in revolutionary action and experiences their sacrifices and "pays the bill" in full, namely the renunciation of the most basic human needs. But romantic perceptions do arise among amateurs—although perhaps not all of them—who enlist in revolutionary action without a full sense of what awaits them and what they must pay in the course of the struggle. When the experience begins to transform them and change their skin, then and only then, do they either acclimate, changing their perceptions and harmonizing their thoughts to take on what they must be prepared to do in the struggle, or they leave for good. In the latter case, the revolutionary movement gains strength through their departure.

Whoever viewed Kan'an's life from the outside and heard about it no doubt saw its romantic aspect: the sense of danger, the mystery and secrecy enveloping it, living a long time like a fox, jumping from one safe house to another, wearing disguises, altering his features, his assignations, the careful way he walks down the street closely examining passersby. However, in Kan'an's eyes, that was not so, especially after over three years living a clandestine life. Its romantic features were there, but its cruelty was now apparent in his eyes. It remained a pillar of his daily life even if its effects were not seen clearly in the course of his routine actions and thoughts. He had begun to reconcile himself with the hardships of his life. Living as a fugitive involved endless deprivations. Having to look left and right and scrutinize everyone leisurely strolling past his house entailed being constantly vigilant, activating his entire nervous system. That was not a natural way to live.

Kan'an delighted in challenging the occupiers by living and resisting despite their efforts. He was elated every time he contemplated that. He used to say to himself, "Here I am! If they really have such an efficient intelligence apparatus, let them get to me!" He felt that the success of his experience demonstrated the incapacity of their government and institutions, revealing its lack of omnipotence. However, he knew, and became increasingly convinced that such a life was a *necessity* more than it was an act of *gratification*. It was a necessity for the struggle of his party and his people to expel the occupiers and build a truly happy and pleasurable life. A clandestine existence is a choice of resistance, not a way of life. If anyone chose to treat a secret life with all its deprivations and hardships as romantic, they may be right in a metaphorical sense, but not in actuality. It becomes a romantic force by its contribution to the creation of an enjoyable and romantic life, but it is not inherently a romantic experience.

The joy of life does not lie in abandoning the requirements of human nature, but in living and keeping with those requirements simply and spontaneously, free of the shackles and rules of an authority that issues and legislates its prohibitions. Every passing day was an affirmation that absolute joy, absolute happiness, lies in liberation from every constraint from living according to human nature. He was growing increasingly convinced that accomplishing that goal required serious struggle. Measures and precautions would have to be taken, requirements and rules followed. His struggle came to demand that he should not meet anyone, not visit anyone, not open the peep window of a door to an old woman from Al-Bireh. The way he judged things now was maturing through the accumulation of experience. He came to know precisely what his rights and responsibilities were, what was possible and what was not possible within the system of his life. Experience forges the man, and his experience was molding him exactly as resistance breeds its professionals, as tolerating torture creates steadfast people, and as battles create heroes. "All soldiers are brave, perhaps even heroes, before the battle begins." Kan'an liked this wise Russian saying a lot when he read it in the epic novel, *The Living and the Dead*.[16] He often thought about it and compared it with his experience and life, noting a lot of similarities.

> *Immerse yourself deeper and deeper into your experience and your life, let its waters wash over you, let it scrub your skin with its soap and brush, let it leaven you with its yeast, forge you in its furnace. Then, and only then, can you say I am the owner of this experience.*

When Kan'an passed the three-year mark of his hiding, he became aware of the mad life he was leading and the risk he was taking in confronting the occupiers. But is revolution anything other than an act of madness and risk taking? A struggle that is serious and deep-rooted in nature requires living the life of resistance passionately, living the revolution madly. A revolutionary pays a very high price to realize an idea—just an idea. Kan'an had paid to realize his idea-vision of the revolution and his adventure. To live life madly was to storm through its tests, difficulties, and adventures. The experience of life molds and teaches. It shakes off apathy and laziness and silly routine. It provides the know-how and experience to dive into another experience, so as to be molded and educated anew. Life was to be lived passionately, by invading it and subjugating it through the madness of diving into the sea of new experiences, which in its novelty and strangeness changes us, giving us permission to ride upon its sea and subdue it ... He saw his experience, his secret life in this way: a mad experience that ground him, mixed him with water and kneaded him anew. He swam in the sea of life and learned from it, he lived it with all his strength, for struggle required that of him.

The madness of revolution is to burn in its oven day by day. We bestow it our entire lives, not merely the hours of our days. We belong to its makers in thought and deed. Either victory or death, there is no third alternative. It is not a revolution if we devote half of ourselves to it and half to something else. Revolution does not abide within the revolutionary individual alongside a second wife; it is not a revolution if it is divisible by two. The madness of revolution is becoming a professional, and becoming a professional revolutionary means living the revolution madly. The interest of the revolution requires professionalism of this sort, he discovered.

Once he grasped this concept and this conviction about life and the revolution, it became his personal religion-creed. His religion had a trinity consisting of life–woman–revolution, joined by a common denominator, a single secret thread: the act of madness and adventure. Life by storming it, revolution by being its professional, and a woman by experiencing her. His inner self was debating him.

> *What about a woman, Kan'an? How does one experience her? As a dream, a picture, imaginings, suppressed instincts? What sort of experience is that? Are you castrated or impotent? When a woman becomes a reality to you, a fact, an aspect of daily life, a joint experience, companion and elation and pleasure, only then can you say "I experience her." When*

> *you experience elation and pleasure with her and through her, when she is elated and takes pleasure in you and with you, when the feeling overwhelms and intoxicates you as though a wine imbibed, only then can you say: "I experienced her madly!" Have you found her so that your religion, your trinity, can be complete?*

His religion was not complete, he knew. His hypostases were still looking for a third. In its long contest with him, his inner self had scored a point in its favor and so he withdrew and was silent.

❖❖❖❖❖

The days and weeks went by in the house of the damned Sakinah and loneliness was killing him. Kan'an wished he could speak to a human, any human. He would observe them from the eastern window, either as they stood in front of the house across from him or as they crossed the street leading to his house, separated by the ten meters' long dirt path. Oh, how far he was from humanity! During one stretch at damned Sakinah's, eleven days passed without him talking to or sitting down with another person. Humans were far away from him, and even if they came close and knocked on the door of his house for some reason, he would not behave with the foolishness of an amateur and open the door. His loneliness was not just the kind that results in the erosion of one's humanity, that is, the loneliness of missing another. His loneliness was utter absence, the loneliness of not finding anyone to talk to. It was as though he was the only human being on earth. He was like Adam before The Creator created Eve from his rib, according to the religious legend. However, he was not in the Garden of Eden, he was in the house of a strange creature called the damned Sakinah. He was like Robinson Crusoe in English literature. But even Crusoe had animals to keep him company, even if they could not talk like he could.

For the first time in his three years of hiding, Kan'an spoke with the wall. He was walking and thinking out loud until he found himself addressing the wall! And why would that deaf and dumb cement wall answer him? He had begun to see it as a friend ever since he reconciled with himself over two years earlier, but now he was losing his mind: why wouldn't it answer him?

The letter from the party did not satiate his thirst. He accepted that he had to be still now so that he could move about freely later, but he was unable to make that conviction seep into his tense emotional state. Why was he not deployed at the time of confrontation? Was he to continue walking and listening to the radio and reading while the party was in *sahat al-shabeh* undergoing torture? He would talk to himself and the tension increased. The sense of loneliness and constant tension resulting from his long isolation was as terrible as it had been in the first months of his experience—no, it was even more terrible and menacing.

That damned Sakinah insisted that she should play a role in vexing his hours and days—she would have it no other way! She had to practice her hobby of frustrating him and making his days more distressing. She came once, twice, even three times a day to inspect and tidy up. She would knock on the eastern door with such force it seemed as though she wanted to unhinge it.

"Open! Open!"

He would hold his breath and not move while she continued to beat on the door.

"Why don't they open up? Open up! I am Sakinah, the owner of the house."

She would identify herself as if the whole quarter could not tell it was her from her voice. In his mind, he lambasted her with the sharpest insults he had in store, and she would begin her routine tour. She would go to the second door, repeating her knocking and shouting while he continued to hold his breath and be still and silent. As he held back his coughs and the rattling in his throat, she would move on to stage three, which was to make the round of the windows, one by one, peering from behind the glass and tapping on it to see if there was anyone at home. Once she began stage three, Kan'an would skip between the room to the corridor to the kitchen, watching out for the bulging eyes staring through the windows.

Once she was done with the windows, she would start her strange hobby of collecting all that her eyes could see, things no one would notice nor give any importance to: a bent rusty nail, a worn out wire, a piece of wood or iron, a plastic bag, an empty and flattened tin box... she ignored nothing! Once the old woman from the house across asked her, having seen her.

"Sakinah, what're you doing in this cold weather?"

"I came to inspect the house. I found no one," she responded before continuing to pick up her fine relics.

"What are you collecting? What use is that box to you?" she asked, amazed at what Sakinah was collecting, in the tone of someone seeing the woman practice her hobby for the first time.

"Everything has a use. It is a waste to leave these things strewn about like this."

Usually, her ceremony of inspecting her "villa" and picking up these precious relics would last between thirty and forty-five minutes, during which time Kan'an would be forced to stay quiet so as not to attract her attention. The only thing that kept her away was heavy rain; Kan'an wished for rain every day. He also wished he could see her dead, laid out motionless, to give his nerves a rest.

He read the letter from the party a second and a third time before burning it, as thoughts ran through his mind.

The cost of resistance must be paid with good will. The clandestine life has conditions which must be observed. Revolutionary life has its own way of washing the self. And here it is, washing the self through the hardship of loneliness. Lay low until activities resume.

He was talking to and rebuilding his inner self. Building the self is a never-ending, lifelong task. The self, like a snake, needs to renew its skin. Once again, he remembered the advice of the martyred thinker Mehdi Amel: "the intellectual must change their skin constantly." He could sense the retreat of his agitated self. It continued to make demands of him, however the demands were now tempered. What was driving him to feel dead was not only his inability to do anything important, but his solitude and isolation. He understood the importance of adhering to and perfecting directives: **"lay low until activities resume."** The time had come for him to understand the orders, and reconcile with the yearning for an end to his solitude.

Days went by. He walked, ate, listened to the radio, sang songs by Sheikh Imam and Marcel Khalife, read and slept. The walls listened and engaged him in dialogue; they were no longer deaf and dumb. He debated his inner self and comprehended its needs and desires. It, of course, wanted its third fundamental. Did he have what it took to tell it that it had no right? He used to tell it to endure. It was no longer firing at him, for it had been defeated and had stepped aside. By becoming revolutionary, his inner self realized its duties and responsibilities. It found itself part of the struggle and secret life, not opposed to it. Like him, it had been molded. Its skin had been washed with a soap and brush. It had become a revolutionary self, but would not stop making demands.

> *It will not stop. It screams at you, demanding the woman, the third fundamental. It expresses your yearning to play childhood games, reflects how you miss staying up at night with your friends in song and laughter, disturbing an entire quarter. You fume with rage since you are not with your comrades, on their marches and their celebrations of the party's anniversary,*

you are not with them in facing the assault. Your inner self carries you far away and you imagine yourself sitting on the threshold of your family home, smoking and drinking tea and bouncing a cute toddler on your lap. Your self will not stop making its demands, in fact its demands affirm your humanity, your deprivation, and they heighten your sensibilities. Only reactionaries spread silly and vile ideas about petrified revolutionaries who are lacking in emotions. Allow your inner self to make demands and do not suppress it, it is your key to opening the door to the outside even if only in your contemplative, dreamy imagination. No matter how long it will be before the door opens, the day will come—it is inevitable. Just do not allow your self to steer you just as the farmer rides his donkey. May you be the rider and your inner self, the donkey. Steer it when it makes demands, even once it becomes revolutionary. In the house of the accursed Sakinah, your inner self has now reduced all its demands to one single desire: that its isolation, your isolation, be put to an end.

Finally, the heavens gave him a gift, humanity in the form of the young woman from the house across from him. Kan'an saw her from the eastern window of his bedroom. She was barely over twenty years of age, tall, slender, with long, coal-black hair. The features of her face were easy on the eyes, not due to any obvious beauty, but because of an innocence they radiated. She had a childish face and voice, soft and delicate when she called her mother, as though her face and voice had come together to affirm her affiliation with the innocence of youth rather than the maturity of femininity. He was pacing between the window and the wall, fiddling with his red prayer beads as was his custom when he was in deep thought. He had just reached the window when curiosity drew his gaze to the house across from him, in keeping with his habit as a man of a clandestine life, scouting the terrain surrounding his secret house.

It was a clear day and the sun had been shining since the morning, spreading its rays over puddles that had formed in the front yard, as well as on the stones of the house across from his, causing the droplets to shimmer off of them. Winter was brewing through the end of February. Just as they say, "February roars and thunders and carries the smell of summer." Those morning rays were born as a challenge from the womb of the murderous winter's gloom, spreading joy in Kan'an's heart. He had always wished, throughout his clandestine life, that winter was a man he could strangle with his bare hands. He peered out his window for a fleeting moment—the time it would take for him to turn before retracing his steps to the wall. At that instant he saw her heading out of the back door of her house towards the kitchen. She paused momentarily to bask in the blessing of the sun's warm rays shining on the entrance of the house. A happy smile formed on her face, a dreamy, innocent smile that at first glance could be mistaken for simplemindedness. She smiled like a child who was happy to receive a gift on *Eid*,* but she did not jump for joy as a child would have. She just stopped and smiled, looking at the sun as though she wanted to thank it!

Kan'an thanked the sun too for its gift, for she appeared with the sun. Who could convince him now that she was not the daughter of the sun? Her face was glowing like the sun, smiling like the

---

* Arabic word for holiday or festivity.

sun, radiating light like the sun: the sun's personification. He was transfixed in place, motionless. She was standing and looking, and so was he, she at the sun, he at her. There was no difference between them in his mind; she was a sun just a few meters away. She moved towards the kitchen. He had forgotten himself for a few moments, and suddenly remembered that he was totally exposed, standing directly in front of her. The curtains were open; had she glanced at the window she would have seen him mesmerized there, entranced in his gaze. As he waited for her to come out of the kitchen, he thought to himself, *Thanks to the heavens for this gift. Thanks to the sun for its offspring. My isolation from human beings is finally ending. My hope now is that the sun will continue to shine, for she comes with it.* He quickly remembered that Sakinah also appeared with the sun for her inspections. After this morning, how could he wish for rain to fall to relieve him from the sight of damned Sakinah's ugly face and voice? He began looking forward to sunny days which give birth each morning to the maiden-of-the-sun at his eastern window. He became aware of how his wishes countered one another and felt frustration that the two appeared with the sun. This abstract comparison was a disturbing and painful one. How could one compare a rhinoceros to a gazelle, or a bat to the delicate and beautiful yellow canary?

Ten minutes passed and she emerged from the kitchen carrying plates of food on a woven straw tray that she took into the house. That was breakfast, as it was not even eight o'clock in the morning yet. She was still wearing her winter pajamas. Her clothes indicated that she was poor. He was pleased that the sun-maiden was a member of his class.

> *Why did you appear so late, sun-maiden? Did you have to wait for February and its smell of summer so that you could be born? Did you have to wait through December and January for the cold and wind and rain and*

sadness to complete their pregnancy so that you could be born? Why couldn't you have been born a month earlier so that I could talk to you instead of the dumb wall?

The party's letter, which clarified things and provided some answers, along with the appearance of the sun-maiden on a February day, gave him a sense of contentment and quiet during the hours of his days. Despite all of the difficulties, he came to live by his religion, his trinity, for days and months. Time was capable of producing beautiful endings if a person succeeded in reconciling with its pressures and coping with its tensions. At the beginning of his third month living in Sakinah's house, Kan'an started noticing the days pass by routinely, no longer congested or subject to tensions.

A second letter from the party arrived. This time it was full of conclusions about the confrontation that it considered to be the fiercest since the previous 1976 assault on the party. It concluded that in the final analysis, "**the most prominent feature was the *sumud* of the organizations' leaders and its principal cadres.**" It described examples of heroic resistance, most prominently Fanoun. As for the immediate results of the Occupation's assault campaign, some organizations were liquidated and the organizational structures of others were destroyed. And as for the circle of potential recruits, the wider popular base that surrounded the party, and the remaining few cadres, the task was not only to rebuild what had been destroyed but to advance what was previously built. This was the case especially in regards to the new experiment (that is, a unified party formation) that had resisted fiercely, having barely just stood on its two feet. The experiment reached the decision that there would be no going back from a unified party formation as a final achievement. As had been stated in the letter: "**The hubris of the Occupation's claim that they had liquidated us has crumbled, as they came to understand well.**"

From another perspective, the letter affirmed that comprehensive confrontation in the life of a revolutionary movement was like a sieve that separates the chaff from the wheat. The party became stronger with the filtering of those who were tested by the confrontation and proved to be fragile and quick to break, just as it was solidified by those who were forged from iron. Finally, the letter reaffirmed the previous letter's conclusion: **"The member who persists with us after this assault campaign will remain with us for a long time."**

To assert the path that the party had chosen after the assault campaign, it issued a letter stating that the experiment had been reaffirmed and there would be no retreat from it. This was the "Guevara letter," which was released in 1986, at the height of the confrontation. It was a preliminary attempt—its final crystallization was to be left open to time and practice—to decide on the party's mass line to build a secret guerrilla movement in the homeland. The letter was based on readings of several revolutionary military experiments: the Russian, Chinese, Vietnamese, Bulgarian, and Cuban revolutions. It emphasized the features of each, and it also examined the demographic and geographic characteristics of the homeland, concluding that the appropriate combat tactic for Palestine should be the establishment of a secret guerrilla movement across the cities and the countryside. According to the letter, the main strength of the movement would lie in its secret nature while its leadership, its cradle, and its base would have a solid organizational structure with political and mass extensions. The structure would reach a degree of development that would enable it to launch the movement, ensure its continuity, and protect it. Finally, the letter focused on the Guevarian revolutionary model and its basic characteristics which aimed to forge fighters and guerrillas.

Spring started to embroider the house's front yard with ripe vegetation and red poppies.[17] A slightly drawn curtain on the window became part of his daily routine. A third letter arrived that referred to the halting of the assault campaign. His comrades were sending him many books and novels, including the complete works of Ghassan Kanafani. Although he had already read Kanafani's novels, stories, and critical studies, this time he reread them in record time—four days. His days went on, filled with voracious reading and happiness that the assault campaign against the party was over. His routine included pacing between the eastern window and the wall, feasting his eyes on the sun-maiden, and listening to the radio. These days were satiated with the sweetness of spring, its green vegetation spread joy and contentment in his soul.

What meaning is to be attached to distant glances between a man and a woman? What message is delivered by the occasional, indirect, shy, secret smiles from a man who finds in the smile of a woman a reprieve from his utter isolation? And a woman, who has waited throughout her adolescent years, having reached the threshold of maturity, for a man to smile at her? What sort of friendship could blossom without conversation, social exchange, joint friendship, the holding of hands? During his daily pacing between the window and the wall he saw the sun-maiden from early morning till noon as she moved between her house and the kitchen. During the afternoons, she had a daily routine that consisted of getting dressed up and putting on red lipstick in a style indicative of her poverty, and then sitting on her chair beside the rear door and spending the hours on her *tatreez*[*] until the March sun began to set.

Kan'an would wait to catch glimpses of her through the window, waiting for her as though they had a date. When she appeared, he would perk up and smile, observing her from afar. He was content with that amount of pleasure that his way of life allowed. How much had it dwarfed his pleasures and desires? From his window he could tell if she had left the house or not. The entrances to her house and his house were the same; the dirt passageway led to both houses. She had not left the house before she was born by the February sun. He never once had seen her walking along the path either going or coming. He was used to looking at the passersby ever since he moved to the house, either to pass the time or out of the sense of curiosity that naturally accompanied his secret way of life.

---

[*] Palestinian embroidery.

She became part of his life inside his house. She would spend her day either in the kitchen or outside of it moving around or sitting and working on her *tatreez*. He familiarized himself with her way of life, which was the same as the vast majority of women among their people. In the morning, she would go to the kitchen to prepare breakfast; a bit later she would return carrying the straw tray to the house. At about nine o'clock she would enter the kitchen to prepare lunch which took about two hours, then she would quickly sweep and clean the house. In the afternoon, either by herself or as a part of a gathering with old women, she would sit beside the door embroidering beautiful, colored figures on a piece of cloth. He learned even more than that about her: her name was 'Abir, and the name of the little girl who followed her wherever she went was Roseanne. He learned that the little one was her brother's daughter. He learned everything about her family: her elderly father's occupation, what her two brothers did, he even learned some specifics about her family and their concerns. Private conversations among the family members when they gathered around the dining table tended to waft out of the home thanks to the popular custom of leaving the door ajar. He had learned to forgive himself for listening in on his neighbors' conversations and consoled himself with the idea that he wanted to be part of life outside his house by being attentive and following the conversations of those living life there. It was beneficial for him to know if his neighbors were raising certain questions or exchanging news concerning their neighbor whom they do not see.

But he had added another important reason for eavesdropping: his desire to learn about the sun-maiden in close detail from afar, since a direct encounter was dangerous. She had finished her high school studies and sat home, like the rest of her contemporaries of the "fairer sex," waiting to move from her father's house to the house of her husband, carried away by a knight on a white horse. That miserable maiden was waiting and dreaming, believing that her dream would come true and that she would consequently find happiness. Meanwhile, her family was waiting on pins and needles for that knight, with a longing comparable to her own, if not greater. "When I will be rid of you and marry you off, then your husband will have to take care of you." That was how her elderly mother had put it during an argument with her that recurred daily about affairs of the kitchen. The sun-maiden was a burden on her family who were waiting impatiently to shift her off of their shoulders.

On a sunny day in March, at ten in the morning, when 'Abir was usually busy preparing lunch, Kan'an was standing at his kitchen window eating an apple and looking at the rear vegetable garden that was full of ripe, green wild grass and beautiful blooming red poppies. He was watching absent-mindedly, his thoughts far away, mind wandering. Suddenly, the sun-maiden appeared standing before him as though she had sprung out of the green grass and red roses. She was only one meter away, looking with astonishment at that strange, bearded face which she had never seen before. The surprise was visible on her face, not only because it was obvious he had not sensed her presence until just then, but also out of shock that she'd never seen him up close before, neither coming nor going. His amazement was no less than hers. *Has she been born a second time from among the grass and wild roses after the sun gave birth to her the first time?* His eyes met her eyes. They were mesmerized for a few seconds while looking at each other. He smiled at her, happiness evident on his face. She returned his smile with a confused and shy one, her face red in embarrassment, joy, and wonder. The meeting of their eyes and smiles lasted only a few seconds, the most beautiful seconds he had experienced in three months. His eyes and face displayed happiness, but her timid, child-like smile suggested that no man had smiled at her before. His smile was an unusual event that took her by surprise, she who was waiting for her knight felt confused and shy, but that did not prevent her from giving free reign to her desire with delight, even if it was with the speed of lightning. For nature has its own logic which only operates according to its own demands.

With the same speed, she turned and retreated, disappearing from his sight. He quickly moved to his eastern window to watch her exiting the entrance to his yard. She looked back when she reached the turnoff and smiled her confused smile again. She knew full well that his smile and his eyes were following her from the window. She quickened her pace, rapidly traversing the distance from the entrance of his house to her kitchen, carrying in her hand a bunch of *khubezeh** that grew profusely in the yard.

He sat down on a chair in his room.

She is beautiful, and her confused smile is even more beautiful. Her face blushing in embarrassment gave her an air of childishness when she was caught looking at him. No doubt the sun-maiden will ask questions that will confuse her more than the confusion of her smile: "Where did he come from? I have been in the kitchen since this morning," she will say. "And there are no more than three meters separating our kitchen from the entrance of his house. I should have heard his footsteps, if not I should have heard the sound a door makes when opened and closed. When did he get here?" she will ask. "Yesterday? The last time the door was opened was two weeks ago, at night. Who is he? Who lives there? I knew the previous tenants and what they did. I used to see them leave in the morning and return in the afternoon. But for three months I have not seen a single one of them. Now I see this

---

* *Khubezeh*, also known as "little mallow," is a type of annual herb, of the genus Malva in the mallow family used in cooking.

bearded stranger, and he is not one of them, standing in front of me, his thoughts elsewhere. Did he sprout out of the ground or descend from the sky?"

A powerful knocking on the door drew him out of his contemplation. He had learned to recognize those knocks three months ago. *I won't open the door. Let her repeat those confusing questions in her mind, confirming the strangeness of my life and conduct. I have no choice!* The cursed Sakinah had begun her accustomed ritual. She knocked on the first door, yelling in her ugly voice, and he did not answer, acting as though he had not heard. The sun-maiden was watching the spectacle. Sakinah moved to the second door and repeated her mad shouts, and he did not answer. She went to the windows and pecked at them, trying to claw them open, sticking her face up to the glass in an effort to see inside. He was being careful not to be seen. Meanwhile, he saw the sun-maiden standing at her kitchen door, laughing in clear delight. She was happy at the torture that the cursed Sakinah was going through! She understood that the bearded stranger did not want to open the door and she came to his rescue.

"Auntie Sakinah, there is no one at home," she said. "They went out this morning." She was confirming that she was on his side in his affliction with the crone.

"Where are they? What are they doing in the house? I don't understand anything. For the last three months I have not seen the face of a single one of them."

"They come home every afternoon and they leave in the morning. I see them." She was reaffirming her spontaneous solidarity with him, and continuing to lie for his honor.

"I come twice, three times each week but no one responds to me!"

"Must be a coincidence, they happen to be out of the house every time you come." She said this but was unable to conceal her laughter. She was happy with a childish delight to help him achieve his objective and at seeing the accursed Sakinah suffer. The latter prattled on, muttering complaints one could not understand, as is the custom of the elderly in such situations, and then she left.

> *Thank you oh beautiful, daughter of the sun, the spring grass, and red poppies! You have been true to the smiles we happily exchanged. You have saved me from a predicament. I shall not forget that. But what did you understand from what just transpired? Did you understand that the absent-minded, bearded stranger—whom you have never seen before and who does not open the door to exit or enter—is in reality a wolf lurking in his den? Or is it that the narrow horizons of your life and your limited experience will not aid you in reaching that conclusion? You must think that everything that just happened was all to avoid the sight of the cursed Sakinah? Never mind, it is good that you should think that. You have kept my secret. Once again, thank you for being faithful to our happy smiles.*

After that, the sun-maiden made a habit of responding to the inspection bouts with false assurances: "They are not at home! They left half an hour ago." She was sure that the bearded stranger was smiling, thankfully happy, behind the curtain.

Ever since the encounter at the kitchen window and the garden, she transfixed her eyes on the eastern window whenever she had the chance. She came to spend the least amount of time possible in the house or the kitchen whereas she spent hours sitting at the door or walking with little Roseanne, coming close to the fence separating the two houses so she could see up close when he was behind the partly drawn curtain. She used to sit and embroider, with her eyes looking more at the window than they were following the motions of her hand and the needle. She was aware by now that the bearded stranger never left his house, the door never opened, he made no audible sounds, and there were no footsteps on the pebbles lining the entrance of the house.

She knew the game even if she did not know the reason for it. But, like him, she was only concerned with looking intensely. She would see that the curtain was drawn a little and she could sense his eyes transfixed on her—her youthful face, her coal black hair, her eyes, her body. He knew that she knew, so he continued to stand behind his window watching her as several emotions swept over him. In the morning, as soon as she stepped out, heading for the kitchen, she would turn her head while walking towards the window and smile at the person behind the curtain. As soon as she left the kitchen, she would turn her head quickly and steal a glance at the window, a brief smile would appear on her lips. She walked more frequently near the fence adjacent to his window and became glued to her chair near the door throughout the afternoon until sunset unless someone from her family called her. She would embroider and look and smile. Her smile was no longer hesitant, it became free and bold, as though she was saying: I have the right to smile, and I am doing so!

They had formed a friendship without speaking, without sitting down together. Smiles and looks were the bridge to their relationship. She had learned his secret without knowing the real cause for it, so her smile was a smile of sympathy, solidarity, and friendship. He had learned about her life, so he felt sorry for her and pitied the maiden of his window, the sun-maiden.

✽✽✽✽✽

On a warm March evening, 'Abir rose from her chair and, taking her niece with her, walked in the direction of the entrance to his house. The two of them crossed the entrance as he followed her with his eyes. Entering the yard, she started picking the blooming red poppies. Kan'an moved to the next window so he could see her well. She was moving towards the back of the house as she picked the flowers. He quickly moved to the kitchen and stopped at the window. She appeared, still picking poppies while little Roseanne jumped around her like a rabbit, happy because of the sun, the red poppies, the journey around the house, and the colorful butterflies flitting about. He noted her trajectory: she was walking towards his kitchen window, bending to pick a poppy and moving on. She looked up for a moment when she drew near the window and saw Kan'an standing in front of her, observing her. She smiled at him and he smiled back. She continued walking towards the window and drew nearer so that she was only one step away from him. At that point she chose a blooming poppy and tossed it in his direction. Taking hold of the child's hand while carrying her bouquet with the other, she moved away from the window, turning her back on him. He joyfully caught her flower, which had passed through the bars of the window, and said spontaneously so she could hear:

"The most beautiful flower from the most beautiful flower."

She turned her head towards him, smiling a wishful smile. The red hue had not left her face and she rapidly continued on her way to the kitchen.

You poor thing, with a face red with embarrassment like the wild poppies. You who have been born of the sun, who appears among the ripe, green spring grass and blooming red flowers. The bearded stranger cannot take one step towards you! That is best for you. In not approaching you he is not acting out of fear of the experience, nor is he abdicating any rights he may have to you or any rights you may have to him. The cause is the secret life and its rules. Can you understand the law of his life: measures, precautions, requirements, rules, visit no one, receive no one, don't open the peep window of the door to an old woman from Al-Bireh? Can you even imagine a human being who visits no one and receives no one? How can you understand that, you beautiful creature whose head has been filled with kitchen culture and the nonsense of a school education? For whom do you make yourself attractive each day? For the knight who will come on his white horse and take you to the land of happiness? You are a poor thing if you are holding onto an illusion of happiness. Are you perfecting your role as a bride, performing before the women who visit your house? They come up with a hundred excuses for a visit, but the aim is the same: to inspect the goods! Are you well prepared to play the role of the daughter-in-law for an old and feeble-minded woman near the end of her life? Yes, you, beauty, you will leave one kitchen only to go to another—you were born of the sun but there is no room for you under the sun. Your place is behind the walls, living in tranquil obedience to worn out customs and a predetermined order.

What a difference there is between your walls and mine, behind which each of us seeks refuge. Only in my case I am here out of rebellion and in yours, out of obedience. There can be no meeting of rebellion and obedience, daughter of the sun and the spring! I make my own decisions and am master of my fate, whereas you cannot even smile without hesitation and shyness and perhaps even trepidation. Was it to that extent that your first smile was hesitant? When you took the steps that you did, you arrived at my window by error. "I know your step before it takes its position!" Have you not read Naguib Mahfouz? My dear girl, I do not even have a donkey on which to come to you, much less a white horse. Coming close to me means coming close to the madness of revolution—the madness of life. A woman who does approach will become mad like me, ridden by the demon of revolution. Either that or she would have found her path to madness before I did. Regardless, together we would live and resist and love, ridden by our common demon.

What do you know about a life of love and resistance and madness? You do not make a decent third fundamental for my religion, just a beautiful icon to hang on the wall! My ambition is a fundamental, a hypostasis—not a symbol! You are miserable. Beautiful and miserable. You are kind and you are miserable. You don't know how to love and what is in store for you. You are living a life of marginalization and deprivation, and you have not yet learned to "knock on the walls of the tank."[18] Everything around you is marginalizing you and you don't realize it. The reactionary prescriptions of religious law, school, men, class, family, the Occupation—all of them are marginalizing you. For centuries they have been laughing at your expense by saying, "You are the maker of men and the nurturer of generations." In fact, they have been defining your role: from the bed to the kitchen and vice-versa, pleasing the knight on the white horse, pleasing his stomach and the desires between his thighs! The tale blames you for leading Adam astray, sullying him and dishonoring yourself although you were the one who granted him knowledge, pleasure, and life! Our forefathers were more just to you than all of these legends and religious laws, for the Babylonians granted you the honor of transforming the half-beast, half-human creature into a full human being after seducing him, having sex with him, possessing him and he possessing you, his being elated by you and your being elated by him. You granted man his humanity only for him to turn around and marginalize your humanity!

Kan'an addressed her for a long time, alone and agitated, pacing between the window and the wall, thinking. He offered her a bouquet of red roses. "Take these, for there is nothing more beautiful than red roses. They are everything that is beautiful, from the revolution to women and all that in between." He saw her smile at his bouquet but without any hesitancy now. She planted a rose in her coal black hair. Her innocent face was tinted with the same red color as the roses so that you could not tell the difference between them. The similarity astonished him; he smiled out of happiness and wonder!

In mid-April, the decision was made for him to leave the damned Sakinah's house. She had created a tumult in the quarter with her questions about the strange nature of her tenants who were never seen. The assault campaign was finally terminated, and new arrangements were being made. He was eager for the coming work, so as to rebuild what had been destroyed. He would make a comeback. The confrontations of 1985 had left a deep impression on him, strengthening his belonging, and enhancing his conviction about the need to protect himself behind the walls of his safe house. He would return, having established and enacted for himself the basis for his religious trinity. The time for laying low was over. It was now time to resume his activities. He decided to leave a souvenir for the damned Sakinah before his departure. After returning her possessions to the two rooms and locking them back up, he took ashes from one cigarette, mixed them with water, smeared the black mixture on his finger and wrote on the inside of the eastern door: "**Death to the damned Sakinah –K.**" He opened the door and took with him what he had brought three months earlier: his papers, his packs of cigarettes, his red prayer beads, and his suitcase. Apart from that, he was departing carrying his memories.

It was seven in the evening. His sun had entered her house not knowing that in the morning she would miss that partly drawn curtain and the smile behind it. He looked in the direction of her kitchen as he crossed the pebble-covered entrance going towards the dirt passageway leading to the street.

To whom will you smile after this day,
maiden of the sun and the spring? He

who stood behind the curtain is leaving, traveling is his life. I will forever carry your smile and your red flower with me. You carry the image of the "bearded stranger," standing at his kitchen window. Just an image, no more.

He walked along the dirt passageway leaving the house of the damned Sakinah behind him and, with it, the smile of the sun-maiden and the spring. He said to himself as he walked, in an audible voice: "Well, Fayad, what similarity is there between you and me? Like you, I now have a window-maiden! Will my ending be like yours as well? To be arrested with the party's printing press?" He walked, not looking back, just forward.

Chapter 7

A white sneaker stopped at his head. Through the slightly dislodged blindfold, Kan'an could see the front of the shoe near his head.

He is probably looking at me. There is nothing here that he could be looking for.

It was an Adidas, of good quality. The sneaker was not talking, only looking. It appeared as though it was satisfying its sadism, enjoying seeing Kan'an lying on his stomach. The forest of combat boots and sneakers and leather shoes were exploring his world-house, searching it room by room, corner to corner. He could still hear the sounds of free-rein vandalism: cupboards destroyed, tables broken, sofas, mattresses and pillows torn apart, walls knocked down and tiles pulled up. They were tearing down the wall in his bedroom that separated his house from his neighbor's. He could hear their wrecking tools leveling it and from his position he glimpsed several combat boots gathered next to him.

What would the neighbors say? Their world was not familiar with his vocabulary. Papers, walls, doors, secret action, cells, organizations, party, disguise, intelligence, deprivation, and hardship, pacing from wall to door. Theirs was a world that sees the Occupation from a distance, at a checkpoint, or upon hearing a curfew order or seeing it on television. They did not live the struggle as he did, hour by hour, rebelling against the Occupation. Like everyone else, they were making money, sleeping, reproducing, eating, visiting, and receiving visitors. Nothing united their world with his. He was always observing them from his window or his balcony. Many would consider their world as natural, but he did not see it that way: life under the Occupation's shadow is unusual. He saw his own life as natural compared to theirs. It is not natural for a people to live under occupation as their normal way of life. It not only contradicts the logic of things, but, with time, will also become a danger to the people themselves. His neighbors excelled at the polite social decorum typical of urban bourgeois circles in the central homeland. They did not keep track of their neighbors' lives, the way those descended from the circles of the popular classes did. They did not thrust themselves into the affairs of their neighbors or monitor whoever is going in or out; they did not act like voyeurs at windows. They were model neighbors for someone living a secret existence, which is why he would remain indebted to them all his life for their decorum.

> *Thank you for your decorum. My apologies to the two little girls whose little hearts were terrorized by the stomping of the soldiers' boots and who were torn away from their beautiful dreams. Astonishment will no doubt tie their tongues when they awaken from the terror of this unique night in their lives. What will they say when they learn what secret was lurking between the walls adjoining their houses?*
>
> *"Incomprehensible!" they might say. "All this time between the walls near us and without our knowledge? The same Kan'an who disappeared years ago appears now in our neighborhood? Is it plausible? What is this? Is it credible? What is going on?"*

Indeed, it is plausible! For the sake of salvation from the army of boots that terrorized your daughters, everything we revolutionaries do is plausible. If the expulsion of a people is possible then everything that could put an end to this travesty of history at our expense becomes plausible, no matter how mad it seems.

But what would all his neighbors say? The workers making cinder blocks, the iron carriage loaded with small stones of all sorts in the floor tile factory, the dairy factory workers, the annoying dogs at the barley mill, the people in the unfinished house across from him, the men and women working at the chocolate factory whom he watches as they spend their lunch hours walking in the rear courtyard behind the factory . . . What would everyone he knows say: his family, his acquaintances, his schoolmates, his comrades, his friends, the inhabitants of the city, and his mother! What would his mother say?

She had visited him a week earlier, carrying her bundles, her longing for him, her kisses, her streams of interrogatory questions, her reprimands. "Why didn't you clean the fridge? Son, your ashtrays are garbage dumps. Cleaning them only takes a minute. Why don't you have meat? Be prepared for any emergency. How long has it been since you cleaned the windows? How is the sun supposed to get in? Be quiet and hand me the cinnamon so I can make you *haytaliye!** Look at this picture of little Kan'an. How cute he is! He has learned to say 'I am like uncle Kan'an.'"

She had transported him to her world. He was happy to surrender to the delightful narcotic of her motherliness. They had lunch and she had left after emphasizing a handful of instructions at the door. What would his mother say? She would be both scared and happy at

---

* A type of milk pudding consumed in the Levant and nearby regions.

his arrest. She would fear him being in their hands, but she would be happy that this stage is ending and that he can come out at last, and perhaps she might finally rejoice to see him as a father one day soon. Her happiness would not push her fears aside nor will her fears dominate over her happiness. She too would live her own contradictions.

> *The secret is out now and the veil has been lifted, the stage curtain has been raised and the viewers will see the actor whose fate they have been asking about for so long.*

> *But first, let everyone remember what they said nine years earlier when you turned your back on life and chose resistance and disappeared. Do you remember what you heard and how you responded?*

> *"This guy is crazy! He is crazy!"*

> *The revolution is madness. Without the madness of the revolution and its adventures you will never be liberated.*

> *"He is deserting his mother, his fiancée, and his university. Does the issue merit all of that?"*

> *It does merit it. It does! I have placed the nation above myself, should I then also not put it ahead of my mother and my fiancée?*

"One, two, three years he will spend in prison. Then he will come out and everything will be over. What need is there for all of this?"

You do not understand what is essential. You are only capable of grasping the superficialities. Learn to plunge deeper and you will understand. Learn to look where the finger is pointing, not at the dirt under the fingernail. Look beyond the tips of your noses.

"No doubt now he has arranged an academic scholarship for himself in a socialist country."

Petty people can only see petty things like themselves. It is hard for a small person to imagine a big project.

"He is no doubt in Lebanon with the fedayeen or in Moscow with the communists."

Your imagination is bigger than God's mercy.

"He has revealed his true nature, as an instigator of high school students and facilitator of demonstrations. He has turned his back on the resistance and fled abroad."

Idiots and limited intellects. Your standards are limited. Prison or flight, isn't there anything else?

"Is he behaving like a man? He gets engaged to the daughters of good people and then leaves them and runs! If he has chosen politics, he should not embroil people's daughters along with him. It is either politics or marriage!"

Is that the only choice before me? That I should lead my life and make my choices based on the conclusions and gossip of the elderly? In many cases, were revolutionaries to follow naïve and foolish public opinions, history would not move one millimeter forward. If so, then the student should attend to his studies, the woman to her kitchen and to the pleasures of her husband, the father to the task of providing food for his children, the mother to gathering her daughters under her wings. Public opinion has defined everyone's responsibilities for them. Who will make the revolution then? Who will drive history forward? Martians perhaps?

You would have defeated your inner self had you responded this way to the gossip of those who knew you at the time. Few were the ones who maybe, just maybe, understood your game and

*the game of your party and buried
what they understood in their hearts.*

What annoyed him most was the behavior of the elderly and their never-ending chatter throughout the first five years. He vanished from sight, so they discredited his name. But when they had almost forgotten about him, Muna officially broke off their engagement, and so his name found its way back to their lips. They had barely stopped chattering when Muna got engaged to the "Man with a Position" and they remembered Kan'an's story, heaping disrepute on his name once more. Then she got married, so they repeated what they had grown accustomed to saying until they were finally silenced.

He was not so much bothered by their judgements of what had happened as he was bothered that his name continued to be repeated at gatherings in gossip. His mother used to report to him what was being said. Internally she was saying the same things to herself, but in front of him she relayed what was being said with feigned objectivity. His secret rule was that his name should be withdrawn from circulation once and for all, like a currency that the state has withdrawn from the market. The party followed the same rule. Whoever among party members asked about him verbally or in writing would receive the same reply: "We know nothing about this name." The party informed him of that and he was pleased.

His arrest now changed things, it revealed and uncovered, it implanted a position, a seedling, which remained under the control of the party, it consolidated a conception that had been kept secret, it educated through an experience that had remained secret—perhaps that is the sole benefit of the arrest.

❈ ❈ ❈ ❈ ❈

After Kan'an left the cursed Sakinah's house, he moved to a house at the southern edge of Al-Bireh, adjacent to the land belonging to the village and refugee camp of Qalandia. It was in a new sector where the streets had not yet been paved but which was being rapidly invaded by new constructions. He chose for himself an apartment on the second floor of a two-story building owned by a man and his family, and it had all the necessary characteristics. The landlord is more important than the specifications of the house itself, and the man was the ideal one for someone living a secret life. Umm 'Isa and the cursed Sakinah turned life into hell for the person in disguise, affecting his stability and inner tranquility. On the other hand, a landlord like the one who owned the fig orchard or the one who owned this newest arrangement was tailor-made for the unique experience—it was almost as if these landlords had been individually selected and brought forth by fate to suit the needs of the man in hiding. Through their conduct, they created an atmosphere that relaxed the person in hiding and contributed to their success.

The owner of the apartment was an old man over sixty who wore thick Coke-bottle glasses and walked with a stoop, probably as a result of old age. The white *kuffiyeh* which he wore during the summer and winter covered his forehead all the way down to his eyeglasses. He could barely make out who was renting his house or who was standing in front of him or who was going up or down the steps as he sat in front of his house. If he managed to raise his head, his eyes failed to come to his aid. His wife had the good nature of a peasant who could never be tainted by owning "private property," even though the property in question consisted of four rented apartments which were in relatively good shape by Al-Bireh standards.

The old woman treated the tenants of her apartments the way she treated her children. Hardly a week passed by in which she did not put in front of every apartment what she could from the produce of her small garden behind the house: mint, parsley, radishes, and green onions. Whenever he heard her clamor at the door to his apartment, he would look through the peephole and see her putting down her present; he would remember his mother and her bundles, for she too would bring her bundles from time to time—some strongly-scented rural mint, a must with tea.

When he entered his new house in 1986, he found that the old woman had cleaned it well, the doors, the floor, the bathroom, the balcony windows. Once he discovered the nature of the old woman on the first day, he discovered a truth that he had missed for the last four months: there is more than one sort of old person in the world and this sort was quite different from the accursed Sakinah. He took a quick tour of the rooms to familiarize himself with his house and environment. To the east there were two houses, one three stories high and the other a single floor. To the north he could see from his kitchen window a narrow balcony belonging to the neighboring apartment.

The following morning, he had barely glanced out of his kitchen window after breakfast when he was appalled at what he saw, a human face of unparalleled ugliness. The face looked like it was composed of clumps of flesh that were hurriedly stuck together without skill and without differentiation among its parts: the nostrils, the nose, the mouth and the chin were all intermingled without clear divisions. A face that was nothing more than a bag of flesh! *How horrible the works of nature can be at times. What sort of face is that? It is as though it had gone through a nuclear explosion.* The meaty face quickly withdrew from the balcony, perhaps out of fear of being envied?! He lamented: *I left the face of the young woman in the window, the sun-and-spring maiden only to be greeted in the morning by this nuclear face?* From then on, the name of his neighbor became "the one with the nuclear face." She would not be mentioned in his den by any other title. The next time he saw her was also in the morning, at eight o'clock. This time she had painted her face with an incredible amount of makeup. The fleshy face was like a mural made by a handful of mischievous children who had amused themselves by spraying paint on the wall haphazardly. As soon as she saw him, she recoiled in embarrassment. Kan'an smiled and thought, *You will not be my sun-maiden even if you were the only woman left in the world.*

After those two encounters Kan'an insisted on not being accommodating with her. He had decided that his window should be curtainless. Let her refrain from going out on her balcony out of shyness—he would not deprive himself of the sun out of consideration for her modesty. The other flat adjoining his was the residence of two brothers married to two sisters along with their children. He had not had an occasion to see either of the two families until a wintery night at one o'clock in the morning. He was watching an Arabic film when there was fierce knocking on the door to the apartment.

"Open! Army! Open, open!"

In mere seconds, the flames of the portable heater had devoured the few papers he had at the time. The tension he was under reached its zenith and questions pounded the cells of his brain. *What brought them here? I did not hear the sound of their cars or trucks. They could not have come on foot for there was no sound around the house.* The pounding and calls were continuous. He was transfixed in place for a moment, then he moved to the glassed-in balcony and looked behind the house, seeing no trace of them. Then the knocking stopped. *I would die to know what is going on! What are these games? They come, they knock on the door, they yell, then they leave, just like that, in less than five minutes? Are the Occupation authorities playing games with the people now?*

The questions that he could not answer were killing him. There is nothing harsher on a revolutionary than the creeping of unknowns into his head, for he feels like a toy being played with in the hands of a ridiculous destiny. He went back and sat down in front of the TV. It was the month of Ramadan and the TV broadcast continued until dawn. In keeping with his habit, he did not fall asleep until after the broadcast ended. In fact, he would wait for Ramadan each year to watch the month's special TV series, films, and programs with the joy of a child. But he was not following the film even though his eyes were fixed on the screen. His thoughts were anxious and agitated, darting here and there without settling on anything. At five in the morning, he dozed off a little and then got up at seven thirty. *I must find out what happened yesterday. There must be a way to strike up a conversation with one of the two sisters.* On almost every sunny day he would hear the voice of one of the sisters as she went up to the roof to hang up the family's laundry to dry. He took a few items of clean clothing, wet them, and arranged them in a washing basin. At eight o'clock he heard the door of the sisters' apartment open. The morning foretold a sunny day. He looked through the peephole and saw one of them going up to the roof so he hurried and followed her and found her hanging the children's clothes up to dry.

"Good morning, neighbor. I live in the apartment next to you."

"Good morning," she answered, the surprise of seeing her neighbor for the first time in months was visible on her face. She was not apprehensive or shy about his presence, which he was relieved by because it meant he could ask her questions. "Let's just hope today will remain sunny so that the laundry dries. On the news they said that today would be clear. A family with children like ours must wash every day. What can we do? That's how it is."

She was receptive to talking to him, unusual for a traditional woman when meeting a man who she does not know.

"I woke up last night to sounds of shouting which I didn't understand. I hope all's well. Did the sounds come from your apartment or the other one?"

Fortunately for him, she was true to the ingrained habit of traditional women: gossiping. She quickly unburdened herself of everything she had to say as she laughed, trying to apologize for what she was about to reveal.

"Oh! You heard the noise. It is our fault, neighbor. My husband's younger brother, that rascal, came to have *suhur** with us, and he felt like playing a prank on us by imitating the sounds the army makes. Oh! You heard. It's our fault, neighbor." She laughed. "We have no interest in politics, and we were expecting him around one o'clock. Forgive us, neighbor. He disturbed the whole building. We

---

* The Ramadan meal eaten before dawn.

laughed a lot. Well, I guess we woke you up for *suhur* with us so you must have *futur** at our place one day to make it up to you."

She laughed again while Kan'an suppressed an overwhelming desire to pick her up and throw her off the top of the building and break her bones. He put on a smile with difficulty.

"No problem. I just wanted to make sure everything is alright, neighbor to neighbor," he said.

"May God reward you. It's our fault. We weren't scared—"

"No problem, neighbor," he interrupted. She was continuing with her news broadcast. "No harm done."

Kan'an quickly turned and went down the stairs to his apartment. His apartment was large and sparsely furnished. He had only furnished the room that he used as an office and bedroom while the other rooms remained empty, so it was natural for loud knocking on the door of the adjacent flat to echo in his apartment as though it were knocking on his door. He had wasted his papers and the repose of the night and the serenity of his nerves, all that because the younger brother had to play a prank on his brothers. Their horseplay had cost him a lot. Once again, he remembered his mother's prayer that he had taken with him since 1982 and had heard her repeat each day: "Go, my son, may God be pleased with you." His neighbors—people in general—had their lives, their amusements, their horseplay. He had *his* life in which there was neither amusements nor horseplay.

❖❖❖❖❖

The attack on the party and its institutions continued until April 1986, ending with the tearing down of the party organization at Birzeit University. Up to that point it had been a favorite arm of the party due to its solid foundation and productivity, its rearing of a handful of revolutionary cadres, and its influential position in student political and syndical activities, in addition to its friendly

---

*   The meal eaten at sunset to break the Ramadan fast.

democratic organization. The party organization at Birzeit had a prominent influence outside the university, whether at the level of agitation and propaganda through its publication of *Al-Taqaddum* newspaper—a specialized student monthly which was distributed at educational institutions—or through its formation of party branches and extensions among the masses in various areas of the homeland. Later on, these extensions were to be used by the party to build more cells and to expand.

The party began to pump new blood into the arteries of its activities. A year of daily clashes with the Occupation and its intelligence agency had stiffened the backbone of many cadres and members, cultivating fertile ground for rebuilding what had been destroyed. Committees whose members had been arrested were restored and new cadres were produced to rebuild the organizations that had been liquidated. Neither the networks of friendly circles nor the democratic organizations for workers and students had been hurt. Thus, the party was able to take on a new expansion campaign to rebuild its organizations using these relationships. In areas where party organizations had been liquidated completely or paralyzed in their political and popular role, the democratic organizations took over such that they became instruments of the party in their activities, speaking on its behalf among the masses.

The expansion was based on a directive: "**The response to an arrest shall be further party expansion!**" This was stated in several letters and leaflets to committees, organizations, and individuals. Following the period after the attack, the party began issuing statements which would serve as a compass for all future party activities: political, organizational, security, and public relations statements. These statements gave detailed analyses of the circumstances of work in the four spheres and united the tangible tasks for each sphere so that all of the efforts of party organizations would be dedicated towards them.

Naturally, the differences in the levels of experience, structure, and maturity of the organizations were reflected in the performance of each organization's tasks in the new period, not to mention the extent of its response. The Gaza organization was not yet able to stand on its own feet, for each courageous and daring attempt on its part was quickly liquidated by the intelligence agencies. Meanwhile, the Ramallah organization was in the lead in terms of experience, structure, and maturity. The attack ended, and with it, the boisterous claims of the intelligence service inside the interrogation rooms—that 1985 would witness the liquidation of the party—were discredited. The prominent Israeli military commentator Ze'ev Schiff admitted that the expectations of the Occupation authorities, which he himself had been convinced by at the beginning of the attack campaign, were illusions: "We thought that the 1985 blow would liquidate the Popular Front, but we now find that its influence is increasing."

The party estimated, at the height of the attack campaign, that the damage it suffered had set it back two years. By the end of 1986, however, it was clear that its structure had been rebuilt more quickly than the initial estimate, and that it possessed the power and dynamism which enabled it to enter the battles of the following year with a clear force at the national level. During the 1987 local elections, the party was able to maintain its influence, and in other cases make important gains on some of the institutions. For example, the party reaffirmed its status as the second power in Bethlehem University and was recognized as the most powerful force in the electricity company's elections. In the Palestinian Red Crescent elections, the party received 1,700 votes which translated to 37 percent of the votes cast. However, the most prominent battle at the public level was the Birzeit University elections which were held at the beginning of 1987.

For the first time in the history of the party's presence at the university it faced a united opposition. It entered the elections as a single bloc facing a coalition of three national blocs and a single Islamic bloc. The party decided to work on enhancing the prestige and influence of the organization and its bloc even though it had not yet had adequate time to recover following the painful blow it received eight months earlier. It was clear there was no chance that the party's bloc would win, however there was an opportunity to demonstrate its influence. In the wake of the long and bitter attack on the party by the Occupation authorities, demonstrating the party's continued influence would have a large effect on the morale of the party's base and friendly forces. The university elections had always had an influence that extended beyond the university itself. It was invariably considered a barometer of the mood of the general public despite the imperfect nature of this measurement. Consequently, it was a way of influencing the formation of coalitions and tactics in other institutions, not to mention the media buzz that surrounded these elections. The university held a venerable standing in Palestinian society due to the prominent national role it played and its position amidst a wide network of international institutions.[19] Therefore, the party mobilized the weight of its organizations and certain individuals in this election, Kan'an being one of them.

Kan'an considered this battle to be his battle, given that the tradition of the party at the university had been an important part of his political formation. He felt that the most successful response to the attack on the organization would be a frank letter to the intelligence services titled "Your Attack Had No Effect on Us!" He had written many letters and circulars on behalf of the party to committees, members, and the friendly base. "You promised the party that you would secure four hundred votes," he wrote to his comrades. "We will not accept one vote less, otherwise move to Jordan and never return to the homeland," a tongue-in-cheek message to underscore the gravity of the battle. He wrote and wrote and never tired. He formulated dozens of directives, instructions, and words of advice, squeezing everything he could out of his years of experience in dealing with student activities and placed it all before them. He argued tactics, mobilization, agitation, and issues of party-political significance, even technical issues of electoral battles, slogans, stickers, festivals, and propaganda. He knew that the sense of being in the "minority," with successful mobilization, could be used to create a great deal of energy and dynamism. His comrades accepted the challenge and, addressing the party, upped the ante in the challenge: "Four hundred and thirty votes. Otherwise, we will submit our resignations from the party."

On the day of the electoral battle Kan'an was restless. He was unable to do anything in his den. He would pace and sit, he tried to pass the time any way he could, but his mind was at the university. He asked his comrades to see to it that the results would reach him the minute they were available, although he knew they would not come out before eleven at night. He waited and the anxiety drove him mad.

The news came at midnight. The party bloc had won 480 seats but lost 20 for technical reasons, overall constituting 24 percent of all votes cast. It was a massive victory for which the party rejoiced in the homeland. The electoral battle at the university had just ended when the party's organizations found themselves engaged in a different sort of battle in March of that year, that of supporting the struggle of prisoners in West Bank prisons who had declared a hunger strike demanding improved conditions.

The struggle of prisoners has a special impact on a person. It is a struggle where the simplest things for an ordinary person—air, water, food, medicine—must be paid for in blood. Men are martyred for the sake of an extra half hour of outdoor recreation; the prisoner's intestines twist in knots from the pain of hunger for extra minutes to the visits from his mother, wife, or son. Emaciated prisoners suffer from illnesses associated with hunger strikes— weak bones, hair falling out, the loss of teeth—all in order to have hot water to bathe in, or to kiss and embrace their child during the semi-monthly visits, or to be allowed to bring in oil or soap or cigarettes, or so that they can keep their academic notebooks, or so that they can get hold of those books in the first place, or so that they are not condemned to isolation for demanding their rights. Things that are trivial or paltry or routine to a non-prisoner can become an aspiration and objective in prison, requiring heroism, sacrifice, or martyrdom. Imprisonment and a clandestine existence both transform the ordinary into a dearly desired ambition. The prisoner is subject to the coercion and repression of the jailor, and has no alternative but to follow the tried-and-true path to secure his desires. The one living a secret life is under the compulsion of secrecy, its "**measures, precautions, requirements, and rules**," so that he has no choice but to follow the tried-and-true path, namely "suppressing the ego and its needs and desires."

No sooner had the strike been declared than the entire nationalist movement—including the party with its branches and extensions in universities, cities, rural areas, and refugee camps—became deeply involved in a campaign of solidarity with the prisoners, although it realized that whatever it could do as a national movement and party would fall short of securing the prisoners their rights and would not end the historic calamity that has befallen them. Resistance activities against the Occupation, sit-ins at Red Cross headquarters, demonstrations, marches, public gatherings, celebrations, and appeals to legal human rights organizations . . . All this went on for the duration of the thirty-day strike until some of the demands were met.

The organizations were strengthened by the clashes in the streets. Along with their political and communal activities, these daily acts of resistance helped them to expand, gain new members, and establish new cells which grew, formed cadres, and became party organizations. On another front, the democratic organizations grew and expanded to new locations, developing their institutional structures and holding conferences; eventually they became a network which served as an arm of the party and threw its weight into another important battle: the popular movement against the siege of the people and fighters in Lebanon by the AMAL Movement from 1986 to 1987.[20]

The Occupied Territories were on fire in 1987. As one battle with the Occupation authorities ended another began, but the revolution was regaining its unity which had been torn by the February 1984 agreement.[21] The Unifying National Council was convened, further reviving popular morale and thus intensifying the battles. Meanwhile public sentiment sensed the Arab and international neglect of the Palestinian issue, further proven by the "Harmony and Agreement" Arab summit in Amman[22] and the meeting of the Soviet and American giants in Sydney, Australia. Despite all that, the political circular issued in July 1987 by the homeland branch of the party determined that the homeland "was sitting on a cauldron which could explode at any moment."

❖❖❖❖❖

In the midst of this turmoil and these changes, Kan'an's tasks expanded and became bifurcated. He struggled and moved from place to place, holding meetings and making contacts. The events did not kill his tranquil spirit that year, except for an encounter one day in November 1987. On that rainy day after the conclusion of a meeting, he was moving from one safe house to another in a car, moving slowly in heavy traffic and rain along the main Ramallah–Jerusalem road near the Shurfa quarter. Kan'an was closely examining the passersby, the passengers, the people standing in front of their stores—peering closely in the hopes of seeing someone he recognized. It was at that moment he saw her.

At the intersection of the main road, which had a side street leading to her family's house, he spied Muna sitting next to the "Man with a Position." He had stopped his car, waiting for his turn to cross the street. She was wearing a heavy winter coat and wiping her nose with a tissue while the "Man with a Position" looked straight ahead. Kan'an looked at her with his mouth agape, sinking his gaze into her as though he wanted to devour her. She had stopped wiping her nose. He looked at her (*Did she recognize whom she was looking at? Did she recognize me, could she tell it was me?*), heart racing, privately happy, not turning his face away from her even for a second! He had grown a beard and was wearing different prescription glasses than the ones she knew. Did she recognize him? He could not tell. They were looking at each other while Mr. Man with a Position was looking to his left hoping to slip through to the main street. Kan'an's heart almost burst as he looked at her. He wanted to jump out of the car, go to her, break the head of the

Man with a Position, and snatch her away to his safe house, to his world! He knew he could not carry out his foolish wish and sighed. His car moved on and the scene changed.

For days after, a sense of anger never left him. He paced from wall to wall—not as he would when contemplating quietly and deliberately as was his custom for many years—but, this time, in pain. Feeling defeated, he cursed everything he encountered: the walls, the doors, the books . . . He cursed with all of the words in his vocabulary. Seeing her face destroyed his composure. What a coincidence! Why did chance conspire against him so that on the one time he saw her in five years, her husband was beside her? He saw her not as his dearly beloved, but as the wife of another man. Why did chance not present her walking by herself in front of his house? He might then have violated all the rules governing his life . . . Who knows? He might have shelved the law of "don't receive anyone" and received her for hours. In the final analysis, she was not just "anyone." She was Muna. Who knows?

The last time he saw her she told him, "I can't. I can't." Now when he saw her with him, he wondered: "Is this what she can do?" And what is that in the final analysis? Becoming the wife of so-and-so, officially appended to him as a subordinate by the marriage contract, with a limited role in life. No special place for her. She became like any wife—known by her man and not for her achievements. She is the *haram*,* the sacrosanct possession of so-and-so according to the Egyptian expression. He remembered her sentence which almost made him lose his self-control: "You must decide, either me or the party." Could he have replied any other way than how he did, decisively? "You have a choice and I have a choice." Definitely not! He had continued replaying the tape of that memory for the last five years.

> *But is it not possible to postpone a categorical response? Perhaps to give*

---

*   *Haram* is a word in Arabic that means sacrosanct possession and is used to describe someone's wife.

myself and to give her another chance at dialogue? Wasn't my rupture of relations then a reflection of the level of my maturity at the time? If that dialogue were to take place today, if I could go back armed with my present level of awareness, would I have dealt with the situation as I did? Could the result have been better? Did I give my love for her a chance to continue, to live on, or did I give it a fatal blow, the coup de grâce, out of compassion for myself and for her?

Many questions buzzed around in his head like a bees' in their nest as he paced from one wall to the other, as he stretched out in bed, as he ate . . . remembering her face, her features, everything about their last meeting, her words many years ago. He cursed his circumstances and the complications of his resistance many times and tried hard to forget that meeting—assuming it was even possible to forget.

A year later he had to leave the house. Construction had expanded in the quarter, which came to be known as *'Ain Umm Al-Sharayet* to the extent that it had encroached on the outer limits of Al-Am'ari Refugee Camp. As such, the quarter had become afflicted with the same ailments as the toiling youth of the nearby camp: traps were set for patrols, which were showered with stones and Molotov cocktails; slogans were written on the walls; crowds chanted and burned tires. The quarter became one of the hotbeds of activity in the city, and the military patrolled it day and night. For all these reasons, he decided not to give chance an opportunity to ambush him.

Chapter 8

The shoe moving in front of his face tore him away from Muna and their last encounter. The shoe turned right. His eyes could now furtively glimpse it. *(Where is the shoe looking? What is it doing? There is nothing on the wall except for a straw plate woven by a skilled peasant woman using the leftovers from the wheat harvest. Is the shoe studying that? There is no furniture in that corner for it to tear apart or destroy. So what does the shoe want by standing like this over my head?)*

    A voice from above his head announced the white shoe's purpose: it was fooling around with the tapes of music and songs which had kept Kan'an company for years. He could not have survived without music and song—life is meaningless without them. Even early man had barely learned to walk upright before he started beating on drums and conversing with nature through music. Some tapes were fairly quiet, others were loud and boisterous—tapes of Sheikh Imam, Marcel Khalife, Fairuz, Magda Al-Rumi, Sabah Fakhri, and 'Abdel Halim Hafiz which he listened and sang along to as he paced from the wall to the door, or as he reclined on the sofa on the balcony, or as he walked on the roof of the house at night, or while cooking, reading, writing, or as he sat on the couch. He would listen and listen, becoming relaxed and chasing away the fatigue of his body and nerves. Singing and music never stopped in his safe house, and he could not imagine himself living without them. The shoe was opening and closing the cassettes. *(Can the shoe read Arabic? Unlikely. So what does it want? Is it really searching over there? Does it expect to find a cache of arms inside the cassette box? Or a stack of secret newspapers and printed material? Or perhaps some third thing hidden in the cassette between the wheel and the tape wrapped around it?)* The shoe opened the cassette player, Kan'an heard the click of the play button.

> "Between Rita and my eyes, there is a gun
> and those who know Rita
> kneel down and pray
> to the god of her honey-coloured eyes"

Oh, Marcel!—Oh, Darwish! Oh, Palestine's Homer!

> "and I kissed Rita
> when she was young
> and I remember how
> she clung to me and I was covered
> from my shoulder with the most beautiful braid
>
> "and I remember Rita
> like a bird remembers a brook"

For the first and definitely last time Kan'an thanked the intelligence officer, the one he knew not by his face but by his shoe! He thanked him for transporting him to the magical world of poetry. The shoe stopped the tape and resumed fooling around with the recorder, so he cursed it. Kan'an waited for a burst of sound. The shoe pressed the play button:

> "All the hearts of the people are my nationality
> So take away my passport"

Kan'an rejoiced. It was a song that transported him to another day, another time, another circumstance. He forgot the pain caused by the shoe pressing down on his face and the bleeding from his left eyebrow that was staining the tiles.

❈ ❈ ❈ ❈ ❈

It was 10:30 a.m. when Kan'an finished his morning exercises and had breakfast. Eggplant fried in local olive oil and covered with a layer of wine-colored sumac. He sat in the room adjacent to the iron door with his legs stretched out on the small table. He picked up one of his novels, the three-part *And Quiet Flows the Don* by Sholokhov, and lost himself in the world of its protagonists: Grigory, the rebel who repeatedly changes sides from Bolshevik to Menshevik and back, a man with noble sentiments, who however held on to the small private property of the peasantry; Aksinia, the wife of Grigory's neighbor, who is led by lust in her love not for her husband, but for Grigory; Pyotr and Darya, who are anti-Bolshevik to the core, all to defend a plot of land, their private property; the father of Grigory and Pyotr, the reactionary peasant with Turkish blood in his veins, and the one who sought to tempt his daughter-in-law Darya; Dina, who is passionately in love with the communist youth, Victor—a poor impoverished worker.

He lost himself in the novel, while nearby Marcel sang the poems of Mahmoud Darwish with his deep, breathtaking voice. He had begun reading the novel for the second time, enjoying it, but vexed by the fact that he had been unable to lay his hands on the fourth and last volume; he had waited for it for years and was always asking his comrades about it. One question intrigued him: How far did Grigory get in his fluctuations between the revolution and its enemies? Kan'an roamed the vast steppes of the Don with Sholokhov, fighting the December cold and its rains and raging winds. His mother used to sum up December's well-known weather in a popular saying: "The cold of December and January kills the lizards, cover yourself well, your house is large and cold." Despite his best efforts, Kan'an never reconciled with December, or with winter in general, in his secret life. He hated its arrival. He finished the section where Grigory and Aksinia achieved a few moments of secret delight atop a haystack, defying the sword of the Cossacks which never dulled. He contemplatively put the book aside as the sound of droplets of rain pecking on the windowpane took him back, despite himself, to the memories of December.

Oh, December, what an effect it has had on my life. In that month a French midwife pulled my head out of my mother's womb and announced the birth of a new life—do I consider this a good event?! What sort of silly and meaningless question is that? I was born again in December when I found my way to revolutionary political action—a turning point in my life! In that month, the party to which I have dedicated my youth was formed. I was reborn a third time in December when I began my secret life and clandestine existence. The course of my life changed once more when, in December 1985, I was tested with hardship and challenge in the months of the comprehensive attack—the months spent in the villa of the damned Sakinah, when I formulated my trinitarian religion, my trinity of fundamentals!

Am I the child of my parents or the child of December? That would make me the Son of Rain and Wind and Clouds and Snow, like a Native American? Perhaps my name corresponds to one of their names. It is as though the books of fate had recorded my name and my life at the top of one of its pages: "Kan'an Subhi— important changes in the months of December and January!" Is the date of my death also recorded as December? It is as though fate placed December as a womb in the course of my life: in my first birth, December presented me as a sperm; in the second as a blood clot; in the third as an embryo; and subsequent Decembers will be responsible for seeing to it that my bones become clothed with flesh. December will continue to give birth to me. For how long will December continue to shape me? When will my bones be clothed with flesh? Are the party and December in agreement that one gives directions and the other carries them out?

Despite all of that, Kan'an of flesh and blood, tucked away between the walls, despised December and winter, and as a man leading a clandestine life, he had good cause for this hatred. As soon as he woke up at 9:00 or 9:30 a.m., he struggled with an overwhelming desire to stay in bed and enjoy the warmth. But he would rise, work out on his exercise bike and have breakfast afterward. Then he worked for two or three hours, had lunch, and then practiced his ingrained habit of napping for an hour after lunch. After waking from what he called his "afternoon sweetener," he would resume work. By then the counterfeit winter day would be on the retreat, having been kicked in the buttocks by the early January night. No sooner did the shy sun rise at whatever hour on whichever day than it was obscured again by clouds, hiding like a thief as though it were the black sheep of the winter family. Closed windows, heating, kerosene, damp cigarettes, restrictive clothing, heavy woolen coverings, a large and sparsely furnished house whose corners were inhabited by a surly cold, the torture of preparing food and washing pots and clothes, not being able to see passersby, the disappearance of the color green from sight—all these made him feel twice a prisoner, of his secret life and of winter.

But Kan'an enjoyed two pleasures dear to his heart during winter. The first was to slip under the woolen bed covers early and read a novel for hours on end, forgetting that he was living in wintertime. The second was drinking a glass of Latroun wine with lunch. It was hard to imagine one without the other: the way a woman's breasts precede her to announce that she is approaching, the appearance of winter signaled to him it was time for Latroun wine. Once he drank a cup, he would remember his mother. He used to return home from the university between five and six in the evening and find her putting the pot of food on the kerosene heater so that his meal would stay hot the way he liked it. They would eat lunch together and he would have a cup of wine in a ceramic cup as though they were in the Middle Ages. Once, Kan'an had commented innocently about his frustration at having to eat alone, so his mother changed her well-entrenched, decades-long habit of eating lunch at noon and would wait for him to return from the university in the early evening. What is a mother? She is a human being who is hard to describe no matter how well-armed we are with the riches of language and literary forms, a human who always offers her love for free, demanding nothing in return. Even now in his secret life he didn't miss out on the joys of a wintertime glass of wine with his mother, for she would save him some and bring it to him every time she came to visit.

Kan'an thought about December as he sat there with a closed book in his hand, remembering his mother and how he missed kissing the wrinkles on her cheeks and playing with her hair. Apart from his two winter rituals, there was nothing he liked about the season. *Why couldn't nature have organized its laws and operating system so that the whole year would be like April and May? Did it have to transform my life into a prison within a prison?*

He protested in these moments of resentment against winter and improvised his own "astrological calculations" to console himself, calculations which were as weird as his life. "October carries the scent of summer and is not troubling. November does not really count as a winter month for it brings neither plentiful rain nor raging winds and still contains some residue of the smell of summer. Many farmers harvest their olives during November. As for December, it is a month of work and festivities as it marks the launching of the party. One does not feel the passing of the days in December. That leaves January, where a few days pass and one finds themself at the end of the month—it reaches its end after barely starting. February is truly full of thunder yet it carries the hint of summer's eventual arrival, no sooner is it over than spring arrives with March and its sun and the blooming of roses and red poppies. In sum, winter is over quickly."

Such was his laughable calendar that he used to draw strength from in his battle against winter and the depressive episodes it brought. Those who heard them remarked, "So there is no winter in our country according to your astrological calculations!"

"If I did not calculate things this way, the son of a bitch called winter would spell my end. As soon as winter arrives, depression overcomes me."

The days of winter dragged on, and his calculations were expelled, tossed to the side, axed once and for all by *Al-Marbaa'niyat** and their calamities. February, the *khabbat*,** does carry the scent of summer, but the month essentially brings lightning and thunder. February addresses its cousin, March: "Oh, cousin, three from you and four from me will make the old woman in the valley with her sheep sing." March, despite its sunny days and the blooming of roses and red poppies, is still the month of "the seven large snowstorms."

---

* In traditional Palestinian culture, *Al-Marbaa'niyat* (literally translated as "the forties" in Arabic) refers to the first forty days of winter, which are typically the harshest days, starting from December 22 and ending on January 31.

** *Khabbat*, which means "the slam" or "the clap," refers to the month of February which usually has thunderstorms accompanied by loud sounds.

December of that year, however, decided to bring joy rather than sadness in Kan'an. It promised him happiness in its early days. December 1987 was an entry in the record of the Palestinian people in the Book of Fate, which is somewhere with Him who watches over human beings for eternity. Kan'an turned his gaze away from the windowpane on which raindrops were landing and he left Grigory and Aksinia to ponder over the solution to their love problem among the Cossacks, who had a tradition of wiping their lips with the flat edge of a sword dipped in blood. He turned up the volume of the radio to hear the twelve o'clock news on the Monte Carlo channel, the reporting announcing in his familiar intonation:

"Massive demonstrations and marches against the Occupation broke out, involving thousands of Palestinians in the Gaza Strip, specifically at the Jabalia Refugee Camp. Israeli forces responded to the demonstrations with live fire and so far an unknown number of victims have fallen."

In the thousands? What is happening? It is true that the situation had been near the boiling point since the beginning of the year, but demonstrations involving thousands—and in a single camp—that is something qualitatively different, a serious development!

He was fixated on the news without knowing what was really going on.

The monumental popular Intifada had decisively broken out. The boiling cauldron which the party had glimpsed in July had exploded. A new prominent event had been born not just in his life, but in the life of the people, and he was experiencing that birth. Two weeks after the outbreak, it was decided that he would move to another safe house. Shortly after sunset that day, he climbed into the car that had been sent to transport him.

"Pray that God protects us," said his comrade, who was driving him, as he put his hand on the ignition. "The side streets are totally closed, cars can't get through them, and the army is not particularly concerned with reopening them. We will have to go through the main streets, they are pretty much the only ones open to traffic. You will see what is happening in the city."

Kan'an was shocked by what he saw. The city was like a ghost town. A few cars passed through the streets in an agitated hurry. He pictured himself as a thief trying to escape, looking around in fear of being caught. Large and small stones carpeted the streets except for paths down the middle which the army had opened to facilitate the passage of its vehicles and to chase the demonstrators, but these paths were not entirely free of stones, so his comrade still had to dodge and weave like an acrobat to get around them—at one point his comrade drove over small stones and later the car's tires passed over the edge of another stone sending it shooting off like a projectile. It was as if he was competing against another driver in an obstacle course. The streets were smeared with soot and the remains of burnt tires, some of which had not been entirely consumed by flames and still held their shape. Young men had begun to paint political and provocative slogans on the walls. Everything he saw was a testimony to the rebellion of the quarters of the city in which he had spent his youth—Manara Square, Sarayyet Ramallah,[23] the Old Quarter, Rukab Street, Abu Iskandar's shawarma shop, Al-Saa'a Square, Al-Jamil Cinema, Qaddura camp, Al-Shurfa Quarter, the Ramallah–Jerusalem Road. They all bore testimony, by the appearance of their streets and quarters and walls, to their rejection of the Occupation.

Kan'an was silent as the car moved from one quarter to the next, attempting to find a path between the stones. All the way, he did not utter a single word or emit a cry of wonder or a comment as he usually did whenever one of his comrades took him for a ride around the city once every few weeks, a tour that used to please him because of how much it elicited memories of days gone by. On those rides, he would disguise himself and go to the street of his family home seeking to catch a glimpse of his mother sitting on the balcony or looking after her flowers before the sunset. He would go to Qaddura camp to remember and lament his old love and to go for a spin in the city center like he used to do with his peers in the mid-1970s, from the street behind Rukab ice cream shop he would turn left to get to the Karam Al-Sausau store, and then from there left again to the Rukab ice cream street, completing the grand tour. Kan'an recalled that whatever could be said in the days of youth was said during walks in that square. He and his peers would buy *ka'ak*[*] with sesame seeds from Al-Khalili at Al-Saa'a Square and continue walking. One would hold a quick organizational meeting, another would walk with his girlfriend, others would engage in debate, yelling and laughing . . . The city was noisy after six in the evening as a result of the commotion made by those touring around the famous square in Ramallah.

He was never able to keep quiet when he went out on these excursions during his secret life. Like a child seeing the sea for the first time who starts to jump up and down, yelling, he would point his finger at every discovery he made:

"Here, on this street, we held secret meetings years ago."

"I broke this barber's shop window in 1976 when the stone I threw missed the patrol. He complained to my father who yelled at me to no avail."

"Look! Look! It's so-and-so. He used to be a member of the party but left before we joined. There is not a hair left on his head," he would laugh raucously.

"Take a detour to the street with the hospital so that I can reminisce," he would ask with a sorrowful smile on his face.

"There's my mother. Look, she is working in the garden. Where is the little one? Why isn't she popping up?"

"Oh my! So this is Ramallah!" he would say upon seeing a boy and a girl walking on the tree-lined street leading to the library, a street which was suitable for all secret relationships.

---

[*] A large, ring-shaped bread with a sesame-seed-crusted exterior and a soft fluffy interior, commonly eaten in Palestine and especially famous in Jerusalem.

"My God! What has become of her after marriage. Do you remember her? At the university all the boys ran after her. Is this what marriage does? She is a living bulldozer!"

Nor did Kan'an forget how the comrade that was driving him around once joked with him: "Look, it's that human variety called 'woman.' Do you remember them or have you forgotten, you poor soul? Summer is here, and this is a variety that is abundant in the summer."

He looked around and saw a slender young woman walking, confident in what she possessed as if she was the only woman on the surface of the earth. He laughed and laughed until his waist hurt.

"Thanks to the party, comrade. Television offers enough of this variety so that the memory of them will not be obliterated."

But today he neither spoke nor shouted out. He just sat silently looking at the stones, the walls, the remnants of tires. He kept his thoughts to himself as the car drove around Al-Saa'a Square.

This is a normal condition for a city
under occupation, anything else would be
forged and not worthy of us as a people.

He arrived at his new house on the main street, near the Al-Am'ari Camp in a rather new quarter called Sateh Marhaba.

"This house isn't perfect, but we'll soon get another one ready for you," said his comrade, turning off the car engine.

The Intifada began to have an impact on his daily life and his resistance activities due to the new tasks, decisions, and mechanisms it required and the party's response. It affected his lifestyle—as a human being and a resistance fighter—as was the case with all the people. The party issued the first memo of directives to him in January 1988. The party deemed it to be the urgent task of party organizations to advance the city's participation and to involve the countryside in the Intifada, for up to that time, the refugee camps appeared to be the only stronghold of the Intifada. The city's participation was ineffective and the countryside was crouching like a lion, waiting, while containing enormous labor potential within it.

The party identified its main political mission by formulating a program of the Intifada's demands that would serve as a fence to protect the Intifada and as a compass to direct its activities. It would also provide a point of entry for mobilizing all classes and groups in society to join in its activities. The program included municipal elections, an end to the confiscation of Palestinian land, the cancellation of the value-added tax, the return of money deducted from the wages of Palestinian workers in Israel, the lifting of restrictions on imports and exports, the freeing of detainees, a halt to the intervention in and closing down of the education system in terms of policies, curriculum, and staffing, and many other demands which were put forward as the demands of the Intifada ...

On the other hand, the state of political thinking had not yet reached the stage where it could raise the ceiling of possible political demands and explore the horizons of the Intifada. These demands might have included international protections, an international conference, the implementation of all UN resolutions relating to Palestine, and finally, the demand for an independent Palestinian state. This latter absence was significant considering "Freedom and Independence" was the organizing banner of the Palestinian people's struggle and that it was the first unified statement signed by the national forces.[24] Inspired by the Algerian revolutionary experience which raised this very phrase in the face of the French colonial project of "self-rule," the party had sought to get this slogan included in the statement.

The party decided to take up the organizational task of safeguarding and repairing its fragmented communications and account for the losses during its period of discontinuity—all while showing full force in the streets, but keeping in mind that this would not be the final battle. The second and more important task was to quickly expand the establishment of organizational forms which would guarantee the energized mobilization of the masses in the future, similar to the early years of armed resistance in Gaza and Jordan following the defeat of 1967. And lastly, it was decided that the efficiency of cadres would be assessed by the speed of their response to the tasks demanded of them by the Intifada.

And so, all of the details of Kan'an's tasks and daily life were altered due to the Intifada. With the Intifada came the boycotting of Israeli goods; the formation of popular resistance, popular, and quarter-specific committees; the establishment of new organizations and cells; the planning of organizational and popular expansion to new positions; the program of the Unified National Leadership of the Intifada, which directed the activities and resources of the organizations; and the organization of marches and demonstrations. Thus, all of the resistance's activities, tasks, and decisions had changed. By the third week of the Intifada, this new political, organizational, and popular reality of resistance shaped the work of the party's organizations and their members, including Kan'an.

He was never as happy and overjoyed as he was during the first months of the Intifada. He came face-to-face with the fact that the efforts of years of delicate organizational, popular, political, and resistance activities among the people—years and years of mobilization and organization—had produced a political capacity to command the streets. You reap what you sow, although it may take years.

Disappearance and evasion—an act of madness little understood by quasi-revolutionaries during the late 1970s and early 1980s—had been transformed into a collective experience, undertaken by an entire people. They refused to surrender, running away from the quarters and rural areas to the mountains and the alleys the minute that their homes were raided. This act of rebellion had become the choice of the people as a whole, not dictated by this or that leader. According to the eloquent expression attributed to Jesus: "The stone the builders rejected has become the cornerstone."

His body withdrawn within the walls of his den, Kan'an was experiencing the events of the Intifada from the rear ranks; however, the effect of his tasks and activities and the decisions that he had helped to formulate placed him on the frontlines. He discovered in the Intifada, more than at any time in the past, the utility of his role and his direct influence in translating decisions and directives into action in the street—actions by the public against the Occupation. Often the Intifada would encroach on his safe house due to his proximity to the Al-Am'ari Camp. Not only could he hear the voices of the demonstrators and the sound of the firing of live ammunition by snipers among the Occupation forces, he also had occasion to curse the smell of tear gas which invaded his lungs and burnt his eyes, drawing tears. Standing by the window and hearing the shouting of slogans, he would see the black smoke rising from burning car tires and the white clouds of tear gas. Just moments later, he would feel a burning in his throat and his tears would start flowing. It was the best smell in the world—after all, it signaled his participation in the Intifada.

❈ ❈ ❈ ❈ ❈

She showed up on time. She looked across the street carefully, appearing to have perfected the maneuver that had become routine after years of secrecy. Making sure there was no one in her vicinity who could recognize her, she made her way to the entrance of the house. She was about to knock on the door when he opened it for her. Each time she came to visit him, he enjoyed watching her engage in clandestine activities; she double-checked before entering, and wore sunglasses and a scarf that covered most of her face. He welcomed her, laughing.

"After years of experience with my safe houses, you qualify as a secret member of the party."

"You and your party be damned! Is this what's in store for the rest of my life?"

She laughed and embraced him with warmth, kissing him until she had her fill. The complaints she had expressed during her earlier visits—which were passive complaints anyway—she no longer brought up, unless he started joking with her, as was his custom.

"Not all mothers are like you. You are the mother of a resistance fighter in the Popular Front!"

"Damn the PFLP and the day it was founded! Habash only established it so that he could make me worry."

He laughed and because he was laughing, she laughed. Imagine that! In her opinion, the decision to establish the party was to achieve one principal objective: to cause consternation to Umm Kan'an. The Arab Nationalist Movement decided to establish the Popular Front for the Liberation of Palestine in order to burden her life. She was perfecting her dealings with his life and with his safe houses each time she came with whoever was assigned to bring her and with whatever bundles she brought, whether he needed them or not... She laid down the sack containing her bundles and panted as she resumed speaking.

"How are you living during the Intifada? There isn't a single house they have not entered."

"They will not enter my house. Your prayer years ago, saying, 'Go my son, may God be pleased with you' blinds them so they do not see my house. Are you still repeating it as we agreed?"

"I always pray for you, day and night." As she spoke, a tear managed to force itself out against her will. "This house of yours is not suitable. You are next to Al-Am'ari. You need a different house. Don't you see what's happening in the street?"

"I'm aware of the smallest details. The comrades tell me everything," he interrupted her.

"Hearsay is not like seeing it for yourself. The youth are turning the soldiers' hair gray. The shops close exactly at eleven o'clock, the army forces them open, the young men shut them down, and they reopen them. They remain open but no one goes near them. The calamity is in Gaza. What is happening in Gaza is happening nowhere else. The West Bank is okay, but Gaza—" she paused for a moment. "What is happening in Gaza is a disaster."

"Poverty and suffering create rebellion which breeds a hardy people," Kan'an replied to her news report. "Look at who is resisting and making sacrifices in the street. They are not the pampered children of the upper classes, but workers in the camps and villages. In Ramallah, the most active quarters are the old town, Al-Am'ari, and Qaddura, in Al-Bireh it is the eastern quarter . . . Those workers are our guys."

She nodded her head in agreement. The Intifada had taught her some things, as was the case with every Palestinian. People learn a lot more from their own experience than they learn from propaganda and agitation. That day her conversation was not dominated, as usual, by news of the family and the neighbors, whose news he was not particularly interested in, but naturally she was ("so-and-so got engaged to so-and-so, a neighbor went on a trip, a relative quarreled with someone"). That day, the topic of their conversation was political, which spared him to a certain extent from questions about events in his life, from being interrogated by her and being subjected to her advice and reproach. Unfortunately for him, her mood was spoiled, which in turn annoyed him because then they left the world of politics and the Intifada and returned to her world: the world of her detailed motherly concerns.

During her previous visit, they had agreed that she would make him some *kubbeh*.* She had asked him to get the required ingredients, the most important being *burghul*** which he was supposed to soak in lemon juice the night before.

"Come on, let's see the *burghul*. Did you soak it in lemon like I told you to?"

Embarrassed, he was silent for a moment. "I forgot to," he said regretfully. "I was busy yesterday and stayed up late and only woke

---

* *Kubbeh* is a meat and bulgur pie, stuffed with ground lamb or beef, that is prepared in a variety of ways.
** The Arabic word for bulgur, a form of cracked wheat.

up half an hour ago. Soaking it now will delay you. Let's put it off till the next visit."

"We won't postpone. There is time. Quick, bring the *burghul*. Just like you think of the party and your work, you should think of yourself and your food."

She decided to do what they had planned on. Even if this would delay her for hours, raising questions upon her return home as to why she was late, she would not leave his safe house without cooking what he had asked for. He picked up a sack from the pantry and handed it to her.

"Here! What's next? The meat and pine nuts are ready. Shall I dice the onions?"

"Fry the meat with the diced onions and toss them in olive oil. Don't use too much oil, this way it will be easier on your stomach." She said this as she was opening the sack of *burghul*. Suddenly she slammed it down on the table, her face contorted by anger.

"This is semolina, not *burghul*. Semolina. *Kubbeh* needs *burghul*. Have you forgotten? We have worked all of our lives with wheat. Did you forget?"

What could he say? He had been stupid. He had made *burghul* for *kubbeh* on the hand mill hundreds of times. How did he get himself in this mess? He thought the situation was funny and could only joke about it to distract her from his mistake.

"Am I a cook on Hamra Street[25] to know that Lebanese *kubbeh* requires *burghul* and not semolina? It's all wheat!"

"*Burghul*, son. *Burghul*!" she clapped her hands once.

"I am not about to die in the near future, at least not before your next visit in two weeks. I will get some *burghul*," he added.

She was angry because he had mentioned death. But she did not waste her visit. She took the semolina and made a dessert out of it which he had not had for twenty years. He had forgotten all about it—how, as a child, he used to pester his mother for change to buy it whenever the street vendor came by carrying a large tray of the sweets on his head. He enjoyed eating it and she taught him how to make it, so he added another recipe to his repertoire.

"It's easy and doesn't take more than fifteen minutes. It's rich and fills the stomach."

They lunched on what he had in his fridge: frozen fish stuffed with almonds and garlic.

"Really, you are active," she said as they discussed the Intifada. "You guys have a lot of marches and your slogans are on all the walls." Kan'an was happy to hear her say so. He ruffled her hair playfully as he used to do in the old days when she loved nothing more than that.

As he was hugging her farewell at the door, she reminded him, "*Burghul*, not semolina. Write it down on a piece of paper and don't forget. Just like you remember party issues and record them on bits of paper, write down *burghul* too so that your comrades will bring you some."

"All right. I'll write down *burghul* along with party matters."

She thought that he was just appeasing her and that he would not do it. "Do you think you are fooling me?" she said reproachfully.

"I promise by my honor as a party member that I will write *burghul* down right next to party matters on a piece of paper. This is a man's promise."

She was pleased, and left in the same manner she arrived. She checked her surroundings before slipping out the door, wearing sunglasses and the strange scarf over her head. He watched her as she crossed the street and sighed. *Oh Hajeh*—in spite of myself you dragged me into your world, my world six years ago!*

He closed the door and hurried to fulfill his promise to her. He picked up a scrap of paper, one of many on which he had written bullet points concerning his work. Under the heading "Matters concerning Popular Resistance Committees," he wrote "Two kilograms of local *burghul*." She had imposed her logic on him through her insistence, a reflection of her hope. *Burghul*, just as important as

---

* A term of endearment for an elderly woman, sometimes used to refer to one's mother, wife, or aunt.

the Intifada, the party, and revolutionary action. In fact, if someone snuck into her head and heard her frank and unfiltered thoughts, derived from tender affection for her son, they would have learned (insofar as the matter concerned her son) that *burghul* was *more* important than the whole world! Life has its logic and a mother has her logic. Life's logic may crush whatever stands in its way without mercy or consideration, but on some occasions, there is something that pushes back against life's logic, something that is stubborn and will not budge, that cannot be pushed out of the way—that is a mother's logic. In the end, however, you will find that a mother's logic is precisely (or actually) the logic of life itself.

❁❁❁❁❁

Months after the Intifada's outbreak, one evening at 9:30 p.m. as Kan'an was watching television, the doorbell rang. Kan'an looked at his watch worriedly. He was not in the habit of receiving anyone at night without an appointment unless it was an emergency. *God forbid it's bad news. What has happened to make them come at this hour?* He opened the door and his comrade entered.

"Good evening, I'm sure it startled you to hear the doorbell ring at this late hour, huh? Rest assured. The situation isn't critical, but it would be best for you to move this evening, before dawn."

"You bring good news, I hope. What's happened to force us to move at night and under such circumstances?"

"As you must have noticed there is a lot of activity in this quarter. We've received information that some individuals belonging to organizations with safe houses in the area have been arrested. The location of their safe houses may come out during their interrogation. Consequently, the level of danger to you has increased. We have a good house for you in a quarter which knows nothing of the Intifada, even if it were to go on for a hundred years."

Kan'an's quarter was indeed a beehive of activity, and he was living there only temporarily until a new house could be prepared.

There were a lot of stone barricades and tires on fire and graffiti and there had been repeated operations nearby conducted by the Occupation authorities.

One night, in the early weeks of the Intifada, his ears picked up the familiar and nerve-wracking sounds of military vehicles so close to his den that he was able to hear their knocking and yelling calling on the residents to come out quickly from their homes. The army was conducting a campaign to erase resistance graffiti from walls across the quarter, which they usually undertook on a weekly and, occasionally, daily basis. It was only by chance that they did not come close to his safe house, otherwise he would have been in a real predicament. Naturally he would not have opened the door, but they rarely accepted that; the problem was he did not have a hiding place in the safe house. Within two hours the soldiers had accomplished their mission and left. He slipped outside to inspect the walls of his safe house and found that the slogans had been erased by white paint. However, since they had been written in red, they were still almost clearly legible underneath the white paint. They had been signed with the initials PPSF (standing for the Palestinian Popular Struggle Front). *Has the homeland shrunk, and have its walls become so scarce that the PPSF has to write on my walls?! How did the PPSF come to be here?* It was quite strange that the slogan was signed by the PPSF. In reality, the PPSF did not have a presence in the homeland as a force, with no hope of becoming one—there were only some members scattered here and there was already a density of well-established organizations. After that incident, he bought some white paint and snuck out every night to check the walls of his house. No sooner would a slogan be written than he would paint over it. Nor was he deterred by the scribbled warning he saw once: "Woe to him who erases a PPSF slogan."

He arrived at his new safe house within fifteen minutes. The following day a military unit raided the houses of active PLO and Communist Party members in the quarter that he had just left. After that, who could convince him that it wasn't the invisible influence of his mother's prayer and the party's "**measures, precautions,**

requirements, and rules" that always seemed to save him from what could have befallen him . . . Or it was just a coincidence!

His new den incorporated the specifications that all safe houses had to satisfy after the Intifada broke out: safe houses should not be close to the lines of settlements often targeted by groups of youths; they should be as far as possible from youth activities; they should not be close to the residences of activists in political organizations or the safe houses of wanted persons; they should be far from places suitable for traps set by the youth to target the vehicles of patrols and settlers. The Intifada had added its conditions to the list of rules for secret life and he had to respond quickly. Progress does not spare those who do not acclimate to its logic, in fact, it crushes them.

At six in the evening, he finished his work for that day—a quick meeting, a writing task for two hours or slightly longer, reading and briefly commenting on some papers to prepare them for a fuller review later, and burning papers that needed to be destroyed. He had listened to a news broadcast an hour before: the main headline was the extensive negotiations in the corridors of the PLO's Palestinian National Council meeting in Algeria. This meeting involved the discussion of two essential documents which had dominated the thoughts and concerns of the people and the organizations of the Intifada for weeks. The first document was called "The Palestinian Peace Initiative," which included the acceptance of UN Security Council Resolution 242—a resolution that did not recognize the Palestinian cause as a question of sovereignty, but only as a border dispute between the Arab countries and Israel.[26] The second document was a declaration of independence which was viewed by popular consensus as seizing the opportunity of the Intifada to reaffirm the Palestinian people's sovereignty over their homeland before the world. This declaration could de facto serve to fill the legal and administrative hiatus created by the sudden Jordanian decision—without any prior coordination with the PLO—to sever legal and administrative ties to the West Bank.

The party had voted against the Peace Initiative and sought, at a minimum, to forge a large minority opposed to it, because it contained some gratis concessions and constituted a hasty exploitation of the Intifada. On the other hand, the party supported the declaration of independence idea, grudgingly accepting UN General Assembly Resolution 181[27] as the legal basis for the declaration, in addition to the legal, historical, and national dimensions. Kan'an turned on the TV and cycled between channels but could not find anything worth watching, nor could he find any programs on the radio to soothe himself. He settled on listening to Marcel Khalife, putting a cassette in the player:

"Upright, I walk
With my head held high, I walk
In my palm, I hold an olive branch
And on my shoulders I carry my coffin"

As the singer chanted Samih Al-Qasim's spirited anthem,[28] Kan'an stood at the window, contemplating his neighborhood. The quarter he had been living in for five months was inhabited by wealthy families and had not experienced the Intifada in the real and direct sense of the word. From watching them, he concluded that, for them, the Intifada meant exploiting the days of the universal strike to get together every afternoon in the gardens of their fancy homes, guzzling down wine in front of their barbeque grills ... *No doubt they want a nation-state*, he ascertained as he watched from the windows of his house, *but they want someone else to fight and sacrifice in order to secure it and then hand it over to them; and if they cannot get that peacefully, they will resort to arms to secure their mastery over it.*

It was rare for the streets of this quarter to be closed or blocked by a burning tire. For that reason, the military patrols never came. This was why Kan'an thought it was the ideal place for a man in hiding to live, for neither did the inhabitants intrude on your privacy nor did Intifada activities create an atmosphere propitious for clashes. He lived in an apartment on the fourth floor of a building near the center of the quarter, and next to his building was a large field where a farmer would plant during summer and winter. Not only was the farmer industrious, but he was also uncompromising—he couldn't care less about the proprieties of the rich who lived adjacent to his field. During harvest season, he would bundle the stalks of wheat together and set out, with the help of his mule, to thresh the wheat in the midst of the cross section that led to all of the houses in the quarter. Once he finished threshing his wheat, he would put the grain in sacks, which resulted in him blocking the road used by their fancy cars. Kan'an watched him, admiring his actions and thinking about this strange combination: on the one hand you had a bourgeois quarter inhabited by the big capitalists of the city and, on the other, a farmer in the middle of that same quarter behaving as though he was on the threshing floor of his village.

That morning, the sky gave full vent to its plentiful anger, pouring down rain and sleet, accompanied by flashes of lightning followed by thunder. It was mid-November of 1988 and winter was still a toddler, yet the heavens did not hold back their bounty for the people of Palestine, such that the field, the intersection, and the side roads were covered in a beautiful white cloak of hail. Meanwhile, the old fig tree stood in the middle of the field alone and naked, resisting the cold and the winds of winter while its solid trunk stood motionless like a tower, its roots burrowed deep in the earth.

"Had I been an artist I would have painted a natural tableau of the white field and the fig tree," he told himself, contemplating the beauty of nature before him, focusing on the tree. "We are like you. You sink your roots in the ground, you absorb water from now till spring when it is time for you to sprout leaves and bear fruit. You have to be patient for time to take its course. Like you, we have been sinking our roots into the soil of the people for years and years. We suck up the people's rich, revolutionary experience. One day our leaves will sprout and our fruit will bud. Everything is good in its time. Our people's wisdom says so. Look, our leaves have already started sprouting. The time will come for us to harvest the fruit of our revolutionary action, so that the workers and those struggling will rule over their homeland."

Time and experience have their logic. I have been undergoing this experience for six years and it has tossed me from one safe house to the other, like a baker kneading a wad of dough, tossing it up in the air and stretching it before putting it into the oven. It has been years and years, broken down into months and weeks and days, minutes and seconds, while the contradictions within me were being decided in favor of the choice of professional resistance and a clandestine existence. What a time! What an experience! How much can a human being endure? No more than what experience can make of him after he gives himself without reservation, turning his back on what came before and giving a full-throated shout, "Here is my self, my being, my thought, my identity—reformulate them as you wish, I grant you everything . . . After my mother's, you are my second womb; feed me, give me drink, pump the blood in my arteries and the air into my lungs . . ."

He remembered the time and looked at his watch. It was only minutes before seven—time for the detailed news bulletin from Monte Carlo Radio channel. He stopped the cassette player and moved the dial to 1200. The ads ended and suddenly the familiar rumble of Arafat's voice could be heard: "In the name of the Palestinian people, I declare the establishment of the Palestinian state over the land of Palestine."

With this one pronouncement, the voice signaled the spontaneous outburst of a joyous atmosphere: a people mad with happiness. Hundreds of fireworks shot up into the sky, ululations, yells, and hurrahs were heard—just about everything a human throat can produce. The people rejoiced that day and the quarter of the rich took part. He was overcome with joy, but could not shout, yell hurrah, or chant slogans; he had no fiery and happy fireworks to shoot into the sky. All he could do was to say to himself, "I am with you, your joy is my joy. For years I have been cooped up here, fighting alongside the party and the people to bring about such a day and more days to come. How can I celebrate with you?"

Without much thought, Kan'an picked up the cassette player and placed it on the window sill. He scrolled back to the beginning of the reel and raised the volume to the max:

"Upright, I walk
With my head held high, I walk
In my palm, I hold an olive branch
And on my shoulders, I carry my coffin"

He participated in the joy of the people in his own way. Hail was falling and the ground was covered with a fine, white layer of frost. The sounds of fireworks and joyous people reverberated in the streets and Marcel Khalife's voice rang forth. The night was decorated with fiery sparks; the cold of winter had given way to the warmth of giddy happiness. He stood at his window and all he could think of was that his struggle, the efforts of years, was starting to bear fruit—the small contributions by himself and thousands of resistance fighters over the years was starting to blossom. He was experiencing the reality that his choice of professional resistance for the sake of the people was absolutely right.

The Intifada had taken on a new impetus with the declaration of independence. To the people, the declaration of independence was certainly a capitalization on their heroic struggles over the course of the past eleven months. It was also evidently the natural response to the legal and administrative disengagement from Jordan. But above all else, the people saw it as a definitive step towards the establishment of a Palestinian state, which would emerge presumably as a result of the Intifada and its doings. However, they did not pay enough attention to the need to develop the Intifada and radically escalate it. The notion that it was enough to create a Palestinian state was nothing more than an illusion. This illusion arose, not only as a result of the legitimate yearning for an end to the Occupation and its crimes, but also (and essentially) as a result of political mobilization—a method employed by the forces that believed that an Intifada of such magnitude would inevitably lead to an independent state. Therefore, these forces came forward with the political slogan: "a state is a stone's throw away." Palestinian political thought was sliding down a slippery slope and reshaping popular consciousness, which weakened the people's preparedness.

In the homeland, the party debated this issue. During the eighth month of the Intifada, it put forward the slogan of "Freedom and Independence" to act as an organizing goal for the people's movement and prevent its capture by Shamir's[29] "self-rule" proposal. The party added its understanding that the Intifada was a qualitative turning point that transformed the idea of an independent state from a historic possibility to a realistic one. However, it did not think that the Intifada was quite at the level that would lead to the creation of a state. This assessment was repeated to its members and the public through the party's bulletins and its secret newspaper. The party concluded that the Intifada had to first be escalated and developed so that it could inflict casualties of all sorts on the enemy and turn the Occupation into a losing project. Only then could one earnestly view the Intifada as a mechanism for building a state.

At the end of 1988, the political bureau issued an in-house circular on the same subject, titled "The Intifada and the State." The circular initiated a large dispute between the party's political bureau and the national cadres. The cadres thought that the party had not presented a clear link between the establishment of a state and the extent to which the Intifada would have to be developed to yield that result. This was followed by a call for the Central

Committee to convene at the beginning of 1989. At the convening, the party's homeland branch presented a paper to the Committee to correct the political position on the issue.

What made matters worse were what the party considered to be "concessions" in the so-called "Peace Initiative"—in it, the Palestinian National Council of the PLO offered recognition of Resolution 242 as the basis for a solution. Resolution 242 ignored all of the UN resolutions that provided for the right to a state, the right of return, the dismantling of settlements, the withdrawal from Jerusalem, and the international security guarantees. Regardless of whether the "Peace Initiative" added the provisions for self-determination in Resolution 242, the issue at hand was that the Intifada had not yet reached the stage where it could continue on its own politically. In fact, it needed to resolve some of its problems so as to provide a basis for the popular uprising to continue escalating.

The Intifada was at its height—the possibilities for its development and escalation were open-ended. The people were adhering to the program of the Unified Leadership down to the letter: Israeli goods that had a local substitute were boycotted; good progress was being made towards land reclamation and the return to disciplined ascetic home economics; the network of popular committees and all the new forms of organization throughout the West Bank, Jerusalem, and Gaza were working. The ranks of the hunted were growing. From its womb groups of armed fugitives were born: the Falcons,[30] the Black Panther,[31] the Red Eagle groups,[32] the Izz Al-Din Al-Qassam Battalions,[33] the Red Star.[34] Abstention from taxpaying was quasi-universal, and daily clashes were taking place throughout the homeland.

The Intifada was at its height, but political disagreements began to weaken the internal front. At the end of 1989, Palestinian unity was threatened—the PLO determined that they would engage in direct negotiations with the Israelis through Egyptian intermediaries in Cairo without Israel proposing anything other than self-rule. The PLO had been deceived by Israeli propaganda that claimed Palestinians were a negative force, always refusing what was offered to them instead of coming up with their own initiatives. This propaganda obscured the fact that at the height of the Zionist entity's political dealings with the Intifada, the Israeli mindset did not want to propose anything other than limited self-rule. It was as though the victim was required to take the initiative to propose solutions to convince the criminal-murderer of his own civility. This was capitulation. Instead, the victim should have built the foundations for his response to the criminal assault and wrenched his rights straight from the murderer's fangs! This was the party's response to the initiative.

The party's organization and members in the homeland were deeply involved in the Intifada through all of the organizational forms and instruments which the Intifada had given birth to—from the local level of the city quarter committees to the Unified Leadership itself. A major organizational effort was undertaken in 1988 on three fronts. The first front concerned the rapid formation of the new organizational vehicles that were appropriate for the conditions of the Intifada: the Popular Resistance Committees, the Martyr Ghassan Kanafani Squadrons, and the Red Eagle groups. The Red Eagle groups became active in the north of the country and in the Gaza Strip, and the names of its martyrs became famous: 'Alam Al-Din Shahin, Abu 'Arab and Mustafa Jawabra, 'Ali Sawalmah, Ayman Al-Razza.

The structure of these organizational vehicles was built at the expense of the party's established syndical democratic labor and student organizations which were no longer suitable for the Intifada's needs. Internal debates about their status and transformation took place. There were some who thought the establishment of new structures was a threat to the democratic bases that had taken years to build. This debate was settled on the basis that such a position was rigid and denied the necessity of altering the party's organizational structure to take on the tasks at hand—rather, the organizational form should stem from the objectives and needs of the Intifada.

The second front concerned the need to deal quickly with the gaps in the party's structure, a result of the arrests of hundreds of party cadres and members, as well as the manhunt for dozens more. It was imperative that the party prevent any breaks in its linkages that could inhibit it from fulfilling the tasks of the Intifada and constructing new organizations. The third front concerned the expansion of the party in dozens of locations where it did not have either an organizational or a popular presence previously. It was crucial to create greater capacity for the Intifada effort by fighting on the three fronts and resolving the organizational and grassroots issues.

By the end of 1988, the party had successfully advanced its approach to the three fronts and expanded its membership in the homeland by 70 percent. The party came to play an essential role at all levels in the Intifada, as well as a leadership role in many locations. The Intifada transformed the organizations of the homeland. making them sites of resistance with political and grassroots power. This occurred not only at the level of the national movement, but also within the party, where the branches on the ground in the Occupied Territories had greater influence over the party's decision-making in general.

❉❉❉❉❉

In 1989, Kan'an's family life intruded on his secret life. He heard that his eldest sister was visiting the country. Her homecoming had a special impact on him—it was the first time in about thirty years that she had returned to Palestine. Her time abroad was almost equal to Kan'an's age, so he had barely seen her and did not know her at all, although he had memorized her features from photographs. Growing up, he had heard a lot about her: her kindness and easy temperament, that she was a second mother to his brothers, that she had planned to visit the homeland every year, but her poor luck always upset her plan at the last minute.

> *My eldest sister is here. I don't know her to begin with. I want to meet her, what do you think of that? I cannot say for sure that there will be another chance like this.*

He got in touch with the party and told them that this might be his only chance to see her. Was it reasonable, despite all his secret calculations, that two individuals who were born from the same womb and suckled on the same breast, should not meet and get to know each other? The party approved the meeting, as he expected.

> **Yes, it's natural that you should see her. Make the arrangements, but it is essential that you make her understand the realities of your life, so that she will keep your secret safe. Make sure! After all, she is a stranger to our world—she is not like your mother!**

"My mother can take care of that," Kan'an replied. "She is best situated to explain my situation to her. I don't want to waste some precious hours of our meeting explaining secrecy and their rules." Kan'an asked his mother to bring her.

The bell rang at 9:00 a.m. as agreed upon. His heartrate increased and nerves raced through him. For days he could not stop thinking about how the meeting would go and how they would feel. It had never occurred to him throughout his clandestine existence, even in his daydreams, that he would meet her under such circumstances. She left him when he was six years old. He was meeting her now as a man of extensive experience in resistance and its challenges. She had always been occupied with her little brother, showering him with presents that made him attached like a son. One question nagged him: How would he address her?

He went to the door and opened it, and she clutched him in her arms before his mother did, kissing him and crying while he succumbed to her. She was shaking as her lips kissed his cheeks and her hands felt his head and shoulders, then his back, his chest, as though she were blind and exploring him with her fingertips. His mother was panting from the climb to the fourth floor.

"Are you satisfied?" she said, sardonically. "Here he is in the flesh. If you've had enough, pass him on to me." Then his mother turned to him. "Ever since you sent for me to bring her, she has been bugging me: 'Is he a real grown-up man? I'll finally get to see him and kiss him.'"

Kan'an smiled. No doubt his mother also said that to herself before their first meeting, but now, after long suffering, she appeared accustomed to his life and experience—so accustomed that she was making fun of his sister.

"The life I lead, and before that, the way you raised me, have made me a real man." He wrapped his arm around his sister and addressed his mother. "Are you convinced now—I'm a real man, all grown up? I am as tall as my father and my face resembles yours, which means that I have nothing from outside this noble family. But no one else in the family has gone mad like I have."

His sister was a true replica of his father. When he saw her, he thought he was seeing their father seven years after he passed away: her face, her tears which flowed easily whether there was an occasion for tears or not, her good nature, and her compassion. She asked him everything about himself, but not by interrogating him like his mother did, perhaps because she had not yet resumed the role of being a motherly older sister to him, or perhaps because she was not contrarian by nature. His mother carried out her customary endless stream of questions about the details of his life—what he ate, what he drank, how he slept. These were the same questions she asked each time she visited and each time she received the same answers, only to return back to the same questions again. A mother is the only being on the planet who does not get bored repeating the same questions, remarks, reprimands, and bits of advice which usually relate to her child's life. It is as though a mother giving up on that ritual would be giving up her very motherhood—a sun deciding not to rise in the morning or stopping in place at high noon.

His sister sat beside him throughout her visit. His mother relinquished her right to that spot under protest that showed on her face but remained unspoken. He had made lunch for them but they had other plans: they had brought grape leaves to stuff with rice. His sister, whom he did not want nor expect to join in, got to work, and joined willingly as sous chef. Theirs was the strangest way of wrapping vine leaves that he had seen. His sister arranged the vine leaves all over the table, quickly placed the stuffing on top of each leaf and then used both hands to wrap the leaves, her practiced hands resembling a machine, working almost too fast for the eye to follow.

"You have combined grassroots authenticity with industrial technique," he said while laughing, impressed by the display. "Do you have wrapping machines in the United States?"

The visit lasted hours and the farewell was warmer than the initial welcome, accompanied by the customary set of directives from his mother at the doorway.

❖❖❖❖❖

It had been a month since the declaration of independence. The resistance was escalating and joy was widespread. On a wintery day at 5:30 a.m., he got out of bed. It was unusually early for him. He could not get back to sleep no matter how hard he tried; his eyelids refused to obey him. He ate a piece of bread dipped in olive oil and za'atar, then carried a cup of tea and a cigarette over by the window, contemplating the dawn and smoking, barely listening to the announcer on the radio. The party's activities were at their height then, celebrating the anniversary of the Intifada's outbreak. Huge organizational efforts had gone into making the celebrations an occasion for various forms of resistance. The Intifada had reached the height of its efficacy. On the one hand, some of the Intifada's mass activities had begun to dissipate: the retreat of the popular mobilization in the battlefield, the halt to the boycott of traffic offices, the weakening of the tax boycott. On the other hand, there was an escalation of the phenomenon of armed groups, particularly the Black Panthers, the Falcons, and the Red Eagles.

Around 6:00 a.m., he caught a glimpse of a child crossing the street carrying a bunch of newspapers in a plastic bag under his arm to protect it from the drizzling rain. He opened the window and whistled. The child, who was standing in the street looking miserable, looked up. Kan'an signaled to him.

"Come in. Have a cup of tea to warm up your stomach and then you can go back down."

He had only meant to buy a copy of *Al-Quds* newspaper, but the sight of the child made him feel pity. He was wearing a tattered coat that neither protected him from the cold nor the rain. He was wearing a plastic bag on his head which was his sole protection against the December weather. He had stuffed one of his hands in his pocket and was using the other to carry the bag of papers. His clothes were wet, down to his worn-out shoes. He was quivering from the cold as though this was something ingrained in his limbs. His early morning activity did not seem to have chased away the remnants of sleepiness which were apparent in his small eyes.

"That will delay my sales," the child hesitantly replied.

Kan'an noticed in his tone a fear that he might lose out in the competition to sell a few newspapers in the early morning.

"I won't delay you. Drink a cup of tea and you can leave. Besides, I want to strike a deal with you that will be beneficial to you. I will buy the paper from you every day. Come in. Come in."

His comrades supplied him with the paper but not on the day of publication, just haphazardly, whenever one of them happened to be passing by. He would angrily remind them of the importance of the newspaper when they forgot to bring it, but without dwelling on it for long. Now he had the chance to read the paper when he woke up which he considered to be a true victory. Kan'an started a conversation, sitting down at the kitchen table after putting the kettle on the burner and moving the space heater near the boy.

"What's your name?"

"Mahmoud."

"Where are you from?"

"From Al-Am'ari Camp."

"How old are you?"

"Eight years and three months."

He replied as children do. Kan'an looked at him, feeling sorry for a childhood of wandering the streets at six in the morning and playing the role of an adult.

"Do you make much profit from selling newspapers?"

"Eh, it isn't always the same amount." The reservations and shyness of the vendor had transformed the conversation into an interrogation similar to that between a suspect and a policeman.

"Meaning how much?"

"Depends on sales. It's not always the same amount."

"Don't worry. I'm not going to compete with you in selling newspapers. About how much profit do you make?"

"Thirty-five shekels, sometimes forty. When Abu 'Ammar declared independence last month, I made fifty shekels in two hours, from five to seven in the morning. Then I went home."

"You mean the declaration of independence helped you financially?"

"Yes."

Kan'an got up to pour him some tea. "Don't you go to school?"

"I stopped when the Intifada began."

He handed him the tea. He put together a breakfast so that they could eat together—bread and white cheese, olives, za'atar, jam, and *labneh*. "Eat!"

"I've had breakfast. I am not hungry," he said shyly.

"No, eat. I haven't had breakfast yet so we'll have breakfast together. Come on, eat!"

He complied, and Kan'an handed him bread, not leaving him an opportunity for discussion. "Tell me, why'd you leave school?"

He began to eat and tell his story. He was hungry. Kan'an thought he had not eaten in a week, or perhaps it was the hunger of poverty, transformed into a chronic hunger that could never be satisfied. He ate from the plate of white cheese more than the other plates.

The boy's story reflected phenomena Kan'an had heard about as a result of the Intifada. There were frequent school closures, and his father had stopped working in Israel because he thought that the decision of the Unified Leadership to boycott work in Israeli settlements applied outside the West Bank and the Gaza Strip as well. Or perhaps he feared that the youth of the Intifada would extend the ban to work inside Israel, so he chose to stop beforehand. When the neighbors explained the facts about the decision of the Unified Leadership to him, the child's father said, "I will not work for the Zionists. I won't work one day and then not work for ten days. If we escape the army checkpoints, we run into the checkpoints of the masked youth and get degraded and demeaned."

In this way he became unemployed. Mahmoud's older brother, who was seventeen and would help his father with household expenses, was now sitting in jail after being arrested on suspicion of throwing a Molotov cocktail at an army patrol and shot in the foot. He also had three younger brothers, and a fourteen-year-old sister. As a logical consequence, Mahmoud left school and devoted himself to helping his family. An eight-year-old child supporting a family. That was also a prominent Intifada phenomenon: childhood being transformed into early adulthood.

"But there are popular education schools, don't you have one in the camp?"[35] The child nodded affirmatively. "Well then, why don't you attend school after selling the papers?"

"There was a school, but then they arrested the teacher."

"They arrested him because he was teaching you. The Occupation authorities don't want you to study and learn because if you learn, you will be better able to resist the Occupation. Try Qaddura Camp, they have a school too."

He nodded his approval and finished his food; the breakfast dishes and the hot tea and the warmth of the kitchen and the conversation had made him forget himself.

"What time is it?" the child asked.

"A quarter past seven," Kan'an replied. Mahmoud got up quickly. "The boys will beat me to the sales."

"Okay. Let's make an agreement before you leave. I don't usually get up this early. Since you pass through this street, come up and slip the paper under the door. Each Thursday I will pay you for the whole week. The paper is worth eighty agorot, I will give you a shekel. That would make six shekels a week, but I'll give you ten. What do you think? That's extra wages for your trouble. Do we have a deal?"

"Deal. We start tomorrow."

The agreement did not last two months. On one occasion, Kan'an had no shekels so he gave the boy five Jordanian dinars, worth eighteen shekels at the time.

"Exchange the Jordanian currency for shekels, take ten shekels and I will see you on Thursday."

The boy left and never came back. Did he consider the payment a chance to make off with the extra cash? That child—a failed merchant. Did he steal a few shekels and lose a permanent client? Or was he arrested while throwing stones at the army—a form of resistance turned favorite pastime for children? Perhaps. Or he might have found steady work at a car repair garage, or in the vegetable market helping the elderly carry things, or as a busboy. He had often heard of the "battle tactics" of young newspaper vendors in clashes with the army near Manara Square. Many of them competed to sell copies of their papers during the morning rush hour, yelling and jumping among the people and the cars, calling out *"Al-Quds!"* As soon as an army patrol showed up, they began pelting them with a shower of small stones which they carried in their newspaper bags. The soldiers responded with a hail of bullets from their automatic rifles, stirring up a wave of turmoil and chaos among the people who would start running around aimlessly; cars honked their horns and shops closed their doors and the soldiers arrested whoever they can lay hands on. As for the younger among the newspaper vendors, they would take part by withdrawing quietly, putting on a show of being terrified to deceive the soldiers of the Occupation all while having a laugh at their expense. Or maybe the boy was caught selling the party bulletins or its secret newspaper and got arrested as a result? This possibility worried

Kan'an, having remembered what he had heard about a party member making a deal with newspaper vendors to insert a bulletin between the pages of the papers they were selling as a novel way of distributing a secret communiqué.

By the end of 1989, there was a turning point in party activities in light of the major expansion in its ranks and its extension to dozens of new locations, along with the building of new cadres baptized by action in the streets, the numerous innovations of party organizations, and the rise in the percentage of publications, bulletins, and newspapers distributed. All of this led the party to uplift a slogan: "Transform the party into the primary force." This was detailed in a document dedicated to articulating the political, popular, resistance, and organizational pillars of the slogan.

This was a massive and historic ambition, seeing as the party's transformation into the top power marked the beginning of bringing about a qualitative change in the balance of political-class power. This would lay the foundation for the achievement of a historic objective, namely that the revolutionary left should move to a leading position of the resistance. It was clear to everyone, as the slogan articulated, that the most important work, the most fundamental lever to ensure the success of the project-slogan, was the launching of the secret armed guerilla movement as explained in the "Guevara letter" of January 1986. Without this more developed form of political struggle, it would be hard to imagine the majority of the people rallying around the left, especially given the high morale of the resistance under the circumstances of the Intifada.

Thousands of party members and supporters were in captivity, hundreds were wounded, and over 120 had been martyred—sacrifices on the altar of the Intifada. Considering these sacrifices and the party's growing capabilities and influence, it proposed scenarios that reached up to the heavens, even if they were far-fetched or even impossible. On July 8, 1989, as organizations commemorated the anniversary of Ghassan Kanafani's martyrdom,[36] comrade Yasser Abu Ghosh—a favorite of the party and the people—was martyred in Ramallah.

In the morning, as Kan'an was busy writing, the doorbell rang and his comrade entered without an appointment. She threw herself onto the couch and burst into tears. Kan'an urged her to tell him what had happened, for he sensed some kind of catastrophe.

"Comrade Yasser has been martyred. Yasser Abu Ghosh. An hour ago. They killed him near Al-Manara."

The news came like a lightning bolt and her voice rose in lamentation. Kan'an had been standing and he sat down, sighing. He didn't say a word. His comrade was crying and he was silent. Yasser had been admitted as a member of the party before he had reached the qualifying age of sixteen. By the time he turned fifteen, he was a candidate for a party cell for student members in high school. He was the most prominent organizer in the democratic organization for secondary students, the "Union of Committees," and later became the head of its Ramallah branch, an organization that had the distinction of providing the first martyr of the Intifada, Hatem Al-Sisi, in the Gaza Strip. Later on, Yasser's name outshone those of his comrades in the Ramallah party organization. Once the Intifada broke out, he became the central topic of conversation in the city: he was involved in every trap for the Occupation, he led every demonstration of high school students. Yasser was a tall, blond, courageous youth who stole the hearts of the girl students with his daring and confrontational attitude. The whole city cried for him. No sooner did the news of his execution by the intelligence services spread than the whole city was in an uproar: drivers stopped their cars and wept, young women wailed in the streets, the shops quickly closed, violent clashes broke out. In the afternoon, at the demonstrations outside Abu Ghosh's house, his comrade Raja Muhammad Saleh was martyred. The city mourned twice.

Chapter 9

Their voices were coming from the next room with the typewriters. The binding on his wrists hurt. Blood was pooling and whenever he moved his hands for any reason, even from boredom, the rubber zip-tie tightened and the pain increased. *The similarity is complete, Fayad, my comrade in this experience! What are you thinking about, Hisham? What are you contemplating? Are the shackles hurting you too?* As the ropes bit into his wrists, he remembered the line by Mahmoud Darwish, sung by Marcel Khalife, in his distinct epic voice: "I am the one whose shackles engrave the shape of the homeland in my skin!" On hearing that line of poetry he felt the moral incentive swell within him. *Where will my chains lead me now?* Several voices, scattered words, sounds of feet moving came from the room with the typewriters.

"Hisham!" said a commanding voice in the adjacent room. "To whom do these typewriters belong, you or Kan'an?"

His Arabic was broken, so he must be an intelligence officer. They, the sneakers, alone ask the questions. Those who wear combat boots only open fire or kick doors with their heels and beat bodies with the tips of their combat boots.

"I don't know. I have nothing to do with any typewriters."

I am in solidarity with you, comrade, as you resist with a will of steel. Kan'an sensed his solidarity and love for his comrade, the person most familiar with his experience, as his mind drifted back to the beginning of their relationship.

❖❖❖❖❖

"Right! Right! Your request is legitimate. We should assign a comrade to be your regular assistant for social and party matters to support you. Hisham is available. What do you say? You know him, don't you?"

Kan'an had moved to his safe house-den in the industrial zone of Ramallah in 1990, and his duties required an aide.

"I can't say I know him. I used to see him at the university, but because of my duties at the time, I restricted my relationships and haven't spoken to him. But I've heard of him and his activities in the Intifada—he has a practical spirit, just what I need in a companion."

In fact, Hisham's most distinctive trait was his practical spirit. The Intifada brought out Hisham's dormant potential as it did with others. The battlefield is and shall remain the soil which not only grows resistance fighters, but also reveals their natural dispositions and brings out their inherent potential which the party needs only to capture quickly. Ever since joining Birzeit University at the beginning of the 1980s, Hisham had established ties with the party as a friend and comrade. He worked with democratic student organizations as well as with cooperatives, visiting farmers in rural areas to supply them with seedlings and seeds while working with popular committees in the city. Hisham also supported foreign press delegations that visited the homeland to cover the events of the Intifada. His boldness and skilled driving allowed him to take a team of journalists to a remote village through several checkpoints and roads, under surveillance and occasionally even under curfew. His daring, courageous, and practical spirit—particularly in the face of critical situations—would be useful in the life of the man in hiding. He also had a deep-rooted allegiance to the party, and his previous arrests added new dimensions to his personality. So, in 1990 it was decided that Hisham should enter the life of secrecy, known only to a limited number of members and bodies in the party.

One evening, a week after the decision, Kan'an stood at his bedroom window watching the street, waiting for Hisham. For him, the visit of anyone to his safe house constituted an important event, like the arrival of a married couple's firstborn, or someone preparing to receive a bride in his home. He usually waited by a window of the house while carefully preparing a hearty meal for his guest. He always paid attention to feeding his guests whether they were new or repeat visitors. He would shave if he was not growing a beard, dress neatly, and if he could, tidy up the house. Preparing a hospitable welcome for any new guest was a general rule for him, even if they held little novelty in his life. So how would he receive someone he would depend on to be his hands, tongue, and feet: his right-hand man?

At the appointed time, Hisham appeared on the street leading to his house. He was astutely looking around to check if he was being observed or tailed. Kan'an immediately noticed that his clothes were at odds with the standard of good grooming and care; his jeans were well-worn, giving them an authentic American look, along with a light summer T-shirt and sneakers—a fashionable young American man. His clothes reflected his practical spirit. When work requirements forced him to change out of his typical attire, he would put on woolen or cotton pants, a shirt, and leather shoes. Kan'an thought he looked funny in his disguise. Once Hisham completed his task, he wasted no time getting out of his cover and returning to his natural state.

Once Hisham slipped into the house they gave each other a long and warm hug, and sat down to talk. They spoke at length about their memories and the university and the fate of the Intifada and the conditions of the Soviet Union. They ate lunch, a dish of *maklouba*[*] with yogurt made from sheep's milk. They sat on the eastern balcony

---

[*] *Maklouba* is a popular Palestinian dish which translates to "upside down." *Maklouba* is cooked in the one-pot style, in which rice, vegetables, and meat are placed in a pot and cooked together. When served, the pot is flipped, like the name suggests.

listening to Sheikh Imam, drinking tea, talking, and reminiscing. Like Kan'an, Hisham was obsessed with the Sheikh and, like a bloodhound, chased after every song of his that made it to the homeland.

"Do you know what? There is an issue that I lose sleep over: Who is better, Sheikh Imam or Marcel Khalife? Even now, after having lived with their music for the last fifteen years I find it difficult to make up my mind."

They had started walking while listening to the song *"Balah Abril, ya Samara."*

"Don't overthink it. The two are on the same level, they are both the best." Hisham had settled the issue with a simplicity that did not take into account Kan'an's dilemma.

"Can't be. I have to take a definite position."

"This isn't a partisan issue, nor is it disputed among the forces and organizations," Hisham said satirically.

Kan'an laughed. "The issue is tied up with my mood and my taste in art. I must know where I stand. That's what I'm like and that's all there is to it. At any rate, I believe that I've found the solution, as captured in the English expression 'the first between equals.' The two are equal and the first is Sheikh Imam. I think that's a reasonable solution."

Kan'an made up his mind and the two kept pacing back and forth on the balcony. The Sheikh was singing:

"Processions, processions.
Men of the creed . . . . Allah!
They wander through the stars,
With the light of the truth . . . . . . Allah!"

The sun was setting. Hisham noticed the peculiarity of how they strolled on the balcony. Only those living a secret life can appreciate the importance of this way of walking, a custom of one who leads a clandestine existence. He contemplates, thinks, empties his frustrations, and waits. He exercises his legs and his back so that they do not seize up from long periods of sitting.

"I sit from morning till evening and so my rear is worn out; that is, if there is something left there to wear out," Kan'an laughed.

"There is another who shares this habit of walking," Hisham remarked.

"Who?"

"A man in a prison cell. He and you are in agreement on this point."

"True, true. Now tell me about your life, your work, your wife—describe her to me. What sort of woman is she? How did you come across each other before marriage?"

Kan'an was showering Hisham with questions. He wanted to draw close to his world, get to know it, try to become part of it. Hisham did not hesitate to open up, and he spoke at length about his wife and family and his work, enough to reassure and make Kan'an feel as if he knew him well, as if he was experiencing it himself.

"And now," Kan'an said, in a tone he did not wish to sound official, "allow me to explain the nature of your partisan responsibilities towards me, your standing in the party, the rules for dealing with this house, and some aspects of my secret life which you should know."

Kan'an spoke for about an hour as they walked, only stopping to emphasize a point or directive and gesture with his hands. As was his custom, he did not saturate his words with details; those, he felt, were best left to be addressed in the course of daily work instead of repeating them like a teacher impressing upon his students. He spoke and Hisham paid close attention, interrupting only to ask about things that needed to be clarified, or commenting to indicate that he understood a particular point.

"And now comrade, having heard all about your responsibilities, your position, your circumstances, and the secrecy of the work, do you accept the job within these parameters?"

"A man would be crazy not to accept such an opportunity." Hisham replied without hesitation.

"Good. I am glad. We expected you to say that, otherwise we would not have chosen you. I had to ask due to official considerations and partisan candor. To be candid regarding another point, I am in the habit of asking people who work with me a straightforward question. In view of the dangers involved in the life I lead, you are a former prisoner and you have had ties to the party for years, so I expect that you will understand my question and answer me truthfully—there is no offense intended."

"Go ahead and ask. I have no sensitivities regarding issues related to the party."

"If you should be arrested for any reason, should I leave my house or not? It is important for me to know where I stand. I don't want to put you on the spot, I will understand your answer no matter what it is."

"Don't leave it."

He did not add another word. "Don't leave it," he said, decisively and with a clarity that left no doubt. He did not explain or justify, as many do to convince others of their position; they talk a lot and repeat their sentences, chewing on their words to the extent that they raise suspicions about what they are saying, like a man who disguises their lack of confidence and cloaks himself with the noise created by his words. Hisham did not do that. He spoke in a way that made Kan'an feel he was with a comrade who honors his word. You hear it from him and that's the end of the discussion; you trust him and it is over. They were still walking on the balcony, and it was nearly 9:00 p.m.

"Now it is my turn to ask."

"Ask what you like."

"How can one bear such a life over so many years?"

"The beginning is difficult, it's very tough. But with time, over months and years, such a style of life becomes very ordinary because one gets used to it and there is conviction. Not that this is a good life ... Because leading a clandestine existence is a choice of resistance, not a choice of lifestyle. Let my position be clear. Certain factors must be available that make it successful and stable, and ideological conviction, which is so important for the activities of our party, is crucial. Without it, the experience will be shaky, as will the person's faith in the life he is leading. Then the elements of weakness will triumph over the elements of strength. There is also the total commitment to struggle, meaning revolutionary professionalism. One must put aside anything that could get in its way. Finally, there is the party's stewardship, solidarity, and support with whoever chooses to take on this clandestine experience. With all that, there is my mother's prayer: 'Go, my son. May God be pleased with you.' If all that is understood, then there is no room for doubt."

❃ ❃ ❃ ❃ ❃

The zip-tie still tore into his flesh. The combat boot carrying the pig came and went, kicking Kan'an in the waist, the thigh, and the foot . . . wherever it desired. Kan'an's burning spite grew and festered until it was enough to consume the world in flames.

> *Who came up with that song? The one that became popular in the Intifada, which goes like:* "Prison for me is an honor and the chain is an anklet."

He disliked the song when he first heard it.

> *That song is suitable for uplifting the morale of a prisoner facing the weight of imprisonment, weak and in danger of descending into total collapse. However, it is strange that a prisoner should take pride in his imprisonment and his chains and to sing happily about them; it is aberrant, even silly. Such concepts should not be the introduction of a revolutionary's training.*
>
> *A revolutionary should cast off his chains, not sing about them as though*

> *they were ornamental anklets. Chains are a humiliation, should we be singing about our debasement and humiliation? If a revolutionary is taken prisoner, his organization should hold him accountable by reducing his rank; his imprisonment should not be regarded as a step up. That is the same mentality that transforms defeat into victory through shouting and clamor and feigned initiative.*

He took a deep breath in while his hands continued to hurt, bracing himself for the pig returning to kick him.

> *What anklet? Look here, a revolutionary fighting for his people, whose heart reaches out in sympathy to every just cause in the world. My throat is pressed to the ground, my hands and feet are tied—and I'm supposed to feel proud?! There is a difference in this case between pride and rancor. The former disguises the bitter truth and embellishes it, whereas the latter sees the reality of humiliation and debasement and transforms all that into spite against the oppressors and injustice.*

The rancor within him against the combat boots, the sneakers, and the rubber shoes was mounting—mounting against all kinds of shoes and boot heels of the world.

❖❖❖❖❖

The summer of 1990 foreshadowed dangerous developments taking place across the Arab region, set in motion by forces that no one fully understood at the time. On August 2, the Iraqi army swept into Kuwait which fell without serious resistance. Iraq then declared Kuwait an Iraqi territory, the country's nineteenth governorate. The Americans and their supporters in the world began assembling a force of over half a million soldiers in Saudi Arabia, and gave Iraq an ultimatum to withdraw by January 15, 1991 or suffer a military defeat.

Capitalists throughout the world mobilized when they felt that their companies would no longer be able to plunder the sea of oil in the Gulf region. The oil was bought cheaply to churn the engines of the capitalists' industries which produced commodities, then sold to the Third World, of which the Arab World is a part. What the capitalists pay for oil, they win back through their exports or in the form of Arab petrodollar deposits in the capitalists' banks in London, Tokyo, and New York . . . sums upwards of $750 billion at the time of the Iraqi invasion of Kuwait.

No wonder then that the move by Iraq was popular among the Arabs. No one at the time was concerned either with the fate of Kuwait, which was swallowed up in less than twenty-four hours, nor with the opinion of the Kuwaitis and how they were transformed into Iraqis in twenty-four hours. At the time only two facts were at the forefront of public opinion: the first being that Iraq was fighting to regain Arab petrol for the Arabs, and the second was that the Western states were spitefully amassing their armies in Saudi Arabia to protect the thrones of the Gulf's tribal sheikhdoms, which were euphemistically referred to as "states."

The political communiqué released by the party in the homeland reflected this public mood and further declared that all efforts should be dedicated to confronting the imperialist invasion of the Arab region—quite aside from whether the move by Iraq in overrunning Kuwait was sound or not. The secret party organ in the homeland, *Al-Thawra Mustamera,* focused its agitation and mobilization of public opinion on a group of central points. Perhaps most important was the call for the confrontation in the Gulf not to be restricted to conventional warfare, but to include guerrilla warfare to deal with the tremendous military machine being amassed against Iraq. While the party communicated that Iraq was an irreplaceable support for the Intifada, it also called on the Palestinian people to rely on themselves and not bet on other factors.

Developments in the Gulf not only preoccupied the daily thoughts, concerns, and wagers of the Arab public, but they also dominated the coverage of world media. These developments entered the spotlight for the world as well as the Palestinian people, displacing the Intifada, which had lost a great deal of the grassroots character that had distinguished it during 1988–89. Meanwhile, the armed wings of Fateh, the PFLP, and Hamas—which were basically formed out of the fugitives of the Intifada—became more active, specifically in the Gaza Strip.

As for the Iraqis, they had taken a nationalist political turn and tied the Gulf issue indivisibly to the Palestinian issue, calling for a solution to both on the basis of international legitimacy. The American-Israeli hypocrisy was clearly exposed: in the Gulf they cried crocodile tears for the Kuwaiti's right to self-determination and human rights, whereas in reality it was all an inter-Arab affair. But in Palestine, they coddled Israel, which was refusing to acknowledge the Palestinian people's right to return, trampling on their self-determination.

The coupling of the Palestinian and Gulf issues was given concrete meaning at a press conference with Iraq's Foreign Minister, Tariq Aziz. Asked whether or not Iraq was serious about retaliating against Israel if their forces in Kuwait were attacked, he replied, "Absolutely, yes!" and unambiguously affirmed the indivisibility of the two issues. His reply struck all Israel sympathizers who heard him like a thunderbolt. The Palestinians cheered this categorical affirmation, even if there were many among them who doubted it, having heard many Arab threats dissipate with the wind, leaving no effect other than the media clamor ringing in their ears. The question that posed the greater challenge was how the Palestinians would respond to their cause being related to the Iraqi cause. Would they affirm this by fighting on the ground?

"I still believe that matters have not reached a dead end from a purely rational point of view. There must be a way out, some kind of solution. I cannot imagine a war that would mobilize forces on a large scale. What is happening is pure madness or more precisely, an American imperialist plan."

"There are only a few hours left before the American-Atlantic* deadline given to Iraq. Under these circumstances, war will break out. The question is when will they strike Iraq—tomorrow morning? If not that, when? Why doesn't Saddam announce that he will withdraw? By overrunning Kuwait, he affirmed his claim to Kuwait. Let him withdraw and exploit the situation to demand Kuwait while continuing the consolidation of his economic and military power." Kan'an discussed this with Hisham hoping that the Iraqi leadership would make the decision to withdraw and avoid a military confrontation which could destroy Iraq.

"I think Iraq is betting on military options unknown to us, perhaps some sort of arms—ultimately states have military secrets. Perhaps he is thinking about the Soviet position, particularly considering the mutual defense treaty between them . . . although I believe this apostate Gorbachev will only stab him in the back in the interest of America."

"There is a *mawwal*** playing in Saddam's head. Once one understands it, can one understand his tactics; to withdraw or not to withdraw is a tactic. The important thing is what truth lies in this *mawwal*: is it a regional Gulf *mawwal* about swallowing up the oil of the sheikhdom-protectorates,[37] which, incidentally, would be a good thing from a historical economic perspective; or is it a nationalist awakening, liberationist type of *mawwal* about unity? If it is a nationalist *mawwal*, should we think of Saddam as an Arab

---

* Atlantic here is referring to the North Atlantic Treaty Organization (NATO).
** Plaintive love song.

Bismarck, or as Muhammad 'Ali Pasha[38] in military uniform at the end of the twentieth century?"

"If this is his *mawwal*, then he is truly a Bismarck, proposing united nationalist renaissance slogans, building a center of production by Third World standards in a serious fashion. It seems to me that he is trying to achieve what the Arab bourgeoisie failed to do: industrialization and the end of dependency on the West. Even if he cannot end it categorically, Saddam is improving his position and acting more like a partner. He is also attempting a comprehensive renaissance in education and importing and developing technology..."

"As to whether his move on Kuwait could be the beginning of a comprehensive nationalist project, then he could be a Bismarck, I hope that is the case. What could be better than a leader who unites the Arabs even if blood is spilled? For history's sake, that would be better than being split into twenty-two states, most of which do not even satisfy the prerequisites for modern cities. But I think there was a different scenario in which his nationalist movement could have entered Jordan, where the king would welcome them seeing as his greatest fear is Jordan becoming 'The Alternate Homeland.'[39] Furthermore, the monarchy has the right to protection which Iraq is capable of providing under treaty. Then let him open a battle front with Israel. Militarily and in terms of the human potential of his population, Saddam can undergo a lengthy war with Israel. As they are primarily accustomed to war by blitz, a lengthy war is the type that Israel's army cannot endure. Israel has a small, besieged population. It cannot afford a war of attrition, particularly considering that Iraq's military technology, which compared to Israel's, is not bad. At any rate, a tribal chief in the Gulf cannot demand repayments of loans to Iraq dating back to the Iraq-Iran War, nor can Djibouti be so presumptive as to send its army to participate in the war against Iraq. Besides, the international position would change seeing as the Arabs are at war with Israel to begin with."

"This scenario would make Iraq the unrivaled leader of the Arab World, enabling it to impose its logic on the region. Approval of Arab leadership, first and foremost was and remains to be gained through the Arab-Israeli conflict. That was Abdel Nasser's experience when he occupied his prestigious position, and that was the reason for the prominence of the Palestinian revolution in its heyday. The persistent question has not changed. What are the horizons of the Iraqi invasion of Kuwait in Iraqi strategic thought? In addition to the previous question: when will Iraq be struck? There are many questions waiting for events to answer."

His comrade, who was a leader with extensive experience in resistance and capable of analysis, was not unaware of the fact that war was inevitably coming. Hisham was just unable to morally accept that hundreds of thousands of troops were in possession of advanced military technology for annihilation at the level of lasers, infrared technology, and computers.

"They will clash in a military campaign of killing using the most modern means. It is human madness created and fed by the widespread desire to enslave and monopolize. The Iraqis need to make their calculations well. It is not possible for the people of a Third World nation to defeat a great power in a conventional war. Only guerrilla warfare, a people's guerrilla war, is capable of neutralizing and rendering the use of military technology pointless. We have already learnt something from the Intifada: fighter planes, tanks, and artillery are of no use against stones and Molotov cocktails and pistols."

Those were his comrade's comments as they debated continuously throughout the day starting in the morning. They discussed as they ate breakfast. As they listened to news broadcasts, they would comment before the announcer had finished reading the news item. They would remain on the same topic as they prepared lunch.

"But they say Iraq has developed chemical and nuclear weapons and that should redress the imbalance and could deter the attackers," Kan'an replied.

"Those weapons, if they exist, are not at all easy to use. Iraq knows that if it tried to deploy those weapons, the US could wipe it off the face of the earth. Those weapons are for resistance. They are a means to apply pressure, but using them is not an easy matter. The international situation cannot handle the use of nuclear weapons."

They were not the only ones engaged in such a debate. The whole world, including the people of the homeland, were caught in similar discussions. As per usual, everyone turned into a political analyst and a military commentator. Nor were the effects of these international developments restricted to stimulating debate—they impacted the life of the people as a whole. Both the people and their occupiers considered the homeland to be the arena of a probable war. People were consumed with the effort to buy supplies for storage and the materials necessary to fortify rooms against a probable Iraqi chemical attack. As for the merchants—that breed of people committed to their customary role as thieves under dire circumstances—they raised the price of everything, from a sack of flour to duct tape for safe rooms. As a result, the already downtrodden became even more so as their pockets were squeezed for every last penny. Vendor carts were everywhere, selling everything for unbelievable prices. The municipality handed out gas masks. Those who had initially made light of the situation began to think of what would become of their children, if not themselves, as the American deadline to Iraq approached.

In the early days of 1991, the party distributed a circular containing directives that members work in two main directions: the first was to escalate resistance in the street against the Occupation, and the second was to offer services to people in the areas where they were stationed. As an exceptional measure to facilitate activities under the circumstances of war, it was decided that all members would work together in their areas regardless of their position in the party so that they would all become field operatives.

If everyone was to become a field operative, where did that leave Kan'an? Action, according to this conception, does not extend to those who are confined within walls. For eight years he had not been considered a resistance operative in the field.

"If the war takes on a new direction such as the involvement of Israel or if there are collective expulsion campaigns against our people, I shall not remain in my safe house. I will go down to the street with my comrades, and I shall probably join my efforts with our rural comrades."

He informed the party of his decision and his proposal was accepted. His safe house also underwent preparations for war, and Hisham carried out a mission to supply the safe house with provisions sufficient for a family over several months! There were dozens of cans of food, meat and fish, fava beans, hummus, rice, sugar, salt, oil . . . When the municipality car distributing gas masks came to the area where he lived, he could not risk going down to receive his mask, but Hisham thought of a way to get him one. As for preparing a sealed room for protection against chemical gas, Kan'an ignored the matter, despite his conviction that the war could take a dangerous turn, until the last minute, just a few days before the warning period was set to expire. After he prepared his room, he entered it once and tried sealing the door with tape, just out of curiosity. He cooped himself up in the room with a bottle of water, a can of food and a few loaves of bread. He felt silly doing that and did not return to his room afterwards.

At 11:00 p.m. on January 16, 1991, Kan'an slipped into bed. His anxiety was at its height. It was one day after the American deadline and everyone was anticipating that something would happen. He wasn't the only one feeling the tension—everyone was wracked with anticipation. The old inflammation in Kan'an's foot had flared up and he could no longer walk without difficulty. This bad luck only exacerbated his worries and reminded him of hard times, the likes of which he had not experienced in eight years. What made things worse was that the inflammation was accompanied by a fever, and his head was heavy with delirious hallucinations and troubled thoughts. He had barely fallen asleep when he woke up again for no apparent reason at 1:45 a.m. Without thinking he turned on the radio. The dial was turned to an Israeli station. The announcer was reading a news bulletin in her familiar voice at a point in time when the radio station should have been off the air. He sat up and listened, fighting off sleep. The tremendous, bloody attack on Iraq had begun on the dawn of January 17. The tone of the announcer, who was relaying the presumed facts of the battlefield, was noticeably confident. Planes and airfields, tanks, missile launcher platforms, troops, and anti-aircraft centers . . . all had been destroyed . . . in other words there was nothing that had escaped the destruction. He felt anger boiling up in him. *Could it be? Did they place their aircrafts, tanks, and missile launchers on the tops of trees so that they could be easily picked off and destroyed in the first hour? Could this son of a bitch be believed when he says that Iraq had been defeated in just hours? Is Iraq the Egypt of 1967, Saddam in the role of Abdel Nasser?*

He was speaking out loud as he walked towards the kitchen, tolerating the pain. *Why didn't he strike Israel? Tariq 'Aziz had said "Absolutely Yes!" When will they do it? It would be a disaster if what he said was just psychological warfare!* Kan'an ate two bananas, poured some milk into his cup, and returned to bed to listen to the news bulletins. He was smoking voraciously. All of the stations were singing the same defeatist tune as the Israeli station, except for Jordanian one which held out some hope. At 4:00 a.m. military patrols were roaming the streets, announcing the usual Israeli order: "To all the people of Ramallah: a curfew is in place until further notice!" The Occupation was also treating the homeland as a potential site of war. A state of emergency was imposed in anticipation of any mass or military activities against the Occupation in solidarity with Iraq.

The war was changing Kan'an's life inside his safe house. He had no tasks to fulfill or meetings to hold. The tasks at hand were all in the field. Each of his comrades were at their stations, carrying out orders to help the population mobilize and confront Israeli propaganda, assuring the people that Iraq would fulfill its promise.

There would be gestures in this direction: in fact, in the early hours of January 18, Iraq fired three Hussein missiles—upgraded Scud missiles—at West Jerusalem. Kan'an had taken to sleeping during the day and staying up at night in front of the TV, following news bulletins and waiting to hear warning sirens. He had spread his mattress on the floor next to the radio and the TV, with his cigarettes and medicine next to him. When the siren would go off, he would rise with difficulty and run, sometimes hopping on one foot, at other times leaning on his injured foot as well, racing to climb the sixteen steps from the door of his safe house to the roof, propping his hands against the wall. He would look to the east, rubbing his hands together, partly out of anticipation and excitement and partly because of the cold. After four or five minutes there would appear from the east a shining, burning red mass entering Palestine, coming from Iraq across Jordan, headed towards the depths of the Israeli interior. He would follow the beloved missile with his eyes, gleefully, like a man who sees his love crossing the street after a long time apart. Once it was out of sight, that failure—also known as the Patriot missile—would attempt to intercept it. But it would fail, and the Patriot would proceed to follow a descending arc. Seconds later, the frightening sound of an explosion would be heard in Tel Aviv,[40] Haifa,[41] Ramat Gan[42] . . . Kan'an would then descend quickly hopping on one foot, the same way he had ascended. He would turn on the TV and the radio to learn exactly where the missile had hit and what casualties it had caused, and most importantly, if it had a conventional or a chemical warhead.

The people developed their private rituals of joy and exhilaration for the Iraqi missiles, which became dear to the hearts of the Palestinians. The people altogether took to climbing to the roofs of their houses and saluting the missiles by whistling and yelling, as if they were fans cheering on their team in a stadium. Once the missiles hit their targets and the explosions were heard and people saw the bright flashes the rituals would reach their peak with shrieks and yells piercing the silence of the night and drowning out the sounds of the rain, and occasional thunder and hail. The people had the right to celebrate: striking the depth of Israeli territory was of great historical and political significance. For forty-five years of the Arab-Israeli conflict, Israel had been out of reach while Arab capitals—Cairo, Damascus, Beirut, Baghdad, and even Tunis—had been hit by the warmongering Israelis.

The people had the right to feel exhilarated as they saw Israeli panic become the dominant trend, not just amongst the masses but on an official national scale. It began with Israel's Foreign Minister David Levi, who had become discombobulated while making a direct broadcast on television. He had heard the sirens, cried "*Mazi mazi azakut*,"[*] and then the screen had gone blank, replaced by the shuddering TV announcer slapping her cheeks in fear while reading the news broadcast. This scene had led the youth to sing:

Announcer we wish you well,
Perhaps you need your mask as well.
Such a pity, such indignation,
If only it would hit the broadcast station,
Toot, toot, toot,
The Patriot is of no use.

With every rocket, the "ordinary citizens" crowded into their shelters and safe rooms, putting on their masks. Our people did not worry about missiles carrying chemical warheads! No one went to their room and put on their masks. Everyone was on the roof whistling, shrieking, and cheering and directing the missile as though they were steering it: "*Yalla*, muster your strength," "Hurry, be careful," "The Patriot's been fired," "Go right," "Go to Tel Aviv," "Hurry, hurry"!

As for that old woman from Al-Bireh, she said on an international TV network what the whole people were saying. She asked the journalist while the viewers watched:

"If I say something, will Saddam hear me?"

"He will hear you! Speak, *hajjeh*!"

"Listen Saddam, strike and don't worry if it hits us along with them, hit them and hit us!"

But the resistance of the people in the homeland was paralyzed and they were unable to rejoice in their struggle. As a result, the

---

[*] Hebrew for "What is this, what is this noise?"

limited capacities of the resistance factions became apparent in relation to the needs of the moment." The curfew inhibited any possibility of the emergence of any real resistance, whether armed or not." That is what was said! Not all factions lived up to their slogans and the calls they made before the war broke out. A revolutionary does not search for a suitable occasion to resist; circumstances are always averse according to the true international revolutionary Ernesto Che Guevara. That is what the real fighters said. In Lebanon, the party's combatants along with other factions opened a new front in the north within the first two days after the war broke out, marking the moment with thick volleys of Katyusha rockets.

That attack, however, did not last more than forty-eight hours as all the involved parties, including the Lebanese National Movement, made them stop. Nor were American interests hit wherever they could be found—that turned out to be an empty slogan, baseless in terms of actual capability. As for the Molotov cocktail hurled at the American embassy in Rome, for which the party claimed responsibility, that could not really be considered a strike at American interests, except as a joke!

The incapacity of the man hiding in the safe house during wartime has its own fragrance. Incapacity was the master of the situation: the incapacity to participate in any party activity and the incapacity to walk straight. The abscess on his leg had burst so that the old wound opened and pus ran out. He treated it each day as he had been accustomed to for years, squeezing out the pus, cleaning the wound, and wrapping it in medical gauze. When his body temperature exceeded thirty-nine degrees Celsius, he would quickly undress and take a cold bath for hours to bring his temperature down only to have it rise again. He would repeat this cold treatment regularly. He needed a visit from a medical specialist. Once the doctor heard Kan'an's history with the disease, he dispensed with a full examination.

"You need to undergo an operation as soon as possible," he said quickly. "That knee needs to be cleaned out."

"I can't go to the hospital. I am one of the Intifada fugitives. Find me a solution that does not involve surgery." Kan'an's firm tone cut short any protest from the doctor. Kan'an was well aware of the difficulty of getting to a hospital within the short timeframe that the doctor wanted. At the very least, security arrangements would have to be made to ensure that the operation would remain secret, which could not happen quickly. On top of that there were still the circumstances of war, the curfew, and the open opportunity for the conflict to develop into a regional war. The doctor did not argue. It seemed to Kan'an that he understood.

"You are in no danger of losing your leg now or later. However, you need to clean it properly. Squeeze out as much pus as you can and clean the wound well. I will prescribe you six months' worth of medicine. It is a strong antibiotic, perhaps it will contain the infection. During that time, you will have to make preparations for surgery. Okay?"

Kan'an's illness physically hindered him from performing the simplest necessities of life: walking, preparing his food, washing the dishes. When he did make food, he chose something that only required minutes to prepare and then he would lay back down. Walking too much or standing for a long time would increase the pus and his discomfort. Hisham, his right-hand man and support, was there whenever he could be. Whenever the curfew was lifted for a few days, he would visit Kan'an for a couple of hours and help him clean. He would bring ready-made food or something his wife had cooked under the impression that they were for "miserable" university students missing home-cooked meals! Hisham was a comrade at a time of need; he filled the place of an entire family. Kan'an felt proud of Hisham despite his frustrations with his own circumstances and resentment of his infirmity.

In those days Kan'an lived with the difficulty of another illness, an illness that afflicts a man living alone. This illness was not merely a pain in the organ, but a sharp stab in the back at the hands of his enemy. As if it wasn't enough that he had to bear the loneliness of his safe house and was deprived of the third fundamental element in his trinity—his body was also stubbornly resisting him. He would complain and get into bad moods and seek solace in a film, but as soon as he needed to move again, his bad mood returned and he would be back to his complaints and vexation. He never thought of his third fundamental as a maker of tea or a preparer of hot meals, nor a maker of cold presses for his forehead, a reminder to take his medicine at dawn, nor a cleaner of the kitchen floor without whom it would be left dirty. Until he entered the ninth year of his secret life, he had seen this fundamental element as he wanted it to be: a revolutionary, deranged person like himself, afflicted with the madness of revolution, life, and love, a person in whom he discovered himself, whose company he relished in, someone closer to a poetic spirit, as though music had created them specially for Kan'an ... But with the war waging on, and as he walked, leaning against a wall or a chair, the fever in his head upsetting his balance and making him delirious, he brought down this fundamental element from the heights of revolution, love, poetry, and music—down to the mundane world of everyday life. He now wished for someone to help him with his boring house chores, someone to ask when there was something he needed, someone who he now just saw as a sick man would find any woman before him. He was not happy that his fundamental element was transformed in his imagination from a tableau he had painted with his brush, full of hope and desire, into what he needed and wanted in that moment: a housewife.

During this time, Kan'an did not forget the words of his comrade and teacher, Muhammad Qatamesh, who died following the onset of paralysis, a result of being tortured and the circumstances of captivity: "The incapacitation brought on by sickness is a killer. Even Lenin himself, had he passed through a similar period, would have experienced moments when he turned against everything he believed in." Kan'an had not fully understood the meaning of these words which he heard some months before he began his clandestine existence. This confirmed an axiom in Kan'an's life: it is one thing to hear a statement, quite another to experience it. Now, in the moments of his impotence, experiencing weakness and pain—even if much less than the martyr experienced—he understood perfectly what Qatamesh meant. A moment of human weakness can creep up on us; if it strikes us, we collapse and if we strike it, it makes us stronger.

His inner self intruded every now and then, as it was wont to do, but as usual he silenced it. For years he had been heaping abuse and curses on his situation, but he would quickly forget all of that when it was time for a news bulletin or a report by CNN journalist Peter Arnett, or when Hisham would show up, expressing his solidarity and camaraderie, or engaging him in a quick discussion of the military situation in the Gulf. At such times, Kan'an reverted to his true nature: a clandestine resistance fighter in hiding.

It had been a month since the war started and the situation had become quite confusing. There were no battles in the military sense of the term, only air raids, long-range missiles, artillery bombardments of Iraqi-fortified positions, and military installations in Kuwait and Iraq. Sa'd Al-Din Al-Shazli[43] provided analysis backed by his experience as a savvy military commander and tactician. He inspired optimism by saying: "The battle has not yet begun. All this is just preparation for an American invasion."

But gradually it was becoming clear that the United States was fighting with the advanced technology of the turn of the century. Its pilots pressed buttons from heights that could not be reached by Iraqi ground-to-air missiles. From the Red Sea, the US was hitting their targets precisely using remotely-guided and computer-directed cruise missiles. When they felt it necessary, the American "defenders of human rights" were not averse to bombing civilian sites like the 'Amiriyah shelter[44] in an attempt to shake the unity of the Iraqi internal front. From behind their advanced equipment, it was clear the American soldiers were only fighting as technical experts, while the Iraqis, sheltering in their fortifications in Kuwait and Iraq, spent a month and a half under attack without the possibility of imposing the "logic of battle" in the way that they had been trained.* On the

---

* Rafeedie writes here that this style entailed "armies and weapons and tanks facing each other in the battlefield, open battles in the style of World War II, using Soviet tactics of tank warfare."

political front, the people did not act to shake the stability of reactionary regimes, nor did the Soviets mobilize under the leadership of Gorbachev.

As for the people engaged in the Intifada, they had placed all their bets on Iraq's military capabilities and an Iraqi victory. Here Palestinian political thought was caught in its second predicament, thinking that Iraq could do the job of the Intifada. For a month, Kan'an's life had followed a unique and regular, seemingly normal, pattern. Any unusual conduct, once it was repeated day after day, week after week, could turn within a short time into a routine way of life. He would wake up at six or seven in the evening and have breakfast, then eat lunch at one or two in the morning, and dinner at eight in the morning and then go to sleep. The timing of the missiles fired at Israel forced this new routine on him, seeing as they were fired at night, and he of course had to wait for the air raid siren to go off and then climb to the roof hopping on one-and-a-half legs. He was one of the people and he refused to give up the right to do what they were doing, even if he had to climb to the roof crawling on all fours.

One evening the sky was bountiful with the rare combination of heavy rain and thick fog. He climbed to the roof as fast as he could with no time to put on his wool sweater, and stood there gazing at the east while trying to shelter from the rain near the door to the roof. He wasn't even wearing socks to protect his feet from the cold surface. The beloved missile did not appear on schedule—*Where had it gone? It should have been visible? Was the siren a mistake? Did the missile lose its way?* Two minutes later he heard an explosion and stepped out into the rain, searching in all directions. He saw a quick flash to the south. The Hussein missile had gone in the direction of Jerusalem this time and he missed it! He used all of the swear words he could remember at the time and went back inside feeling defeated. He slipped into bed after changing out of his wet clothes but continued to shiver from the cold.

He ate, sitting on his mattress on the floor. In order to move as little as possible, he lived off of salted fish for two weeks because they could be eaten cold. He relaxed and enjoyed the simple meal. He watched two films by the famous Italian director Federico Fellini and sketches by British comedian Benny Hill. When he had no luck with television, he turned to the radio and tried to find songs by Abdel Halim Hafez, Mohammed Abdel Wahab, or Fairuz . . .

His comrade who had come to visit him commented on the movements of American forces near the border with Iraq: "By opening this front they wanted to cut off Saddam's line of retreat. He carried out the withdrawal under the smokescreen created from the burning oil wells in Kuwait before declaring his intention to retreat. The objective of the war was to crush Iraq's forces. In Kuwait, Americans were chasing the retreating Iraqi forces from behind while attacking along their path from the direction of Saudi Arabia. It was a pincer move."

"Will the Americans risk invading Iraq?"

"That is a different question. It would be an occupation. Even the Shi'ites of the south[45] would resist this invasion, in my opinion. The area is also suitable for guerrilla warfare. The Americans would drown in the quagmire. The field in southern Iraq is like that. Prince Hassan[46] has hinted that developments in the war would take a different dimension in the event of an invasion, and Mudar Badran[47] frankly used the term 'guerrilla warfare.' The important question, however: Have the Republic Guards[48] stationed there trained to fight a guerrilla war? Has the public been mobilized and armed for this option? A people's war requires a comprehensive policy at all levels and on all fronts of society."

"I imagine matters will take that course. Otherwise, why did the Iraqis not leave a few thousand special forces in Kuwait's capital to engage in urban warfare, even if only to confuse the Americans and inflict some casualties on them? That would have sapped their morale and opened an internal front. The capital, Kuwait City, is very large—bigger than Beirut. Why didn't they leave pockets of resistance there? Is it because of the difficulty of fighting in the midst of a hostile population?"

The ideas, questions, and unknowns were abundant. However, it was clear that Iraq had suffered a military blow that had depleted its power and set it back several years, which would leave its imprint on the Arab region, favoring American-Israeli arrogance. At first glance, the Iraqi project appeared to have been defeated, for some time at least.

The war ended and its bitter particulars no longer occupied Kan'an's mind in his safe house. What remained was the defeat. It was over, and the joy departed to be replaced by frustration and lamentation of the moment of withdrawal. The missiles coming from the east, Peter Arnett's reports, the reversal of night and day and their subsequent return to their normal cycle, the military synonyms of war—Al-Hussein missiles, Patriot missiles, air raid sirens, missile launchers . . . Nothing was left of them except for the Iraqi challenge to the most formidable military power in the world and the destruction of Iraq's infrastructure which had taken twenty years to build. One precious memory remained: the missiles striking the Israeli interior. What was also left were the handful of ill-advised political wagers and tactics, and the failure of the Palestinian factions and people to support Iraq in its war. The infection in his leg and the pus had gone, and his strength gradually returned. As for the Palestinian people who had placed all of their bets on Iraq because of their attachment to the spirit of confrontation and to the missile strikes on Tel Aviv, Haifa, and Jerusalem—their Intifada was broken as well and its activities were being scaled back, apart from those of the armed groups.

The Americans capitalized on the defeat of the Arab's effort to improve their situation internationally and in the market. They lost no time in affirming their political hegemony after having asserted it through the force of arms and war, or in harvesting the fruits of that hegemony by putting forward a project for the "resolution" of our national cause, tailored to suit their interests and in line with Israel's old plan, the "self-rule" plan. In March 1991, US Secretary of State James Baker brought with him a plan that undermined the national program and the Intifada. The leadership of the PLO snatched up the plan and instructed its prominent leaders in the homeland to receive him. The PFLP refused to take part which increased divisions within the PLO and the Intifada. It appeared that a new era was on the horizon.

Within the party, the debate among the ranks of the cadre and the leadership became more boisterous. The intractable crisis in the Soviet Union which threatened its own future as well as that of the collapse of socialism in Eastern Europe, the collapse of the official order in the Arab World and the defeat of Iraq, the declaration of agreement with US policy by the PLO leadership, the increasing weakness and retreat of the Intifada, specifically in the area of popular participation, and finally, the unwillingness or inability of some factions (specifically the leftist ones) to give the Intifada the push it needed by augmenting its capabilities against the Occupation . . . All of these developments were indicators that a new and difficult period was coming in the wake of the Gulf War. The left was on the threshold of national and historic tasks which would test it and its capabilities to play the role of alternative to the political right.

There was a clamorous debate within the party. It was discovered that following the three-year trial, the project of transforming the party into "the Leading Force"[49] was far from a project that could be implemented in practice considering the party's level of development, not to mention a whole string of other objective reasons. Still, the efforts to implement it had played a tremendous role in stimulating activity, increasing membership (up by 80 percent in 1990), and establishing new organizations and opportunities for action, such as instituting committees and organizations for professional revolutionaries, developing the party's information effort, and publishing the secret party newspaper on a biweekly basis.

However, the development of the party illustrated its strength new structure with two branches: one in the homeland, and one outside of it. Therefore, the natural conclusion decided at the end of 1992 was that the branch in the homeland should assert its weight in preparing to hold the party's fifth national conference.[50] The homeland branch could do so by delegate participation from the homeland, or the drafting of resolutions, or the structure of the new leadership of the party, which would be on the conference agenda.

The party's organizations in the homeland discussed the proposed program, formulated for the first time, as well as the military report, which clearly reflected the crisis faced by the party. This crisis was exacerbated by the inability to launch a clandestine armed guerrilla movement in the homeland due to the inadequate accumulation of organizational and mass power on the one hand, and the dominance of political concerns over the party's activities on the other. There were also other matters concerning the party outside the homeland. All of these factors caused the importance of the project of transforming the party into "the Leading Force" to be diminished, or rather revealed its inadequacy as a slogan. It was also clear that without a guerrilla movement there was nothing that could transform the project into a political reality.

Kan'an contributed to some of the clamorous debate going around. He started thinking about the special arrangement to send him to the conference as a delegate, eagerly awaiting the success of his arrangements and imagining his successful arrival and participation in the conference. He would bear the nation's concerns, struggles, and experience, meet leaders of the party, understand new dimensions of the struggle, and finally gain some measure of relaxation after many months of incapacity. After this, he would return to continue his walled-in existence as a professional revolutionary during a stage of difficulties.

One of those difficulties lay in the crisis and collapse of the model of actually-existing socialism. Since Kan'an had found his way to leftist Marxist thought he had devoured everything he could lay his hands on, including books, studies, and magazines about the Soviet Union and socialism. He had hungered socialist knowledge since his early youth in the mid-1970s while he was in jail, and his appetite had only increased throughout his clandestine existence, where neither time nor reading materials were in short supply.

After Gorbachev's rise to the position of Secretary General of the party and given his positions and statements, Kan'an's desire to follow what was going on in the Soviet Union increased. Kan'an's party did not close the door to discussion or freedom of thought, but its ideological program was clear and should not be violated— whoever disagreed with it should find another option. Even though the party's cadre was largely raised on the publications of the Soviet school, the party nevertheless encouraged cultural diversity in its program and through bilateral dialogue. He read many theorists who disagreed with the Soviet school of Marxism (György Lukács, Antonio Gramsci, Leon Trotsky, Mao Zedong, Che Guevara, Mehdi Amel . . .) and he kept up with many periodicals (*Al-Nahj, Al-Yasar Al-'Arabi, Al-Tariq, Al-Thaqafa Al-Jadida, Qadaya Al-Selm wa Al-Ishtirakiyah*[51] . . .) in an organized manner, although the effort was strained at times by his clandestine existence and the possibilities it offered. His socialist conviction was unshakable in his heart and mind as the historical choice for those who toil, but he could see that criticism of actually existing socialism was one thing, while the rush by the Gorbachev leadership to substitute socialism for capitalism was quite another.

Kan'an understood Gorbachev's diagnosis of the real situation of the Communist Party of the Soviet Union and its relationship with the state, democracy, and workers' supremacy in the factory. But he had also glimpsed Gorbachev's unprincipled wooing of capitalism and his nixing of the revolutionary principle of "class struggle!" He had read everything he could find on what was happening in the Soviet Union and the socialist bloc. In 1989, he had read Trotsky's most famous book, *The Revolution Betrayed*, and observed the singular genius of that communist leader and pontificator who wrote in the 1930s about his expectations for the future of socialism after first analyzing its rise, and saw these predictions come true in the 1980s and 1990s. Trotsky is one of the most masterful authors who was able to predict the future of socialism through an analysis of its contradictions, namely the disruption of the relationship between the trio—"party, state, and class"—as well as of socialist accumulation, capitalist siege, and the resulting extreme centralization, the worsening of bureaucracy, and the absence of workers' democracy, alienating the worker from his production, and thus enabling the authority of bureaucrats from the top of the pyramid ("the state") to its bottom ("the factory manager").

That same year, Kan'an had read Isaac Deutscher's trilogy about Trotsky: *The Prophet Unarmed, The Prophet Armed,* and *The Prophet Outcast.* This helped him to understand that in the 1920s and 1930s, the Soviet form of socialism had been encircled and under siege, trying to effect a rapid qualitative transition in manufacturing and agriculture while warding off the claws of the capitalist beasts. Such a socialism had no other option than to centralize within the state apparatus and everything else in order to rapidly construct a socialist economic base. This would inevitably lead to a political system in which bureaucracy would flourish; and as a result of this centralization, democracy would be marginalized. This made sense to Kan'an: no one demands that a state in a time of war and siege be a paragon of democracy.

On the one hand and for this reason, Kan'an had come to admire Stalin's personality, as a man of secret action, the leader and follower of the socialist experiment who had managed not only to construct its model but also to defeat the Nazi beast. On the other hand, Kan'an could not accept Stalin's power grabs and tyranny, which had produced the assassination of historic leaders of the revolution and the party, such as Trotsky and Bukharin whom Stalin had described as traitors and hung from the gallows alongside two-thirds of the central committee. . . . Kan'an had read and read and formulated his own points of view about these events, reinforcing his conviction that there was no substitute for socialism—through humanity's historical experience, socialism would prove itself to be the best model.

In general, the party in the homeland was united on one position. Reflected in the political bureau circular issued in December 1989, this position concerned a speedy resolution of the crisis in the Soviet Union. The circular registered its frank criticism of Soviet foreign policy and raised questions about how much Gorbachev's actions constituted a service to socialism.

Chapter 10

"You have a jovial disposition. You sing along with your Sheikh in rapture, you hum, you delightedly tap along with foreign songs, you joke and tell funny stories. That's good, very good, especially after nine years hiding between walls. After all of the difficulties that have been heaped on us for some time now, you seem relaxed." So said his comrade who visited him in May 1991, unexpectedly broaching the topic while Kan'an was slicing a tomato.

"Maybe that's just my nature. My temperament is cheerful, perhaps that is my way of defeating the difficulties of life and this experience. Do you know, I sometimes surprise myself: 'How can I be merry despite the cruelties?' I am committed to the golden rule of the Intifada, 'offense is the best defense,' and so I attack my woes before they get to me with merriment and jokes. To smile in the face of difficulties is to make light of them, which is the prelude to defeating them."

"Makes sense. That is a good approach. But tell me, do you want for anything? What is it that you need most after all these years?"

"To sit on the threshold of our family house with a cup of tea and a cigarette, with the pretty little one in my lap—of course, unfortunately she is no longer little." He corrected himself, speaking out loud. "I want to sit there watching the passersby. To partake in the bad habits of our elders, sitting there idle. I actually wish I could do that."

"Your requests are quite modest, comrade, but they are impossible, quite impossible to satisfy. That is what it means to be in hiding; it places simple human demands in the pigeonhole of the impossible. I thought you were going to speak about something else, about the most basic human need." His comrade winked as he said this, giving a knowing smile, which Kan'an understood. Kan'an warned him with a look.

"My inner self demands those more basic human needs, but I silence it with difficulty. Don't remind me of it, don't let it get the better of me. Leave it be!"

"Your third fundamental element insists on not appearing."

"My religion stands on two pillars, two fundamental elements and that's enough. I can't give such high honor to the desires of the flesh, that would require three fundamental elements—leave it alone."

"Does Muna still ever cross your mind, or has she been displaced?"

"The past, history, is never displaced. There remains a fuzzy image of her, fragments of memory, laughter, arguments, and whispers. It is a transitory apparition, in the hours of solitude; an incitement before breakfast in the early morning. Although I do not dream of her, I do not relinquish the components of my history and personality, of which she is a part."

"I see. Has it occurred to you, then . . . I mean, do you think about the future of this experiment?"

Kan'an looked at his comrade in astonishment.

"Has the party decided to interrogate me? What's with you today?"

His comrade chuckled and opened the fridge, taking out a second tomato.

"I am just trying to figure out what you're thinking. Have you considered your future as a fugitive in hiding?"

"Oh. As if I don't have the time for that." Kan'an had finished slicing his tomato. He placed the knife down on the table and pushed the plate aside. He looked at his comrade, who was standing by the refrigerator munching on the tomato with appetite. "I see only four scenarios: either I am arrested; or we are successful in establishing our state while I am still alive and I am delivered from this confinement (of course we know that the state is far off); or I say I am tired, or you say to me, 'pack your bags, we will smuggle you out for we can no longer protect you'; or, lastly, I could die while I am between these walls."

"The first three scenarios are reasonable. Forget the fourth one."

"Why?"

"I can't discuss it, I can't even listen to that so don't talk to me about it. Put it aside."

But Kan'an had already gotten the idea into his head.

"It is a possibility and you have to take it into account."

His comrade had finished his tomato and said firmly, "I will not. Enough!"

"You are free to do that, but I do think about it. Incidentally"—he felt provocative—"will I be treated like a martyr if I die a natural death while engaged in this experience? For instance, as a result of a heart attack or a brain tumor? Will you put up posters ending with the phrase: 'Glory and eternal life to our martyred comrade Kan'an Subhi'?"

"Stop kidding around! Your jokes are getting on my nerves. How do you assess your ability to tolerate the coming years of this experience?"

Kan'an sat down on a chair, lit a cigarette, looking serious. "I will endure; the party can have confidence in that. I am used to leading a clandestine existence . . . Although I am choosing resistance, it is not a preference for a way of life. I fear I may never be able to leave these walls," He said with a smile on his face. "I mean I have grown accustomed to this curse. I have come to fear that I may be in love with this secret life as if it were the woman of my dreams." While his jokes concealed his serious intent, his facial expressions gave him away. His comrade knew Kan'an and knew what was behind his sarcasm.

"There is no romance in struggle or in such a way of life," Kan'an continued. "Instead there is deprivation and hardship and challenge. Of course, I am here out of necessity, not enjoyment. You know that, you know my position and we've discussed this before." He took a long drag from his cigarette. "The experience has become part of me, and I am a part of it. Rather like what that great Sufi, Al-Hallaj, said to his Creator: 'I am You and You are me, we are two spirits inhabiting the same body.' Similarly, I cannot imagine myself without this cursed life—in the full sense of the term. It may be hard on my health, on my mind, but even if I had to forsake it, I wouldn't do that until a few days after the beginning of the new millennium."

He was now speaking of his own experiences after nine years of struggle and hardship, years which had formed him. What he had to say now was in sharp contrast to what he had had to say during his first months of the experience. "You will get used to it!" his comrades used to console him.

"How? You don't know what you're talking about. How shall I get used to no life?" Kan'an would respond.

"We know more than you do. The experience of the collective is more significant than the experience of the individual. This will pass and nothing will remain of this house except stones. You will look back at what you're saying now and laugh. Be a man and bear up!"

And he did get used to it. Now, he spoke in the name of what had been carved in his psyche and on his skin, not in the name of his hesitations and weaknesses and his inflated inner self. The party knew a great deal about his suffering. All he could see before him during those early years was the party and its expectations. The collective always has more experience than the individual. Kan'an endured. He endured for the eight years that had gone by and here he was crossing the threshold of the ninth, committing himself to hours and days of resistance and struggle in the years ahead.

His ninth year was eventful from the start: a crisis in the USSR— the first socialist country—a devastating war and military defeat for Iraq, American hegemony over the region, Baker's plan,[52] and the PLO on the verge of splitting . . . He was amused by the impetuousness and frivolity of his early behaviors, the tense expressions he used to fling in the face of whomever he was addressing and in his letters to the party. Now, even if he could, he would not forsake this lifestyle until after the year 2000, not a day before.

"Why the year 2000?" his comrade asked.

"That is the year that scorns Gorbachev, that counterfeit communist who penned the *Guidelines for the Economic and Social Development of the USSR until the Year 2000*. While he spoke of achieving what he called the 'reconstruction of socialism,' the result was that only five years after its passage he had destroyed it and paved the road for the return of capitalism. I, too, will honor that commemorative date, but in defiance of it: I will seek to achieve hiding in a clandestine life to the year 2000 plus a few days, in affirmation of our party's experiment of constructing a revolutionary model of evading the enemy's capture from within the homeland."

"So, why a few days *after* 2000?" his comrade asked, without hiding his joy.

"So that I can respond to the question, 'When did you go into hiding?' by saying, 'In the last century, the twentieth, and I came out of hiding in the twenty-first.' Wouldn't that quip alone make the sacrifice worth it?" Kan'an had quickly returned to joking. He appeared intoxicated as he spoke of his "two centuries," as though he was butting against them with his head, affirming his willpower. He threw away his cigarette after it had burnt all of the way down and singed his fingertips.

"That is tempting, very tempting. So that would mean that you will have spent eighteen years in this experiment? You will be over forty years old by then." Kan'an nodded his head in agreement. "But where is your third fundamental element in this plan?"

"God damn my third fundamental element and when I declared my sacred trinity of fundamentals. Leave it be. Can't you smell the aroma of *mulukhiyah* with fried garlic? Remembering my third fundamental element makes me lose my appetite. That would be a disaster. *Mulukhiyah* with spicy pepper, my friend, is the adornment of earthly existence, especially when the leaves are plucked during the first round of the harvest."

"You will solve the problem of your third fundamental element someday. We will talk after eating, as I have something to say," said his comrade with clear sympathy. "And if you fail to solve the problem you will become a monk. Don't you Christians have room for monasticism?"

"Becoming a monk befits a Christian whose life is dominated by the afterlife and who embraces Christ. I, on the other hand, am a Marxist—have you forgotten? This worldly existence dominates my life and I embrace the revolution. As for the future"—he nodded with a nonchalant smile on his face—"the party said it to me nine years ago when Muna chose the Man with a Position instead of the Man with the Resistance: 'Don't despair, the future ahead of you is vast!' But I found it to be narrower than the prick of a needle, comrade. In brief, if the problem of my third fundamental element is solved, of course, my religion will be complete, but if it is not"—he turned to the pot and stirred the *mulukhiyah* with a wooden ladle—"I shall live as if guided by Umm Kulthum, singing the words of the tenth century poet Abu Firas Al-Hamdani: 'If I should die of thirst, let no raindrops fall after me.' I shall perceive all of the third fundamental elements in the world and all of the feminine nouns[53] to be hostile and conspiring against me and I shall curse them until Judgement Day. In the final analysis, one can live with a religion that is incomplete."

Kan'an said the last sentence with resignation to his circumstances. He picked up the pot and went on. "Now, let's have dinner. Afterwards, I'll amaze you with my favorite dessert, *tamari** with *balluza*,** fried in local olive oil. My mother makes it best, she taught me how to make it last year."

"Great," his comrade pursed his lips, "*mulukhiyah* followed by *tamari* means we'll have a feast, as you like to say. The best thing for you is to keep your attitude up, you'll need it to deal with everything. Let us have dinner. Let me help you."

---

* A sweet made from dates.
** A layered gelatinous dessert usually consisting of milk, starch, and sugar.

Kan'an ate but with no appetite, and he made little progress on his food. He did not enjoy the sweetness of life nor that of the *tamari* he had made following his mom's recipe. The discussion about his third fundamental element had chased away his appetite, and his mood turned sour.

❖❖❖❖❖

She disguised herself well for fear that the woman in the house next to Kan'an's might see her, since the neighbor knew both her and him as well. She wore her traditional disguise: a scarf that covered her head and parts of her cheeks, and dark sunglasses. After she got out of the car driven by Hisham and started to walk along the path leading to the front door, she lowered her head further to conceal her face.

For some time, she had been urging Hisham to arrange a visit. He answered her in the way he and Kan'an had practiced—words that were ultimately callous to her desire to see her son: "He is busy and cannot receive you, he sends you his greetings. If you'd like to send him anything I can deliver it to him . . . "

Kan'an was receiving her care packages but that was not enough for her—she wanted to hug him and, like any mother, she could not help but be worried about him. Even the briefest maternal happiness found itself interrupted by her heart's return to apprehension.

"I haven't seen him for four months—you said it was the war and that made sense to me, but the war ended two months ago. Can't work and the party take a break for four or five hours?" A logical question. She did not know that he didn't want her to visit him while his leg was still fighting the remnants of the infection, that he did not want her to see him limp. But she gave in quickly. "Okay. Send him my greetings. Pass by this afternoon under the pretext of wanting a book from the study and I'll give you some things. I will prepare some grape leaves with chicken which he has not had for some time. Shall I prepare a bottle of carrot juice to help his vision?"

Hisham interrupted her. "Carrot juice is abundant in the market; I will buy him some."

"Forget the market," she replied. "Commercial carrot juice is no good." She had made up her mind on the juice and Hisham acquiesced. Now she could finally see him. She came in through the second door and took Kan'an's head between her hands, kissing his cheeks in a frenzy. Hisham came in behind her carrying a sack.

"When shall I come back for you? One o'clock as usual?"

"No, come back at three. I haven't been here for a long time." Hisham left and she got to work. She opened the sack and began to take out its contents. "We haven't met for five months. All the work that has to be done. Was it really that much work?!" She was clearly tense. "How is your health? How's your leg? Your stomach? I prepared some grape leaves. You haven't had that for some time, huh? I brought *malatit*[*] You could have some for breakfast with white cheese and tea? This is mint from our garden. Next time I will bring you a za'atar pastry. Have Hisham buy you some za'atar and some cheese and put olive oil on it. Hisham told me you haven't had fresh cheese all this time, so I brought you two blocks . . . "

Out of habit Kan'an either nodded his head in agreement to humor her or smiled out of admiration and enjoyment, or he made quick comments as he listened to her questions, reprimands, and complaints about what he ate, who got him involved in politics, his life between and behind walls, the fact that he had not gotten married . . . She had brought these things up many times before, but that didn't stop her from returning back to them. Deep down, she was still agitated from their time apart. Her worries followed her around at home, she was reminded of him whenever she went to his bedroom or study at mealtimes, she would toss and turn in bed every night and these apprehensions followed her around their family home . . .

She had become one of the singular constants of his safe house and his way of life; she had a unique role in his world that no one else could fill. She would travel to the United States for months on end and when she would return her connection to his secret

---

[*] Vegan anise cookies.

life would be restored, bringing back their pre-1982 memories, reviving his heart and lifting his spirits, and so the cycle continued every time she left and came back throughout his nine years in hiding. When she was away, he would feel desolate and miss her. Once she entered his house he would come out of his secret life and be transported to her kingdom, her old house. When she returned, he would discover that she had aged many years in just one year or even over a few months. She came and went and resumed the practice of her clandestine habits during her meetings with him; she would conceal her trips out of her house and hide what she knew about him from his brothers. She came to understand the rules of secrecy in his life—where it was appropriate for him to live, how he moved from one house to another, what methods he used to disguise himself when he moved or made contact with people whom he did not want to be recognized by . . .

❊❊❊❊❊

The boots and sneakers were still investigating his house, vandalizing the contents of the next room, the one with the machines, while he was remembering his comrades and his mother. Suddenly he heard the sound of a sharp knife tearing fabric nearby. The knife was being thrust in and out of something, tearing it and creating a sound that put one's nerves on edge. He turned his head to the right as far as he could manage, his right pupil straining to see. The boot next to Kan'an's head noticed the motion of his head. It touched its toe to Kan'an's right cheek, pushing his head back so he couldn't see again. The knife was still tearing. *I should wait quietly until the boot leaves. I have to see what the shoe is doing with the knife.* The boot left and Kan'an turned his head to the right again. Now he could see what was happening—a sneaker was leaning over the long couch and tearing its fabric with a practiced hand, pulling out the innards, searching.

Kan'an was offended; it felt as though the knife was tearing his intestines. With their knives, he saw them tear up the daily routine of his life which had stopped only three hours earlier. That couch was where he used to sit most evenings to watch the television that he regularly moved between rooms—not for any specific reason, just a desire to change the routine of his life. He had a habit of dozing off on that couch for an hour after lunch each day. He used to sit there with his papers, he would read and write for two or three hours without ever tiring... there, on that roomy, long couch, the one that was now being torn by the knife and letting out a whimper.

His memories began to percolate. Their tearing was like a pail drawing up memories from a well, pouring them onto him in his present state—surrounded by boots and sneakers, on the floor tainted with the blood seeping from his eyebrow and his bloodied hands. Time had not lowered its curtain so that Kan'an could snatch up recent events and call them memories—these memories had not even aged long enough to become memories in the full sense, he was still living through them. Only a few hours earlier his teeth had chewed, his tongue had turned over. He had devoured the last of his recent memories, of what reminded him of the previous weeks.

> *Why the tearing? Is this the time to want to feel torn up?*

His inner self, his enemy, was testing him and mourning his comrade, but it was also full of criticism and blame—Kan'an did not entertain it.

> *You met here for the first time and for the last time. You had a short experiment, a mere phosphoric flash. The percolation of memories is burning you like an acid. I understand that you have no say in which ones seep through your storage of memories. I understand that. But the tearing, why the tearing? What is wrong with you?*

He did not answer these questions. He remembered the words of her song. He sang her favorite part and he hummed it silently.

> *Kan'an! Bearer of my suffering for years. What is wrong with you? Did the sneaker reopen your old wounds, my old wounds?*

Leave her song aside for now, forget it.

He let out a deep sigh, causing the sneaker that was tearing up the couch to grumble and look at him.

> *Your wound is my wound. I am now your revolutionary self. It is I who says, like the martyred Al-Hallaj did, "I am You and You are me." We are a revolutionary pair sharing one body which has hidden for years in this den, living between its walls, swallowing the bitterness and deprivation of his days and struggling, hoping.*

Then understand me, be understanding and leave aside my short-term memories.

They say the song you do not forget is connected to an occasion or a perspective. Her song was her perspective. Signs of frustration appeared on his face, mixed with the blood that was seeping incessantly from his eyebrow—bloody features, an indicator of what was building up inside him.

> *A hesitant position, followed by a 'but.' A false promise as a means of evading a decision you fear.*

The sneaker is surrounding me, his knife is tearing up my world and my memories. The boot is unhinging the doors of my life, flipping it upside down. Its toe is pressing on the reservoirs of my short-term memories and spilling over into my present. You want the shoe to take down my affidavit, my confession, and ask me to sign it? Forget it.

His inner self continued to vex him while he was surrounded in the barracks. In this moment, it had returned to being headstrong and agitated, just as it was nine years ago.

Do you think you can? Do you think I can? You remembered her and her song just a few hours ago. Will you forget her now? Time has not yet transfigured her with its curtains. The boot came to invade your liberated territory—our liberated territory. The taste of her last kiss on your lips by the door has not yet faded away, can you forget her? She was our mutual desire for years; can I avert my face from her memory?

✱ ✱ ✱ ✱ ✱

(1)

The image in his mind: her eyes laughing, self-confident and strong, perhaps liberated; an unaffected mouth, naturally smiling as though she had been born with a smile branded on her face; her eyes, he returned to them, wide pupils always staring, discovering him; an astonished smile drawn on her small dewy lips shaped like fresh green almonds of spring. All of these features gave her face a look of childlike happiness. Kan'an could almost imagine her head separate from her body as it danced away in the distance. He smiled as he looked at her, imagining her head, examining her with his eyes, discovering her as she stood before him.

It was as if he was experiencing the incarnation of the woman from this image. The experience was delightful, but not free of confusion. He took this in stride and smiled—imagining her head unmoored from its torso and dancing. She was wholly taken aback by him, flustered and breathing quickly, she spat out her words like rapid projectiles.

"I am so happy I could dance. But why me and not someone else?"

"Why shouldn't it be you?"

"Because the story is about you—the years, the experience, the name, you . . . I don't know."

"You are the woman born of the picture in my imagination. I've had the image for years, but now you are flesh and bones, a woman."

"Wasn't there a woman before me—what you are calling a picture?" Her eyes betrayed a desire for discovery.

"I had what was left of a woman, what was left of her image: laughter and arguments, whispers during moments of solitude, and the appetite before breakfast in the morning. The human in me asked for her and the revolutionary in me rejected her for her perceived weakness. She addressed me with the polite plural 'you'—she could not say 'we.' In the end, the latter triumphed over the former, and the woman was rendered into bits and pieces, becoming the picture of a human being in this den. Six years ago, I saw the maiden of the sun and spring. She was born of the sun, out of its yellow morning rays in the space it left for her below. The earth grew her from its green, ripe vegetation and red poppies, then buried her underneath them. Her birth was miraculous and her life miserable. Her hand was chained, and she did not have the strength to "knock on the walls of the tank," the reservoir of her misery and hardships. She asked me to come riding in on a white steed, but the poor thing did not know that I did not possess even a lame donkey."

"I am not like the sun-and-spring maiden!" she said confidently.

"That is why you are in my den. The picture I created is of a woman who is always under the sun, a woman who stands above the ground and is not buried underneath it, who is able to knock on the walls of the tank. As for the *hareem*,* they are a third sex destined for the past like the Turkish *fez* and the manual coffee grinder, leaving behind those women who belong to the current age. A woman who severs her ties with history, should do so with no regrets; there is nothing worthy for her in the past."

She lowered her staring eyes; her demeanor was strange, as if she was outside of herself.

❖❖❖❖❖

You must avert your gaze to help me do the same thing. You who claim to be revolutionary—support me so that I may erase her image, forget the memory of her. I am the revolutionary and no longer have a need for her now.

Can you erase the image from the first and last time of your experience together? The fact that she laid her head on your shoulder and that your fingers toyed with strands of her hair behind her neck? I cannot erase her, in fact I can only ask for her. You're the one that won't be able to.

The tone of confrontation in the voice of his inner self indicated that it was confident in what it had just asserted.

---

* *Hareem* is the plural of *haram* which is the word for someone's wife.

I have to be able to do so, I must. The image that I happily asked for has been torn to pieces and has become painful.

Another shoe had joined the first one in the tearing campaign. They were tearing out the innards of the couch, shredding them into tiny bits and scattering them across the floor of the room, and with it, scattering bits of her image too.

❖❖❖❖❖

(2)

She looked on sympathetically until he finished explaining.

"I understand, I do, the reason for this arrangement. You are not like anyone else. Because you are not living in this world, I am required to do what is unfamiliar to me. and what's required of me is unfamiliar. But we live and we see! It's all strange to me, yet I understand your situation, I support it, I do but . . . I need to think about it."

"Think about it!"

"This arrangement . . . it is all strange to me." Words that reflected her hesitancy, enthusiasm, and reluctance, drawing near with trepidation. He was attracted to the one who belongs to this age, not to history. Consequently, he had to bear it. She was not like the *hareem* waiting for the horseman on a white horse, rather she chose her horse and its rider too. She was independent, and he always considered this to be the essence of her personality and of his image of her, a woman of this age. So it was on him to bear it! He existed between the walls, not in the real world. In the real world, there would be no image to dream of incessantly such that his only refuge became the special arrangements and channels that made seeing this image a reality; she would have been born a woman, not born from his image. In real life, a man and a woman would not need party decisions and rules and secret arrangements in order to meet.

You exaggerate! You like to play the martyr. You imagined yourself more than once as a martyr, you like the role of the martyr.

She was like lightning, passing in a split second and momentarily illuminating the darkness of a winter's day, only to disappear just as quickly. Like a tourist visiting the sea for the day, enjoying the breeze and the waves, then turning her back and departing at sunset while the sea remained in place, immovable. Like a weary woman climbing a mountain to its summit and breathing in the pleasant air, only to descend a few hours later to her exhausting daily life. Her image in pieces, her astonishing smile always artificial, her song hesitant.

❖❖❖❖❖

Hubris! How conceited of you. Her image has not been shattered—it is whole, present in all its visible splendor, shining across millions of your brain cells, inebriating you with her presence. Her smile is the last thing that toys with your imagination, fatigued by contemplating her as you fall asleep. Her smile reminds you of all her facial features, her eyes staring at you with the full force of her personality and confidence, her freedom, her small dewy lips like fresh green almonds of spring. Her song transports you to glimpses of her, hour by hour, minute by minute, glimpses that play with your head like aged house wine.

❖❖❖❖❖

(3)

"Tell me: How do you live?"

"I live according to the rules '**visit no one, do not receive anyone**'—to which I once added 'and do not open the peephole on the door for an old woman from Al-Bireh'—and '**measures, precautions, requirements, and rules.**' Between this and that, I resist and I cook, I sleep, I dream, I sing, and I contemplate, I jump from one safe house to the other. I escape from bad coincidences by virtue of a prayer my mother made nine years ago: 'Go, my son, may God be pleased with you.' I get bored and talk to the walls on occasions, I work and feel tired, I laugh and I curse. Before and after all that, my tasks dominate my thinking—my resistance is my life. The self that pushes me towards bad things has fought me and I defeated it, so it fell silent."

"What about solitude?"

"My social affiliations keep it from killing me. Solitude has been my companion for nine years."

"Can you convince me that solitude does not bother you?"

"I said it does not kill me, not that it doesn't bother me."

"How is it then? How can you live with it all these years?"

"It's fine, I do not see solitude as living alone between the walls. It's the loneliness of the human being who misses others, and in doing so misses his humanity. He senses this absence so he turns in on himself, arguing with his inner self, having a dialogue with it, bargaining with it, silencing it so that it is stifled within him. So, he lives in solitude with his stubborn, crushed self within him. Loneliness is not failing to find someone to talk to, it is when the human cannot find himself while with others."

Her eyes signaled bewilderment. She was thinking.

"Is it the absence of the woman, then? And what about resistance and the missions for the party? Where do the party and your comrades fit in?"

"They are present, and their presence prevents loneliness from killing me."

"Does that not satisfy you? Does it not relieve you?"

"Nothing obviates the need for a woman. She is our opposite, the one through whom we men discover ourselves. Could I possibly renounce myself, for instance?"

"What about monks? Don't they live without women? Have they renounced themselves?" she asked with disapproval.

"I speak of the living, not the dead!"

"I would have gone mad had you chosen someone other than me."

With that statement, she ended the discussion and rested her head on his shoulder.

❋❋❋❋❋

From now on, I shall not sing her song,
I shall not repeat her favorite passage. I
need something else; I shall sing along
with my Sheikh who is dear to my heart:

> We will sing, we will always sing.
> We bear good tidings, we are hopeful,
> We go around the revolving world,
> To the sound of the thundering tune
> We have the scalpel and the balsam,
> In the awakened, enlightening word.
> This is how we are, and how we shall remain:
> Knowing and understanding,
> With whom, and against whom we stand
> We are always awake,
> Not wavering from this and that

> *In a harmonious personality, there is no contradiction between the revolutionary and the human being. There is no contradiction between your old revolutionary Sheikh and Fairuz. The*

gazelle and the rifle, the rock and the apple—the revolutionary sutures the difference between them.

I know. I know. But each moment has its song, each phase has its song. The current moment demands the Sheikh, not Fairuz—the moment of the encircling barracks and the phase of a new confrontation.

The tearing and the couch awakened a memory, and a memory too has its song—it demands it.

I shall freeze my memory even if the weather is hot and summery. I insist, Kan'an.

You won't be able to. If you evade her eye, you run into her smile. Try elsewhere, and you are met with her wet footprints on the floor of your house. Where can you escape to, you who were besieged, closeted between walls for years? You are surrounded by two eyes, a smile, and wet feet just as you are surrounded by soldiers around your house. You are between the sea and the enemy, as in the story of Tarek bin Ziad.[54] So, where is the way out?

Wherever he went there were traces of her. Where was the way out? They had lunch together in the kitchen, suited to her tastes. *Laban kishk** with meat and rice. In the room where Hisham now lay bound, they had a long discussion about the party, the Intifada,

---

* A form of preserved yogurt.

life, the Gulf War, information and the press, municipal elections, poetry. They discussed everything. They sat at night, with her head on his shoulder, on the eastern balcony listening to a new recording of Fairuz's *"Kifak Inta."* Her wet barefoot footprints are all over the house. Once she slept on this couch like a child after an exhausting day. Wherever he went, her traces knocked on the door of his memories and forced their way in.

> *You won't be able to!* his inner self said, challenging him.

Yes, I will! Kan'an insisted.

> *Then we are disputing once again! We have gone back to the games of the first year! How long will this mutual contradiction between you and me last?*

You have become a revolutionary, so learn your lesson well and do not challenge me. We were not playing games; we were facing each other behind shields, in combat.

> *No, we are not behind opposing shields now like we were at the beginning.*

I am a revolutionary.

> *I am the human in you therefore I ask for the picture of . . . Please, for me. I want to be happy.*

That does not make me happy. So shut up and don't exhaust my brain.

Kan'an fidgeted and this motion smeared his face with the blood on the floor. The taste disgusted him.

> *You are back to your loose tongue and your boorish behavior towards me. When will you stop? You call for reconciliation and yet you call me names? You are insulting yourself and attacking the human in you.*

If my own self tries to stab me in the back, I will shoot it. You are always inciting me to evil, he replied, almost shouting.

A sound jolted him out of this dialogue with himself. He adjusted the position of his head and stole a glance in the direction of the sound. The soldiers had finished opening a hole in the wall separating him from his neighbors.

My heart is with you, little neighbor girls. But don't worry. The parts of your brains dedicated to memories still have room for many more. Remember this night well and learn to hate, be saturated with it.

> *I excuse you. You are tense and you discharge your tension onto me,* his inner self said in a conciliatory tone. *For years I have yielded to your wishes, I—the human. You are the revolutionary and yet you want to execute me, the human in you? I am you; will you commit suicide? Have you become so hardened as to kill the human in you?*

Has your personality split, or your feelings turned hostile? You weren't like that with her, you were tender, she said so. Then why does it seem now that you have coarsened?

❖ ❖ ❖ ❖ ❖

(4)

"I am getting to know you and your life. Each day for the last two weeks, I have discovered something new about you. The question of how you are able to withstand the hardships of life has been preoccupying me. Don't you miss walking in the street, don't you miss your relatives and friends . . . ? How do you cope with all that?"

"Of course I miss those things, but I endure. My life is not enjoyable, but I was molded to endure hardship. Man has immense potential, expanded by ideological conviction. Normally people do not discover this until they decide to join the battle. When a person is embroiled in that turmoil, everything depends on his own decision, whether he attempts the impossible or he hesitates, his determination faltering and his body collapsing—there is no in between. Either we rise to the challenge of the revolution or we don't. Hiding and clandestine struggle are ways of rising to the occasion of the revolution. Either we enthusiastically engage in the revolution's daily battles, each in their own field, or we are defeated. The collapse of our determination will defeat us before the enemy does."

"But the Intifada has lost a lot of ground; the revolution is over in Lebanon, revolution is over as a phenomenon of overt struggle . . . a state is further away now, socialism is collapsing, Iraq has been defeated, and the PLO is going to be attending a regional conference about 'self-rule' . . . How does that fit in with what you are saying?"

"Those are the headlines of our times—we are in the stage of retreat and collapse. But we were here before the Intifada broke out, and we will still be here after it is over. The people who made the Intifada and made the revolution after it can renew it with even greater vigor. The PLO may go where it pleases but we will go only to one place: towards our national objectives. In order to get there, we must hold on to the only correct and sound logic: that of the revolution."

"Sometimes, I feel that things are moving in a different direction than the party and its revolutionary position. You speak of a revolutionary project and of struggle, but the PLO leadership speaks a different language—that of a political settlement and a regional conference. You speak of clandestine action and going into hiding, meanwhile things are headed in the opposite direction. Public personalities sprout up every day like mushrooms. Precipitating forces and trends are emerging; some are calling for openness and visibility from beneath the shadows of the Occupation. Isn't the party being isolated? We are moving against the tide."

"But not against the tides of history! What you are saying affirms only that we are a revolutionary party, it makes our identity distinct. Read Mehdi Amel and you will understand exactly what I mean. Our distinctiveness is not only in our program but also in our activities. We oppose a settlement by resorting to armed struggle. We oppose openness and its drawbacks by constructing models of secret experiments that we seek to consolidate and develop. We oppose producing and publicizing leaders who have no political capital by building up revolutionary leaders molded by experience and the hardships of struggle. We reject what is, and strive to construct an alternative; we give shape to the historical alternative."

"But we are butting our heads against the rocks, swimming against the current."

"'The revolutionary' is about swimming against the tide, not making peace with the current state of affairs. If 'the revolutionary' loses their critical, rebellious spirit they become castrated—like the impotent man who finds his counterfeit manhood exposed from his first moment with a woman. In this way, a revolutionary that seeks to compromise with reality will be exposed as false in the first battle, resulting in defeat. As for butting our heads against the rocks, that has been our duty as revolutionaries since the time of our forefathers, since Spartacus, the leader of the slaves, the Qarmatians in the Abbasid state, up to Che Guevara who set to Bolivia to make a revolution, and ultimately up to our people unsheathing the sword to confront the sixth strongest military power in the world.

"All revolutionaries have butted their heads against rocks and shattered them into pieces, bit by bit, through endurance, perseverance, and patience, and that's the key here. Everyone looking for an excuse to drop out of the struggle repeats the idiom and slogan 'the bare hand is no match for the awl.'[55] Our palms must push back against the awl until we break it. The palm will be bloodied, well and good—are we seeking independence and liberation while expecting a path strewn with roses? This stage is difficult, very difficult, and there is no alternative to endurance. Our day will come, I don't know when, but it will come, and our efforts will not be wasted."

She listened very attentively although she looked like she was not fully embracing everything that he said. "You are the alternative to those I see around me: the secretive against the public, the pure revolution against the widespread chicanery. I enter your den and leave one world behind so that I may live in a different world with you."

"Beware of romanticizing my world, my revolution is not romantic. Neither is my experience. My experience is about daily revolutionary action that is tiring and exhausts one's nerves, the same as the experiences of thousands of Palestinian revolutionaries. As to whether my experience is an alternative to those you see around you, I am the image of the party before you. That is how you should look at things. Meanwhile those you see around you are a picture of decadence."

"I think of that a lot . . . I mean my coming here, your project, our meeting, the probability of us being together. Over there I am in a different world, a world of shiny stars."

"Do you want my world or the other world consistent with some of the demands of your profession and your life?" He made a point of asking her this question directly and frankly. This is how one should always handle sensitive issues. His eyes bored into hers, suggesting the seriousness of his question.

"I want your world," she replied. "Today, as I was coming to you, I thought of the possibility that I might never come again for some reason and my body shivered, and I could not bear to think of such a possibility."

"But can you handle the consequences? I mean the consequences of establishing ties with my world and the one who lives in it? That is not an easy matter." He asked her the same question as before, dryly and frankly.

"I could commit to you, your experience, your life—all that appeals to me. But will this affect my life, my profession, and my job?" She asked herself this but did not answer the question. She was no longer thinking out loud, confusion apparent in her eyes. Kan'an did not ask any more questions that could demand an unambiguous response. He respected her right and her attempt to arrive at an answer. He was engulfed in thought, sensing some kind of defeat. Silence reigned over their meeting . . .

❃❃❃❃❃

> *You did not concede, perhaps I crushed you, silenced you, defeated you! I have crushed, silenced, and defeated the human who used to fortify me when my revolution became romantic, dreamy, and brittle as glass! Remember that well!*

Kan'an was constantly confronting his inner self throughout their last two hours in the den together.

> *No, my concession, me the human in front of you, to you, the revolutionary, is the most prominent token of your expe-*

> rience. Call it what you wish—crushed, silenced, defeated, executed several times—but won't you carry out my last request of your experience, which will end any moment now? Evoke the image, the song, the smile. I, the human, implore you: don't let me down.

I will not! I cannot extract my memories now no matter how recent, for I am surrounded, you are surrounded, Hisham is as well, so are the memories besieged. Everything around me is surrounded. I fell into their hands and so did everything along with me.

> You have extracted everything from the besieging circle, from under their boots, out of their military barracks around your house. You liberated the party dialogues you had with you, the Intifada, the Gulf War, the fortifications against you and me, even the "breakfast arousal." They were liberated by the wrinkles in your mother's cheeks, her warm embrace, her interrogations, the cup of local wine, your pen, your papers, your books, the sun maiden and the window—your whole life. Will you give up now and leave Hind's image, her song, and her smile in their hands, inside the barracks, under the boots? Your evocation of her liberates her. Evoke her, free her, fight to release her.

❖❖❖❖❖

(5)

Hind embraced him, and a tear fell from her eye onto her cheek. Kan'an wiped it away and kissed her eyes.

"Why are you crying?"

"Out of happiness. Happiness with you." She sat down and rested her head on his chest in a gesture of farewell.

"I share the most beautiful moments of my years of experience as a human being with you." His words spilled out of him spontaneously, like a child addressing his mother.

"Your spontaneity entangles me, makes me lose my bearings."

"I will not resort to inauthenticity and fakery."

"Be careful not to do that. Maybe our emotions are running away with us, all this in one month?!"

"Since when does a person schedule the flow of their emotions according to a calendar?"

"But I fear for myself from you, and I fear for you from myself. I am mad!"

"I have been living this madness for years. With you my madness—my religious trinity—is complete."

"I'll exhaust you. Whoever loves me becomes weary."

"I am used to fatigue."

"You don't know me well."

"That is why you are here. You have become part of the vocabulary of my den."

"What have you learnt about me?"

"Enough for me to say I found in you my image, constructed years ago by my weary imagination."

"And what do you think of this image?"

"She is mad, tiring, and beautiful. She has a place under the sun and she is adept at banging on the walls of the tank. Her eyes stare and her smile is one of astonishment. Above all this, her lips are small and dewy like spring almonds."

*****

I do not want to leave my den while under the snares of ruptured feeling. I fear if I do, I will be overcome by the enduring pains of memory; far better, perhaps, to leave with a smile on my lips. There is no room for those pains, I want only challenge and confrontation, nothing else.

> *Your thoughts went to her when they surrounded the door to your house and began practicing their beastly ritual—the battle over the papers was your first confrontation. There was no room for fear and falling apart then. You confronted and challenged them while the taste of her letter was still in your mouth. Your strength is apparent, so what's next? Arm yourself with her smile, she will give you strength. Her smile is beautiful, and you will need beauty to assist you against the ugliness of what you will face. Remember the passage from her song that she sang while she was happy. You will need to remember that feeling in the interrogation chambers or on the truck that will transport you away from the homeland. That happiness will be your strength; it will allow you to scoff at the noose they will use to hang you and declare, "He committed suicide." Carry*

> *that happiness, the smile, the beautiful moments, the song, on top of everything you are bearing and you will triumph in the coming confrontation. All that inspires optimism. Didn't you say to their intelligence guy a few hours ago, "I am a revolutionary Palestinian optimist." Be optimistic and you will win! Be pessimistic—lamenting your memories and surrounding them with melancholy—and you will lose. Do you want defeat?*

> *I will not be defeated. That issue was settled five years ago. I will win, of that I am sure, just as I am sure that I am Kan'an Subhi. Yet I have metabolized her beautiful moments, the most beautiful moments of my nine years, into a single painful one, when I could have carried them as they first appeared. Do you remember, oh, inner self? Not enough time has passed for me to forget that moment. How am I supposed to evoke the memory of the most painful moment of my experience?*

His tone indicated a sense of great pain, buried inside him.

> *You are back to exaggerating. You are sensitive to everything: living with sensitivity, thinking with sensitivity, feeling with sensitivity. Sensitivity will kill you one day if you remain like this.*

My "sensitivity" was out of sympathy for you. Wasn't it you, my inner self, that kept making demands? Up to the last hours you were still asking for this and that. I wanted you to be happy, you who were crushed between the walls. I would have hated for them to hurt you. I wanted the human in me to emerge from his loneliness, I wanted you to discover the other self so that you would discover yourself. I never forgot the price that I paid, nor the sacrifice that was made many years ago. My search for my third fundamental element is a search for your happiness—you who have never been happy—a striving for the "other" whom you always asked for.

❖❖❖❖❖

(6)

"Come, let us sing with Fairuz," she said suddenly, as though she had just discovered her music. Hind stretched out her arm, turned on the tape recorder, and that mesmerizing voice rang out. She had brought him the new tape of *"Kifak Inta."* She sang along with Fairuz many times until that tape inevitably became part of the vocabulary of his existence. She would sing along happily with Fairuz, looking at him and swaying her head—her eyes radiating desire, striving to perfectly imitate the singer's intonation. She was at the height of her beauty.

"Sing with me, sing!" she implored him.

"I like to look at you as you sing. It is your eyes, not you, that sing—your eyes which have captivated me for over a month."

"Forget my eyes"—she reprimanded him coyly, and went on—"Sing! Sing!"

"*Tomorrow I will stand with you again,
If not tomorrow then the day after for sure,
You tell me and I will hear you,
Even if the sound is far away!*"

"I would rather sing another song. A different song suits my third fundamental element better."

"What is it?"

"It is a song by Marcel Khalife, your friend, and the lyrics are by Mahmoud Darwish, my friend:
*I am sipping the kiss
from the edge of the knives
Come let us join the massacre!*"

She stretched out her arm and turned off the tape recorder. Fairuz's voice faded away. She kissed him with surging passion and tears came to her eyes, tears of joy? Sadness? Sympathy, longing, or sorrow? He did not know . . .

❖❖❖❖❖

So, it is for my sake that you are suffering?! His inner self exclaimed, having made this late discovery, and it went on. *Finally, we have made up. You have understood my demand and sympathized with me. What trouble you have given me, Revolutionary Kan'an. Oh, how I have been isolated in your inner depths, suppressing my desires, my needs, and my screams, rolled up into myself, hiding my head so that it does not look on over the world of "***measures, precautions, requirements, and***

> ***rules.*** *Now I understand you—before and after being a revolutionary you are a human being and you have not relinquished the human within you. You will be victorious. You will certainly be victorious. Despite the brief depredations of melancholy, you will be victorious!*

❖ ❖ ❖ ❖ ❖

(7)

"I told you from the beginning that I fear for myself, and I fear for you from myself, but you did not listen to me."

She said it by way of apology, as a prelude to her decision. Hind's tone had changed. It was tension, not tranquility, that hovered over their sixth week together. Kan'an remembered her song, her drawing near and drifting away, her approach and retreat. His image of her was swinging in his head like a pendulum, right to left and back again while he was in a state of confusion and observation.

"I would be lying if I said that I had feelings for you," she went on to say. "I am not your third fundamental element. Don't torture yourself over me. I pity you."

"I am not looking for pity, because I am strong. Solidarity, sympathy, yes; but pity, no. Pity is for the weak, and I am not one of them.

"I'm sorry, that's not what I meant, I can't help what I feel." She then fell silent.

"You are the one who decides the reality of your feelings. Typically, in order for there to be a meeting of feelings there must be a meeting of worlds. But we belong to two different worlds," he said truthfully, and continued with resignation. "It is not important here what I saw, felt, and experienced with you over the past month and a half." His words marked the end of their conversation and the end of the brief flashes of lightning that momentarily illuminated his den. After nine years, the only thing left was a wound.

She rose from the long couch in the spacious room, picked up her leather bag and swung it over her shoulder, heading for the door, where she stopped. With tears in her eyes, they embraced warmly, and she spoke.

"Although we shall not meet after this day, know that you have a very close friend in solidarity with you, whose name is Hind. For my part, I know that I have a wonderful friend called Kan'an who lives between the walls somewhere, who dedicates his life to the revolution. I am happy to have met you. Since there are no bonds of love uniting us, let us be content with friendship."

She said these words and followed them up with a kiss planted quickly on his lips. He smiled a bitter smile, a feeling he tried to conceal. He kissed her, tears welled up in her eyes. She left quickly, and he closed the door behind her, the bitter taste of her last kiss still on his lips. *Is she the type who will be true to a friendship that arose between the walls? Is she in fact capable of appreciating its greatness?* He was wondering between him and himself, doubting, leaving it up to time to answer. He could not get rid of the feeling that perhaps all those signifiers—her smile, her tenderness, the tears in her eyes, her words—might simply have been the product of etiquette, aristocratic table manners, and formality. He sat at his worktable in the kitchen, with his pens and papers before him, and addressed them directly: *You, and the rest of the vocabulary of my house and my life, are the only ones whose friendship I can rely on. Everything else is counterfeit and artificial.*

He lit a cigarette and took a long puff, feeling the smoke burn his lungs, stinging. He had not felt that in seventeen years of smoking. He sat like that for an hour or more, chain smoking. His gaze traveled from his papers to the wall in front of him, which he examined closely, then to the bottle of oil on the table. He cycled through many feelings, congestion in all its senses welled up inside him. One term dominated all others: rupture! He felt something inside him had been torn, once and forever. He felt like shouting, but he did not know at whom. He wanted to curse, but he did not know at whom. He only knew something inside him had been torn once and for all.

You are miserable, Kan'an. You waited for your third fundamental element to find enjoyment and it resulted in pain. This is the second time you bid farewell to a woman at the door to your house. You kiss her, open the door, and she leaves. But you stay, retaining only a picture in your imagination and your memories. For the second time, your needs are squeezed in within the walls, your desire is buried inside your safe house—your den. The first time it was Muna, an incomplete life, transformed into the shrapnel of an image and memories. The second time it was Hind, a transient moment. A flash of lightning bestowing you with the memory of a wound. Between the two stretches, a secret life of nine years. They are bookends: you kissed the first one, bidding the first phase of your life goodbye, just days before beginning your secret life, and here you are kissing the second one goodbye just days before the end of your secret life. Between the first and the second are years of unrealized desire and need, years of deprivation and hardship and resistance too.

Your story in hiding began by bidding farewell to a woman and being deprived of her, only for it to end by affirming that deprivation and that farewell—as a secret resistance fighter, is that the law of your life? Is it an inevitable requirement that you should shelve the human in you in order to storm into your life as a revolutionary who finds no humanity in the other self? Is that due to circumstances or chance? Or is it a bad choice in both cases? Or perhaps is it a case of forsaking feelings in order to make that life succeed, confining the third fundamental element in your life to your imagination rather than a lived, palpable reality, a realized desire? Or Kan'an, have you tamed me so much that we have made peace in these final hours?

Have the womenfolk conspired against you, or was it the hardship of experience that prevented you from bringing together your three fundamental elements: life, revolution, love? Are you addicted to farewells and kissing at the door? It is as though you were adding an extra function to the door of your secret house: that it should allow women to slip out of your life. What door is this that has assumed all these functions and roles for years and years?

Kan'an was busy trying hard to expel the drop of blood that was touching his nostril.

What next, my revolutionary inner self, surrounded along with me by boots and sneakers and rubber shoes? Do you still see her smile as a source of strength for me? Passages from her song, a source of happiness? Her beauty, something I shall need to face to the ugliness of those who are surrounding me? Understand that I derive my strength from my party and my struggle, the solidarity of my comrades, and the love of my people, and not in the glint of an electric moment, a moment of pleasure that turned into a moment of pain ... If you don't realize that, you have not yet been well-formed.

Fine, I will leave you alone.

Fine, you and I face a new experience which will begin within a matter of hours and through which you will be shaped further. But from now on, don't bother asking me to evoke her image for you. It is enough that I have to bear the weight of the collapse of my experience and my capture, and on top of that, endure the moment of pain and the wavering song and the insincere smile! Don't ask me for anything from now on.

Having consolidated his alliance with his revolutionary self, Kan'an was prepared to enter into the new phase of confrontation.

Chapter 11

For hours, Kan'an lay prone on the floor of the spacious room, blindfolded, bound hand and foot. Memories flooded from the arteries of his brain, mixing with the blood seeping from his left eyebrow. The two merged; the plasmatic mixture filling the small den as he lay there, waiting and watching with the faint hope that he might escape.

His arteries were depleted from the last few hours of bloodletting. What a long cinematic reel they had produced, loaded with the memories of his past and stretching out before him like railroad tracks. Kan'an had lived to the fullest over those nine years: they had been his formative years as a man, spanning his youth, stability, and maturity. He was aware now—bidding his past life farewell as he stood on the threshold of his new one—that he had not lived his life in vain. At his desk in elementary school, he had grown attached to an objective that was veiled in fog. Abstract and ill-formed, this objective had become clearer to him little by little until his conviction firmly took shape. He had lived as part of a noble revolutionary movement, one that he had joined early on. He had seen its ranks swell over the years, the ripe fruits of his labor joining with that of his comrades to decorate a tree that grew taller and taller clutching for the sky.

He was filled with pride, for he had chosen a place for himself in the camp of workers and toilers, connected to their values and hoisting their banner. A feeling of contentment was enveloping him, from bloodied head to bound feet; it surged forth despite the agony of his experience coming to an end and despite the bitterness in his belly from the phosphorescent residue of Hind's image. That feeling of contentment dislodged the lump in his throat and the bile in his body. And he was not yet dissuaded from his plan of "disappearing until the year 2000 and a few days."

The only thing left was the radiant truth, as radiant as the deep red blood that had been seeping from his eyebrow for hours now, a truth that could be summed up by an equation: Kan'an versus the combat boots and sneakers and rubber shoes. *Him versus them.* Apart from that truth, everything else was trivial and secondary. This was the indivisible reality of the confrontation today, where the inevitable and long-simmering struggle between the two sides of the equation had finally taken the form of blood.

He was aware of his own contradictions. He had often measured their depths, uncovered them, contemplated them, and suppressed them so as to free himself from the tension in his head. He had done so at a furious speed, prioritizing stability and an upbeat mood in his day-to-day life. That stability had reigned over his life during the long years he was concealed between the walls, reasserting itself every time it was violated in an act of self-preservation. Throughout his experience, he had always known where he was stepping before he put his foot down. He had taken the advice of Naguib Mahfouz. Since the construction of his internal bunker, Kan'an had engaged in defending his experience-choice from his agitated inner self, who had incited to evil behind its own bunker of needs and desires. It fired its bullets, complaints, groans, and screams. It mobilized his tense, short-lived experiences with the image of his third fundamental that deepened every contradiction. He lived those contradictions to the fullest, and they did not push him to a madness that would lead him to betray the values he had he had spent years honorably fighting to adhere to. Once he overcame them, he could say then, just as he did now, laying on the ground: "I am pleased with my life and my choices." Man cannot separate himself from his inner contradictions, even more so for the revolutionary fighter, for they are part of his essence, posing questions according to his years, his days, and his life... No sooner did he finish with one would another rear its head! Man is wedded to his contradictions in an inescapable Catholic marriage, bearing them like a cross! He will face the same questions about those contradictions: what was the effect of their battle within him? Did he retreat before them, defeated, sinking low like a mouse entering its hole, or did he advance forward, upright, head held high?

There were no sounds coming from the adjacent room where Hisham lay. Like Kan'an, he had been reliving his memories, imaginations, apprehensions, anticipations, and contradictions. Like Kan'an, he was bound and blindfolded, surrounded by combat boots, sneakers, and rubber shoes. Then a sound came. There was congestion and noise and shoes of all sorts going in and out, with voices calling, angry, warning.

Once again, Fayad, our experiences converge, coalescing with our shared contradiction of the strength and weakness within each of us. The window-maiden brought us together, and the wolves of our loneliness and desire sharpened their teeth and tore us to shreds. We once diverged, but our experiences merged in the end, nevertheless. I did not return to a homeland I never left in the first place. I did not feel the cold wind of exile gnawing at my bones. I felt the warmth of Ramallah that embraced me from my first day to my last night. Now we have met again, Fayad, a comrade of my experience, arrested with the party's printing press, tucked away in a stone den. Will my arrest make a splash in the media as yours did? Will tales be told and rumors spread such that elders may spend many hours of their monotonous days chin-stroking about them?

The last thing he wrote and printed was a hasty internal letter to the members warning them about the escalation of the intelligence agency's assault campaign on party organizations. They anticipated that the Occupation authorities' would attempt to sway public opinion for the success of the "regional conference,"[56] the date of which had been set for a month and a half after the raid on his den. And here he was caught in the very assault he had warned about! At the end of the letter, he wrote: "**Don't let them cover you in detention hoods. Rebel against the detention orders. Do not turn yourselves in!**" They will find the original still attached to the drum of the printer.

Nine years ago, Kan'an had concealed himself between the walls, refusing to turn himself in; and there he had been, two days before the end of his secret life, just two days short, writing the last of what he was to write there, calling on his comrades to conceal themselves as he had done, and not to turn themselves in:

> **I do not ask you to bear what I have not borne myself.**
> **I do not demand of you what I am incapable of doing.**
> **I invite you to a rebellion I live, and I urge you to live**
> **a life I have chosen, for I am on the path ahead of you**
> **and you are the following behind. So, make haste!**

Kan'an addressed all his comrades as he wrote his last missive; he had no way of knowing that he would not be taking up the pen again between his four walls after that day. He had read two novels recently. First, he had finally gotten hold of the fourth volume of *And Quiet Flows the Don*. He put aside the work he was doing for the party and returned to the world of the Cossacks. Having fluctuated between the revolution and its enemies, Grigory had settled on joining its enemies as a model peasant. When the revolution was victorious, he became headstrong and refused to turn himself in. He turned the page on the past, and the blood between him and the Bolsheviks turned into a sea. He mounted his horse and became a highwayman only to be killed by the militias. Aksinia died of a fever after she had gotten her things together and deserted her husband to join her lover, Grigory. The second novel was *Undesirable Alien* by Regis Debray, who had been an associate of Guevara and embraced the revolution in Latin America only to betray it, like many of the educated bourgeoisie, becoming an advisor to Mitterrand! When he got to page eighty-one of the novel, he paused at a passage: "One can only be sure that someone is made up of the stuff of revolutionary fighters after the age of thirty, when he has to give up having a family, a name for himself, a career, and ambitions forever."

A perpetual uncertainty for life, a gloomy atmosphere on routine days; watching friends get married and raise families, observing classmates become important personalities, successful in their professions—yet one knows they are trivial people. He would have been far more successful had he been in their place. He doubted they could have locked themselves in a basement of their own free will and watched life pass them by from the window, noticing the happiness of others that would never be theirs. He doubted they could have done this knowing the keys to their dens were in their pockets and that they could climb out and mingle with the public any time they chose; doubted they could have handled not knowing in the morning where they would sleep that night, or if they could even sleep that night, or whether they would still be in same place in the morning. One could do this for six months, perhaps, but not for ten years straight.

Kan'an put the book down once he had read the paragraph and started pacing. He too was over thirty and was about to enter his tenth year living in his den. *The professional resistance fighter, the man of clandestine action, no matter where he is fighting—in Bolivia, Palestine, Sudan, Venezuela—remains who he is . . . He carries his cross, the weight of his resistance, and marches on,* he thought. He was most captivated by the character Manuel, the anarchist who gave himself to the workers of the world: wherever the workers' struggle was found, he was there with his printing press, producing their pamphlets.

The voice of the *muezzin*[*] startled Kan'an from his thoughts. It announced the arrival of morning, and that there was enough light to distinguish the white thread from black. With the break of dawn, Kan'an began to hear the chirping of birds from the direction of the kitchen balcony where they had built their nests between the drain pipe and the wall of the house near the top of the balcony.

Occasionally dawn would catch him by surprise like this, when he was kept up by insomnia as he sat reading or writing or sitting on that balcony, drinking tea and smoking until six or seven in the morning. In those moments, he would watch the birds begin the journey from their nests in search of food, flying back and forth with sustained energy. By virtue of their proximity to his balcony, they became his friends, nesting in his vicinity, enjoying the security and taking care of their hatchlings until tender fuzz turned into feathers. They would then fly away to begin a new cycle.

He could still hear sounds from the adjacent room. Many shoes and combat boots passed near him, headed for the iron door. He could hear them go down the steps then return and leave once more. They were taking their loot from his den: his books, mechanical equipment, reels of music and song, and anything they thought was worthy of examination, study, and confiscation for one reason or the other. He could now begin to see through the blindfold, not only the movement of combat boots and shoes near him coming and going, but also the faint sunlight infiltrating his house-den. Soon the workers of the neighboring cinder block factory would begin arriving for work. Shortly after that, the noise of the machines would announce itself, rending asunder the peace of the entire quarter.

---

[*] Person who makes the call to prayer.

Kan'an had often felt anger toward the factory and its machines, its owner, and its workers. He would curse the day that man had invented cinder blocks! His work had sometimes required him to stay up late, past midnight, up to two or three o'clock in the morning. No sooner would he struggle to fall asleep for a duration of two or three hours, than would he be awakened by the loud noise of the machinery, as though hammers were beating on his skull. Occasionally, the factory subcontractors would begin at one or two in the morning so that they could finish by 10 a.m. before the blazing summer sun could scorch them, as though this was a smart thing to do, becoming utterly exhausted from their work. He could not understand the workers' arrangements and needs, but he wanted to sleep because he too, had work and his own arrangements and needs. He could do nothing at the time except curse and lambast them or, consumed by tension, address them sarcastically: "I am fighting for you! Can't you show some appreciation and let me sleep a little?"

He would move from his room to the opposite room to get some sleep, but it was like jumping out of the frying pan into the fire. In a few moments the tilemakers would begin work, and they had an even more disturbing and distinctive routine that consisted of scooping up various size pebbles with an iron shovel and collecting them in an iron cart that ran along platforms to the interior of the factory—an operation which produced a cacophony of provocative noises.

A pair of sneakers stopped near his head, its toes pointing towards his head. "It's him," one of them said. "It's Kan'an Subhi."

"So, you are Kan'an Subhi!" said the other. "We have been eager to make your acquaintance for years."

"I do not share your excitement," Kan'an replied.

"You seem to be stubborn!"

"You will get to know me well. No hurry."

That was the totality of their exchange in his safe house. He heard the sound of the military trucks declaring that they were prepared to leave. Someone freed his feet, making him stand up and steering him towards the iron door. *Why aren't the cinder block factory machines working? Aren't they going to bid me farewell, burden me with their memory? I want to take their noise with me. I want it!* He had reached the door.

His new journey—his new life—had begun. Here he was now, opening a door he had spent years hiding behind. After he emerged, he knew it would close once more. A new experience awaited him, of that he was sure; he had spent his youth in the kiln of experience after all. Kan'an Subhi had entered through the door, remained behind it, but the man who emerged later, was no longer himself. He left with history trailing behind him. Carrying it on his shoulders, he embraced his experience in the depths of his heart.

I return to life, born again! What will my new life be like? Years of captivity? Deportation from the homeland? Or will I be killed in cold blood? I don't care. It is enough that I lived true to my convictions, values, and objectives. I don't care. I do not care! He reached the first step while chanting to himself: "I don't care. I do not care!"

One of the men guiding him was trying to make him bend his head by pressing on it, perhaps because he was short, or out of a desire to humiliate Kan'an, or to keep anyone from seeing Kan'an's face as they walked down the steps.

> *You will not achieve that you son of a bitch. I will not exit my clandestine life with my head bent. I began it as a rebel and will end it the same way. I will lift my head high even if you were to break my bones on the steps of my den. Let the workers in the cinder block factory see how I descended, how I behaved while in their hands, so that they will know what kind of resistance fighters we, the members of the party, are!*

He summoned his will power and raised his head in spite of the combat boot pressing it down. The combat boot pressed down again, and he raised his head once more. This struggle continued until they had walked down the last step, at which point the soldier stopped pressing. Kan'an had reached the iron door, and before he had taken the last step the noise made by the cinder block machines started. His heart rejoiced and he yelled in his mind, "The dear things are saying goodbye, they are saying goodbye." The workers replied, "Excuse us for disturbing you, you who concealed yourself between the walls! It is our responsibility to make cinder blocks for building, just as it is your responsibility to build, with your comrades, a free homeland. We are all building, as we are children of one camp. Here, we are carrying out your wish and bidding you farewell in our own way. We entrust with you our voice and memory, oh, neighbor-comrade of the same camp." How he wished he could return the workers' salutation, to bid them good morning: "Young men, may you be granted good health!" But the trucks were waiting to carry their precious cargo to his unknown future. He considered his upright walk with his head held high to be a salutation to the workers; he knew each and every one, although they had never seen his face.

As soon as the door closed, he heard the distant voice of Sheikh Imam, warm and poetic:

"How beautiful the breaking of dawn,
The roaming light enchants our eyes,
The birds sing to the Lord,
Whose power is exalted.
Beautiful melodies revive the melancholic heart,
To all you workers, have a blessed morning!"

As he slowly exited the outer door surrounded by the soldiers, Kan'an was accompanied by chirping birds, the voice of his blind, revolutionary Sheikh, and the noise of the factory. He made his way onto the walkway and down the four steps, then, as his foot touched the street, he held his head higher still. Now the workers could see him well.

"Farewell, you most cruel and revolutionary years of work!"

As soon as he let out that shout, Kan'an felt as though the memories of the past years had suddenly dissipated from his mind, as though he had spat them out. He left them behind as he walked, dragged by the combat boots to the trucks. There, he left behind the years of strength and weakness, those decisive years and the image of Muna, Sakinah, and the sun-and-spring maiden. He left behind the assault of 1985, the confrontations between organizations and members, his desires and needs, his bouts of tension, joy, anger, his anecdotes, his waiting . . . the image of Hind with her dewy lips . . . the years of the Intifada and the Gulf War . . . his sadness, revivals, moments of pleasure, pain . . . All of it ceased to inhabit the reel of his memories. There were only these words ringing in his head, gushing out of his mouth:

"A new phase requires a new confrontation—and a new challenge."

He was thrown into the truck and the door slammed behind him.

—Al-Naqab-Ansar 3 Detention Center
February 1995

Glossary

Organizations

Popular Front for the Liberation of Palestine (PFLP)
A Marxist-Leninist party which emerged out of the Arab Nationalist Movement, was founded on December 11, 1967. It remains the leading leftist Marxist organization in Palestinian politics.

Palestinian National Liberation Movement (Fatah)
A secular nationalist movement, launched on January 1, 1965. Since 1969, it was and remains the leading party of the Palestinian Liberation Organization.

Democratic Front for the Liberation of Palestine (DFLP)
Founded by Nayef Hawatmeh who split from the Arab Nationalist Movement and formed the DFLP.

Arab Nationalist Movement (ANM)
A pan-Arabist Marxist organization founded by George Habash and Hani Al-Hindi in 1951. It is the progenitor of various leftist nationalist formations, including the PFLP and the DFLP.

Palestine Liberation Organization (PLO)
A nationalist coalition of various Palestinian political parties, including Fatah, the PFLP, and the DFLP, founded in 1964. Today, the Fatah-dominated PLO controls the Palestinian Authority.

Palestinian National Council (PNC)
The PNC is one of the highest decision-making bodies of the PLO, forming the legislative body of the organization. This branch of the PLO debates and determines the PLO's policies and elects the PLO's executive committee.

Unified National Leadership of the Intifada
The national leadership committee that was composed of a coalition of popular committees spontaneously formed to mobilize and meet the needs of the people across cities and villages.

United Nations Relief Works Agency (UNRWA)
The United Nations agency responsible for relief and human development of Palestinian refugees. It was established in 1949 by the UN General Assembly. Today, UNRWA supports more than five million Palestinian refugees, more than seven hundred schools, and over 140 health facilities in Jordan, Syria, Lebanon, and Palestine.

Places

The Occupied Territories
Refers to the lands occupied by the Israeli state after the 1967 war, which include the West Bank, East Jerusalem, the Gaza Strip, and the Golan Heights. This does not refer to all of the Palestinian lands occupied by the Zionist entity.

Al-Bireh
A city in the West Bank, Palestine which along with Ramallah, forms a governorate.

Ramallah
A city in the West Bank, Palestine, which along with Al-Bireh, forms a governorate. Currently and since the signing of the Oslo Accords (1993–1994), Ramallah is the administrative "capital" of the Palestinian National Authority.

Qaddura Camp

A Palestinian refugee camp east of Ramallah that was established in 1948 during the Nakba. Qaddura camp is comprised of Palestinians from various villages and cities—such as Dayr Tarif, Ramla, Lydd, Qalunya, Imwas—which were either destroyed in 1948 or remain occupied by the Zionist state. Like other Palestinian refugee camps, it remains unrecognized by the United Nations Relief and Works Agency (UNRWA).

Al-Am'ari Camp

Established in the Al-Bireh municipality following the 1948 Nakba, this camp houses refugees from various cities across historic Palestine, including Ramleh, Lydd, Haifa, and Yaffa. Located less than 1 kilometer from the illegal settlement of Psegot and 1.3 kilometers from the apartheid wall, the residents of the camp have suffered repeated atrocities by Occupation forces and remains a site of resistance to Zionist aggression and colonization.

Rafah

A Palestinian city in the southern Gaza Strip. It is the district capital of the Rafah Governorate, located thirty kilometers south of Gaza City.

Qalqilya

A city located in the northwestern side of the West Bank.

Bin 'Amer meadow

A large fertile plain in the northern region of Palestine. It is the shape of the triangle, with its edges marked by the cities of Jenin, Haifa, and Tabariah.

Jenin

A city in northern Palestine, located at the southern point of the Bin 'Amer triangle. The city has a long history of resisting settler-colonialism dating back to Napoleon's invasion of Palestine. It was the first city to organize armed resistance to fight the British in 1935 under the leadership of Izz Al-Din Al-Qassam. After the 1936 revolts, Jenin along with the cities of Nablus and Tulkarm were referred to by the British as "the Triangle of Terror." In 1948, Zionist militias attempted to capture the city, but failed due to the fierce resistance of Palestinian fighters with assistance from Iraqi soldiers. Over fifty years later, on April 3, 2002, Zionist occupying forces invaded the Jenin Refugee Camp in a failed attempt to quell the resistance. Four hundred fifty-five homes were completely destroyed, eight hundred homes were partially destroyed, and fifty-eight Palestinians were martyred. To this day, the city continues to play an active and central role in Palestinian resistance against settler colonialism.

Nablus
A city in the northern part of Palestine with a long and proud history resisting settler-colonialism. In 1799, Napoleon's troops needed to pass the valleys of Nablus to reach Acre. In response, the Palestinians of Nablus burned their groves to obstruct their path, earning the city the title of the "*Jabal Al-Nar*," or Mountain of Fire. After the Palestinian revolution of 1936, the British named the city, along with Jenin and Tulkarm, "the Triangle of Terror." Nablus continues to uphold its tradition of resistance to this day.

Qalandia Camp
Established in 1949 and located within East Jerusalem between the main checkpoint between Jerusalem and Ramallah, this camp is one of nineteen refugee camps in the West Bank. It is the fourth-largest and eighth-most-populated camp in the West Bank. The refugees in Qalandia Refugee Camp are mainly from al Lydd, Haifa, Al-Ramleh, and Al-Khalil cities.

Jabalia Camp
Established in 1948, Jabalia Camp is the largest of the Gaza Strip's eight refugee camps. It is densely populated, and Palestinian refugees in Jabalia Camp hail largely from the occupied lands of Beer-

sheba, Ashdod, Jaffa, Al-Lydd, and Ramla. After the launch of the First Intifada within the Jabalia Camp, it was declared a "closed military zone" and was a site of Israeli brutality as well as resistance.

Events

1982 Invasion of Lebanon

In the summer of 1982, what began as an Israeli invasion of South Lebanon became, in just six days, a full-scale occupation of Lebanon and siege of Beirut. For three months, the joint Lebanese-Palestinian forces confronted the occupying forces. By August 1, the number of bombs dropped over Beirut was estimated at 185,000 (more than two bombs per second) in 210 air raids. As a result of this military defeat, the PLO evacuated their fighters from the capital. By August 23, West Beirut bade farewell to the last PLO *fedayeen* under the supervision of the Multinational Forces, composed of troops from the US, France, and Italy. Fifteen thousand PLO fighters dispersed from Lebanon, and the PLO's leadership relocated to Tunisia.

Reagan Plan

A regional policy plan introduced by US President Ronald Reagan on September 1, 1982. The Reagan Plan delegitimized the PLO as the representative of the Palestinian people by designating Jordan as the negotiation partner with Egypt and the Zionist State. Through its naturalization of the latter and its embrace of a capitulationist version of "peace," the plan was one of the first building blocks for the state-building project represented in the Oslo Accords.

First Intifada (1987–1993)

Refers to the period of mass Palestinian resistance against the Israeli occupation. The popular uprising was sparked on December 9, 1987 in the Jabaliya Refugee Camp in the Gaza Strip before it spread to the rest of occupied Palestine. The Intifada was and continues to be a historical product of Palestinian anti-colonial struggle in response to years of Israel's efforts to suppress Palestinian national identity through colonial occupation, economic exploitation, political suppression, and violence. Israel responded in brutal fashion by instituting an official policy of breaking the bones of Palestinian protesters, and by killing over one thousand Palestinians and arresting over ten thousand.

Individuals

George Habash (1926–2008)
The founder of the PFLP who served as General Secretary from 1967 to 2000. Habash is also known by the name Al-Hakim, which means "the wise" in Arabic.

Yasser Arafat (1929–2004)
A founding member of the Fatah political party, as well as Chairman of the PLO from 1969–2004 and President of the Palestinian Authority from 1994–2004. He is also commonly referred to by the name Abu 'Ammar.

Sheikh Imam (1918–1995)
An Egyptian Arab musician and singer, famous for his revolutionary songs in favor of the popular and working classes.

Marcel Khalife (1950–)
A Lebanese singer and composer who celebrated revolutionary causes causes, including the Palestinian struggle, through his music, famously incorporating the writing of the Palestinian poets Mahmoud Darwish and Samih Al-Qasim in his song lyrics.

Mehdi Amel (1936–1987)
Hassan Hamdan, popularly known by the pseudonym Mehdi Amel, was a notable Arab Marxist thinker and a member of the Lebanese Communist Party. A teacher, intellectual, and militant, Amel's historic contribution to the field of Marxist theory was his exposition on the "colonial mode of production."

Endnotes

Chapter 1

1. Qaddura camp is a Palestinian refugee camp east of Ramallah. It was established in 1948 during the Nakba and is comprised of Palestinians from various villages and cities—such as Dayr Tarif, Ramla, Lydd, Qalunya, Imwas—which were either destroyed in 1948 or remain occupied by the Zionist state. Like other Palestinian refugee camps, it remains unrecognized by the United Nations Relief and Works Agency (UNRWA).
2. Muhammad Yousef Al-Khawaja was from the village of Ni'lin, located in the Ramallah Governate. He joined the Popular Front for the Liberation of Palestine (PFLP) during the beginning of the 1970s. In 1976, he assumed responsibility for central organizational work in the Ramallah organization. He was martyred that same year while in the cells of Ramallah prison under torture from the Zionist intelligence. He died in defense of his party and nation, preserving the secrets of the PFLP and the revolution [footnote from the author].
3. PLO fighters evacuated the camps under guarantee of the Reagan administration that they would not be harmed. The forced withdrawal of the Palestinian fighters left refugees of the camps unarmed and defenseless. The Sabra and Shatila massacre, which took place between September 16–18 in 1982, was planned and carried out by right-wing Phalangist militias under the supervision of the Zionist army who invaded the Shatila Refugee Camp and massacred over 3,500 Palestinians and Lebanese. This massacre was carried out with the green light from the United States administration.
4. Following the 1982 Israeli invasion of Lebanon, the Lebanese National Resistance Front (LNRF), often referred to as *"jammoul"* through its Arabic acronym), was created on September 16, 1982 with the call to action from the Lebanese Communist Party and the Organization of Communist Action. The Front was joined by the Syrian Social Nationalist Party, the Arab Socialist Ba'ath Party, and other members of the Front of Patriotic and National Parties. The Front gained full support from Palestinian groups such as the PFLP and the DFLP. The LNRF formalized the

resistance activities of those parties, and conducted hundreds of operations against the Zionist enemy with the last recorded action taking place in 1999.
5   The Palestine Liberation Organization (PLO) created robust civilian infrastructure aiming to provide social and political services to Palestinians across the diaspora. Following the 1982 invasion of Lebanon, the Israeli military systematically destroyed PLO institutions including archives, cultural bureaus, hospitals, factories, research centers, and orphanages. This deliberate attack on infrastructure was part of the Zionist entity's objective in liquidating the Palestinian national movement.
6   The Muslim World League is an international organization founded in 1962. It is based in Mecca, Saudi Arabia and funded by the Saudi government.
7   Naguib Mahfouz is an Egyptian writer and novelist (1911–2006).
8   *How the Steel Was Tempered* is a work of socialist realism and one of the best-selling books of all time that centers around the Bolshevik working class revolution in the twenty-first century. A central theme is revolutionary transformation into a "New Man," like iron into steel, alluding to the title of the book. *Kaifa saqailna al-foulath* is the translation of the title in Arabic. Kan'an playfully changed the title with a slight alteration of the letters, changing it to "irrigating the fava beans."

Chapter 3

9   *Al-Taqaddum* translates to *The Progress*. The student newspaper was issued between 1984 and 1987 by the Progressive Student Labor Front in the Occupied Territories. A digitized archive of the publication can be found on the *Institute for Palestine Studies* website: https://archive.palestine-studies.org/ar/node/1043

Chapter 4

10 Fatihi Al-Ghirbawi (1955–1984), was an inspirational local leader and resistance fighter in Gaza. He was martyred in a resistance operation that left three enemy soldiers dead and many more injured.
11 The "phased" policy or "policy of phases" refers to a strategy adopted by the Palestinian National Council, the legislative body of the PLO, at its twelfth meeting held on June 8, 1974. The policy called for the establishment of a national authority over any liberated Palestinian territory in service of the long-term goal of total liberation. The policy, which is said to have introduced the concept of a two-state solution in the PLO, was rejected by the left-wing of the national movement. The PFLP's eventual approach to this phased national goal differed from the Ten Point Program in that it aimed to liberate as much land as possible without negotiating with the enemy.
12 On February 11, 1985, King Hussein and Yasser Arafat signed an agreement in Amman representing a common approach to the so-called peace process. A Jordanian-Palestinian delegation was to be formed to negotiate with the Zionist entity at an international conference. The PLO was expected to accept UNSC Resolution 242, which meant the recognition of the Zionist entity and a renunciation of armed struggle.

Chapter 6

13 The policy of deportation of leaders of the Palestinian liberation movement began under the British mandate and in the 1936 revolt, and has continued until the present day. Between 1967 and 1980, over 1600 organizers and community leaders were exiled by the Zionist authorities.
14 A reference to *No One Writes to the Colonel*, a novella by Gabriel García Marquez, a Colombian revolutionary socialist novelist, journalist, and author of *One Hundred Years of Solitude*. It is the story of a colonel in Colombia living under martial law in the years of La Violencia (a ten-year civil war in Colombia from 1948 to 1958) and waiting for a letter about a pension he had been promised.
15 Zakariya Nahhas is a former PFLP member who went into hiding for seven years. Mahmoud Fanoun is a former PFLP member who went into hiding for five years and was one of the co-authors of the PFLP book *Philosophy of Confrontation Behind Bars*.
16 A trilogy by Konstantin Simonov, the first novel in which is *The Living and the Dead* and the second is *Nobody Is Born A Soldier*.
17 The red poppy is a spring rose with red petals, black-and-white-center, and a green stem. The name of the flower differs depending on the region, where some call it *"hannoun"* or "passionate" and others call it *"shakiq"* or "brother." To the Palestinian people, the poppy represents political and cultural consciousness and symbolizes sacrifice.
18 The phrase "knock on the walls of the tank" is an allusion to one of the most popular short novels written by Ghassan Kanafani, *Men in the Sun*. The novel follows the stories of three Palestinian refugees who aimed to enter Kuwait from Iraq with the help of a smuggler. All three Palestinian refugees endeavored to alleviate their own hardships or the difficult circumstances of their families by seeking new lives, jobs, and financial security. The refugees were being smuggled into Kuwait by hiding in the tank of a water lorry in scorching summer heat. At the end of the novel, the smuggler was delayed at a border checkpoint from returning to the lorry. After finding the refugees dead from dehydration and suffocation, he laments, "Why didn't you knock on the sides of the tank?" *Men in the Sun* serves to illustrate the struggles of landlessness, persecution, and adversities experienced by Palestinian refugees. The author's use of the phrase is meant to represent the powerlessness of the sun-maiden.

Chapter 7

19 By 1980, Birzeit University became a member of the Association of Arab Universities and became the first Palestinian university to join the International Union of Universities under UNESCO. During the 1980s, Birzeit University further developed its academic programs, which included community education for adult literacy and housed the first graduate program in Palestine; a master's in education. As a result of Birzeit's academic and international achievements, the university became increasingly recognized by the Palestinian masses for its merit in high-quality education as well as a symbol of national achievement in defiance of the constraints set in place by colonialism and occupation.

328   THE TRINITY OF FUNDAMENTALS

20   The AMAL Movement (its acronym in Arabic spells out "the Lebanese Resistance Regiments") was founded in 1974 by Musa Al-Sadr, originally as "the Movement of the Dispossessed" advocating for further political power for the Shia sect. It gained more momentum following the Israeli invasion of Lebanon in 1978, then in 1982, and following the Iranian Revolution. The party has been led by Nabih Berri since 1980.

21   The February 1984 agreement (also known as the Amman Accord) refers to the meetings which took place between King Hussein of Jordan and Yasser Arafat, then Chairman of the Palestine Liberation Organization and Fatah, and which sought to formulate the principles and steps needed to negotiate with the Zionist entity. The signed agreement included "the formation of the proposed confederated Arab states of Jordan and Palestine," as well as the formation of a joint Jordanian-Palestinian delegation to all future negotiations. The Amman Accord was thus largely seen as a Jordanian attempt to usurp the right of Palestinian representation and self-determination by other Palestinian political parties. The PFLP and dissident parties indicted Yasser Arafat with treason and capitulation to the alliance of right-wing Arab regimes and imperialism (*Democratic Palestine*, PFLP 1984).

22   The November 1987 Arab summit held in Amman, Jordan, declared its convening was in pursuit of ensuring "Arab solidarity" in the face of renewed Iranian offensives during the Iran-Iraq War. The summit gave little priority to the Palestinian struggle despite the presence of the PLO. This intensified feelings among Palestinians that they could no longer rely on the Arab states to take any meaningful steps to advance their cause.

Chapter 8

23   Sareyyet Ramallah–First Ramallah Group (FRG) is a Palestinian nongovernmental community-based independent organization established in 1927. They offer services like scouts, summer camps, arts, and sports. The facilities of Sareyyet Rammallah are also used as a place to gather for the community and families.

24   Throughout the course of the First Intifada, popular committees were spontaneously formed to respond to the needs of the people across cities and villages. The Unified National Leadership of the Intifada was the national leadership committee composed of a coalition of popular committees spontaneously formed to mobilize and meet the needs of the people across cities and villages during the First Intifada. Through their communiqués, they called for general strikes and boycotts, made arrangements for secret clinics to treat the wounded so they would not be arrested, called upon teachers to do their jobs out of their homes as the schools would be closed, and encouraged people to grow their own vegetables so as to become quasi self-sufficient.

25   A famous street in the center of Beirut with many restaurants and sandwich shops, and a popular hub of social and political activities during the 1980s.

26   UN Security Council Resolution 242, or UNSCR 242, was a British-sponsored resolution designed in November 1967 which proposed mutual recognition of legitimacy between the Zionist Entity and Arab states. According to the resolution, Israel would have to withdraw territories it conquered in the 1967 War and the Arab

states would have to recognize the Zionist Entity on the basis of its pre-1967 borders. This resolution became the basis for all peace negotiations and normalization attempts with the Zionist Entity, and strengthened colonial "land-for-peace" paradigms. The organizations of the Palestinian Revolution, especially the more radical wings, considered it an extremely dangerous development, an attempt by imperialist powers to preside over "the liquidation of the Palestinian cause."

27 United Nations Resolution 181 was a non-binding recommendation passed in November 1947 which called for the partition of Palestine into Jewish and Arab states. The partition, supported almost exclusively by Western powers, proposed to offer more than half of the land of Palestine to the Jewish settler population, which at the time comprised only a third of the total population in Palestine. The partition plan was proposed after decades of Zionist colonization and the political and economic disenfranchisement of Palestinians. The Palestinian political leadership and the masses rejected the partition plan as a transgression against their national rights. The PFLP's begrudging acceptance of Resolution 181 was a result of its strategic considerations, in pursuit of its "transitional policy" of national struggle as well as attuning to the 'popular nature' of the Intifada.

28 Samih Al-Qassim was a Palestinian poet and communist who lived inside the Zionist entity with citizenship. He refused to leave his homeland, quoted as saying: "I have chosen to remain in my own country not because I love myself less, but because I love my country more." He was jailed several times for his political activities and dissent against the Israeli regime, starting in 1960 when he refused to enlist in the Occupation Forces—which is required of Palestinian Druze with Israeli citizenship. He spent many years under house arrest, and was also incarcerated in Al-Damoun prison. One of the poems he wrote in prison was "Enemy of the Sun," which spoke of his steadfastness and refusal to cease resistance despite terrible conditions. Marcel Khalife's song referred to in the text is from Samih Al-Qassim's poem, "Muntasib Al-Qamah Amshi."

29 Yitzhak Shamir, the Zionist entity's prime minister at the time.
30 Military formation of Fateh.
31 Military formation of Fateh.
32 Military wing of PFLP.
33 Military wing of Hamas.
34 Military wing of DFLP.
35 This is referring to the popular education schools of the Intifada, which were an alternative run by the parties in the face of school closures by the Occupation.
36 Ghassan Kanafani and his niece Lamees were assassinated by Israeli agents in a car bomb in Beirut, Lebanon on July 8, 1972. As a writer, artist, political theorist, and PFLP leader, Kanafani was targeted for his commitment to the cause of Palestinian liberation and anti-imperialism.

Chapter 9

37 This is referring to what are now known as the "Gulf Arab states" in the Arabian Peninsula, including the states now known as Kuwait, Qatar, Bahrain, the United Arab Emirates, and Oman, which were "protectorates" of the British from between

the late nineteenth century, early twentieth century, and the early 1970s. The British backed particular families as rulers in exchange for control over their foreign relations and maritime trade routes, including control over eventual concessions signed between ruling elite families and oil companies for exploration and extraction rights.
38 The ruler over Egypt from 1805 to 1848, often thought of as the reason behind Egypt's renaissance and known for building up its military.
39 The Alternate Homeland is a known phrase among particular circles which includes Zionist propagandists. It is used to argue that Jordan should serve as an alternative homeland for Palestinians given its post-Nakba Palestinian majority. These suggestions are, of course, categorically rejected by the Palestinian people.
40 A settlement founded in 1909 and located atop the historic lands of Jaffa, Al-Shaykh Muwannis, Al-Jammasin Al-Gharbi, Al-Mas'udiyya, Al-Manshiyya, and Salama, among others.
41 A Palestinian city located on the northern part of the coast, that was ethnically cleansed in 1948.
42 A Zionist settlement originally built in 1921.
43 The Egyptian chief of staff in the 1973 October war.
44 A shelter in the 'Amiriyah residential neighborhood in Baghdad, located near a school and mosque. It was directly targeted by the United States using guided bombs that targeted the shelter as US planes roamed above it for two days. The attack resulted in the complete destruction of the shelter and the death of over four hundred Iraqi civilians.
45 Referring here to Iraq's Muslim Shi'a majority, numbering around 60 percent of Iraq's population. They live mostly in the southern half of the country, centering around Najaf, Nasiriya, and Basra.
46 Crown Prince of Jordan.
47 Jordan's Prime Minister.
48 The National Guard of Iraq that is loyal to Saddam.
49 The slogan of "the Leading Force" was proposed and discussed across the party in 1988 due to the expansion of the PFLP base and membership during the first year of the Intifada. Due to this expansion, the PFLP became the leading force in multiple cities and villages like Ramallah, Beit Jala, and Beit Sahour. As a result of this, the following question was proposed in 1988: Can the PFLP become the leading political force across the entirety of occupied Palestine? To achieve this position, the PFLP further considered their strategies on various popular, political, and military fronts. The party reached the conclusion that this goal can be achieved. In the end, the PFLP was unsuccessful in becoming "the Leading Force" due to the raid campaigns against their organizations and branches in the early 1990s, during the end of the first Intifada and the signing of the Oslo Accords.
50 The PFLP's fifth conference was held in February 1993. The political program that emerged from the conference is electronically archived online.
51 The titles translate to *The Method, The Arab Left, The Path, The New Culture, and Problems of Peace and Socialism* (a monthly theoretical journal published by the

Information Department of the Communist Party of the Soviet Union from 1958 to 1990).

Chapter 10

52 This refers to a five-point plan, presented in 1989 by US Secretary of State James Baker, to facilitate negotiations between the Palestinian Liberation Organization and the Israeli state through Egypt.
53 In Arabic, nouns are distinguished as masculine and feminine. This is referring to the rules regarding how they are differentiated.
54 The Berber Muslim conqueror of Al-Andalus (Spain) who reportedly burnt the ships he and his men sailed on from North Africa to the Iberian Peninsula, to the spot that became known as Gibralter (*Jabal Tarek*, Tarek's Mountain), confronting them with a choice between fighting and winning or losing and drowning: "The sea is behind you, the enemy is in front of you . . . " is the beginning of his famous speech.
55 An awl is a stitching tool that you poke holes into strong material like leather.

Chapter 11

56 The October 1991 Madrid Conference marked the advent of a new stage in capitulation by the rightist PLO, the Arab states, and Israel. It was considered a "breakthrough" in Middle Eastern diplomacy due to the spectacle of Israeli, Palestinian, and Arab leaders negotiating in public view. The Madrid Conference also made transparent the growing world hegemony of the United States as well as its dominance over the Arab-Israeli "peace process" in that the USSR played a supportive and inferior role just prior to its dissolution two months later.

Milton Keynes UK
Ingram Content Group UK Ltd.
UKHW020134260224
438413UK00005B/146

9 798988 260219